TAKE
WHAT
YOU
CAN
CARRY

ALSO BY GIAN SARDAR

You Were Here

Psychic Junkie

TAKE WHAT YOU CAN CARRY

A NOVEL

GIAN SARDAR

LAKE UNION
PUBLISHING

Text copyright © 2021 by Gian Sardar
All rights reserved.

Published by Lake Union Publishing, Seattle

www.apub.com

Amazon, the Amazon logo, and Lake Union Publishing are trademarks of Amazon.com, Inc., or its affiliates.

ISBN-13: 9781542026895 (hardcover)
ISBN-10: 154202689X (hardcover)

ISBN-13: 9781542022422 (paperback)
ISBN-10: 1542022428 (paperback)

Cover design by Micaela Alcaino

Printed in the United States of America

First edition

For my father, whose stories inspired this novel and whose gracious heart has taught me to find the beauty in the world.

June 8, 1979

She'd seen it clearly: a woman half-over, half-happy with her life. A focused, single snapshot of her future midmark, that moment the hour-glass gets flipped. She'd be forty-five years old and play a mere footnote in her own life: someone's secretary, someone's wife, someone's mother. Just thinking about it made her want to run naked and screaming into the street—which she might have done had she not hated herself naked and had she not been afraid of dying, particularly in the street.

Olivia was twenty-seven when she imagined this future self. Now she's twenty-eight, and what's happened in the interim is proof that life can be condensed into a sharp, horrifying essence, that after years of stagnancy, events can tumble with white-water rage. It's clear to her that her previous worry was born from youth, from an innocence she knew she had even then but tried to keep hidden. After all, to panic at having a job, a spouse, a child? To see a brick house and block parties as punishment? A failing?

Boredom, she was told—and now believes—is a privilege. If she could go back in time, she would, just to kick herself. A pinch in the rib. Without thinking, she'd trip herself to stop her restless wandering, to keep her from boarding that plane.

Be careful what you wish for, her father used to say. And there she'd gone and wished for love. That bottomless, enduring kind of love, the kind in which you see the depths of all someone wishes to keep hidden and yet still you love, relentlessly. And she had wished for her career. To take photographs that would matter, that would catch breaths and make people shift in their seats. And now, in her room, in a folder she's not opened, are photos she's afraid to look at. The wish, she knows, came true.

Her best friend says her eyes are less green. Some days Olivia sees it, that they're not as vivid, that before they were filled with something that on good days she calls *hope* and on other days calls *ignorance.* Her hair as well. Auburn still but wavier then, as if after the trip, the weight of all she'd been through had pulled frivolity and flourish from everywhere it could.

Now she stands in their yard. Baking in the Los Angeles sun and watching the windows of his room, feeling his absence like a draft. When she cranks the knob on the hose, the water arcs from this side to that from their flimsy sprinkler, and the simple fact of this current is a fist clenched within her because she remembers too clearly carrying water in a pail. Each drop precious, each spill a denial. And then she remembers the way white woven shoes looked against the dry earth. The way hands brushed dirt from a new leaf, helping the sun reach through its skin. And the way blood looked on that same earth later, soaking in as if the land itself had made the demand and would take whatever it could get.

Usually the memories are pulled from unexpected hooks. A low-flying airplane, she hears its rumble and instantly is there, teacups shaking and glass rattling in window frames, feeling confused at the panicked reactions around her because to her, in her life and where she was from, an airplane had only ever been an airplane. The scent of diesel or kerosene. A heavy mix of spices. Even the crisp of grilling meat. Any of it places her in the bazaar, his shoulder pressing into hers, *this way, through that alley.* With the rough feel of sequins or taffeta against her skin, a hand is always placed within her own, and without fail, the scent of oleander takes her to the moment of a confession. Heart racing. A rising heat.

Damask rose. She cannot smell damask rose.

Nor can she listen to someone pounding their chest with their fist. A couple of weeks ago, a man from Houston was celebrating his Oilers' recent season while cursing their last game. *Nine turnovers,* he'd said. *You don't come back from that, and man, they'd have killed the Cowboys in the Super Bowl.* He ended his proclamation with a pound on his chest—*next year is* ours. Once more he beat his chest—a macho display, something like a battle cry—and though it was in the midst of a party in her house and the man's breath was peaty with scotch and the room was rising into formations of Ys and Ms to the commands of the Village People, Olivia heard the sound and had to turn away, to lean into the wall and fight to stay where she was. Because to her, that sound was an attempt to beat in understanding. To shock a heart with its grief. And with it, she could hear the women wailing, and once again he was gone.

CHAPTER 1

April 7, 1979

At last there is silence.

The plane's cabin holds a strata of cigarette smoke from the hours in flight, and a stewardess walks the aisle, shutting off lights in the rows of sleeping passengers and nodding at those still awake, as if seeing in them a diligence that's to be commended. The woman's scarf, the Pan Am colors of blue and white and candy-apple red, has loosened around her neck, and when she reaches Olivia, she smiles in recognition of someone like herself: a woman, white. On this flight from Paris to Beirut—Olivia's second flight since leaving Los Angeles—she is a rarity.

The handful of children have fallen asleep. Businessmen chew silently on dates, newsprint on their hands as they turn pages. The woman in the aisle across from Olivia wears a black headscarf and reaches with thick fingers into a bag of nuts, watching the night, as beside her a little girl sleeps with one patent-leather Mary Jane loose on her foot and the other on the floor.

Hours ago, when they boarded, Olivia waited for a moment when the child was looking and quickly made a face. There was a shriek of happiness and heads turned, and though the girl continued to stare at Olivia, expectant and waiting for more, Olivia felt the burning gaze of a man the next row over, a man who appeared to have left his better days and humor behind. Once again Olivia waited, this time until the man turned forward. Then she did it again. There was the shriek. The glare. A repeat of just moments ago, but now Olivia basked in not having let the girl down as well as in her own small rebellion. How good it felt, this slight dissent. From behind her hand, the mother smiled as if something had been said in her defense. But with another beat, the woman's face drew to confusion as she studied the empty seat beside Olivia, as if upon it should sit the reason a white woman would travel alone to the Middle East. Until Delan appeared. Delan who is Olivia's boyfriend and roommate and is taking her to his hometown in Kurdistan of Iraq. *Cigarettes for my cousin,* he'd said as he shook the duty-free bag. With this, the woman had seemed appeased, as if he were an explanation she understood.

"Are you not comfortable?" The stewardess. Hunched over to talk to Olivia, who's in the window seat. Delan, in the middle, is asleep, as is the man on the aisle. "I can get you another pillow."

Olivia shakes her head. "My mind. Doesn't shut off. But thank you."

The woman glances up and down the aisle before turning her voice to a whisper. "Fancy a disco biscuit?" A pause at Olivia's silence. "Quaalude. They shut it all off."

"Oh, I know. But then I'd just worry about being shut off."

"Doesn't work like that, but suit yourself. He looks like a good-enough pillow. Got a nice deal there."

The stewardess's lips shine, glossed and pink and perfect. But when she smiles, there's a smudge of color on her tooth. Olivia taps her own tooth to indicate the streak, and the stewardess nods a thank-you. People who keep quiet in such situations, who let others walk around with wedged-in poppy seeds or toothpaste on their chins, those people are a different breed. The ones who either value their own comfort above all or who feel themselves rise when others fall. Olivia is neither, to a fault. Once, she saw a woman stare into her own eyes in a movie theater's bathroom mirror, as if imparting a pep talk, and then walk out with toilet paper stuck to her heel. Olivia sprang to action, but too late. The woman was already in the lobby, joined by her date, and all Olivia could do was slyly step on the toilet paper from behind. A silent save, it would've been. Had the woman not stopped short. Had Olivia not collided into her back. Had popcorn not burst into the air and the date's eyes gone wide. The woman unleashed a very vocal tirade, and Olivia missed her movie upon realizing the same couple also planned on seeing *Halloween*. Instead, she'd dragged Delan into *Attack of the Killer Tomatoes*, where she suspected much of his laughter had nothing to do with the film.

Delan. Black eyelashes against pale cheeks. Dark hair that's chin-length and wild and long enough to curl. A mustache and beard that's trimmed short yet full. He has passed for Italian, Spanish, even black Irish. *Kurds are not Arab or Persian,* he's told her, *we are our own ethnicity. The largest ethnicity without a country. My brother has green eyes. I have a blonde cousin. Even redheads are in our family,* he added with a nod, as if inducting her into his tribe. Always the last to leave a party, he is a man who refuses to follow recipes and insists on buying roses from the fake gypsy women in restaurants. At thirty-four years old, there are a few early streaks of gray in his hair that lend a refinement to his innate, almost feral quality and a scar by his eye that's shaped like an old-fashioned quill. *Delan is like the land he was born in,* one of his costars from a play once said. *Untamed and loud.*

The land where he was born. Olivia's flying into the unknown. A landscape he's compared both to the mountains in *Mork & Mindy* and the hills of *Little House on the Prairie*, everything an almost illogical, startling contrast to her image of the Middle East, where camels are silhouettes on sand dunes and hot air wavers in mirages. His stories have made her long for nights under a darkened cap of stars, to bite into figs still warm on trees, and to walk the crowded paths of a bazaar, breathing in twists of spices and the honeyed glaze of pastried treats.

It's shocking, his world. And splendid. But also, she realizes, possibly incorrect. Because when he speaks of home, he speaks like someone in love, someone blind to faults and entranced by the mundane. Someone whose heart has learned to lie.

This is a hazard she's familiar with: when you love, you see what you love, not necessarily what's there. The artful blur of affection. For her, in relationships, it was always a matter of time before someone was left faltering in a less-than-forgiving light and truth was exposed, connections built upon a desire for true love rather than a presence. An eager heart's ruse. Certainly not the trajectory of love's lasting arrow.

You worry that if you really love someone, they will be taken, her father used to say, the only person who didn't view her parade of short relationships as the result of unrealistic expectations. *It happens when you're not looking.* An infuriating cliché, made even more infuriating by the fact that after two years of living platonically with Delan as roommates, she was indeed not looking when everything changed. When in a still and silent garden, she'd felt his hand.

Is what she has with him the real thing? She's convinced it is but is aware that her past determinations have led her down broken roads. For now, the only certainty is that they're at that brink. The five-month mark, her longest relationship yet. And here, in this new territory, a new and significant worry has risen: they are from different worlds. Not just in the details but in the weight.

Only months ago, she'd walked in to find him and his friends watching the nightly news, a colorful, choppy map of the Middle East and a monotone newscaster who wrapped up a segment that had to do with two Kurdish groups. The empty bottle of gin was closer to Delan than the others, and when the news switched to a commercial, Olivia asked what had happened. *Clashes between the Kurds,* his friend Alan said when Delan kept quiet. *So much to fight for but they fight each other. No wonder he's fucking depressed.* When Delan looked up at her, he stayed silent, and she saw, like a shape on the horizon, the fact that the friends he'd had for more than a decade, who'd been with him when the fighting back home was bad, might know him differently than she ever would. Because they'd lived through rough times with him, and since those times were not something he wished to conjure again, they'd since been swept to the corners of his conversations. The fact was, she realized, he would tell her tales of mountains and wildflowers, but there was a chance he would never talk about the rest.

The rest: the space between them. The weight of his past.

Is it possible to truly know someone if you cannot comprehend that which made them who they are? Can one truly love another without that understanding? She wondered then. She wonders now. In the past, she dated men from Texas, from New York, from Idaho, and once even from France. In all cases, she could close her eyes and picture their homes, their mothers, could ask them what their Christmases or birthdays were like and see the same celebrations in her mind. But with him? Their differences are profound. His is a world where men cherish their Brno Rifles, Fridays are a holy day, and war has never just been fought on foreign soil. And though his words have painted magic and bravery, there have always been omissions. The starts or ends to stories he tends to swallow down, leaving behind only a silent aftermath.

All he's left unsaid, the *why* of him, that's what she wants. Why she's on this plane. To truly know him. To prove that they can work, and *different* does not mean *over*.

To pass time during the flight, Olivia entertains herself with imaginations of her own hidden magic. Daydreams in which she'd be at work, lost in the chaos of the newspaper's bullpen, when suddenly she'd sense the jumble of something in the air and drag her coworkers to safety before the earth begins to shake. In her mind, she sees the looks on peoples' faces. The way they'd turn to her, glimpsing power in someone they'd thought powerless. It's ridiculous, she knows. Both the daydreams and the feeling within her, a joyous lift from a force she doesn't have. But it doesn't matter. The crux of these daydreams is a righting of wrong, those who've underestimated her pausing and seeing their mistake within her strength. Just as often, she imagines the photographs she will one day take, images that will make people stop as they're about to turn a page, fingers letting go as they lean in closer. Lately, those fantasies have happened more frequently, ever since a photo contest was announced at work in which the winner is promised a position within the department. No one expects her, a secretary, to enter. After all, her one job has been to make sure someone else lives up to his greatness, her own just a quiet stirring offstage.

Suddenly, an announcement jolts her back into the present. Eyes around her open. Words are spoken by the captain in French and Arabic, two languages Olivia doesn't understand, so meaning for her is gathered by the change in people around her. Newspapers are put away and seat backs straightened. Hand-rolled cigarettes get mashed into metal trays. The mother in the aisle next to them finds her daughter's shoe and wrestles it onto the small, still foot, her face unreadable under the overhead light.

Almost as an afterthought, the captain remembers his English. "We will be making a landing in Switzerland."

Switzerland. Olivia glances at her watch, still set with the Paris time. At some point they changed course. There must be a reason. A certain hospital, perhaps. But though she listens, there's no call for a doctor on board, and the stewardess, who not long ago acted as though they were friends, suddenly won't meet her eyes.

Even months later, Olivia will be shocked at how long her mind kept the word *bomb* at bay. It was 1979 and Lebanon, where she would change planes, was thick into its civil war. Los Angeles to Paris to Beirut to Baghdad. *A journey of airports,* she joked before boarding the first flight. Now her heart beats faster and the back of her neck goes damp.

But all around her are calm faces. Nothing can be that bad. *Turbulence,* she decides, though the wine in her glass is still.

Beside her, Delan continues to sleep as if the dead press upon his chest. Suddenly the plane pulses, and something rattles by the front of the cabin. She nudges his shoulder. "We're landing in Switzerland."

He raises his head slowly, glancing out the window, as if perhaps the reason for her words should be found in an alignment of stars.

"Delan. Can you find out why?"

"Switzerland." There is a whiff of wine on his breath, and he now focuses on the orange upholstery before him as if still crawling from whatever dream had pinned him to his seat. When he puts his hand on the knee of her corduroy pants, his light touch changes, his fingers curling, short nails finding the tiny trenches. A leap within her chest. Even before they'd started dating, their chemistry was like a quiet rage, something that lit even the most banal activity, and touch, though then under the guise of friendship, was constant. Whenever he could, he walked with his arm around her. At any opportunity, they sat too close on the couch. Sometimes she missed an entire episode of *Barney Miller,* simply because she couldn't take her eyes off the place where his leg leaned against hers. Drawn to each other from the start, they'd been held back by a fear of ruining a friendship *and* a living space—her fear—or making a move too soon and scaring the other person—his fear.

Now Delan turns to the man in a gray suit next to him.

There is a flurry of talk between them, in Arabic, Olivia assumes. All hushed tones and hand gestures and strangely—perhaps she's wrong?—the word *Disneyland. My Arabic is rusty,* he told her when they'd booked their tickets. *I need to brush up. Speaking Kurdish to the wrong person could get us killed.* He laughed then, and despite what he'd told her about his homeland, she'd thought it a joke.

He turns back to her. "We're making a landing in Switzerland."

"But why? What does that mean?"

"It means my mother gets chocolates." He smiles.

"Mechanical trouble?" In her mind, she sees a flock of pigeons blending into the night, sucked silently into an engine.

"Sure," he says. "Mechanical trouble."

"But you don't know? You were just talking to him for five minutes."

He lowers his voice. "He's a Kurd. He used to buy shoes from the shop where my brother worked. His wife's a professor at university and he was just in Los Angeles for business. He didn't get to Disneyland but he got the Mickey ears for his nephew."

A kaleidoscope of mountains exists within Delan's eyes, a turn of deep brown with bits of faraway trees. She watches them now, the way they spin tales. "All that just happened."

"Don't be mad, but we might have tea with them when we land in Baghdad."

This quality of his—to be generous and affable and see the world in a series of potential friendships—it's one of his greatest draws. What people love. What she loves. But it's also what challenges those closest to him, because he can't say no. Can't look into someone's eyes and allow his own image to shrink, lessened by their disappointment—even when his money or comfort or time is put at risk. Thanksgiving dinner, random Tuesday nights, someone new it seems is always in their house. *Just once, I'd like to know the people in my living room*, Rebecca, their other female roommate, has said. Rebecca, the only woman financial manager at her firm, bold and midthirties with bobbed hair and a low threshold for strangers. *Am I to feel honored that the bartender from the Formosa raids my fridge and the mailman carves the turkey?*

Then there is the crackle of another announcement. This time to fasten seat belts. Something's wrong. Olivia feels it now. Can even hear it, a sort of murmur in the engine's hum.

"Olivia Anna Murray," Delan says, and the names sound into one, *Oliviaannamurray*. "Why worry? What can you do from up here?"

"Pray?"

He smiles. "Sure. Then pray."

When the envelope with news of his cousin's wedding first arrived, crammed with stamps and containing a letter that was heavily redacted by the government, as if decorated with black rectangles, Delan's face went wistful. Constantly he spoke of going home, and when asked what was stopping him, he cited money, time, or politics, and the words tended to transform into a heavy drink that got poured and an early night asleep on the couch.

As he read the letter, Olivia chopped garlic. The wedding, he said, would be a party for days. There would be four different kinds of rice, and each dance would last for twenty minutes. The cousin, Ferhad, the one getting married, was an amazing flute player who once hid in a tree with Delan as they waited for Delan's brother to have his illicit first kiss. For an hour they crouched on a limb, cramped and irritated but knowing this would be the secret spot, till Soran at last appeared with the girl and leaned in for a kiss, and Ferhad started playing and Delan tipped a bowl of paper confetti into the air, releasing a flurry like snow on a hot August evening. Ferhad was the cousin who chased an older boy half across town because he'd stolen Delan's pocketknife. The cousin who'd spent summers with them in the mountains at their mutual aunt's house, training *Hawshar* dogs how to tend sheep. This was a wedding Delan should attend.

And she'd heard it was better there. He'd told people that. Already, though she'd barely conceived of the idea of going to Kurdistan, it felt like a challenge. Both to know him and to knock herself off the safe ledge from which she viewed the world. Because while others made a difference, she sat at a desk. Reserved in her risk, her electric bolt of curiosity constantly kept in check by a heavy layer of caution. And going to Iraq would break that. Though even the idea made her nervous, the fact was, she was far more terrified of *being* scared, of forever being that person who didn't experience life because of fear.

"Take me," she said.

He was surprised, and she saw it flood his face—something she knew was happiness. He *wanted* to take her. But then it changed. "I didn't say I was going." He paused, drumming his fingers on the letter. "I don't know if I should."

"Why?"

"It's hard, facing what you've left."

"Because you have it so much better than they do?"

The green clock on the wall ticked. "To say it like that."

"But that's it, right?"

He folded the letter along its original creases. "Having left anywhere, for any reason—it's a lot to return. But you don't want to go. It's not a vacation."

"It doesn't need to be a vacation. It's going home. It's important. And you said it's not that bad."

Though he was calm, she saw it in him, a tightness about to unwind. The flip side of his charm, the other angle of the two-headed snake— that passion that drew people in, that kept people glued to their seats, was the same that fueled his words and could make a pleasant dinner party go awry with rants on the Kurdish plight—though, she'd noticed, not his own. His peoples' story, but not his.

"*Not that bad.* America's tolerance for what is bad, it's different from ours. Kent State—people will talk about that for decades. How could the National Guard do that to their own people, they cry. Iraq's government, the Ba'athist government, they used *napalm* on us. Bombs. You name it, they got it and used it on us."

He paused, and she saw the anger had already moved into his eyes. Quick, lit like an anonymous fire, present in a matter of seconds. She'd seen it before. They all had. But because it was usually gin-fueled, their solution was to walk away or help him to bed. But now she stood there. She wouldn't move. She would listen, and he would take her. She knew.

He continued. "Villages incinerated. Faces of children burned off. Did anyone take to the streets for us? Were there signs, picketing? Did anyone know?"

"I know."

"Because *I* told you. Not because you read about it. Here, the Weather Underground, the New World Liberation Front—they bomb in protest. Power stations, banks. For impact. For interruption. Not to kill. There, it's to kill. To destroy a people. For genocide."

Moments like these, she tried to extract the truth from the tendency he had to constantly find himself upon a stage. Not that she didn't believe him, but his words often swelled with drink, and an audience riveted with joy or fear was what he craved. Already there was a ring of wet on the kitchen table from his gin and tonic's base.

"The fighting," he said. "There are clashes still."

"But where your family is?" Because he'd made it seem that they were fine. And again she saw the fact that though his stories were often passionate or angry or despondent, very few were ever personal, as if he could tread upon a territory only just outside his own. And if it was indeed dangerous where his family lived, that, too, would be something crucial he'd held back.

"They're fine," he said at last. "But only years ago, we were at war. You feel that still."

"But if it's safe, I could meet your family. I could see where you're from. What if this is it? The best chance we get? The best chance *you* get?"

He watched her, and she saw it once more—he *wanted* to go, and he wanted to go with her. Then he shrugged and sat back in the chair, and in his eyes she saw the beginning.

And now she's on a plane she's realized is making an emergency landing, and understanding that the *calm* she saw on the faces around her had really been *acceptance*, and that for people who grew up where she was going, a flock of pigeons was not often the cause of trouble. Prayer beads have begun to slip through hands.

"Another five things," she says as the plane makes a sudden dip.

"Mulberry trees. Sweet like wine right on the branch. Caves with Neanderthal bones and fields with huge chunks of white marble. And waterfalls. Springs that go right through houses—"

"What? Why would you love that?"

"Who doesn't love running water? And the people. This is the best part. Generous. Friendly, like nothing you have known. The hardest thing is saying no, because they will invite you into their houses and feed you even if you've never met them, even if they don't have food for themselves."

Despite her rising panic, she smiles. One part of his personality explained.

"Now, tell me about Washington," he says.

"I can't. You go again."

"Just five things you love."

"No. I'll cry."

Turning to face her, his eyes flicker to the window. The ground feels closer. She wonders what he's seeing but won't look.

"Knock-knock," he says.

At this moment, a knock-knock joke. She laughs, a strange laugh of release and incredulity and fear. "Who's there?"

"Control freak. Now you say, 'Control freak who?'" A pause. "Did you get it? The control freak is telling you what to ask next. You got it?" A jump as the plane lifts before a sharp descent. "Don't worry. I won't let anything happen to you."

"You'll catch the plane? The Kurdish Superman?"

"Nothing will happen. I promise."

The plane tilts, city lights replaced with a large patch of nothing. *Mechanical trouble,* she thinks. An engine. They've made it this far, but there's an issue with the landing gear. "Lake Geneva. That's water. Is that better or worse?" *If the plane crashes.* That last part unsaid, a tremble beneath her words.

Delan cranes his head to look but says nothing.

A grab at logic: the stewardesses have simply told them to remain in their seats and given no further instructions. No crash-landing tutorials or warnings. But with another beat, it's the *lack* of information—ominous or otherwise—that looms suspicious.

Delan sits back. "My brother, Soran, when I visited him in London, he'd just started university and had this roommate from Switzerland. It was not my fault, but they both left for class and I was stoned and ate all the guy's chocolate from home."

"This is what you talk about when it might be the end?"

"It's not the end."

"And that *was* your fault, if you ate all his chocolate."

"No, because before that, I found a brownie and ate it, but no one told me what was in it. And it was very strong."

"But they didn't give it to you. You found it."

"I'm just saying, I have experience with Swiss people. And chocolate. That guy was okay. And my brother, you'd like him. He's serious like you. Not much fun. Top of his class."

The walls rattle, and the plane seems to compress with noise. Then the aisle lights flicker as her mind retrieves what he just said. "I'm not fun?"

"When you give yourself permission to be fun, you're the best. You're fun in a very ordered way. Like him. An architect. Did I tell you? Not even graduated and firms are after him."

"Not fun and now ordered," she says, knowing of course that she is. Her greatest pride and shame.

"He didn't like it when I told him that either. Too bad he's in England. You two could make lists of fun things for us to do."

He's distracting her. She sees this now, because suddenly they're about to land. Closer and closer. Noises louder, that feeling of compression intense. A flash in her mind: the plane will tilt and the wing will catch and they will flip into a cartwheel of orange. Now her mind sees only this. Feels it. Everything gathering, drawing to that moment.

Again, lights inside the cabin flicker—until all at once, they shut off. The world gone black. There is only sound. Encompassing, gripping sound. And within her—not tied with coherent thoughts or words—is something she will later remember as a feeling of all she would trade, all she would give up. Because the only thing that matters is living and that the man beside her live as well. A split second of undefined, borderless, and desperate bargaining.

Then a shot of bright. The lights back on, the world returned. All the people are still there, faces drawn with concentration or eyes closed—but no one panicking. She wants to cry from relief, just because the lights are on.

But it's not over. Sounds grow louder, everything gathering, collecting. Then a rumble begins. The plane shakes. She can't remember if this is normal for a landing. A high-pitched whirring starts, then the sound of flaps rising up against an impossible wind. She realizes she's not breathing only when she feels something on her arm and looks to see Delan with a pen, connecting three freckles above her elbow. *What,* she starts to say, but with a *thud* and a lurch, they hit the runway. The plane makes a sound like a crowd saying *ooooh,* and everything seems to rock back and forth but then, mercifully, straightens.

"I've always wanted to do that," Delan says. "A perfect triangle."

And he's right; there is now a triangle on her arm.

Wind pushes the walls of the plane as they taxi past stands of trees, toward a line of trucks with red and blue lights flashing. With that sight, she understands that something *was* very wrong, and somehow, by some miracle, they are lucky. Delan shows her the half-moon dents in his palm from her nails, and she looks up to see distant buildings that seem to float in lit-up beauty along the hills.

They are alive. But as they taxi away from the airport, not toward it, she understands something is *still* wrong. All at once she needs to be off the plane, to be walking—no, running—running to the airport. She's shocked that no one else appears to feel this, and even more shocked when the line to exit the plane is peaceful—something she also will think of later, how everything was orderly and it was the Lebanese businessmen who offered to carry the sleeping children.

Lights are bold on the tarmac. As they walk toward the airport, his arm around her waist and the plane at her back, she feels an increasing happiness with every step, a severing from whatever calamity held them. When she turns back once more, she sees that all the suitcases are outside, everything being opened one by one.

"We might not get our luggage tonight," Delan says.

Already she's thinking of a small bottle of damask rose oil he gave her for the trip. For every big occasion, she buys a new perfume. Certain scents for certain events. The day before they left, bottle in hand, Delan had instructed her to close her eyes and then drawn the oil over her wrists and the hollow of her neck, touching it lightly with his finger, then tracing it around the Celtic tree-of-life pendant she wears as a necklace, strung on a dark leather cord. Made of copper, the tree clutches a green jasper stone, and its wavering boughs stretch and lift like lightning, appearing to connect to the heavens just as the roots connect to the world below. As Olivia inhaled the scent, Delan pushed the symbol to the side and leaned forward, placing his lips upon the spot that was lighter from lack of sun.

Now he glances over his shoulder. "They need to find what they're looking for. Or make sure it's not there."

"What's not there?"

"A bomb."

"A *bomb?*"

"Not so loud," he says as they enter the airport. "I want a bed, not a cell."

Everything now makes sense. Through the window, the plane is still far removed, kept at a distance on the tarmac.

"*Threat,*" Delan says when the airline finally fills them in. "Key word. Bomb *threat*. So really, there was no bomb." He says this like someone mentioning it wasn't chocolate in a cookie but carob. *Surprise.*

"I thought pigeons," she says.

Half his mouth lifts in a smile. "The way you see the world."

She feels foolish. Her hope, her innocence, is something she tries to cover like an ill-fitting shirt. Delan is six years older than she is, around the same age as most of her friends, and only recently has she understood that this has her operating from a youthful, inexperienced deficit. "So you knew."

"Of course," he says. "But what could we do? Get off the plane? You panic when you have a choice." With his arm around her, he pulls her toward him, giving her a squeeze, and then turns to the woman behind the counter, taking on a charming smile. "Luggage. Please. Tell me it will find us at the hotel. I have gifts for my family, and I cannot replace them—and I will need to know where the chocolate is."

His gifts. A movie poster from his first job in the United States—a minor but key part in a huge film, and though he's not on the poster, his name is—and reviews of plays, which are his real love, though television and commercials and a job at a restaurant pay the bills. Also packed is a playbill from a production he was in last year, from before he and Olivia started dating, his face on the cover alongside that of his costar, a woman with a ski-slope nose and blonde hair that always looked slightly wet, a woman who'd once ended up at the kitchen table for breakfast. As well there are six necklaces, two men's gold-plated watches, and one watch with leather straps like dampened wood and a compass. When Olivia saw it, she'd known exactly who it was for: Aras, his best friend.

An *Amir Hez*, the head of a large unit of *Peshmerga*. *Those who face death,* he's told her of the word *Peshmerga's* meaning. *We grew up next door. He's been there since the start. If I show him a scar, he remembers the blood.*

"And we have to pay for the hotel?" Olivia now asks. Already she's adding up the cash in her wallet. In the Paris airport, she'd spent far too much on a Christmas ornament of the Eiffel Tower, but all things Christmas are her weakness. She's been known to sing carols in July and to carry around a small twig of fir tree to convince herself of another place and time.

"A bomb threat can happen to any airline," the woman says, eyes on the line behind them. "Like a blizzard. We don't pay for that either." A glance at Delan. "Your luggage will get to you at some point. Don't worry."

"And there's no flight soon to Beirut?" Olivia asks.

"It's a war there. They close early."

The perfume. Olivia thinks of it again. From where she stands at the counter, she looks back, toward the plane, feeling the scent that was to mark this trip left behind. Its absence twists with meaning, and there is an illogical worry within her that what's to come are days that were never meant to happen.

CHAPTER 2

Often Olivia tries to find the start of things. The true start. One that stretches past first meetings. After all, the real beginning is what led to a moment, what drilled the course, and so for everything big in her life—her move to Los Angeles, her love of photography, her relationship with Delan—she likes to revisit the past to find the markers that created the paths.

Her start with Delan began, in a way, with her job. Or, rather, even further back—with her decision to major in English in college, despite an unrelenting and consuming love of photographs that had her spending more time with images than the articles she read. Still, with this decision and a degree that said *English*, she figured any job in publishing would lead to a chance at writing and the future she'd signed up and paid for.

The first week at the newspaper was magical. The building itself was charged with life and energy and movement, and she sat in a bullpen of cigarette smoke amid phones that rang nonstop and metal file cabinets that clanged open and shut. Everyone's steps were hurried. To get in the way was a sin. Always organized, the person who dreamed of school-supply shopping, she lined up her stapler and tape dispenser and arranged her favorite pens, Parker's "Big Red," in her desk drawer. An ordered desk was an ordered mind, and her mind was nothing if not ordered. She was ready.

But by the end of the week, the glow was gone. She heard them called "office wives," the women who sat at the desks just beyond the glass, even though they had degrees and ideas and for the most part had taken the job, like she had, as a first step. They were made to order flowers and send gifts and told to be sure the scotch was stocked and the paperweights shone, while privately they listened in on meetings and submitted spec pieces that were shuffled to the bottom of piles. Feminism had taken hold, but the good old boys still held the reins in certain companies, and breaking in meant going through a wall that might be painted a different color but held all the same. *That's a sassy one,* Olivia'd heard an editor say about a woman in advertising who'd come in for a meeting. The men with him laughed.

There were only a few female reporters, and they worked hard and kept to themselves. Passing through the hall once, Olivia heard one of their names thrown out from behind a door left ajar. *You want to send in Holliday? It's a financial piece—and you're gonna send in a skirt?* The moment was made worse by the fact that Beth Holliday was actually walking from the other direction in the hall and heard it as well. There was a falter in her step, and her hand went to the wall beside her where she paused. An internal countdown perhaps. When she met Olivia's eyes, there was understanding and anger and commiseration and embarrassment, and, sure enough, the eventual byline of the piece was that of a man, and Beth Holliday avoided Olivia whenever she could.

But what did it, what really charted the course, was that Olivia found herself drawn to the photo department and watching the photo editor, a man named Peter Darrow, whose face was all but lost to his ever-expanding beard and whose love of hockey kept him pacing with a stick. There were no women on his staff, but his eyes stayed level in the hall, and once she'd seen him making coffee. When she could, she paused at his door, listening to debates: *No, no, not this one. Look how it's organized—everything competing with everything. Shit, who did this? I'm getting hives looking at it. No, really, look. On my arm right here.* There was a kind gruffness to him, like Santa in a bear suit. He cared little for decorum and his office was a mess and frequently there was a stain on his shirt from the food he tended to eat while walking, but his words about photography hooked her. She listened and looked at the secret collection of photographs she found inspiring, a collection she had hidden in a green Trapper Keeper in her drawer, and tried to see if they fell in line with his parameters, with what he thought made a photo stand out. She hoped they did.

And then, a bit over two years ago, it hit her that she didn't just want to appreciate good photos but to take them. That perhaps she could do it. That perhaps it wasn't too late. That night, she told her father she was interested in photography and pictured him pacing as he did when he got to thinking, his corduroy pants *swish*ing. "It's only too late when you believe you can't do it," he finally said. "So do it. Do whatever you want. Just do it big and bold and brave."

From Washington State, he made a call and bought her a professional camera. Instructed her to go to the bookstore a few blocks away, where he had two books set aside and paid for: Andreas Feininger's *Principles of Composition in Photography* and *The Complete Photographer*. The fact that he did this, purchased these gifts even from more than a thousand miles away, meant he'd have to set the heat in his small house at sixty-two and walk with a blanket around his shoulders. Meant that he'd buy cans of beans—*cheap nutrition, always have some for when rent is due*—for months and leave the car parked unless he had no other choice. She knew this, and his generosity meant she had to act, and that same day she registered for night classes at the community college.

Mornings before work, evenings after work, weekends, and holidays. As often as she could, she studied and saw the world through her viewfinder, developing an obsession with texture and a need to seek it out. Tree bark, cracks in dry soil, the craters in an orange rind. For days she'd play with capturing mood in one location, turning a luxurious and inviting pool when seen in early-morning sunlight into a place that was solemn, cold, and haunting through the blue light of dusk. Playing with high- or low-key printing, distorting perspective or using color filters, her tests turned her view of the world into a series of potential photos.

With this turn, she had hope. Suddenly her slog of a job was made palatable by the proximity to her desire. Just down the hall. She was there but not there, and she learned to repeat the phrase *This doesn't matter* in her mind when the noose around her days seemed to tighten. Sometimes she took a ruler to measure her handwriting, determined to keep it straight and small, fearing the day when it might shoot up or down in loose script, the moment she let the job defeat her. On mornings when the editors were behind closed doors and everyone was to be quiet, she felt a rising scream itch in her throat and had to hurry away.

But classes, supplies, lenses, film, even the considerable number of batteries needed for her MD-2 motor drive and flash, all of it was expensive, and each time she knew she needed to print just one more negative, or perhaps a dozen more in order to bring out a quality or effect, she felt her wallet tighten. Taking photos of anything in motion demanded a need to snap image after image, and one couldn't be afraid of wasting film, since with a dynamic subject, each shot would be different—and a missed shot could have been *the one*—but her budget made her fearful. Even using an acquaintance's darkroom— for those photos Fotomat could never do justice to, for the ones she wanted to put in her portfolio—even that sapped her checks. And her portfolio itself, all printed on glossy double-weight white paper, the cost was adding up. When she asked her boss about a raise, he looked at her hard and said he'd see what he could do but then added, *I thought you had someone; isn't this money for fun?*

A raise did not come through. And so an ad in the paper was answered. She was to meet a man at a diner on Vine, a man who owned a house in Hollywood and had two roommates but was looking for a third and told her she'd know him by the slice of chocolate pie with two forks he'd have waiting.

"Is one fork for me?" she asked, wanting to laugh.

"If a person doesn't like this pie," he responded, "they're out. So yes, a fork is for you. And then we'll see about the room."

She suspected the room would be the size of a closet and he sounded crazy, but the savings in rent would buy film and a new telephoto lens this month alone, so she had her foot on the clutch of her Rabbit within minutes, wishing she were hungry.

There, on the sidewalk by the diner, was one of the fattest dogs she'd ever seen. A golden retriever whose rolls slunk around his haunches. Olivia, who'd once missed an entire day of high school and spent all the money she'd had on turkey to lure a kitten from under a building, a calico her father still has, could never stop herself from greeting animals.

"Hi there, handsome," she said to the dog. The dog looked up, and she smiled.

"Hello," a voice said.

She'd not seen the man holding the dog's leash, but there he was. In patchwork brown velvet pants and a white linen shirt that roped across the top of his chest. More than handsome, in fact. The kind of good-looking that makes you take a step back, which she did.

"I was talking to him," she said, pointing to the dog.

The man's skin was slightly olive toned yet still managed to hint with red. Instead of looking away, however, he let his smile grow, as if the twist had both embarrassed and delighted him. "How do you know I wasn't saying hello on his behalf?" he asked as he tied the dog to the base of a phone booth.

"Then hello." She gave him a small wave to get him moving, heat resting below her eyes, and let him go into the diner first to avoid further humiliation. Five minutes she waited, scanning the street for anyone who looked like they had a room to rent, anyone who might like chocolate pie, and then she went in.

There, of course, was the same man, sitting in the first booth with chocolate pie and two forks.

"I was wondering when you were gonna come in," Delan said. "Thought you were stealing the dog."

"You didn't say you had a dog."

"I don't."

"All evidence to the contrary."

"His mother is shooting a scene for *Laverne & Shirley*. He is my child for one day only." Then he watched her, silently, that unwavering, unapologetic gaze of someone who's made it their job to study people. "You're tall," he finally said. Her eyes must have showed her surprise because he quickly added that she was lucky.

Sliding into the booth, she was aware his legs were inches from her own. The space beneath the table suddenly seemed smaller than it should be, in part because he was right—she was tall. Distracted, she started talking. "I was the one forced to buy beer. Let on roller coasters when I was way too young and way too scared, and I can't blend in even if I try." She stopped, hearing her own reveals. "Lucky is a matter of perspective."

He smiled widely. "You're right. You don't blend in."

She shifted in her seat, unsure if it was a compliment, though her face seemed to interpret it as such, her cheeks again filling with heat.

He pushed the slice of pie in her direction, and as she cut down with her fork, she felt his gaze, intense and curious, and realized that this bite was actually the interview and that this man was going to be her roommate. And he had a girlfriend, she figured. Which was good because she'd just started dating a musician named Ted, who at that point hadn't yet begun to bother her, and she knew that if there was a line that could not be crossed, it existed within a living space. *Off-limits,* she told herself, but even then watched his fork as he brought it to his mouth.

Delan's house became hers. A peeling Craftsman in the heart of Hollywood. The site of parties where artists of all types smoked and talked and often sang on the couch or the patio and once from the roof, which was ill advised. After only a few months of living there, she felt the restless lack in what she had with Ted and called it quits. Because Olivia wanted love. Romantic, consuming, distracting love. The true kind. But she kept this to herself; most of her friends were women who relished in their freedom, in their lack of ties, and so the desire to love and be loved made Olivia feel youthful and unevolved. Made her feel as if all the progress women had made with sexual freedom simply slid from her like something that wouldn't stick, because commitment was what Olivia wanted, what she'd always wanted. She could take care of herself but craved someone's caring.

That night, after ending things with Ted, she made a neatly lined list in her steno pad of qualities she wanted in a man. On a new page she wrote *FOR ME* and underlined it three times. It was a night when the air held a green shock of rosemary from the neighbor's dog's wandering forays, Delan was at rehearsal, Rebecca on a date, and Mason—her other male roommate, an artist and activist who'd gone against Vietnam and ended up in prison for more than a year—was out prowling for women. Olivia's room felt tower high in its isolation, and she worked on the list for over an hour. When she was done, she went into the bathroom and burned all but the bottom part, which she held between her fingers, attempting to send her requests into the ether, into the heavens, to her mother, or to anyone, and in the process set a hand towel on fire. Frantic, sweating, she stood in a bathroom doused in water and laughed at her eager, all-encompassing desire and then cried because most people just went to bars when they were lonely, while she was the kind of person who'd set a bathroom on fire.

Then there were the creaking sighs of Rebecca's footsteps on the stairs. Rebecca, at this point, was single and exuded a take-no-prisoners quality with her sexuality, a fearless older-woman sophistication from having lost the love of her life to the war, and truth be told, she was the last person to whom Olivia wanted to explain the charred remains of this particular wish. But to throw away the remainder seemed like a bad symbolic message to the universe, so by the time Rebecca was on the landing, Olivia had slipped into her room and hidden what was left. Safe.

Time passed. Life in the house became set and cherished. Delan and Rebecca, the people she most wanted to see, the ones who lined bad days in silver and gave her more reason to stay home than to leave. Then, almost five months ago, she couldn't sleep and ended up cleaning out her desk. There, under a notebook, she found that partial bit of the list that hadn't burned. The edges were blackened and crisp and left a trace of dark on her fingertips, and there was a faint scent to it, something that hinted at aftermath. Then a knock on the door and Delan was standing in the threshold.

"*The Tonight Show*'s on," he said. "I'm making pasta."

She was wearing her nightgown. Knee-length white cotton with white embroidery on the bodice and braided satin straps. Her *Little House on the Prairie* nightgown, as he called it, which was the reason she usually had it covered. But now she wore nothing else, and in a split second there was the lowering of his eyes, and she felt a shiver and a thrill and then a shyness. So she looked down to the paper in her hand, grateful for the distraction.

And that's when she read the words: *Someone to watch* The Tonight Show *with.*

Certainly it was timing. But maybe it was more. Whatever it was, the room seemed to fill with a pounding, and her hand shook as she put the paper back in the drawer. Other items from the list came back to her—*someone who is bold and not a wallflower, someone who knows his way around a kitchen, someone who's artistic*—and she realized what she'd done: described him. Her roommate. The person she'd told herself was off-limits. The person she'd been attracted to but passed off as a playboy, a ruthless flirt whose interest in whomever he was with swelled and faded with the moon. He was not someone to fall for, but in that moment, she realized it was too late. That clearly it had been too late for some time.

"What's wrong?" he asked as she passed by. "Something's wrong."

Not knowing what to say, she stopped walking, as if her words might catch up to her. He waited and then said her name, his voice rising slightly at the end, arcing into a question.

Within minutes, she was watching as he stirred tomato sauce on the stove, then nodding dully when he said he could use some oregano and basil from the garden.

"What were you looking at?" he asked as she was about to walk outside. "That paper."

He faced the stove and so she studied the paisley of his shirt, the collision of patterns where it creased at the elbow. "Part of a list. One of the things I wanted in a man."

Now he turned, watching her, holding an open palm under the spoon to catch the drips. "What was it?"

"Someone to watch *The Tonight Show* with." She thought he would laugh.

But he didn't. His gaze was steady as she opened the back door and even as she stepped down into the garden. And all at once, it hit her. What she'd said, it was just enough to ruin the ease they'd always had with one another. With this, everything would change.

Rocks on the path pushed into her feet. Her shoulders tensed with cold. She wondered how long she could stay out here before he checked on her, and that thought made it worse—knowing he would check on her. Because he would. He always did. He brought her blankets on nights they sat by the firepit and made sure her umbrella was by the door on days it rained. He observed. He noticed. They both did. They always had. What would this do to that routine? How would it affect the way kindness was felt? How would it make them second-guess caring?

Pots were lined along the wall, and the herbs inside had gone wild. Already the basil had begun to flower, so she pinched farther down on the stem like he'd taught her, then brought it to her nose. There was that fresh, slightly licorice scent, and she heard him on the path.

"Liv."

A last breath in of the basil, the flowers bright with streetlight. She lowered her arm, needing to face the moment. But then his hand was on her wrist. She turned to him, and he stood there, making a decision. And she saw it in him, a sad curiosity and his need to be kind to her, to let her down easy, and with this she was about to cry—not just because she wanted him, and *want*, once recognized, is a ruthless accomplice— but because already something had ended.

Then she heard him breathe. A deep breath in and an exhale out that seemed to catch slightly with sound. Barely there, but in the silence of the garden, she heard it. A sound that made her heart beat faster. And at that point, she realized that his fingers were still on her wrist, moving as he felt her skin, and that the sad curiosity had actually been a search- ing curiosity, and then his grasp tightened as he pulled her toward him and his other hand went to her hair, fingers curled against the strands.

That electric brink of anticipation. He came close but not close enough, and time spread out, and with it came an increasing heat as the space between them slowly thinned. Then there was the warmth of his breath as his lips were almost against hers, but still he held back, until all at once she pressed into him, kissing him and present in every inch of her body in a way she never was. The surface of her skin felt charged. Her toes, even. She moved a bare foot so it was against his, and her skin flared.

Everything was still and silent. Just a bit, she opened her eyes to see that this was him, that this moment was real, and when she did, she saw him do the same. Still, his right hand was in her hair and his left was wrapped around her wrist, fingers pressed into the center where the vein pulsed.

CHAPTER 3

"I bet we were diverted here for a reason," Delan tells Olivia now as they drive the streets of Geneva without their luggage.

That scrap of paper from her list, the one that mentioned *The Tonight Show* and led to their first kiss, is currently framed and on his bedside table because he is the believer in fate, the one who sees the roots of events, all that grew and gathered and had to be just to create one beat where words spoken would match words written, all so the rest would unfold.

"Something might've happened in Baghdad," he continues. "An accident maybe."

All they have are Delan's backpack, inside of which is a change of clothes and some toiletries, and Olivia's purse and camera bag, inside of which is her Nikon F2 Photomic—improved automatic film advance and a wider shutter-speed range, her black-and-silver best friend—and the MD-2 motor drive that allows six frames per second and automatic film advance and rewind. *You have nothing to wear,* Delan had said earlier, *but at least you have twenty pounds of lenses and color filters and film.* To that she had agreed, because the thought of being separated from her camera was truly upsetting. She'd realized he was being sarcastic only when he started laughing.

Photography is a start she feels she's still in. Caught in a perpetual state of *ready*, like a quivering crouch at a starting line that's gone on too long. But that could change. Just a month and a half ago, after the tickets to Iraq had been booked and paid for, the contest at work had been announced. A bit of in-house fun. Selected anonymously in the middle of June, the best photo would win its owner a spot in the photo department, courtesy of an employee who gave his advance notice for the middle of the summer. A chance based on merit. There were months to prepare, and an undercurrent of competition wedged itself among the rookies and those who manned the desks. *And now this contest,* she'd said to Delan the day it was announced. Because with the timing of the trip, she had a chance to take photos that would stand out, that would be different from those of the scenery just outside the office door. *Fate,* Delan had replied. *Opportunity,* she'd countered.

Ornate buildings and cafés and streetlights like full moons. For a while they watch it all streak by, this detour on which they're captive.

"So where are you from?" Delan asks the driver.

"Mumbai."

"Mumbai," he says with drawn-out wistfulness. "I had a girlfriend from Mumbai. Her hair was like onyx, like the chiseled side of onyx. So shiny."

The man's eyes find Olivia in the rearview mirror, and she smiles to assure him it's okay and then feels Delan squeeze her hand.

The hall on the hotel's second floor is long, with impossibly high ceilings. *Eighteenth century,* the clerk had told them when Delan asked the building's age. *With drafts to prove it, I bet,* Olivia had added.

"What did they do in the eighteenth century that demanded such high ceilings?" she now asks.

"Their hair," Delan says. "Three-feet-tall hair. Powdered white and dangerous."

"With peacock feathers."

"Or peacocks."

Inside the room, there is a window with a view of two streets that seem to branch from the spot in which they stand. "You," he says, turning her so she's facing the window, his fingers on the rise of her hip bone. "You and me here. Look at this."

And she does. There is the dark luster of streets and the city in the glass, and the feeling of his lips along her neck while their reflection hovers before them in a faint overlay. This moment. It wasn't supposed to happen. They exist in the middle of everything, this night like an accidental slip in time. It makes her think that yes, they can be forever, and she was right to hope and believe their differences won't matter because if you want something enough, you make it happen. You find yourself in an unexpected place, something shared. This, this is what they need.

After loading in black-and-white film, she opens the window and leans out while Delan holds her waist; then she twists to capture the row of buildings beside her, pulling against his grasp. "I'm not gonna fall."

But his grip tightens. "You really think that's the only reason I'm holding you?"

For a second, she loses her focus, feeling only him standing behind her and the points of pressure from his fingertips and even his smile that she knows is there, and she must remind herself that he is not going anywhere, but this view will be brief and in her life for only one night. So once again she finds her focal point in the spread of buildings next to her: a sign with the white cross of Switzerland. *Click.* In black and white, with the diffused light from the streetlamps and the ancient building and the cross, it will feel like a long-ago plea for help.

Minutes later, she watches as he pulls off his shirt. At the airport, she'd bought a white T-shirt and red sweatpants, since her nightgown is stuck with her luggage, wherever that is, and already she's changed into them. When he moves his arm down, shirt in hand, the face of his wristwatch flashes with the streetlight's glare.

"This is the last night we'll be sleeping in the same bed," he says, nodding to what she's wearing. "Which means you wasted good money."

A smile as she pulls the covers back. It's supposed to fade, she knows. Chemistry lasts only so long. The fact that what's between them is still so present, so remarkable, is a slight, nagging worry, as if its brilliance is only due to a dullness elsewhere within their relationship. Or, worse, perhaps he was like this with every woman he's been with—an equally nullifying thought. But of course, this is what she does—invents problems—and so she wills herself to stop thinking.

"Will they be worried," she asks, "when we don't show up as planned?"

"Do you know there's no word in Kurdish for *plan*? You get worried if someone's on time, because it means they have bad news. Or they want something. Also, I said I might come. Not that I would."

A car's headlight flashes through his hair. "I think what's most surprising is that I'm not surprised."

"But if I say I'm coming," he continues, getting in bed, "then the government ears that listen to the calls know I'm coming. And know to start watching us in case Aras visits. It's fine. My mother knew what I meant."

"And me? Did you say I *might* be there too?"

"Of course. Don't worry. They'd expect you."

"You and your American girlfriend."

"They will love you."

"But they'll wish I was Kurdish."

"They will love you," he says again.

She curls into him, her hand on his chest, fingers dragging against him. Beyond their door is the rumbled roll of a suitcase being wheeled.

"Olivia."

Her hand stills. He never calls her that. Always Liv. The sound of her full name from him is beautiful but unnerving, and his accent—slight after all these years—is somehow heavier on the O. It makes her think of all the accents he can do so well—Irish, English, South African, Spanish—which then makes her realize that in fact what she hears from him every day could be an accent, an act, or an effort.

"If I tell you something, will you not make a big deal of it? I just need to hear myself say it so I can decide what I think."

She's about to chide him—*you only want to hear yourself talk?*—till she realizes he's serious. "What?"

"Last year, I had a dream."

She waits. Delan is notorious for his dreams, long tales told over breakfast or in bars that involve symbols and metaphors, nature always a main character, so in-depth that there are intricate plotlines and places he's never been to but where he returns. Almost always the dreams can be interpreted—by him—in such a way as to prove they came true. An entire catalog of hindsight prophecies.

"In the dream, my brother wasn't in England. He was back in my hometown. Nailed to a tree in our yard. A big fig tree we have. Blood dripped down the trunk onto the rocks. He was left there, barely alive, and all I could hear was my mother's voice calling me to help him, but I couldn't move."

Olivia waits for more, for the thunder or lightning or earthquake, the drama that always accompanies his dreams and renders them simply great tall tales. Instead she hears only his heartbeat, and there is a feeling that this dream is different from the rest. Still, she wants to reassure him, so she props herself up on her elbow and gives him her attention.

"Anxiety. You feel disconnected. They're far away. That's why you felt helpless, why you couldn't move. You talk to your brother after the dream?"

"Sure. He was in London, happy. Everything was good. Good grades. He's got a girlfriend there. The *one*, he said."

"There you go."

"But the dream was one of the reasons I agreed to go. My mother calling me. There was something wrong with my family. I feel like I should've told you. All disclosure."

"You dream in metaphor. He's not there, and your mother wasn't needing you. That was guilt and your general inability to help, your worry that *if* something did go wrong, you couldn't get there. And it's *full disclosure.*"

"I have a feeling we shouldn't go."

Now she lies back, and as he speaks, she studies the tin-tiled ceiling.

"I read the dream wrong."

"It was a dream."

"We should stay here. Forget the trip."

"You're serious?"

"Would you do that? I would make it up to you. You and me, here. This in itself is amazing. Maybe it is fate. We just have to listen to what it's saying."

Destiny, he likes to go on about, referring to it like a friend he'd run into who'd whispered ale-soaked secrets late at night. But it's strange, this twist in him. Usually so bold, he's the first one out of the car, the first one through a door, the first to speak when tempers spark the air. That now he lies there, asking her what she thinks, admitting he's essentially scared, it undoes something within her.

The part that will shame her later is that in this moment, there is a certain appeal of being, for once, the one who is brave. But it's more than this. Only a month from now, she will sit in her father's car back home in Washington, a May day of rain and not much else, and watch the drops hit the windshield. In one spot on the glass is something invisible—grease, a light dust—something that makes the drops skirt around it, dividing off into little jagged explorations down the glass. And it's this moment in Geneva that she'll think of, this seemingly invisible moment that caused the course. *But your tickets were bought,* Rebecca will say on the phone that night, *you were on your way; you didn't* make *the trip happen in that moment.* Which would be true but also not true. *I could've stopped it,* Olivia will respond. *He wanted me to stop it. He was asking me to stop it.* To that, Rebecca will also say what she knows is right: *You wanted to know him better. Wanting to go there was not wrong.*

The crux of everything: *I need to prove that we are not so different. That this stands a chance. I want it to stand a chance, so I need to see what he's afraid to show me.*

True. All true.

But not in this moment. In this moment, she sees her camera bag on the floor and opportunity. A chance to prove herself. A ticket into a club that so far has not even noticed her hovering by the door. She sees the one interview she'd had with a well-known photojournalist who was looking to mentor someone, a low-paying lackey gig that would provide hands-on experience and keys to a future. For an hour, she'd waited in a lobby that seemed to seethe with orange furniture, hoping that her portfolio would speak for itself, and then saw the man exit the elevator and walk right past her to the doors. The day was overcast with shots of bright, and he squinted with his hand over his eyes before finally turning to see her standing behind him.

"You're Murray," he said.

"Olivia Murray."

He nodded slowly, then motioned to the couch. When seated, he studied the first image in her portfolio for a while and then quickly flipped a page and then another, and was only three in before he stopped. "Thing is, I have people with experience who want this. Who've put themselves out there and proven they're up to the task."

"I'm sure. But it's hard to get experience when you don't get a chance."

A smile. "They made their chances. That's what they'd say. Bottom line, though, I need someone who's gonna be around."

"I'm not going anywhere."

He studied her. "You're how old? Because I'll be honest, your stuff's good, but I don't want to put work into someone only to lose them to a clock."

"A clock?"

"*The* clock."

He made a *tick*ing sound, and she felt herself redden and looked down at the coffee table with its sharp glass corners and vowed right then to tell no one at the paper of her dream. Not till she had images that proved she could do it, despite her lack of experience, despite her being young and a woman with some clock others thought they could hear.

So in this moment, she sees this and hears the ticking clock that has had no effect on her life whatsoever but that prevents her from work. And she thinks of the contest. How in Los Angeles she can take photos Peter Darrow will nod at and pass off, or she can continue on course and do something different and take photos that would make him lean in, photos that would stand out and maybe even negate the strikes she apparently has against her.

Hannity will get it, she overheard the day before she left for her trip. Hannity, who was actually a junior editor in advertising and had shown off his photographs during lunch one day, all Jack Garofalo knockoffs of community found within the streets, just swap out Harlem with South LA. Also top in the running was Kyle Rudger, whose father was LAPD and promised him adventure in a ride-along. And Trevor Miller, a gadgeteer who always had the latest equipment. Miller's grandmother was in a home with *at tops a week left,* he'd mentioned, as if adding that she would levitate for the camera. The boys, as they tended to do, spoke freely in front of Olivia. No one knew she was submitting; no one saw her as competition or noticed her studying the flyer on the door that outlined the rules of the competition—*Submit three photos by June 1 to Peter Darrow . . . and don't waste his time!*—which made it worse, to be so not-thought-of. Suddenly she'd felt jittery with hope. And bold. All they didn't know about her and her future bunched beneath her skin.

"I take photos," she'd said. It was lunch in the break room, and the kettle on the stove began to whistle. *I take photos.* Not even *I'm a photographer* or *It could be me who gets the spot.* Downplayed. *I take photos.* A statement like *I take baths.*

"You do?" Hannity said. "I didn't know." Despite his arrogance and his derivativeness, he was a polite man, and his insults were never found in what was said but rather whom he chose to say it to. He turned back to Trevor Miller to continue his conversation.

"Anyhow," she said, already feeling a deep hook of regret. "I'll be back in a few weeks. Maybe with photos." *Maybe.* Another soft, feathered word.

"A little vacation?" a voice said. "Some sand and sun?"

Ben. She'd not seen him enter the room. Not a fledgling like the others—a boss. An editor who'd started almost a year before. Her *mistake*, as she'd started calling him.

"Trying to get away?" he continued. A loaded, coarse question, given what had happened between them months prior to that night in the garden with Delan.

He smiled, and maybe that was all it took. Olivia felt defiance vine into her words. "Some sun and sand, maybe. But northern Iraq is supposed to be different from southern, so we'll see."

And with that, she'd walked out of the room, departing through a layer of silence. The feeling carried her on broad shoulders the rest of the day.

What would she say when she returned? That she never made it? That the Alps weren't as snowy as she'd thought they'd be? And Delan, what would happen from losing this chance to really know him? Will she one day be just another one of his girls, a story to tell a cabdriver on a darkened street, a part of someone else's vacation?

"You've been back twice in fifteen years," she says to him. "And now you're almost there. And I know you're nervous, but—"

"Nervous is waiting for a callback. Nervous is parking the car to pick up your date. This isn't nervous. This is a pit I keep getting in my stomach."

"Delan, it's a different nervous. It's bigger. Mixed with so much else. Guilt for leaving? Sadness for having missed out on things?"

For a moment, he says nothing. "Did you know," he says at last, "I came to America on the same plane as the Beatles? Their first tour in America. When I told my mother that, she cried because she thought it was a sign that I'd be famous. And then I cried because I knew she'd one day die never having flown on a plane."

Always she'd heard the story of his arrival to the country, the women screaming from the tarmac, how he'd—*for just a moment*, he'd be sure to add in, laughing—thought they were there for him. But never had he told her the part about his mother.

Now he waits for her to speak, to allow him this turn of events. But she doesn't want to, because she believes it will be fine and that at his core, he is just nervous, and there is simply too much riding on this trip—for both of them—to go home. So she gets up and turns, sitting beside him to face him. "It's good for us to go. You know it is."

At first, he doesn't look at her. Just watches the ceiling as the lights slink across the surface. "And you're not worried?"

"A little. Of course. But tonight? I'm alone with you."

Now he meets her eyes. "For the last time."

His gaze is steady, and just that, the way he's looking at her, makes her feel as if everything has come loose within her. *For the last time.* She hears it again and is brought back to just minutes ago when she'd stood at the window telling herself to only think of taking photos, since he wasn't going anywhere. And with the recollection, she feels it. A ripple of unease.

"For the last time *in weeks*," she corrects and sits up again so she can rest her right leg on the other side of him.

Her fingers stretch along his stomach, and she hears the sound of her own breathing and through the open window, a car door that slams and a dog that barks at someone's return. Then his hand is against her chin, and she turns in to his touch, feeling his eyes steady upon her. And even when he sits up, when he's slid his hand beneath her shirt and pressed his palm hard between her shoulder blades as a brightness flares against them from a turn of headlights, even then she knows he's not looked away.

CHAPTER 4

Baghdad. Hot even in slender strips of shade. Wide streets with no lane markers. The swerve of cars pitted from sand. Date palms sway past rooftops or lift high above billboards, the clusters of fruit like pollen on giant flowers. At times, it feels as though Olivia's found herself caught in the pages of a magazine or history book, until the noise and dust and the smell of buses and grilling meat plant her where she is. All of Baghdad is a work in progress and a collision of centuries, with unfinished buildings and white houses, everything seeming to *move* but against itself, the whole city caught in different, conflicting currents of motion all at once.

Though some men wear *thawb*, white tunics and white headdresses encircled at the top with a black cord, most are dressed as they are in the West, just as the women are both in shapeless *abaya*, long black cover-ups, as well as in short-sleeve dresses that hit their knees, their hair loose in waves. At a light, a young man in flared brown pants and a striped button-down shirt that's left open at the top watches Olivia, his toes tapping, the bones of his chest showing through like a pattern.

"The Tigris," Delan says as they approach a bridge.

When they're stopped, she opens her camera bag, trying to focus on a boat capsized in the reeds. Then her attention's drawn to a boy jumping in from a pile of rocks, joining his friends who float nearby. *Click.* Her early-childhood summers were spent in lakes or rivers as well, and at once she feels that really, truly, the differences between her and Delan could be negligible. Since they've arrived, she's started gathering similarities. Coca-Cola. Oleander that grows against high walls. Swimming in rivers.

He nudges her. "You see? Every country had a British invasion."

She turns and catches a red double-decker bus cutting off a pickup truck. The driver honks four times. Hot air pushes fumes into their car.

They have no luggage, so Delan gave the airlines his aunt's address in Baghdad, which Olivia remembers having used for her visa application to not draw attention to the Kurdish area she'd be visiting.

"Will she be mad that we're just showing up?" Olivia asks.

"Mad? She would be mad if we didn't stay with her. She's my favorite aunt. And we have chocolate."

A mosque draws nearer, the four minarets on the corners rising up like giant birthday candles. "Al-Kadhimiya Mosque," Delan says. "You should see it up close. The tiles. If you didn't believe in God, you would then."

She turns to him, surprised. "Really? And not in the power to create?"

"And who gave you that?"

"My father."

"Everyone has a father. Some fathers are just not on this earth."

The city streaks behind him. In the last decade, most of her friends—even those who'd not gone to war—had let the concept of God be beaten away in torrents of Vietnamese rain, burned in the jungles, or obliterated in a blast that claimed a village. A world of such atrocities could not be under the jurisdiction of a compassionate God, and who wanted to believe in an uncompassionate God? That Delan believes is something she'd never considered. "I didn't know you believed in God. Allah?"

"My family's Muslim but not practicing. Most Kurds are Muslim, and most were converted ages ago at the end of a sword. But we have all religions. I'm Zoroastrian, or I was. Now I don't believe in anything, as much as I believe in everything. But I like to be convinced."

With that, he places his hand on her thigh, out of the view of the cabdriver, and she closes her eyes to his touch, wondering which side of the argument she represents.

Soraya is his aunt, a short woman with short, dark hair and a midsection that seems equally distributed, chest and stomach plentiful. A smile breaks upon her face when she sees Delan and flickers only once upon seeing Olivia. A confusion. Delan wasn't expected, much less a red-haired American. *Give her the chocolate,* Delan had told her moments ago as they pressed the buzzer, and so now Olivia presents the box like roses from a suitor.

It works. The small hallway cracks with excitement, and words are spoken between aunt and nephew until the woman takes Olivia's hand in her own, pulling her through her door, into an apartment with walls that are painted like a garden. Every surface has a yellowing ivory background covered in painted plant life: blooms and stems, vines and trees. With the old furniture and aged Oriental rugs, it's like stepping through time to an abandoned garden world.

Olivia lifts her camera bag. "Can I?" she asks Delan. He turns the question to his aunt, who nods an approval, pleased, it seems, that this room will make it onto film that will be carried overseas.

"My cousin," Delan says as Olivia focuses on a framed black-and-white photo of a man, full stalks of blue hyacinth painted on the wall in the background. "Don't worry, my aunt doesn't understand English. She was sick, cancer. All this he painted to cheer her up. He was an artist, one of the best. But he had just started teaching. Without his job, there was no money for her treatments and his job was in our hometown, six hours away. Tall, I remember that. He must've been six two."

The man's face is smooth in the photo, though perhaps softened by the black and white, the haze of the soft focus and diffused light. Still, he's young. Too young to be referred to in past tense.

"The government wanted him to speak out against the Kurds," Delan continues. "He said no, and one day went to buy yogurt. They shot him on the sidewalk. In the back of the head."

Olivia tries to not react.

"That was a decade ago. Maybe more. He just wanted yogurt." A beat as he looks at the photo. "I hate that. Dying, having been hungry for something."

Before Olivia can say anything, Soraya is there, pressing something into the palm of her hand and then clasping her own hands over Olivia's for just a moment, as if sealing in a gift. A delicate square of soap, tied with a ribbon. Rose, sweet and peppery. If her luggage never arrives, Olivia decides she'll keep it in her pocket, and the scent, as Delan intended, will mark the voyage.

She thanks Soraya, who says something in Kurdish. Delan follows with the translation.

"She wishes she had more to give you, but she didn't know. And she told me that 'a good companion shortens the longest road.' Which means she's thanking you for bringing me home."

"I didn't. You brought me here."

"If it weren't for you, I don't know that I would be here."

Words that will soon, in only weeks, repeat in her mind in an unstoppable refrain.

Delan is given the couch and Olivia a room with a twin bed and a window that's gone gold with the lit-up mosque. The room used to belong to Delan's cousin, a man Olivia sees never got the chance to need a double bed, and now she stands before it, studying the Pacific blue of the bedspread and knowing that tonight she will sleep in the imprint of his ghost.

Shew bash: good night. At last she closes the door to her room, the brass knob worn from the ghost's hands. The window is open, and jasmine's rich aroma drifts from a plant Soraya has on her narrow balcony, its many arms wound around the railing. Directly above the mosque, the stars appear faded but far off are emboldened in a crisp contrast to the kohl sky.

The night curls on its edge. Dark deepening, some sounds muting and tucking away till morning, while others—cars, dogs barking— simply fall into the background. As she rolls over, she catches voices in the other room.

Unable to sleep, she goes to them; Delan is perched at the end of the couch, Soraya sitting forward in a chair, voice a furious whisper and hands a moving blur in the lamplight. Rocking back and forth, as if gathering momentum for the next tirade, his aunt opens her mouth to speak but stops when she sees Olivia. Quietly, she takes Olivia's hands and gives them a squeeze before leaving, her bedroom door clicking in place.

"She's mad at you?" Olivia asks Delan.

"At me, no." He opens the balcony door and steps outside, then motions for Olivia to follow.

The night is a sweet pollution. On the sixth floor, where they stand, they're above the buildings across the street, and the city lights beyond stretch into black, braced by billboards. To the left, the light from the mosque is like nothing she's seen. "I need my camera."

"No, wait. Stay." He's leaned against the gray iron railing, his arms on the spots where the jasmine doesn't vine, and for a moment she wonders if he'd chosen to stand exactly there so he doesn't hurt the plant, which is, she knows, something he would do. "We talked about it, I know. But it was a mistake to come."

"She *was* mad at you."

"Not at me. But it's not as safe as I thought. Better than before, yes. That's true. But areas near my hometown, it's not great."

Below is a teahouse, the metal tables left outside black in the night. Olivia watches the street, trying to process. Of course she'd known it wasn't completely safe. That was where her reticence came in, but in some ways, it was a draw. To challenge herself. To find adventures rather than another day at a desk. To push through what easily could be a hemmed-in life. *Live big and bold and brave,* her father likes to say. When she'd told him about her plans, about the coded call to Delan's mother who said it was safe—coded because the government tapped their phones, since his family is political, just as they censor the letters—she'd felt bad, picturing him at a rainy window, sitting in his green chair after a long shift as manager of Zayle's Deli, listening to someone else's adventure.

"The concept of *peaceful* is relative," her father finally said. "What's been done to the Kurds, if someone only lightly beat them with a hammer, they might call that peaceful." A deep breath, which always signaled a verdict. "Liv. You use excuses to leave people. But him? If you're worried you don't know him—that's not a reason to leave; it's why you lean a little closer." At the time she'd just laughed and countered with, "Why should I bother to listen closer if he doesn't talk about what's important?"

"Is Soraya your mother's sister?" she now asks Delan.

Calm. No anger. He nods. "That's who she's mad at. She thinks she didn't tell me the truth because she wanted me to come home. Could be true, I don't know. I also might've gotten the codes wrong."

A bird swoops overhead, alone in the sky. Olivia starts to laugh, a small laugh that erupts from her like a spill. "*Your uncle is well; I'll pass along your greeting*—that could've meant *whatever you do, don't come?*"

"Maybe. The calls, they're minutes long. I heard clicking; that means the lines are tapped. I couldn't ask."

"*Delan.*"

But he's not smiling. He's not laughing. "Would you blame her? If she *did* mean I should come. If she let us come when it wasn't safe?"

He wants an answer. And in this, she understands that it's not *his* view of his mother that concerns him—it's hers. "She wouldn't have put you in danger. Us. You, you're her son."

"Danger," he says. "It's their *home*. Why should I be so much better than my own parents that I shouldn't walk the streets they walk?"

"I didn't say that. And it's not about being better. It's about a mother protecting her child, wanting what's best for her child. She'd *want* you to stay away if it kept you safe."

Now he turns to her, and what had touched on anger seems more like grief. "And what kind of son accepts that?"

Car horns, music that's faint from open windows. His question hangs, and all his past reasons for having gone home only twice—time, money, a job that kept him in town—are now revealed as half-truths. The convenient, shinier side of the coin. "So why, then?"

For a second, he looks surprised that she would ask him. And she sees it, a gathering of sorts, like a breath before a motion. He's going to reach under that bravado of his, that need he has to rarely admit hurt, and finally show her a part of him he'd thought better hidden. He's going to let her in. She waits, but instead he looks to the sky. To a plane that glows distant and slow. And in his focus, she understands that his resolution is gone.

"Danger is relative," he says at last. "What your father said is true."

"Peace. He said peace."

"I think you should go home."

"Just me? No. If you can stay, I can stay."

There is, for a moment, the start of a smile on his face. Just for a second, though, before he turns away.

The mosque smolders gold in the dark. Otherworldly and alluring. She watches it, the way the light seems to pulse, to emanate, and though the thought of leaving him here, of never meeting his family or seeing his life, is itself a devastation, at this moment the deeper ache is from turning away from a chance to take photographs that could help her career—and the second she realizes this, she feels shame that at a moment when she should be thinking of him, she is instead thinking of herself. And then this shame infuriates her. Why should she feel bad for taking herself seriously? Why, when she allows herself the opportunity and risk for love, should she not do the same for her career?

When she turns back to him, he's watching her, waiting. "I won't go home."

A deep breath. "Liv. There's no official war—but war never needs to be declared. The resistance, the nationalists, they're being targeted. The Peshmerga. Anyone the government thinks is associated with them. And the secret police, the Iraqi military—they're everywhere. And ruthless. What they do to people, to get information. And there are rumors," he adds, "that someone in my family is an informant."

"You think it's true?"

"Of course not. The military starts the rumors. It's a tactic. To break up families."

"So what do the rumors matter?"

"It means my family is being looked at."

"Because of Aras? Because your family is close with him? Or because of your other aunt, the political one?"

"Because we're Kurds. It doesn't matter. You'll go home. I'll pay you back for your ticket. You, of all people, I shouldn't have dragged here."

You, of all people. One night, a couple of months ago, she'd walked in to find him, Mason, and their friend Alan in the kitchen, no one talking. The bamboo light shade cast blocks of shadows, and the faucet's drip was steady. Through an open window were the insistent piano notes of Foreigner's "Cold as Ice." Somber. Everyone was somber.

"What?" she asked. "Someone die?"

Alan nodded, and when he spoke, his voice was loose with liquor. "The rabbit died. I knocked up Cass."

There was a moment when no one spoke, so she reached for words, used to words making things better. "Okay," she said. "I know it'll be hard—"

Mason shook his head. "No. You of all people don't get to give advice on this."

Immediately she'd glanced at Delan, feeling angry and embarrassed. But Delan only refilled their glasses, the scent of scotch an iron fist in the air. Looking back to Mason, she felt fire in her words. "And what the hell does that mean?"

"Don't get bent out of shape. Just means you're a romantic. And romantics can't give advice to someone with real shit going on."

Alan interrupted, holding his hand up to command attention. "What he's saying, in a not nice way, sorry about that, is I'm taking the night-manager job. The one they offered me last year."

"But then you can't do theater."

Delan smiled at her in the checkered light. "You *are* a romantic. You're my romantic. And that's wonderful. But not everyone is as lucky to have choices. I hope you never have to understand that."

Young. Naive. Not understanding life. *You of all people.* The way he saw her, the way everyone saw her—irritation rose within her. "I've done things that would surprise you," she says now.

When she looks at him, he's smiling, and even for a moment she's glad to have lifted his mood. "Tell me."

"I climbed a fence into the Hollywood Memorial Park and smoked at Harrison Gray Otis's obelisk." He raises his eyebrows in a question, and she explains. "One of the original *Los Angeles Times*'s publishers."

"A passive-aggressive fuck-you to your industry. That's cute."

"There was one other time that wasn't so passive-aggressive." He watches her, and even as she says the words, she wills them back. "With an editor, one of my bosses."

"You smoked grass with an editor."

She touches a jasmine bloom. The smell is intoxicating. She could blame her words on that alone, though a need to shock him, to prove that there is more to her, threads right alongside. "No. I slept with him. In a supply closet."

The regret is instant the second she sees his face.

He doesn't look away. "When?"

"Before you and me. Of course."

Now he turns, facing the city. "Then why tell me that?"

You of all people. She watches him, the brightness from the lights in his eyes. "Because maybe there's more to me than you think." The childishness of these words is evident the second she hears them.

"How do you think I see you? And why would it be bad?"

"Naive. You think I'm naive."

"*No.* Innocent, yes. There's a difference."

"Innocent, naive. You said you shouldn't have taken me here. *You of all people*, you said. Because what, I can't handle it?"

He stares at her, angry. "Because *you* of all people, I cannot lose."

The words twist with her misunderstanding. A pulsing, bright coil of regret.

"You thought I saw you as less?" he says. "*You* are here on this trip with me. No one else. The only one I wanted was you." He turns away from her, facing the city. "Tomorrow, we'll see the Hanging Gardens of Babylon and then change your ticket so you can go home."

Regret sits hot within her. His words, her words. What she'd shared about Ben, who was a past mistake, plain and simple. Everything on a replay the second she hits the bed, over and over in that loop of torturous memory.

It was only flirtation—eyes locked in meetings, Ben's hand dragging on her desk when he passed by, once a Bit-O-Honey bar left by her phone—until one afternoon he'd whispered in her ear, *Olivia with the olive-hued eyes, lower supply closet, three p.m.* With those words, that one sentence, that directive without promise of anything beyond the day, she'd felt both elation and insult. Of course she would not go. She grew indignant and sharpened more than a dozen pencils.

But then the clock ticked, and she began to wish she *was* the kind of person who would do this. Who would take the edge of thrill she felt from flirting with a boss and let it consume her, let it swallow up worry and rationale and become her, even just for an afternoon. Instead she was skeptical and practical and always too aware of dangers, those possibilities that somehow only she tended to see, faint, like smudged-out paths in a Choose Your Own Adventure book. Sometimes, she'd found, it was safer to do nothing.

And so nothing was what she did. But with every glance at the clock, she began to feel this person she *could* be, the same as if her arm were against another's. This was what a man would do. This was what Rebecca would do. This was what so many single women who seized their sexuality and owned it and owned their desires would do. They'd take a man they wanted in a supply closet, then grind out a cigarette with their heel and dominate whatever room they walked into.

Hannity, passing by with Kyle Rudger, managed to mention that his uncle had just *shot eighteen with Byron this weekend.* Byron, their big boss. The editor in chief. *Shot eighteen.* Everything in her burned. And craved. And so at 2:57, she felt herself rise from her chair even before she stood, felt herself running down the hall even as she walked at a snail's pace. It was as if there were two of her and with every step, she shed her own restrictive skin.

In the middle of the night, she surged awake with her mistake. She'd slept with a boss. She, who wanted to be taken seriously, had just done herself a massive disservice. Things like this happened to women she knew, but not of their choosing. They suffered and coped; they were tricked or forced. But here Olivia had *caused.* She was a part of her own undoing. An active, stupid part. If this was what men did, it was because they could get away with it—but she could not. That euphoria she had felt from surprising herself had twisted back and snapped at her when she wasn't looking.

So when only days later, Ben whispered, *Supply closet at four*, she realized again the enormity of her mistake. Four p.m. came, and she watched the clock and didn't move. When he returned to his office, he watched her as he went and then found her later in the break room. *Que pasa?* he asked quietly, slyly, by the refrigerator. And she faced him and said far too loudly, *I can't.* A woman by the sink turned, her eyes flickering between them.

And though her point had landed, she instantly regretted her choice in words. Because she didn't mean *can't.* She meant *won't. I won't.*

Minutes later, the edge of her desk gouged a line in her arm, and the late-afternoon sun simmered from the windows and fell short of where she sat. She had wanted to be someone else, she realized, and it hadn't worked. Because she was Olivia. Open, craving heart and all. A person longing to love, the way others were resolved to conquer.

The morning call to prayer sounds in the dark, waking her from staggered sleep. Olivia listens from her bed, trying not to hear their conversation last night, trying to hear only the call that has filled this land for generations, sung into darkness from multiple mosques in the city. Haunting voices that seem to echo themselves, dipping and pausing and rising. A hook to the past. Quietly she goes to the living room, intending to stand on the balcony and let the ancient sound consume her, but stops when she sees Soraya on her prayer rug.

In the kitchen, Delan pours tea into small glasses, liquid the color of rich amber. The time on the wall clock says 4:14.

"I couldn't sleep either," he says. "The call. *Azaan* in Arabic, *bang* in Kurdish."

He won't look at her. Just mops up a spill, then wipes down the counter.

"It's beautiful."

"It's early. Now it doesn't matter, because I'm up. But soon I'll want him dead. There's yogurt." He points to a bowl covered in dampened cheesecloth. Beside it are soft-boiled eggs, a stack of naan bread, and a small dish of honey with a silver spoon. "They do that, head on the ground, to be humbled. To remind themselves to take time from their day to remember God. *Fajr*, the first prayer. There's a line in this one that prayer is better than sleep. Not for me, but I wanted to make her breakfast."

Olivia stands directly behind him. "Delan."

The call goes high, and he smiles. "Right there, we used to say someone grabbed his balls." Finally he turns to her. "I didn't have the right. I know that. Last night. You were with who you were, and me as well."

"But I shouldn't have brought it up."

"You should say what you need to with me."

"And so should you."

He watches her as the muezzin's voice reaches from a long pause, building and going wide. "But that you thought I saw you in a bad way. Why? Why would I be with you if I thought you were naive?"

"That's what I've wondered myself, I guess."

"You don't see what I see."

She smiles. "Probably not."

He reaches for her, pulling her against him. "Then you're the one missing out."

Outside, the sky is still dark, city lights hesitant. "I'm not leaving. I'm not changing my ticket."

A close-lipped smile. "I didn't think you would. You, who wouldn't come inside during the manhunt."

A year ago. Men with rifles and a helicopter that made low, loose loops, who barked out orders to not go outside and to lock all doors—a directive that backfired on Olivia, as it drove her out onto the porch to try to seek a better view. "We were blocks away."

"And told to stay inside. By the men with guns and knowledge. You don't listen to warnings."

"I do, though. That's all I've ever heard."

He smiles, his lips now inches from hers. "If that were true, you wouldn't be here with me."

She's about to ask him what he means—is the location what he thinks she was warned against? Or *him*?—when Soraya appears in the threshold and reddens upon seeing the two of them. Then she spots the tea and breakfast, places her hand over her heart, and looks up, nodding as if something has been answered, as if this whole time she'd been asking for just one morning's help.

Later, they stand in the ruins of a long-ago garden, a gift from a king to his wife, who missed her homeland of lush forests. Rubble that had once stretched to the sky in majestic structures. Terraced levels filled with vegetation that combined to form an impression of a mountain of trees and plants.

"Queen Amytis," Delan says. "The daughter of a Median king. The Kurds, we're one of the descendants of the Medes. The area she missed, that's where I'm from. We used to hike to a Median king burial chamber. Empty, though. The Brits took the bodies in the thirties. But the carvings, you should see them. Maybe you will see them. There was a door that was also taken. It locked from the inside. Slid on a rail. The person who locked it from inside had all eternity to wish he'd picked a different job." With that, he laughs and places his hand on the small of her back, and the move—in this country of studied distance and separation—feels daring and romantic.

Another cab ride. More prayers. Naan bread slathered with honey, the scent of kebab on the streets. Then, at last, a knock on the door and their luggage is wheeled inside, and the next morning a second cousin appears with a car. From the balcony, they watch as he smokes on the street, while inside Soraya covers her hair with a bright floral scarf, tying it at her throat.

"At home," Olivia says to Delan, "you don't leave someone knowing it's the last time you'll see them. Possibility exists, just from proximity. But here, now—what if this is it with your aunt? The one and only intersection with her life? It's meeting someone just to say goodbye."

The sandalwood oil he wears has mixed with a green soap from his aunt's bathroom—olive and laurel oils, an herbaceous, dark freshness—and already she knows this smell to be him, here. Together they watch the morning caught in the gold of the mosque. Men appear at the café below, a game of dominoes set up.

"A small key opens big doors," he says. "One of our sayings." Then he smiles. "Everything, always, is the beginning."

CHAPTER 5

They will drive north to Kirkuk, then to Erbil, passing Khanzad Castle, which Delan tells her was built of stone and gypsum by Princess Khanzad in the sixteenth century and still stands strong. From there, they will drive on Hamilton Road, named after the engineer who connected Erbil to the Iranian border in the twenties, winding through what he calls the Grand Canyon of Kurdistan, until at last they reach their destination in the Rawanduz area. A journey that will take the whole day in a car with seat belts that work only in the back and a fender that once belonged to a different vehicle.

Only Olivia's suitcase fits in the trunk, so the rest get piled in the front seat. Delan sits next to Olivia in the back, knees pressed against the seat before him, and though a few times his cousin tosses a comment toward him, all in all the man seems interested only in the silence the ride provides and the endless opportunity to smoke. Now and then, his hand taps on the open window to a beat no one else hears and whenever they speed up, the wind becomes a wild whip in the car.

Soon, her hair, tied with a clip, comes undone, and she's forced to hold it back with both palms on her temples—catching the heady scent of the damask rose oil she'd found whole and intact in her suitcase—appearing as a passenger who is shocked at what's before her, which, given the condition of the roads and how closely the cousin follows cars in front of them, wouldn't be far from the truth. Beside her, Delan laughs when he sees her.

Small rivers. Flat and bright with blinding sun. Palm trees in low, leaning kisses with the water. Clutches of grass grow from dry ground, like the strange, bold vegetation on a sand dune, and everywhere there are fallen fronds, swept against old trucks or buildings. They pass a car that's been reduced to a burned shell, and she turns to watch it go. It recedes in the distance, a scorched remnant of a day someone would never forget—if they were lucky.

There was a daydream she used to have. On the way to work, she'd think of it, a way to pass the time. She pictured herself coming in to work late one day, her boss angry, yelling, till he'd see the streaks of soot on her pants and the expression on her face. One by one, the entire bullpen would notice. Phones would go unanswered as they looked to her, wanting to know what happened. And so she'd tell them: a crowd gathered, one person with a hose trying to get it to reach a car that had just caught fire. She was passing by as well when just past the flames, she saw a head. A child in the front seat. In a second, she was outside with a jacket she'd grabbed from her car, running to the man with the hose, dousing the jacket in water and then using it to open the door before carrying the child to his mother. And right as she finishes the story, the newsroom silent, the photo editor, Peter Darrow, would burst into the room. *You'll never believe what just happened down the street. I got pics; this girl, she*—and then he'd see her. And everyone would see her. The moment practically came with a trilling sound effect, and as she saw this, Olivia would grin to the streetlights ahead, lost in the magic of a moment that never happened, seeing her once unseen bravery.

For almost a month, she thought of this, every day on her way to work. Now she thinks of that car on fire, the one they passed, and feels a pierce of guilt. Because there would be no man with a hose that barely reaches. Only flames and heat and a desert that seems forever.

The road they're on eventually becomes dirt, and the air thickens when they ride within the path of another car. Mopeds, donkeys, and embattled vehicles, everything dulled with blown sand. Houses with light-colored brick walls and pink and white oleander.

In the distance now, there is something. At this point, it's just a promise, a shape that slowly sharpens. Cars stopped, men with rifles. Iraqi military are both on the ground and up high in lookouts. Cement barricades divide and reroute the road.

"It's just a checkpoint," Delan says. "Don't talk. Our papers are fine; we've done nothing wrong. But don't draw attention to yourself."

Tall grass gone to seed feathers the edge of the road, waving with the wind. When it's at last their turn, a man who wears his rifle slung across his body like a beauty contestant's banner approaches their car. Without meaning to, Olivia's gaze goes up a fraction, just a bit, to the man's eyes, and in the tilt of his head, she understands he's identified her as foreign. A split second, that's all it took.

Delan's cousin hands him their papers, but the man is now leaning into the car, peering at Olivia. His eyes are silty water, a hazel that would be beautiful in any other situation. Quickly she looks down, realizing she's doing exactly what she was told not to, because it's clear he's now talking about her. Beside her, Delan watches the grass along the road as if he's never seen anything so captivating, and that, his marked avoidance, tells her there is something to fear. The fabric under her arms dampens. Trying to get a bit of air, she lifts one leg off the seat to cross it upon the other.

Time passes in a new, tar-thickened way. That's what people said after the '71 earthquake, the one Olivia missed by a year. Still talked about to this day, stories shared late at night—*where were you? What did you lose?*—terror told through wine-stained lips. Early morning, six a.m. Rebecca ended up outside in nothing but a towel she held closed with a fist. *It was only twelve seconds?* Olivia made the mistake of asking, because the damage was legendary and to her, twelve seconds should not still be felt years later. *Don't say "only" to someone who's been through something like that,* Rebecca said. *One second of true fear beats hours of anything else.*

This, Olivia finally understands.

The man still won't take his eyes off her, even as he backs away from the car. Just barely he nods and motions them forward. The cousin puts the car back in gear, tense. Slowly they pull ahead, and no one speaks until the checkpoint is small in the rearview mirror.

"What happened?" she asks quietly.

"Nothing. Just making sure you were you."

"Money," the cousin says.

"You paid him?"

"I'll pay him back," Delan says. "But there will be many checkpoints and many soldiers curious about an American with a giant camera bag. A blanket over it, please."

The camera bag gets covered, and the checkpoints they go through from that point on are fine, though through each one, Olivia's pulse rises and her breath feels shallow. As they pull past another one, Olivia watches it diminish in the side mirror, a fading threat. "There go my spy daydreams. Shaking too badly to take my cyanide pill."

"You'd *want* to be a spy?"

"Like CIA. You know, something fun."

"CIA is not fun."

In her mind, she'd seen intrigue. Red dresses. Handguns in small purses. A harmless fantasy, something that had no bearing on her actual life. But now Delan's cousin's eyes find her in the rearview mirror, and she realizes her mistake. Remembers a Saturday of too much wine at a Persian restaurant where she sat with a group of Delan's friends on a patio snaked with vines. That day Delan had organized a protest at the Federal building, an attempt to shed light on the Kurdish situation. Though the signs and banners had all been left in cars, he carried his anger with him, railing about the portions the *Village Voice* had leaked of the Pike report, the congressional investigation into the CIA. One element had to do with the Kurds: the United States and Kissinger had encouraged and funded them in a rise against the Iraqi government, as a favor to the shah of Iran, but abandoned them when they no longer served their purpose.

"They never wanted us to win," he told his friends. "That's what the committee found. They wanted us only to fight and keep Baghdad busy. We were a pawn. Kurds quit their jobs, school, you name it. Everyone joined in to fight and to die in a battle we were *never allowed to win*."

It was reckless to talk of the shah and the Kurds there, and a ridiculous choice in venue to begin with, but Delan seemed fueled by the setting, his voice loud with daring.

"More than two hundred thousand refugees when they abandoned us, when we were being slaughtered, and not one dollar of humanitarian aid from the United States. Our leader, Barzani, he begged Kissinger for the United States' help. 'Our movement and people are being destroyed in an unbelievable way with silence from everyone.' That is what he said. And Kissinger, he was later asked how he could justify such betrayal." A pause as Delan looked each of them in the eye, and the belly dancer who'd been edging closer caught one look at him and abandoned course. "'Covert action should not be confused with missionary work.' *That* is what he said to the Pike Committee. The man we trusted. When Kissinger got married, Barzani even sent him a necklace and rugs."

As they drive now, Olivia remembers that with those words, everything had changed. Because he no longer looked angry—he looked heartbroken. "A gold and pearl necklace," he'd said. "And three rugs, I remember." Then silence from everyone.

The landscape turns in a slow pivot. Hills erupt like giant seams upon the earth, trees in muted army greens. She asks Delan a question, but the words are lost in the wind. *What?* he mouths, and she leans in close to be heard, her head against his shoulder.

"Are you nervous?"

He doesn't answer. He's looking beyond her. She turns and sees a clutch of partially destroyed buildings, as if someone had grown bored mid-obliteration and simply turned their back. A wall-less kitchen. Dishes still on the table. Left for all to see is that turn, the moment between *then* and *now*, a frozen second in time after which nothing would be the same. She wants to stop and take a photo, but judging by his cousin's speed, the question would not be met kindly.

"Always," Delan says a moment later.

It takes her a moment to find the prompt for his words. *Are you nervous?* A stupid question. Before them, houses now give way to barren land. She stays leaned into him, and with his arm around her, he holds down her hair from the wind.

"There are parts that remind me of California," she says.

"I saw home so often, I thought I was inventing things."

She doesn't tell him she's wondered the same. Instead she falls asleep against him, and when she wakes from the car's swerve, the world's gone cooler.

"An hour away, Sleeping Beauty. Look where you are." He nods to the window.

Everything's emerald green. Verdant. That water-drenched, spring shade, teeming with potential. Even the soil is bold with promise, striped in places with colored veins of minerals. The term Fertile Crescent comes to her, and Olivia remembers Delan telling her that that was where he was from. Meaning, when he said this, was abstract, just a fact on a page or a lesson in a classroom. In no way had it resonated. Until now. Now she feels it. The pulse of ancient civilizations thick and steady. She wants to get out of the car and place her hands upon the ground to sense the life that's been lived there, the stir of ancient footsteps or the faded roar of a long-ago army. Somehow they're still here, she thinks. Those worlds. Ghost worlds that exist just beneath what can be seen. The air, if she were still enough, might quiver from a once-spent arrow.

Past another bend, the landscape opens in low hills and fields, contained by massive mountains. In the midst of the range is a jagged gorge, as if in that one spot, the earth had heaved and split and torn. Even farther back, distant in a way that could be a trick of the eyes, there are snow-covered peaks washed in clouds of the same white, an almost disorienting union.

When they pass through a small village of flat-roofed houses, Olivia remembers Delan's stories of sleeping on the roof during the summer. *Too hot inside. But what better way to know the stars?* Romantic and exotic, the way he told it. Flowers that bloomed at night. Waking at the time nature intended, folded in its arm. Was it just how he sold it as an adult, to avoid conversations that could hook into any uncomfortable truths, or was that how he actually saw it? Children stand in the opening of a partially destroyed stone wall, and as she watches him wave to them, their faces wide with smiles, she realizes she doesn't know. Outside her own window, buildings have been razed and cars abandoned. A dog sits in the shadow of a tall pile of rocks. Life seems to emerge from between cracks or sift from rubble.

When they're stopped at a light, he looks left, searching the street. "The candy store. We used to go to one here. You should see it, stacks of *gazo*, or *shirini*. Sweets, like rolled jellies, in every flavor. Pomegranate, apricot. Raisin with walnuts—my favorite." He taps his cousin on the shoulder, leans forward, and says something in Kurdish. Loudly, despite the silence of the stopped car. In turn, the cousin yells back before hitting the gas.

"Is he mad?" Olivia asks.

"No, we were just talking directions."

"You were yelling at each other."

He's genuinely surprised. "It's how we talk. But we'll stop for a break. I haven't been here since I was fourteen. The old man must be dead, I'm sure. His wife was a beast, but she gave us sweets if we sorted the green rose petals from the yellow for *halway gula zerd*."

"Time," the cousin shouts. "Ba'ath." With his chin, he motions toward the town.

The Ba'ath party. The ruling political party of Iraq, led by Saddam Hussein, a fearsome man whom many said would become the next president. To go to university, you have to be a Ba'ath member. To do anything, you have to be a member. *Everyone has a certificate*, Delan has said, *even just for show. To be safe.*

"No, we're stopping; it's fine," Delan says. "*Shirini* for your family."

"The Ba'ath party is here?" she asks Delan.

"And *mokhabarat*," his cousin says.

The secret police.

"They're everywhere," Delan says. "You want to avoid them, you stay in your house the whole time. But even then, they come to you, so what good is that? Nose to the dirt, we're fine." He turns as they pass one of the few street signs they've encountered. "Everything's in Arabic. All of it, changed." Another turn, and they're on a street with houses. "Wait, wait. Here. *Lera raweste*."

They pull before a house of pale brick, two stories with a gate that straddles the street corner. The windows are narrow and clouded, as if the view is better left unseen, and a tree in the front has lost its leaves. In fact, more bare branches from other trees stretch above the walls, and Olivia motions in their direction. "They're dead, aren't they?"

A nod. He looks worried. As if someone might round the corner and catch him where he shouldn't be. "Those trees were old. Neglect reaches them last. So think of what happened. The whole garden, gone, I'm sure."

"What is this? Whose house?"

In his nervous silence, she understands: someone he loved lived here. A lost love. She sees it in his eyes, that longing for something gone. Even his cousin, always wanting to be on the move, waits patiently, as if aware of the significance of the stop.

After a moment, Delan sits back. "I know how to get there from here."

And so he gives his cousin directions and sure enough, within a couple of minutes, they're in front of a building whose second floor juts into a balcony that hovers precariously above the sidewalk. Below, the first floor is a glass storefront filled with stacks of rolled sweets—green, yellow, pink, white, and orange. Dark centers in some, others coated in seeds or nuts.

"After all this time, it's here. Maybe it's a new owner. But it's here. You have no idea what that's like."

"To revisit your childhood?"

He smiles. "Sure. And find it still standing." As he opens the door, his cousin lights a cigarette and leans against a stone wall. A bell chimes. "I feel like I'll see myself here. Stage right, from the kitchen."

Old pendant lights hang from high ceilings, and a fan wobbles in the center. The floor is tile, stained with time. Every inch of every shelf and wall is crammed with jars and posters, baskets and tubs. Rolls of candy in all shades are dusted with powdered sugar like spiraled clouds of color. When a woman appears from the kitchen, Delan looks up, hopeful, but then quickly studies the choices.

"She's Arab," he whispers to Olivia when the woman's turned to get another box. Olivia looks, and after a moment, Delan leans against her, his chin beside her ear. "There are ways to tell. One is her head. Kurds have flat backs of their heads. From our cradles, when we are babies, the way we are made to sleep on our backs. But look at her head—it's not flat. I don't know where the family I knew went, but she's not it."

An assortment of treats in two boxes. One to bring home to his family and the other for his cousin. When the woman hands them little squares, pale pink and dusted with sugar, Delan becomes like a child with an unwrapped present. "You have no idea. Fresh. She just made it. This is a treat. Eat it now; she wants to see you enjoy it."

Though the outside appeared firm, the inside collapses in her mouth. A burst of sugar and rosewater, a candied garden unleashed. The taste catches her off guard and without thinking, she brings her wrist to her nose, matching the scents.

He smiles, pleased. "One of the oldest scents and one of the oldest sweets in the world."

Just then, his cousin appears, cigarette smoke still caught in his exhale as he leans in to Delan. They glance toward the street, and Delan turns to Olivia. "There's a problem outside."

The problem is a man who's drunk on the sidewalk, yelling. In a dark-brown suit, he sits on the curb, swaying even while seated. He's bald, but Olivia sees gray within his mustache, lines upon his cheeks. His brown shoes are covered in dirt, and a few buttons are torn from his shirt. As he rests his chin upon his chest, the vertebrae of his neck stand out, prominent. It's on noting this, that his chin is to his chest, that she realizes the yelling is not coming from him. In fact, three men across the street stand behind the gate of what looks like a restaurant and are yelling *at* him. Now and then, they lift their fists into the air.

"What did he do?" Olivia asks Delan.

Though he could not have heard, the man looks up to the sky as if in response, and though his words are lost to Olivia, they're loud enough that the men on the corner hear and yell in return. Trails from past tears are on his cheeks, having cut through a layer of dust. It appears as if he's been walking for days just to sit on this curb and cry.

"He lost his son," Delan says. "His little boy. That's what he's saying."

Delan's cousin pulls on his arm as one of the men picks up what looks like a pipe.

"Let's go," Olivia says.

The crying man seems incapable of understanding what awaits him, oblivious to the men who taunt him. They must be Iraqi military. Or secret police. Whatever the case, they seem to be threatening him, and the air on the street is tight with rage.

"Delan," Olivia says. "Nose to the ground, right?"

"His son is dead. We'll get him home." He turns to his cousin and says something hurried, but his cousin shakes his head, furious, and yanks his keys out of his pocket, already at the car by the time Delan stoops down to the man. In one move, Delan has his arm hooked beneath the man's shoulder and despite the danger before them, the trio of angry men who are now unlocking the gate, who are now stepping through the gate, louder and closer, the man on the curb stands wearily and turns toward Delan, studying him as if it were just another day and all the noise was birdsong.

"*Ta'al ma'ana,*" Delan says to the man. "Olivia, please. Take his other arm."

The men, seeing this, perhaps noticing Delan and Olivia for the first time, step off the curb into the street. Their fists jam into the air. And though Olivia has seen street fights, she is hit at once with the difference: this is not anger; this is hatred. And now it is aimed at Delan.

"Shit," she says, bending under the weight of the man. Out of the corner of her eye, she sees one of the men lean over and then rise back up with a large rock that must have been placed behind a car's tire. The car lurches backward, hitting the one behind it, just as the man hoists the rock above his head.

"Move," Delan yells. "Go."

Delan's cousin, one leg inside his car, sees the situation and races back to them, yanking Olivia away to take her spot. Together they hobble to the car under the man's weight, and within seconds, they've shoved him into the back seat, and Delan and Olivia are running to the other side and jumping in. There's a loud *thunk* as the rock hits the ground beside them, and the door shuts against her hip as the tires crunch on gravel and spin before taking hold. Then the car is moving, and the shouting is loud and then lost.

The man stares straight ahead, silenced. The turn of events has sobered him, Olivia thinks, but then she observes his stillness and reconstructs the moment. The man is not drunk. What she'd seen was grief. Pure, disorienting, numbing, risk-inducing grief.

"Now what?" she asks Delan quietly. In the distance there is a minaret, blue and green tiles faded in the sun.

"I ask him where he lives." He turns to the man. *"Wain taeish?"*

The man nods and reaches for his suit pocket. As he does, Olivia sees that half the fingers on his right hand are missing, each digit nubbed at the knuckle. The sight is jarring. Then his wallet is in Delan's lap, open. On one side is a card with writing and an eagle, wings stretched outward, its body that of the Iraqi flag.

And in a beat, everything makes sense.

This man is Iraqi military. Quite possibly the other men had been Kurds—and this man was what they've been warned against. He is, in fact, the enemy. And he's sitting in their car.

The air constricts. The world gone brighter, flashing with threat. What this man could do to them, just in thinking they are Kurds. On a whim, he could drag them in for questioning. Could pronounce them resistance and shoot them on sight. He could decide that she, the American with the camera bag under a blanket, is a reporter or a spy. Does he have a gun? Olivia wants to look at his waist but can't move. Instead, she stares straight ahead at Delan's cousin, who must have also spotted the card because he's nodding, the tendons of his knuckles bulged against the steering wheel.

Only Delan acts as if nothing is wrong. Calmly he reads something off the card opposite the military ID, and the ride goes silent. Cypress trees line the street, bent from years of wind.

At last they reach a house that looks as if it's been poured of cement and shaped into a square with windows and a door. Two pots of geraniums line the path, bloodred against the tedious gray of a low wall. Wordlessly, the man uses his good hand to open his door, and it appears he's about to simply walk from the car. *Go,* Olivia thinks. *Don't turn around.*

But right as he's shutting the door, he stops. And turns. He stares at Olivia, her brown pants and white linen shirt, her brownish-red hair. Then he studies Delan, as if trying to understand something. His eyes trace his features, and it's then that it hits her—he's recognized Delan as a Kurd. *We are our own ethnicity,* Delan has so proudly bragged.

Now Delan opens his mouth to speak, and Olivia can't breathe. The wrong accent, the wrong Arabic words. Anything could be the tipping point.

"*Allah ma'akum,*" Delan says, calmly, as if dropping off a friend.

Olivia watches the man, waiting for any indication. And for a horrible moment, she sees it—something is off, something registered. There is the slightest narrowing of his eyes, like a curtain that stirs with the shutting of a door.

But the man nods and turns. And the car door clicks behind him. No one breathes. A face moves in the house's window, and the front door swings wide. And though it's distant, Olivia thinks she hears the sound of a cry, something that rises and falls. Just for a moment, the man's steps falter, but then he keeps going, his head bent to the ground.

CHAPTER 6

Though she felt nominally prepared, she now sees she was never ready. Never should she have gone on this trip, because the idea of dying was not a true consideration. What she'd thought of was physical or emotional discomfort, hushed voices and downcast eyes. She'd thought of being the only one in the room not to understand the language. His parents not liking her or preferring he be with a Kurdish woman instead. Boarding the plane at the end of the trip suddenly uncertain they could last or, worse, breaking up on the trip and boarding the plane alone. Never had she thought of being in the same car with someone who could have them killed, who most likely had a gun within reach.

"Tell me," Olivia says. No one has spoken since they left the man at his house, and she's angry. She wants this explained, this encounter that didn't need to happen. This unnecessary risk.

"Saddam's man," his cousin says from the front seat. Anger makes his voice high.

In turn, Delan's voice goes louder. "His son was just killed. He was no one's man. He was a father. He couldn't see; he couldn't think; he *wanted* to die. What, I let him be killed on the street because he's so lost in grief, he doesn't know?"

"*Ew sagbabe!*"

"He might be a son of a bitch, any other day he is a son of a bitch, but today he was a father blind with grief."

"You knew?" Olivia asks. "You knew he was military?"

"He knew," his cousin says. He holds the steering wheel as if it might get away, the skin on his knuckles stretched tight.

"Just this morning, his son was killed," Delan says. "Eight years old," he adds and then unleashes a string of Kurdish.

After a few minutes, when Delan has stopped ranting, his cousin finds his eyes in the mirror. His words are soft, which carries a different threat and implication—that meaning alone will land his point. *"Zor dameka roishtooit lera, nazani."*

To that, Delan leans against the door.

"What did he say?" Olivia asks quietly.

For a moment, he rolls his head to look at her, and she sees something in his eyes. Resignation.

"He said, 'You've been gone too long.'" Then he looks out the window, at a car abandoned in a field, a scattering of holes along the doors like the dark outline of a wave.

The afternoon undoes itself like a coiled snake. The problem is that Delan *has* been in the United States too long. She understands this now. Though she accepted it was more dangerous than she'd previously understood, never did she realize that her boyfriend himself would in fact amplify that danger. Unnecessary risk, not reading the situation or grasping the consequences—all the result of his absence, the hazard of the foolish optimism he's picked up in the States. And now, Olivia realizes, that part of him that's always tried and tested her, that part that talks to everyone, invites everyone to his home, that part of him that needs to be loved by everyone, that's what could get them killed. What almost got them killed already. Because this place is an *avert your eyes* place. A place like a child whose only goal is to not be seen by the parent with the whiskey breath. You do not speak unless spoken to—and

Delan could not silence his voice if given a muzzle. This whole trip was a mistake.

And then there is her fear. What she'd felt must have been a fraction of what real photojournalists must feel, and yet never could she have pulled out a camera—even long after the man had gone into his house, even after the door had safely shut. Somehow she thought she'd rise to whatever occasion occurred, the drive to make a difference lifting her arms, focusing her lens, calming her heart. Now she's thinking of her favorite photographers and what they've gone through, and the feeling of being slight in their shadows is overwhelming. Nick Ut and his Pulitzer Prize photo: the napalm attack and the naked girl running. Ut said that the moment he pressed the button, he'd known the photo would stop the war. And her idols, Catherine Leroy and Dickey Chapelle, female photographers who wore fatigues and trudged through rice paddies right alongside troops, who crouched beside men in combat not only to capture the human side of war but to prove themselves in the face of military and male resistance. Sexy rebels, articles painted them as, even though these women had been captured, had been jailed, had taken risks right alongside the men, and—in the case of Dickey Chapelle, who'd covered seven wars—had died right alongside the men. *It is not a woman's place,* she once said about a war zone. *There's no question about it. There's only one other species on Earth for whom a war zone is no place, and that's men.* Never did Olivia want to work the front lines of any war, but she thought she'd take photos that mattered. She thought that if in the right place at the right time, she'd seize the moment, but this is now in question.

Mountains rise craggy and broken before them, everything smothered in green, fields punctuated with patches of yellow mustard flowers. Putting her head against the window, she closes her eyes, letting the vibration of the road sift within her, edging out thought.

"The Grand Canyon," Delan says after a while. "You gotta look."

Now, on all sides of the car are massive rock walls, a former river's carve through stone and time. Striated layers packed with history. Some spots are marked with what looks like spills of dried oil, while other places gleam from seeping water. Where it can, grass grows like velvet, plush and forgiving.

"You're right," she says. "It is like the Grand Canyon."

"I keep hearing surprise in your voice. Makes me think you doubted me."

A small smile. "I've never been to the Grand Canyon. You shouldn't take my word."

They fall to silence, the river below them raging white. When they emerge in a clearing, violet flowers grow alongside the road beside fat, spiked pods. "Thistles," he says.

Land spreads wider, lazy in fields, though still the mountains brace all sides. Without the shadows from the peaks, wildflowers relish in access to the sun, boasting from the green in purples, reds, and yellows, an impression that strikes her like music. They pass a tree, brilliant in white blooms. "And that?"

"Almond. There, a hawthorn."

"You can't put me into something like that. I didn't know; I didn't have a say. I get that I don't know the language and decisions are split second—"

"Stop. Please—it's done." He faces his view, a small hill with a fig tree that leans crooked in the midst, leaves wilted in the sun like broken hands.

"It's not done. You don't *do* that."

"There used to be lions here. They're extinct now. Lions and tigers and bears."

"I'm not over it. You can't do that."

"Oh my?" He flashes her a smile—an offer of charm she refuses to take. "Okay, okay. I hear you."

Another pass through mountains, the river below fed and angry, roiling and muddy. The rain was recent and the streets still dark with water. Minutes pass. Now and then, she catches sight of storm clouds that appear on the move and in a hurry, and every so often their car swerves to avoid hazards in the road, rocks and spills of dirt.

When they emerge through a vee in the mountains, the sky stretches open. Half pigeon gray and white, the other half faded blue. Below them is a valley in new-growth green, surrounded by mountains that rise gradually in some places like legs stirring under bedsheets, while elsewhere they jut up sharply, all cliff face and drops, varied-hued striations packed one on top of the other, a geologist's dream. Splotches of grass give off an aura, a feeling from the mountain. Ancient. Wise. The whole land feels old and tested and solemn. The sight is a salve on her anger and worry, and for a moment she forgets everything but that she knows nothing and that these mountains are in part an answer. Beside her, Delan grasps the door, and in the white press of his fingers and the way he sits forward, she knows—even without a map or signs in a language she can read—that this is where his hometown is. Because he's braced. Excited and yet nervous. Sitting forward, he's ready for the approach of a world left behind, and with this, she understands that place can build or break a heart just like a person.

Wildflowers dot the field. Purple and white irises. Pink, white, red, and purple anemones. Long-legged scarlet poppies. It's stunning and almost surreal.

Her father should be here. Though he himself couldn't grow a cactus, his multiple attempts at gardening left him awed and with an appreciation that never faded. A slight obsession, really, with what he couldn't have. Research for his writing, he liked to claim, as he did with all the subjects he threw himself into: gardening, sailing, Spain and Portugal, locomotives, South America. His studies took him far and deep while he himself stayed anchored to his island and his day job—in part because he'd had to raise her. Gardens, though, those he could experience in his own limited way, talking with neighbors about their vines, doling out advice from his reading, even learning the Latin names of plants. Once, after Olivia's thirteen-year-old heart had been dismantled by her first crush, he'd found her curled against the couch far too early in the morning and, not knowing what to do, had grabbed the car keys. They drove and drove. As if maybe they could outrace this new stage. As if pain could be left behind. She thought it both charming and juvenile, his response, but after five hours of listening to music with the windows down and her feet on the dash, she started feeling better, despite the fact that not a word had been spoken about the boy. Distance, perhaps, really was the answer. They were in the Palouse, a side of Washington she didn't know, when a field of orange flowers slowed him to a halt and almost got them rear-ended.

"Fire poppies," he announced.

Within seconds, he was out of the car, stepping into a wind. His shirt and pants billowed flat against him as he turned to face the flowers, and when Olivia opened her door to the noise and rush of passing cars, she, too, was gripped in the warm gusts that rippled the field. Tall poppy stalks were bent, papier-mâché-like petals quivering as if in a desperate rush to leave.

"They're fire followers," he said. He had to speak loudly, which was not his nature, and so Olivia moved closer. "That's a group of plants that needs heat or smoke to tell the seeds to germinate. Sometimes even ash in the soil. They're rare because of that. People hunt for them after fires." He pointed to the charred skeleton of a tree. Snarled black arms. Behind it, more trees, all charred. "For decades sometimes, the seeds lie dormant. Tucked away and asleep. Then a fire comes along and wipes everything out and *that's* what they need. The challenge. The wake-up call. Like a slap. Everything else is gone, and the world's just recovering, and that's their cue to rise from the ashes."

"You're saying I should be a fire follower."

He turned to her, studying her as if she'd suddenly changed clothes. "No. You got that from what I said? I was telling you about the flowers."

After a moment, he knelt, tracing a finger in the ashy soil, and when he stood, he wiped his hand on his pants, leaving a streak of dark by the pocket. "Loss keeps going, you know? It doesn't just stop with what was taken from you. It grabs new things all the time. You think you're up against missing the memories, all that happened, but Christ if you don't miss all that didn't happen even more."

The wind against her face turned cold with her tears. "I think you're doing just fine. With me."

Maybe she'd not spoken loudly enough. Maybe her words had been claimed, snatched by the hurried air, because still he faced the flowers. But at last he nodded, slowly.

"If you wanna know," he said. "These flowers, they're beautiful, but maybe they're just beautiful because there's nothing left around them. You don't need destruction to shine. And you don't want to be one of those people who thrives when it's difficult. The sooner you figure out easy is good, the better off you'll be."

And here she is. In a country she doesn't know, with her boyfriend who just allowed a man who could kill them into their car. She's not sure if she should laugh or cry. Instead she tries to only take in her surroundings.

"Can we stop?" she asks. "Here?" She wants to capture his home from a distance. This photo, she knows, would be taken differently from one she'd take at the end of the trip.

Delan's cousin glances at his watch and then the lowering sun before pulling next to a hawthorn tree, its white blooms like a snowfall.

The mountain's tinged with red, draped in the start of sunset. Studying the setting, she finds a large boulder with a view and leans against it, facing the valley with her camera in hand. The ground at her feet is slightly red as well, but from iron. Iron and chrome are in the mountains, she remembers reading. Mountains with caves and remnants of the first human settlements. A direct link to the start. And there, she sees, shoved up against the foothills, is a large cluster of rooftops and roads that round another hill and disappear, out of sight. The edge of a large town or a city, where for the next two and a half weeks she'll live.

Above, in the tree's canopy, is a gray bird, the feathers at its throat parting as it sings. "Hawthorn trees are fairy trees," she says to Delan, who's wandered up beside her. "According to the Celts. Other trees, too, if they're alone in a field, but fairies love the hawthorn."

"You know, I did hear you back there," Delan says. "What you said. I got it."

Her anger seeps back. "But you couldn't acknowledge that in front of your cousin? Women can't talk back?"

"You're about to meet my mother. Trust me, talking back is not an issue. But you were right," he says and then pauses, searching the valley. "And so was I. Here, everyone thinks they're right. And they are, in a way. The Kurds. The Turks. Arabs, Assyrians. Everyone. They all have their stories, and the stories sound good." He shrugs. "They should. They've been worked on for thousands of years."

She says nothing, just takes the lens cap off her camera and kneels before a yellow daisy, focusing on the flower as the valley below becomes a distant green blur.

"You cannot make a perfect choice here," Delan continues. "That's what I'm saying. It doesn't exist. It's a mistake to care, just like it's a mistake to not care enough. You may live another day, but you will never win."

On the grass before them is a hawk's shadow, broad wings thinning to a line as it turns on a breeze. "So everyone's wrong."

"Yes. Everyone's wrong." He pauses as she watches the hawk through her viewfinder, losing it behind a tree. "Or everyone's right. Some people are more right than others. The Kurds, I'd say we're more right." He smiles. "You're still angry. I know. I'm sorry." He leans over and snaps a yellow flower from its stem. "Liv. Olivia."

"What?"

"Just saying your name. It's a good name. I'm the only one who calls you Liv, though."

"And my dad."

"Why, you don't like Liv?"

"It's fine. Sometimes it just sounds like a command."

"Like you're being told to live. I never thought of that. *What's in a name? That which we call a rose, by any other name would smell as sweet.* I did *Romeo and Juliet* in San Francisco; did I tell you? I was Mercutio."

A shadow from a cloud moves slowly along the base of the mountain behind the far line of roofs, just enough to provide further separation between background and subject. *Click.* Reaching into her camera bag, she grabs the red lens filter and twists it on. With this, the clichéd blue sky with white clouds will turn dramatic, the blue changed to dark gray and clouds to electric white. *Click.* Tilting the camera, she puts the horizon's dividing line lower so the sky seems to take over, increasing the tension of the photo. Then the opposite, lifting the horizon to make the photo heavier. The rough lines of the mountains feel like the rise and fall of the land itself's language, one intense with emotion and churning with stories of ancient armies and invaders. "The Zagros?"

His shadow nods. "'Kurds have no friends but the mountains.' That's our saying. Our proverb. And that mountain there means 'close friend.' As a kid, I thought of them all as friends. I thought that was what it meant. Then the Elburz Mountains, I thought they were the nice neighbors who look after you if you wander too far. Taurus were the distant-cousin mountains. You might never see them, but if you did, they would still take you in and give you dinner. There"—he nods to the peak before them—"that's my mountain. At the top, you're above clouds, and all you hear are birds and wind. You're so high up, the earth feels round."

Olivia looks at the sheer cliffs. "I'm not going up there."

"No. Now, you're meeting my family." He stands and reaches for her hand, as above them the hawk swoops low, its shadow lengthening upon the grass.

"What does it mean?" she asks. "That the mountains are the Kurds' only friends?"

"The old story is that any time an invader was going through Kurdistan, the Kurds raced to the hilltops and rained stones onto the enemy at night. When the enemy got tired and left, the Kurds returned to their villages. But really, the mountains are the only ones who've never betrayed us. That's the truth of it." A pause. "Also, you've heard *head for the hills*? Think of protection, of people running from tanks or planes. You're harder to kill in a mountain."

CHAPTER 7

An old stone bridge with three arches. A blue-green river with a tuft of white from a current in the center. There must be a drop there, Olivia figures, picturing a cut in the earth that rushes with its own, deeper force. Along the bank, men pull a net with white, sun-flickering fish, and just before the town, there's a trench that's been dug, a scar from past fighting. Iraqi military patrols the streets, and when she turns to watch a soldier, Delan nudges her.

"Best not to look at them."

"Why so many?"

"Military occupation."

Now she studies him, this man with his recklessness and oversights. "You didn't tell me."

"They were always just here. Since '61, more or less. I forgot. It wasn't intentional."

And though she is nervous over this omission, she believes him, because what is daily is often overlooked, and with every hour upon this soil, she's realizing that the baseline of his world is nothing like her own.

Streets are narrow and thick with life. Shoe repair shops. Bakeries. A place that sells birds, peacocks strutting on a roof of patched aluminum. One long, iridescent tail hangs over the awning, and in the background, cinder blocks rise into a half-hearted second floor. All the houses and buildings are right against each other, many made of mud bricks with roofs that are flat, timbers evident in the eaves. And though main roads are paved, the rest are stone or dirt with channels through the center to prevent flooding.

When they turn onto another busy street, something strikes her: the men are with the men and the women with the women. The groups are not mixed. "Men don't hang out with women."

He glances at her, as if he's felt a first step onto shaky ground. "And women don't hang out with men. It works both ways. Because it's not proper."

"So how do you date?"

"There is no dating. Not like in the West." A pause as he taps his cousin on the shoulder, pointing to what must be a restaurant, pictures of food taped to the windows. Something gets said in Kurdish, and he sits back. "Some, they might meet in secret. In groups maybe, if someone has a sister. Just not out in the open."

"And then you get married."

"Or you don't."

"And what if you don't know? What if you need time to figure it out?" They pause at an intersection, alongside a fig tree's low sprawl, the bark white against a shifting evening. Already the start of sunset charms the streets, spilling onto sidewalks in a honeyed light. When she turns to him, she catches him shaking his head as if she's just told him she's unsure of their relationship. "I didn't mean *you*."

He grins. "You only *think* you didn't know at first."

"Lucky for you, I know now, because arrogance would go in the con column."

"See—columns. What is that? That's not instinct. That's logic. You know when you meet someone. *You* talked yourself out of your instinct."

Instinct. That elusive center an overthinker tends to dart around. Now, recalling their start, she remembers that initial pull to him. Not just attraction, though that was there as well. But a whole-being pull. Cells moving. Mind consumed. "The point is, I came around."

"Always better late than never." He gives her hand a squeeze. Up ahead, two boys walk in the street, laughing when they turn to see the car trailing them, then flashing grins and waving with dirty palms.

"Look," he says. "We're almost there. See how close the mountains are? Some towns like this, they lose daylight to shadow. We're lucky we don't have early dark. Because here, when it's dark, it's black. A cloud goes over the moon, it's darkroom black."

"No late-night walks, I guess."

"No walking at night at all. Curfew."

To this new fact, she says nothing. It's as if she's been handed a cryptic map only after having been left in a maze, and no amount of stating the obvious will help. All she can do is stand in the midst and adjust.

"Sunset," he says. "Six thirty. Somewhere in there. It's fine."

"What else, though? What else should I know that you didn't think to tell me?"

"I guess we'll find out."

Delan, who rewired the bathroom after having only read a book, who thinks nothing of eating expired food or giving Iraqi soldiers a ride home, would of course explain in detail about Neanderthal bones and the varieties of fig trees while neglecting to mention military occupation, curfew, checkpoints, and bribes. But *she* should've expected this. Because this was not a trip to Hawaii. They're not in Paris or Rome. She should have better understood the landscape, but instead she romanticized it. A mistake that was hers alone, to have considered danger only from the vantage of privilege.

Then she startles, his hands covering her eyes. "Shh," he whispers, his mouth by her ear. "Don't be mad. I'm sorry about earlier. But this right here, right now, it's important."

She nods, her eyes still covered.

"You remember your first glimpse of what matters most," he says, "right? The Hollywood sign. The ocean. The first time I saw you. I could tell you about all those times. Even where the sun was."

"Is this your house?"

"I never thought I'd be with someone who'd see it. My life. I couldn't admit it was important, but now I know it is. It always has been." He kisses her cheek. "Try to remember this, okay? One day, I'll ask you to remind me. I'll want to see it through your eyes."

Her lashes brush his fingers. Still, his hands are in place, slivers of light between his flesh, until finally he lets go.

Stone at the base. Beige brick as it rises. Two stories. Window frames and the door painted a bright teal. It's only feet from the cobbled street, and cinder blocks flank the door, rising into tumbles of red and pink geraniums from round clay pots. Though the house is actually large, she is struck at once by how small it is. Which doesn't make sense until she realizes that the incongruity is in the impression, not the reality. From the fact that his house means so much and yet takes up so little actual space. Here it is, this speck in the world that is tied to him, that became him.

But the windows are dark. For a moment, she feels an easing of tension, and in this she realizes how worried she's been about meeting his parents. This would of course only be a postponement, but glimpsing his life without their observation feels like a break, some allowance she'd not known to crave. Delan, however, clearly wants no such postponement and is looking behind him as if perhaps his parents are crossing the street, ready to surprise him. But the street is empty, save a yellow dog that sniffs the corner of a wall, its white-tipped tail straight in the air.

"They must be close," he says, facing the dark house. "They wouldn't be out past curfew."

Then there is a quick conversation with his cousin, who seems appeased by whatever plan Delan has and more than willing to leave, and before the plan is discussed with Olivia, their suitcases are dragged to a small side gate to the right of the house and his cousin is pulling away.

"Kurds say goodbye for too long," Delan says as she watches the street. "There's nothing worse. Be thankful. My cousin, I love him, but he's never been good with people."

"He's not driving back to Baghdad, is he?" Because now an idea has kinked itself under her skin. What if his parents are not here? What if they've moved and Delan, recklessness previously disguised as impetuousness, simply failed to ask for their new address, much like he *might* have messed up the codes?

"No, he couldn't. Curfew," he adds, this time with emphasis, as if doubting she understands the meaning of the word. "We have another aunt across the river. He's hungry; he'll go there." He sets the pots of geraniums on the ground and grabs two of the cinder blocks, stacking them. "Stay here."

And just like that, he's got his leg hooked over the gate and is balancing in a slight wobble, then is gone.

"Grab those," he says when the gate swings open. He nods to his backpack and her camera bag while he heads for the suitcases, still searching the street.

Clotheslines stretch along the narrow space between the two houses, green with grass and small shrubs. The neighbor's window is open, the kitchen mere inches away. Something sizzles on the stove—a yellow smell, thick and warm. A woman is there but facing the other direction, a dulled white apron tied loosely behind her back. Olivia pauses just for a moment, hungry—cumin, she thinks, thrilled with the identification—when suddenly a little face catapults up into the kitchen window. Olivia lets out a sound of surprise, and the woman turns and howls. In the melee, the little face disappears and is replaced by a child's shrieking cry.

"What happened?" Delan asks.

He doesn't wait for a response, just sees the woman and goes to her, saying something as she starts crying, reaching through the open window to cup and then kiss each of his cheeks. Olivia doesn't move, scared and then not scared, surprised and then not surprised, when the little face returns. A girl, maybe five years old, with shoulder-length brown hair that curls into wisps at the ends, a pink-and-yellow-beaded bracelet that's far too big resting at her elbow, and a loose red T-shirt that says I'M A PEPPER in white lettering. Olivia smiles and waves, and the girl—though just seconds ago terrorized—grins in return. There's blue on the corner of her mouth, as if she'd bit the wrong end of a marker, and her teeth are small, just tiny white squares.

"All right," Delan says. "My neighbor Miriam. And she tells me this is Lailan, but I say we've got a monkey who jumps onto counters."

Though he follows his words with Kurdish and a laugh, Lailan watches him, serious and captivated. "English," she says. An awed whisper.

"Do you speak English?" Delan asks.

But she doesn't answer. Instead she turns shyly, wrapping herself in her mother's apron, face covered. Miriam says something in Kurdish and pushes the girl forward. Though Lailan nods, apparently in answer to Delan's question, she now looks only at Olivia. "I love doll, she with hair." She pauses, looking for a word, and then motions to her knees.

"You have a doll with long hair?" Olivia asks.

Encouraged, comfortable, the girl nods quickly and within a second is at the counter again, elbows straining as one leg lifts all the way up and a bare foot gets jammed in by the sink. Then she's on the counter. She's done it, though it's clear she didn't expect to. Her face opens with surprise, and she quickly shoots a look back at her mother before once again peering outside, now acting nonchalant, a child feigning cool in front of the older kids. Her eyes are big and brown with bits of gold that catch in the sun.

"Hi-lo," she says, eyeing their suitcases and clothes before fixating again on Olivia's hair.

"Hi-lo," Olivia says back and catches sight of a brass Star of David on the side wall, tucked into a corner and partially hidden.

"Dinner with them at the picnic," Delan says, motioning Olivia forward, toward the backyard. "There's a picnic. There's always a picnic."

Olivia turns once more and sees Lailan with her head out the window, watching them go. Another wave from the girl, and the woman's arm appears around her waist, pulling her back into the house.

We have Kurdish Muslims, Christians, and Jews, Delan loves to tell people, proud that Kurds believe in democracy and religious secularism. But Olivia'd never been sure. When he spoke of his people, she'd suspected that claims and facts merged and expanded and became sweeping statements that may or may not have been true. "They're Jewish," she says now.

He stops, finger on his mouth. "Not loud, please. She is. One of the few left after the government, those monsters, hung them in the squares. A friend of mine, he was in Basra when this happened. From five a.m. to two p.m., they were hanging in the hot sun. Necks a foot long. All to scare people. Show them who was in control. Miriam, she changed her name, everything. Before it was . . ." He pauses, then shakes his head. "I don't remember. But this is not to be known. So keep it quiet."

Necks a foot long. A horror, reduced to a detail. Slowly, she says, "But the Kurds are okay with—"

"The *Kurds*, yes. But not the rest of Iraq. Jews and Kurds, they love each other. It was the Kurds who helped them escape."

Once more, he urges her forward. At the end of the building, the garden is revealed. Large and lush, a sense of sprawl from the creeping vines and branches. Towering sunflowers and hollyhocks. Pink and white blossoms of fruit trees. Passionfruit vines that cling and reach. Enclosing the entire space is an old plastered wall, parts of which have chipped away, revealing stacks of mud bricks underneath. Despite what he's said, how accurately he described it, she's now confronted with her past doubt. After all, peach trees growing in the Middle East? Plums? That he spoke of walking to school in snowstorms or his first kiss under a waterfall, how did she know what was true?

On the left side, there is a trellis covered in grapevines and a green canopied walkway underneath. Scatterings of smaller fig trees grow along the perimeter, and in the center is a giant pomegranate tree, its base gnarled and thick, new red leaves sunset-lit and impassioned with light. A cement bench is underneath, a pair of black plastic glasses on the seat. By the side wall must have been a large tree, but all that's left now is a thick stump, a ghostly footprint of what once was. Then beside it, a rosebush, the canes bare of leaves. Somewhere, chickens laugh, if that were possible, which in this garden, it might be.

Delan points to the hollyhocks. "Pollen from those were found in Neanderthal graves nearby."

Neanderthal graves. Bones beneath her feet, perhaps. The rocks in the garden would've once been larger, bright and shadowed with early-human firelight, and the land around them would've seemed empty and forever. There'd have been no concept of oceans. No awareness of planets. And here, right before her, are those same silhouettes of mountains, the same spikes of peaks. A shared view, glimpsed across time.

He, too, glances toward the mountain. "My parents should be here by now." Then he points to a heavy tree branch that crooks over the fence from the neighbor's yard. "Walnut. Not ready till the end of September, unless there's not much rain. Then later."

Oddly, there's a lightness within her. A buoyancy. Something she now realizes is *safe*. Hidden from the street, lost among plants. A pervasive and underlying fear has been left at the garden gate. Until she sees Delan glance once more to the darkening sky. "What happens if they catch you out past curfew?"

"Whatever they want to happen. Jail, at the least."

On the ground, next to the back door, are woven white shoes, one slightly atop the other as if someone had used their feet to remove them. For a moment, he studies them, placing his foot beside one as if to measure the size. Confused, it seems. Again, she's struck with uncertainty: his parents could've moved, the house now belonging to strangers. But no, the neighbor would've said something.

With a quick glance at the sky, he opens the back door and for a moment doesn't move. Struck, perhaps, with an unfamiliar home. But then he presses his hand to his head, nods a few times as if savoring in a near miss, and waves her inside.

The first thing that hits her is the smell. Heavy and strange. Scents she's familiar with—cooking spices and leather and old wood and must—are held in an unfamiliar palm, braced by a pungent backbone. Almost like diesel. If they'd been outside, she would've thought that it.

"Heating oil," he says. "The smell. Electricity here doesn't stay on. You'll see. So they use oil heaters. Kerosene. To me, this is home. This smell."

Their shoes get left with others by the door, the tile of the kitchen floor cold. Again, the scent. This mix, it's the bits and pieces of his family's world and of his past, what marks his own memories. Never has she smelled this combination exactly. Not in her friends' houses, or stores, or restaurants. And with all the life she's lived, it amazes her how scent can still be discovered, and how despite all she's seen since arriving here, the mosques and bombed ruins of homes, it's smell that separates the place from anything she's known.

One room off the hall is lined with two long cushions upon the floor, each covered in dark-red blankets and pillows in varied, geometric patterns. A wooden plank is in the middle with a sugar bowl and little glass cups and saucers. The dining room. At once, she thinks of the dinners they've had at their house where the table could never fit everyone and so people sat on the floor, leaned against walls or furniture, lost in comfort and hours of talk. She'd not known how much of this world he'd taken with him until now. All the little things he does at home. Now she's seeing the *why*.

"In here," Delan says from the living room. "Leave your bags here till my mother tells us where we sleep."

Family photos. A glass ashtray filled with pistachio shells. A small couch of gold brocade and matching chairs. Next to the window is a table with a radio and a small vase with a single plastic daffodil, leaves beige with dust. *Radio Baghdad spread lies about the Kurds,* he'd once told her. *Right in our living room, we heard the lies.* Even seeing the radio, it feels like glimpsing a celebrity. Everywhere, the details of his stories are coming to life.

And in front of the flower, a black-and-white framed photograph of a man. Mustafa Barzani. The general who stood only five feet six but looms in mythical proportions within the minds of many Kurds. The founder of the Kurdistan Democratic Party, the man betrayed only years ago. He'd led every major Kurdish revolt since the '40s and died just over a month ago from cancer, a result of the hand-rolled cigarettes filled with powerful tobacco from the Kurdish mountains.

"Every house has one," Delan says when he sees her studying the portrait. "In this area, I mean. KDP territory."

Against the wall is a long wooden cabinet with three doors, the outer doors each painted with a peacock and a folksy jumble of flowers. The center, however, is what draws Olivia closer. A mythical creature, a woman's head with dark flowing hair on the body of a winged white horse. She wears a crown, and her tail is a burst of turquoise plumes, her saddle pomegranate red. Behind it all is a sky that's bold and blue, and when Olivia leans in, the glass that covers the images flares with light. Chips and missing paint hint at age.

"How old?" she asks. The woman has white eyes, the black paint of the irises so faded, it appears missing. Something about her image makes Olivia feel that this is a woman who somehow senses everything but says not a word.

"Who knows. Here, if it works, you use it; you don't talk about it. My grandmother had it; that's all I know. We don't have much from when I was young."

She's tracing a line of feathered plumes with her finger when the front door opens.

There stand the clear origins of him, like two branches of DNA once grafted. In his mother he exists in dark-brown eyes, pale skin, and a straight nose. His father has his height, with gray hair that curls but a nose that's different, wider in the middle, and ears that stick out, making him appear sweet and goofy, like a cartoon character who'd grant you a wish. Upon seeing his son, his father's face seems to collapse—the purest expression of love Olivia has ever seen. Unmonitored, uncensored. For a moment she looks to the ground, to afford a bit of privacy as they embrace, studying a rug of bold sienna and blue.

And then his father is smiling, and even while he holds his son, his eyes find Olivia, and he nods as if promising a greeting eventually, as if admitting he is powerless over this moment. His father wears *ranku choxa*, the traditional male Kurdish attire—baggy pants with a matching jacket atop a white shirt, held in place in the middle with a large sash around the waist—and a black-and-white turban, rolled at the brim. Beside them, Delan's mother is in a long dress, her black hair held back in a white scarf. She holds a fist at her mouth, as if attempting to contain the moment.

"Olivia," Delan says when they part. "My father, Hewar."

But he gets nothing else out, as Delan's mother is there, wrapping herself around him, saying something over and over. *My son,* Olivia imagines it to be. Knows it must be. Delan, much taller, rests his chin on her head as she clings to him and spreads his hand against the black of her hair. His father, meanwhile, stands with his hands clasped behind his back. There is a pen in his jacket pocket, and something about that makes Olivia love him right then and there.

"My mother," Delan says when at last she allows him to pull free. There is a hitch in his voice, as if the words themselves caused a certain pain. "Gaziza." Then he says something else in Kurdish, and Gaziza excitedly brings her hands together as if in celebratory prayer.

"Olivia," Hewar says, the word slow and thick with accent. "It is pleasure. Maths, I taught."

"A teacher," she says and glances back to his mother, who now holds Delan's wrist but watches her with eyes that are mahogany dark. Though Olivia goes to her for a hug, there is a pause. A moment of fluster in which Olivia regrets this choice. But then Gaziza lifts her arms, allowing an embrace, hesitant though it is, and Olivia relishes the moment, itself a small wonder. All this way, all this time. His mother in her arms. The root of him. The one who picked him up when he fell, who came to him when he cried. She smells of pepper and something sweet, like sugared tea.

A month before Olivia and Delan started dating, they had a party. It was one of those nights when voices sounded from the path below her window and suddenly there were people in her house, and so Olivia, long used to last-minute parties after rehearsals, threw an old sweatshirt over her nightgown, dabbed on lipstick, and knew to give in to whatever was about to happen. Guitars, the firepit. Food that seemingly appeared from nowhere. Nights like this sparked with unforeseen magic.

Cooking with Delan. He'd take the lead while she trailed behind, watching and observing, chopping and stirring. Oregano and rosemary for when he thawed out lamb. Cumin and coriander for the okra. This night, he sprinkled a red spice on the chicken.

"Sumac," he told her. "I found it at that market on Vine." Dipping his finger into the little bag, he then pressed it against her lips. It was unexpected, his touch against her mouth. For a second she was confused, until she understood she was to taste it. His eyes never left hers as she let her tongue find the spice. Heat bloomed from his observation.

"Lemony," she said. Across the room, a woman who'd arrived on his arm let the screen door bounce loudly against its frame.

When he started on the okra, he turned to the spice cabinet, but Olivia was already there with cumin, garlic powder, and coriander in hand. He looked at the spices and then at her. Steadily. Not breaking her gaze. Then, without warning, he leaned forward and kissed her forehead. His lips stayed on her skin while he breathed in and out, and she felt his exhale on her hair. Around them, people were watching, but she didn't care, just felt his lips on her skin and smelled his sandalwood and the sharpness of the scotch he must've been drinking.

Everyone ate on the living room floor. Plates balanced on knees, bottles of wine by plant stands or speakers, the fireplace lit. Candles flickered, wax a slow creep. Ashtrays filled and spilled over. Then the silver dial on the Kenwood amplifier got cranked further than it should, and while Led Zeppelin sang of silent women in the night, Delan spoon-fed okra to that woman he'd arrived with, a woman with wild corkscrew hair who insisted she didn't like okra and managed to keep an eye on Olivia even while chewing. "You will like it; I promise," he said to her, his hand on her shoulder. Olivia looked away, embarrassed that she suddenly cared, that she was still thinking of the way he'd watched her with the spice on her lip, the way he'd kissed her forehead and how she'd breathed him in, isolating the place of contact on her skin. Always they'd been close, but tonight had crossed a line and she wasn't sure why. Then the woman he was with leaned in to him while he threaded a curl around his finger, and Olivia decided that the line must have been crossed only in her mind. She had been a fool to even give it another thought.

And then a man appeared. Tall, with Mark Harmon blue eyes and a Davy Jones accent. He offered her wine from a bottle he held under his arm, then sat by her for more than an hour, telling her of his difficult childhood with a stepfather who didn't want him and the English fog that swallowed houses and cars. In turn, Olivia told him of the rain she grew up with and omitted the fact of her own father, loving and present. He nodded when she said that back home nothing seemed to dry, then closed his eyes, getting it, feeling that same eternal drizzle. Then somehow she was talking to the woman beside her, facing the bright flare of orange beads that separated the living room from the kitchen, and with her back turned to the man, she overheard him announce that his stepfather had ridden on the Concorde just last month. "London to New York in three hours," he said. "When they pulled the plug on my mom, it took longer than that for her to fucking die."

Olivia was shocked, hearing it said like that, that someone could reveal a horror identical to her own with such phrasing. She'd been six years old when a car had not stopped, when her mother's slight pause in the crosswalk had been just long enough. The next year was spent memorizing the veins on her mother's eyelids as she lay in something like a sleep, the smell of antiseptic becoming forever notched into the memory of the time and the sage color of the walls enough even now to make her cry.

Quietly, she said, "We pulled the plug on my mom too."

He turned to her, surprised, and watched her without looking away. His eyes reminded her of china, something beautiful and breakable with shards that would hurt. "You're stunning," he said, and Olivia felt a confliction of being sad he'd changed the subject to a thrill from his words.

From across the room, she caught Delan glance at her as he opened an expensive bottle of wine he'd been saving. He must have had someone go into the basement to get it, because Olivia was in charge of storing the few good bottles—gifts, bribes—in the basement's shallow but dark depths to keep them out of late-night drunken reaches. *I don't do basements,* he'd always said, and Olivia never questioned it. Now she watched him twist out the cork, his eyes still on her till suddenly he turned back to finish telling the tale of when he'd ridden in a tank to cross a restricted zone, all to be with someone he loved.

When the man with the damp and dark past left, she'd not seen him go. The space beside her was simply empty.

Later, when she and Delan were cleaning the room, bottles clanking into bags, ashes pluming when trays were dumped, she told him what had happened.

"It was this one moment, with this one person who I could tell got so much about me, even our childhoods in the rain, and we just sort of met, connected, and left." She shook the sediment left in a glass, a dark-red sludge. "Or he left. I didn't want him to go. But he's in the cast?"

Delan nodded, then used the edge of his shirt to mop up a ring of water on an end table.

"Don't worry," she said. "I won't pursue it and embarrass you. I got it. He left. He's not interested or he would've stayed."

"Not necessarily." He clicked off a lamp. "Sometimes the last thing you want is to want."

A whoosh in the walls from the pipes—Rebecca was just getting up, readying to start her Sunday. Suddenly it was all too much—this new confusion between them, being brave and alone, the sad routine of it all. "What's the point in any of this?" she asked.

"The point," he said, "is that you're telling the story."

"Because of the lack. I'm telling the story because of the *denial* of what could've happened. The *lack* of a great story." With that, she realized the woman with the corkscrew hair was gone as well, despite the way she'd looked at Delan all night. "Where's your girl?"

"She wasn't my girl." A bottle clanged as he dropped it in the bag. "And despite what you think, most of the time what could've happened *is* the great story." Then he turned to her. "But him? You're young. With possibility. And a good heart. You still believe. I know him; I've worked with him. And a man like that—you're drawn to him, but he would destroy you with his damage."

Now, in his parents' kitchen, she waits at the far end of the counter while Gaziza cooks, opening bags of spices to inhale and identify. Cumin. Coriander. Oregano. Most she recognizes, but then there's one that's tangy, a deep-burgundy-colored ground spice. She breathes it in, feeling an unassigned familiarity, until Delan brushes against her back on his way to the sink and whispers, "Sumac," in her ear. Of course. She remembers that night, the confusion. The hints at what was to come. Everything now—the spice, the heat of the kitchen, the possible Neanderthal bones in the yard, and his breath against her—everything presses into a chill that sweeps her shoulder. *This is right,* she thinks. *Despite the rocky start, being here is right.*

Then he's back to helping his mother, reaching in as a second set of arms until his mother shoos him away while also slyly scooting over so he can do just as he intended. His father, and those ears Olivia loves, steals bites of this and that and is hand-slapped by Gaziza while also being observed by Gaziza, as it's clear he is an unofficial, covert taste tester.

"Sumac," Olivia says to Delan as he reaches for a dish towel beside her. She allows the word to climb at the end, as if leading to a place she hopes he sees, to the memory of the spice pressed against her lip and that night when their attraction had finally reached into action and reaction, though tentatively, confusingly, as all first steps tend to be.

He stops, with his shoulder against hers and a grin that's gone lopsided, a look that's all mischief, one she's glad his parents can't see. "That night," he says quietly. "You in your sweatshirt and nightgown. All I could think of was how to save you from that guy."

She smiles, her words a whisper. Playful. "Too bad you didn't have to. The jerk took off."

"Oh, too bad."

"What would you have done if I'd actually gone off with him?"

"You wouldn't have."

"I think I would've."

With this, his voice goes low. "You wouldn't have. Because *I* told him to leave." A wink and he turns, leaving her smiling, watching him at the sink as he fills a bowl of ice water with mint leaves. Then she sees his parents watching them, drawn in to whatever's happening, though the second Olivia looks in Gaziza's direction, she blushes to the floor.

"I love that cabinet," Olivia says for something to say, something innocent. "The one in the living room." She motions down the hall, where she can see its corner. Hewar points, verifying, and she nods. "It's beautiful. The paintings."

"Careful," Delan says from the stove. "If you tell a Kurd you like something, even a small comment, it's custom for them to give it to you. And be warned, there will be more presents."

Several times already, Gaziza has stopped what she was doing and raced from the room only to return with something hastily wrapped, and Olivia now has three gold necklaces, two rings, and a bracelet of eyes. *Protection,* Delan said.

When the kitchen door opens, everyone turns. A man almost as tall as Delan stands beneath the back porch light. The same straight nose and slightly curled, dark hair but with no beard, which makes him look younger and softer, like someone who'd write the poetry Delan shouts from stages. The man spots Delan and in a second is across the room and embracing him.

Delan, however, looks torn. Genuinely happy but worried. Reaching for the man but stiff. Everything a confliction. "This is Olivia," he finally says. "Liv."

The man turns to her, and his face narrows. A split second. A flash. That's all it is and once again he's smiling—though saying something to Delan in Kurdish, something that his mother catches and responds to happily. Within seconds, the man has both Olivia's hands within his, changed. His skin is soft but his grip strong, and his eyes are a darkened green, like a plant gone wild in the shade.

"Olivia. From California. Congratulations." His accent is slightly British, and the second she hears it, a fear wedges beneath her heart.

"Liv," Delan says, "this is my little brother. Soran."

In the dream, my brother wasn't in England. He was back in my home-town. Nailed to a tree in our yard. A big fig tree we have. Blood dripped down the trunk onto the rocks. Soran was not supposed to be here. She tries to remember the yard, the fig trees, and the very attempt makes her feel both ridiculous and slightly sick. Looking at Delan, who believes his dreams hold an inherent truth, she sees the same consideration. That confliction when his brother walked in, it was a clash of love and worry.

"I thought you were in London," she says.

"He does not write enough or call, or he would know that I am no longer in London."

"School is over?" Delan asks.

"For me."

"But why?" Delan asks, angry. "You were doing so well. You need to graduate. Why—"

"Maybe at Baghdad, I have not decided." Soran glances toward his father. "Things change." Then a smile at Delan. "You look the same, Hollywood."

As if surrendering, Delan hugs him again, saying *bra*—brother.

"If you had told me you were coming," Soran says, "I would have picked you up."

"On what, your bike?"

"I have a car. Part owner. I share it with Baktiar down the street. It is orange. That is all I can say for it. And you remember Sarchal, in town? I do his bookkeeping."

"But *architect*," Delan says.

"Yes. Well, it may still happen. But for now, I decide the hours I work. Some I can do here, from home."

Another hug between the brothers, their mother and father watch-ing them with the happiness of parents whose greatest joy is their children in one room. Olivia, too, is caught up in the moment, till she catches something burning on the stove.

As they sit for dinner, there is thunder. A distant boom, followed by another. And though Olivia waits, there is no lightning. The air outside the open window stays warm and dry. An approaching storm, she figures. Dark, bunched clouds must hover in the distance.

The food is at once known and unknown, much like Delan and Soran look like their parents but different. The same ingredients, done differently. Again she hears the thunder, three claps, but now there is a rumble, a rolling, all-bass sound that reminds her of far-off fireworks, that low, deep-throated growl that happens every Fourth of July. Soran catches her watching the window.

"Cannons," he says. "The Peshmerga and the government fighting. Handren and Karukh Mountains. Close enough to hear but not to worry. They start up in the evening but stop at night." A glance at Delan. "Peshmerga mostly have Handren."

"That's far," Delan says, pouring more wine into juice glasses for everyone but his parents, who don't drink. "Always there is fighting in the mountains."

Already another story is being told. *Fighting in the mountains.* In her mind, she sees the range they passed through, the tall peaks. Where they are now is against a mountain, right at its base. But then there's English. The translation to the story just told. It's considerate, that they do this, but it makes everything take twice as long. Still, she appreciates the inclusion, the way his father or mother will say something and then pause, expectant, waiting for the English version.

It's in one of these pauses that there's a different rumble. Loud and approaching, gathering and building. A tremble she feels within her. Tea and wine shimmer in glasses, and the windows of the room begin to shake. Still it increases, an impossibly loud noise but one she recognizes as a low-flying plane. Still, Gaziza bolts up from the table, and Hewar searches the ceiling with eyes gone wide, while Soran appears to be praying. Trying to understand, Olivia turns to Delan, but he's frantically speaking in Kurdish, grabbing his mother's hand when she starts for the door. His fingers press into her wrist as she pulls away.

And then it is dark. Nothing ticks. Nothing hums. Like the final beat of a countdown. Something is about to happen. Now.

But there's only the plane. Louder, it gnaws through the sky as Gaziza backs against the wall, her face blanched in moonlight from the window, her eyes on the ceiling. Suddenly it occurs to Olivia that low-flying planes drop bombs. She tries to get up, but Delan stops her.

"No. *No.* It's the electricity. Liv, that's it. The power's out."

But the plane. The words, what could happen, they're choked within her. Her mouth opens just as there's a shift in the sound above, noise collecting in what must be the plane's turn, right before it starts to fade. Still, the lights are off. Her heart beats in the dark. Another long collection of seconds and then the silence is complete, the plane gone.

A relief. She sees it on their shadowed faces, a slow, hesitant release from a past that wasn't long enough ago to be forgotten, a time when the fighting was not just in the mountains. Suddenly what feels wrong is that she'd not known. What's wrong is that to her, a plane has only ever been a plane. A fundamental difference even in what they fear.

And then a click. And a brightness. The power returned.

Gaziza presses her hand to her forehead and returns to her seat, eating with unsteady fingers. Rice falls to the table. Soran drinks from his glass while staring straight ahead, and Hewar nods, shyly, to his plate, as if it had just spoken some sort of logic.

"Now I'm telling them about our house," Delan says, refusing to acknowledge anything other than the power outage. He reaches for a fava bean in the bowl near her glass and clenches down with his teeth to capture the beans and the soft, boiled pod. "I said our yard is small and a mess, and they want to know why we don't grow more vegetables in the empty lot behind the house, since it gets all sun."

"It isn't ours," Olivia says slowly, lifting herself from the past moment. She's still thinking of the plane, wondering where it was going. "It could be built up any day."

"A poor excuse," Soran says.

Olivia turns to him. "Can you imagine doing all that work on something that might be taken away?"

"Yes. All the time," he says and smiles timidly to his plate.

And though she realizes what he means, that here—a place where a low-flying plane means destruction—nothing is forever and things and people and places are taken just like that, for some reason she feels that he's talking about a woman. She watches him, and when she looks to Delan, she sees he's doing the same.

There is a single bed in the room Soran has been sleeping in, so he will take the couch, and Delan has been given his room. Olivia learns this as she stands in the threshold to the room she's been given, which has a double bed and a view of the garden. She tells Delan that he and Soran should take this room and share—that there's no reason for Soran to be on the couch when one room has a double bed.

"You're the guest," Delan says. "This is the room for the guests. It's the nicest room. Please, you argue, it will upset them. And," he adds quietly, "if my brother is with me, there's no room for midnight visitors."

She glances at his parents' room, right next door. "No way."

"The couch is best for me," Soran calls from the hall. "I do not sleep well, and from there I bother less people. Come, the garden."

Outside, the moon is heavy and the sounds of cannons have faded.

"The Kurds in the mountain villages, they keep their lights off at night," Soran says. Olivia thinks of electricity, a lack of power, until he adds, "Or they are targets. Hopefully tonight will be quiet for them."

The plane. Was that where it was going? To the mountain villages? What she'd heard might have been the beginning of someone's night. A mere rustle here but chaos on the other side.

"All you can do is say a prayer," Soran adds when he sees her face.

Delan shakes his head. "Prayers were needed an hour ago. A bit late for that."

"It is never too late to wish someone well," Soran says. "And you know this; it is never over."

"Enough," Delan says, draping his arm around Olivia's shoulders. "Our first night. Let's not get depressed."

In the silence, they walk the path. Now and then, Soran points to plants and says their names in English and Kurdish, introducing Olivia to them like a new teacher at school. Olivia repeats their names. *Xiyar*, cucumber. *Kuleke*, zucchini. At the end of the path, a birdcage hangs from a branch. Olivia goes to it, hoping there's nothing inside. Nothing could be worse than having a bird outside, among nature but barred from it. A few more steps and she sees the gray top of a head and then the whole pigeon, sitting in a box with straw. "Why?" she asks. The bird looks up at her with its head tilted, echoing her question.

"He is hurt," Soran says.

"My father fixes them," Delan says. "Sometimes he has three, four birds."

A relief. Already she loves his father with his big ears and the pen in his pocket.

"Finches, pigeons. Once an owl. Whatever falls from the sky, my father will fix."

"And chukars," Soran says. "Do not forget them. Though they will not let you forget them, even if you tried. In the back. By the wall."

"Partridges," Delan says. "We call them chukars."

The sound, she realizes. She'd thought them chickens. Laughing chickens.

They approach the coop, wood and chicken wire under the cover of a large peach tree, and three birds stand for a greeting. Mostly gray but with black-and-white-striped wings, red beaks, and black around their throats like fur collars.

"The food," Soran says, turning back to the house. "They like what we did not eat."

"Fruit," Delan says. "Get them fruit only. They're not pigs for leftovers."

But Soran is already at the back door and then inside.

She turns to Delan. "So the fighting is close."

"Close in your terms. Not in ours." He takes her by the waist, thumb hooked into her belt loop, then touches the hair at her temple with his finger.

She glances toward the house. "We'll get in trouble."

"Not if they don't see."

His lips on hers. She lets her eyes close until she hears Gaziza's voice from the kitchen, calling out in Kurdish. Delan smiles as Olivia backs away. "We're safe. She was yelling at my father because he was about to go to bed. Without dessert."

"I can't eat more."

"You'll have to. She won't stop until you do."

Olivia leads him toward the tunnel of grapevines. In their corner, the chukars laugh quietly, as if they've sensed motivation. "My mother had birds. Or one, I guess. When my dad met her, she had a parrot named Bigelow. My dad drinks tea, and there's a tea called Bigelow, so when he picked her up for their first date, he said he knew. All because of the parrot."

"Your father believes in signs."

Under the vines, light swims on the ground. Ebbed movements from the leaves, a marbled moonlight. She wants her camera, wants to capture it in black and white, this patterned pathway. "My father is a writer. He believes in whatever makes a good story." *Most of the time what could've happened is the great story.* "Did you mean us that night? That what could've happened with us was the great story?"

Again he draws her to him, making the most of their privacy. "Back then, you were the story I told myself." A whisper in her ear. "But I think this is a better one." With a quick kiss, he surveys the green above them. "We should plant grapes at home. We could have a tunnel on the side with the Spanish house. I wouldn't have to take leaves from the neighbors for dolmas."

"But raiding the neighbors' yard is part of dinner at our house."

Though she said it jokingly, his tone is sharp. "I give back. I don't steal. We have an exchange."

She tilts her head as if to question the direction he's taking the conversation, though she herself set the dial. Delan's need to never disappoint, to never place himself first—she's loved it but seen it verge on destructive. As it did today.

"They come and take oranges," he says. "And herbs. Basil, I gave them two plants before we left."

"Delan. *That's* fine."

He steps away from her. "The zucchini. I can't believe we're talking about the zucchini."

Taken from the neighbors' garden when a couple of his friends had been sent to find swiss chard—*not* zucchini, not something the neighbor had been watching and waiting for. But Delan had said nothing to them. Delan, who needed to be liked at any expense, who would bring empty-handed friends home and smile as they ate the groceries he'd bought for the entire week, and who'd helped people move because he was the one with a Vanagon and yet said nothing when the time came to fill up with gas and he'd been forced to stack his quarters and dimes on the counter.

"It wasn't right," she finally says.

"I bought him a dozen the next day, did you know? I knew it wasn't right. I saw it in your eyes."

"You didn't need to see it in my eyes to know. That's what bothers me. *You knew.* You just didn't want to upset that guy, your castmate."

"What could I do, glue them back to the plant? What was done was done; why make my guest uncomfortable? What do you really mean, Liv?"

A vine by the wall shakes from something within. "You want everyone to like you. And everyone does. And they know you as good, because you feed them and love them and pick them up at the airport or help them move—but people take advantage of that. And you let them."

A small smile. "And you want to protect me from that."

"There's no reason to sacrifice yourself just because you need to be liked."

Smile gone. "That's how you see it?"

She regrets this now. How can you tell someone that their goodness is wasted? "Your being nice is a good thing, but when it comes at your expense—"

"The expense of a few dollars. Going to a movie that week. Those are my *friends.*"

Mason, Alan, and only a few others are his real friends. The core, the ones who've proven themselves on nights gone sour with news of home, the ones who won't leave the table when Delan's voice rises above the rest. The others, all the castmates with their months of closeness or the directors with their searching eyes, they're moths that circle tight but are gone by morning.

But the way he said the word *friends.* Like a plea. Like a child hopeful to avoid a truth, reacting to the impending edge of hurt. Just looking at him, this man who is generous to a fault, who loves unabashedly and wholeheartedly, she *does* feel the need to protect him. *Don't confuse your anger,* her father used to tell her. *Sometimes we get mad just because we're forced to feel.* The anger she's felt on his behalf, she realizes, has fallen upon him. An anger for making her care. "Fine. I want to protect you."

He smiles. Just as the back door swings shut and Soran steps into the garden.

"Your brother," she says. "Your dream—"

"That fig tree is gone. The one I dreamed of. I asked my mother, and a branch broke last year and the tree died. Liv, you were right. I dream in metaphor. It's not to be translated as real. Of course. I was told to come here, that they needed me. And I listened. And I'm glad I did." He smiles at her. "This is *good*. Now, let's forget everything under this tunnel, okay?"

By the pomegranate, Soran uprights a pot that's tilted over, dirt in a spill by its edge. In the second-floor window of the neighbor's house, Olivia sees the little girl Lailan, a doll in her hand that she's making walk straight up the window frame, her hands moving the legs, *one two, one two.* Then she lets go of the doll, which falls from view, and even from next door, Olivia sees her face transform into mock concern before she disappears. "She's cute," Olivia says.

Soran looks up to the direction of Olivia's gaze. "She's smart," he says, and Olivia loves him for his correction.

"Soran-*gyan*," Delan says. "You're not telling me something. It doesn't make sense. You were about to graduate. Why here, why now?"

Soran pushes the dirt around the plant, firm, the imprints of his fingers left in the soil. "They wanted me here."

"Bullshit," Delan says and turns to Olivia. "Kurdish parents expect perfection. To give up on school? That's a failure. That, they would not ask for."

Now Soran looks up. "They are old. You might not have noticed."

Olivia doesn't have to look at him to feel Delan's anger.

"*Baba* has trouble walking," Soran continues.

Delan lapses into Kurdish, and Olivia turns to the house behind her, wanting to get away. Then she remembers the seed packets. When they were packing, she'd thrown in three seed packets—California poppies, snapdragons, sweet alyssum. A bit of their home to share. It was only at the airport that she'd realized it might be considered smuggling, a worry that made Delan laugh. Now she goes to her room, where she finds the packets in her suitcase, and listens to the brothers argue through the open window. Sitting on her bed, she begins a count to two hundred but stops when she hears her name. Who said it? Their voices are so alike, though Soran's speech is slower, paced out as if in a marathon while Delan sprints. Though she listens, she doesn't hear her name again.

"Here," she says when she returns. A cloud sits below the moon, scattered and long. "I brought these for your garden."

"She smuggled them," Delan says proudly. "All by herself."

Their conversation has turned. When she looks back to Soran, he's flipped a packet over, lips moving as he reads.

In the dark, she wakes, listening to a call to prayer that's soft and distant. No one in the house stirs. From her bed, she sees lights on in two of the houses behind Delan's property. Within would be Muslim families, knees upon their rugs. Her eyes close again as the call continues, wavering and old, coursing deep burgundy and purple in her mind, leading into dreams she won't remember.

A knock on her door, and she wakes to sun through the window. "Liv," Delan says. "Meet me in the kitchen. Let's get going."

In the kitchen, he's not there, but Gaziza is, on her knees as she cleans the floor with what looks like a short-handled brush. Her wrists are dented, heavily creased with lines.

"Let me help," Olivia says, kneeling down. "Please, Gaziza."

But Gaziza bats her hand away, then turns to sweep in a different direction. Her hair is wispy in the back, patches of gray in the spot that's usually covered by her scarf, areas that must be hard for her to reach on her own when dyeing it dark. Does Delan know she dyes it? Or does he see her with the love of a child, that love that never glimpses death or aging? Already Olivia has seen it, the difficulty the woman has standing and kneeling so much. Always, it seems, there is standing and kneeling. Even to sit for dinner, Gaziza's face tightened, eyes closed as she found her way to the floor. And here she is again, on hands and knees.

Under the sink is an old cloth that Olivia moistens and uses to start wiping the floor.

"Olivia," Delan says, standing in the doorframe. "I don't think my mother—"

"That needs a handle. What she's using, there's not even a handle. Where's the handle?"

"That's always how it's been. How they all are."

Olivia stretches to wipe the corner of the floor. After a moment, she sits back and sees Gaziza's stopped what she's doing and is watching—shocked and not pleased—and it's then Olivia realizes that Delan is behind her and also on the floor, wiping quickly and with much less care but wiping all the same.

"You don't have to do this," Olivia says to him.

"Of course I do. It will be faster; then we'll go."

Quietly, she says over her shoulder, "Your mom hates me now."

He stands and motions to her to give him her cloth. "Give it. Let me rinse." The faucet in the sink comes on, and after a moment, he hands her back her cloth. As he does, he looks her in the eyes. "Ignore it. Mothers never like it when a woman changes their son."

For a second, Olivia stops wiping. Beside her, he is already kneeling, the wide arcs of his arm swiping clean the floor.

Tea that is hot and sweet. Baklava that is honeyed, sticky flakes. From the table at the café in town, the mountains are tall and jagged and capped in white. Soldiers patrol the streets, set up at the next block's corner. Though she and the brothers sit at a table fairly far from others, far enough that no one can hear them, Soran still turns his voice to a whisper as he tells of Kurdish glories. Sheikh Mahmud who they're related to, Saladin who battled Richard the Lionheart, and even the three wise men, the Magi from the bible, who are thought to be three Zoroastrian priests. "That is what the priests were called," Soran says. "Magi. Zoroaster, the prophet who lived in this area, he said a king would be born to a woman who was a virgin. So the Zoroastrian priests, they were waiting, and then they saw the star in the sky. Or so it goes."

"I know where he gets it from now," she says, motioning to Delan. "The storytelling."

"The *goranibezh*," Soran says. His eyes, that sun-filtered green, move between Olivia—the recipient of the tales—and Delan, who takes over now and then as if by cue. "They are our storytellers."

"Our bards," Delan says.

"Yes, Shakespeare, our bards. For centuries. A very special people. Trained for years. More than a hundred stories that they sing from memory, some stories an hour long. It is an art. Started by women too. When someone was injured, they would sing to distract from the pain."

"Two hours," Delan says. "Three. The memorization, even I could not come close. Epic stories, Liv. In Turkey, they could be killed for even speaking Kurdish. So they practice alone, where no one can hear them. Here, they're hired for weddings now. The new wedding singers, telling the tales of old." He turns to Soran. "Maybe there will be *goranibezh* at the wedding?"

"That, I do not think. Ferhad lost his business months ago. His family is in good standing, but the bride-price was—" But then he stops talking, and Olivia turns in time to see Delan shaking his head.

"What?" she says. "What's a bride-price?"

"*Sheerbayee*. Bride-price. What it sounds like," Soran says. "The man's family pays it to the bride's family. They are losing a set of hands, someone valuable in the house."

Olivia turns to Delan, eyes wide.

"My mother," Delan says quickly, "she makes the decisions in the house. All the money, how it's spent."

"But she also does all the cleaning and the cooking."

"And that does not happen in America?" Delan asks.

"Here, it is a patriarchy," Soran says. "And traditional. Less traditional than other cultures, yes. Much less. But roles are slow to break. We are far from perfect."

Delan shakes his head. "Soran-*gyan*, it depends where you are from. Rural, not rural, educated, not educated. Life in the mountain villages, it's not like here. And that is true for any country."

"Yes, that is true. You remember Roza," Soran says. "Wassim's sister? She's a judge."

"See? A *judge*. And family, everyone is different—even in America, that is true. But the struggle for freedom, you admit, *that* has united men and women. Women are respected politically. Think of all the women Kurdish leaders, the women Peshmerga. Our family—my aunts, cousins—many are political—"

Soran holds up his hand, glancing toward the soldiers at the end of the street. "It is one thing to talk of history quietly. Another to talk of our family. Even in English. The walls have ears. No more, please."

Delan, silenced, taps his finger against the table, then glances at Olivia. "Ferhad was to have married someone else, you know. But he didn't. Because of her, his bride. Because he loved her that much."

"He loved her so much, he didn't marry someone else? And he gets credit for that?"

"Arranged marriages are also for love. Love of your family. And he could've grown to love the other woman."

"And what if *she* never loved him?"

"Then he'd miss out."

"As would she," Olivia says. "Imagine, not getting a chance to love. Never getting those butterflies just because you heard someone's name or feeling like everything's better because someone exists. No one should miss that."

Delan smiles.

"What?"

"No, you're right. No one should miss that. But you described *in love*. The *in love* part of the first few months. That is when they can do no wrong and your stomach jumps and everything is bliss. But really, truly, loving someone? To me? What *in love* becomes? That's deeper. That's when they *can* do wrong and it's not always sunshine. You love them for who they are, sure. That's the easy part. But you also love them despite who they are. That's the important part."

Saying nothing, Olivia pours tea into her cup. She's trying to remember what Rebecca told her about her ex-boyfriend's return from the war. Broken in too many ways, he'd not made it easy. But not once had she stopped loving him, even when it hurt. Even when he made a final choice and took away any chance at getting better. Love, in that case, was certainly not all sunshine.

Delan turns to his brother. "And you, what of your girl, the one who was the one?"

Soran shrugs. "I loved to love her. How is that? Can we walk now? Enough riddles."

The day ekes into the afternoon. A drive and a hike to Shanidar Cave, where a stair path zigzags through thistles and tall white flowers to an entrance that's dark upon the mountain, the shape like a gaping frown, as if the mountain silently wails. Inside, the stone walls are streaked and darkened, and Soran tells her of the Neanderthal remains that were unearthed, thought to be sixty thousand years old.

"When I was a kid, we'd come here," Delan says. "At the time, they'd not been found. Imagine the discovery, waiting."

"The skulls," Soran says, "the bodies were covered with pollen. Hollyhock and thistles. It meant flowers were thrown in the graves. The first signs of humanity, in creatures not even fully human."

Right here, where she stands. "My mom's in my dad's den. In an urn, brass with engraved daisies. They were her favorite. Underappreciated, she said." Sitting in the grass in someone's yard, they'd made daisy chains, tying stems so they fit around her wrist. "I want to stay on the earth like this. To be found in a cave that no one will look in for thousands of years."

"Only you would have that request," Delan says. "The most difficult request. Look." He points to the grass outside, yellowed from a light that could only mean a storm. "We'll be here for a while."

Just as he says that, heavy drops bullet the dirt outside the cave's mouth, kicking up dust. Within minutes, it's as if a curtain of water has been lowered before them.

"Think of how many people stood here," she says. "Listening to the rain. These exact acoustics, in this exact spot. Sixty thousand years ago, someone stood right where I am, hearing *this*."

The rain beats the valley. This is what she's wanted, what she's needed. This connection, this tie to the core of humanity—it clenches something within her. After so much war and politics and struggle, here it is, the essence. A cave for shelter. Flowers for grief. Uncomplicated and pure. So basic, what's needed, and yet how easily she forgets.

Delan leans against the cave's wall, his head turned toward the rain. Soran stands before him but faces the mouth of the cave, his hands in his pockets. Both brothers watch the water as it beats the earth. Without them noticing, she has her camera out and focused. The rain on the right of the image will be a soft curtain, the texture of the wall in the background striated and ancient. The distribution of light and shadow has her entranced, like something moving: water seeping, teasing. The brothers stand in postures that are *them*—one relaxed and leaning and the other shy and contained. Both lost in what's before them. She shifts slightly to avoid graphically entangling a dark spot in the background with Delan's hair and feels the photo hook into something deep within her as she presses the button, that thrill she gets when she knows she has it.

Delan hears her snap the photo. "Come," he says as he turns on a flashlight so they can walk farther inside. "Soran, stay there in case we get lost." He glances at Olivia. "Joking. We won't get lost; it's not too big." And then, back to his brother, "Soran, stay there."

The cave is black and cool. Delan takes her hand, helping her over rocks, and in stereo bats squeal, one side and then the other. Holding his hand in darkness, surrounded by ancient life, she's hit with a feeling that if the world spun as many times as it did and somehow they found each other—though they were born continents away—that that in itself is a miracle. That truly, in looking at where they all began and somehow have ended up, that life itself is a miracle. And in this moment, she feels happiness without question, because already so much has been overcome, just in the fact that they stand here together. "Delan," she says. "I'm happy."

He spins the flashlight at her. A cringe as the light hits her eyes before he aims it at a rock. "You should be happy. Why wouldn't you be happy? Why is this an announcement?"

"I was just saying I was happy, that's all."

"You overthink. You *are* happy most of the time. I see that you are, even if you don't. Maybe you're afraid to be happy when you realize it. Afraid that it will be taken. Your mother."

She smiles. "I say I'm happy, and you bring up my dead mother?"

"No, that's the easy answer. I know what it is. It's come to me. You think to be an artist, to be taken seriously, you must suffer."

Now she turns to him. "No I don't."

"You do. I've seen it when we have certain people over. You smile less. There are no jokes. You search your stories for the saddest ones."

"I do?"

"Look, there," he says, aiming his flashlight at two rocks across from each other. "Can't you see them sitting there? After a hunt?" A moment passes, and he continues. "Maybe it's because you're younger; you see life as either-or. But I'm an artist, too, and I have suffered, and I would rather not *keep* suffering, so I smile. And if I am happy, I don't tell myself not to be."

He shines the light under his chin to show his smile and then back to the path before them.

Delan's words stick. Parties they've had—a director here, an artist there, all sorts of creative people who Delan and Mason paraded through the house. He might be right. She shuts down. Becomes quiet, lest they confuse a smile with youth. She wants to be taken seriously when she talks of studying Mondrian or Kline to understand composition. She wants to take photos of the people in the house, reclining by the fireplace and lost in themselves, without being shooed away or dismissed. Somehow, over the course of time, permission for this has become enmeshed with a need to make people believe she has suffered as they have, that she is part of their club, when the truth is she has not. Yes, her mother died when she was young and yes, it was loss, horrifying loss that emptied her of everything for years, but her father's love tipped the scale back to where it should be, and her childhood was, all in all, happy. And yet that, her father's achievement, raising a daughter on his own, that she does not speak of. As if having an amazing father in one's life disqualifies one from being an artist. Maybe it *is* because she's younger that she thinks this—though even that, his drawing attention to the six years that separate them, even that makes her angry, makes her feel less than all the lovely, wounded people who tell stories that make people lean in, that make people respect them because they've gone through so much. The actress with the ski-slope nose, she remembers Mason announcing, *Christ, what she draws from. I heard her mother put her on a diet when she was seven and pimped her to the landlord at ten for a break in rent.* Olivia was horrified, not only at what was said but that Mason knew. Now Olivia thinks of her father again, drawing from his own childhood for his writing. All that past suffering, isn't it true that pain inspires? Doesn't it lead to insight?

"Van Gogh," she says. They're standing outside his parents' house, Lailan playing nearby. Soran walked to his friend's to get the car to take them to an early dinner, and now they wait to see its flare of orange. "He was tortured. A wreck of a human, but look at what he did. And Sylvia Plath."

"This whole time, you've been stewing."

"Dostoyevsky," she says. "Hemingway. There've been so many." Remembering the checkpoints, she's got her camera in her knit purse and pats her bag, reassured of its presence, while Lailan jumps from a spot by a car's tire to a rock and then to a brick, avoiding the ground. Now and then, the girl points a toe and comes close to touching the cobblestone road but draws her foot back sharply. Olivia tries to decipher her game. *"Beethoven,"* she says, watching. "He lost his mother *and* his hearing. A composer whose ability to hear was stolen from him, and from that came total and complete genius. There's a connection."

"So what, you're excluded from that because you weren't tormented? Because you don't have a mental illness? Be thankful you don't. Of course there's a connection. But it's not the only one. I've known brilliant actors who had wonderful childhoods. What pain were they drawing from? Is their performance less brilliant because they've got loving parents? Because they told a joke that day? Of course not. And I've known people who've suffered like you could not understand and they have no more creative ability or desire than someone who sells tennis rackets."

Lailan jumps to Delan, holding on to his leg as if about to fall in, and Delan grabs on to her, saying something in Kurdish that makes the girl's eyes go wide.

"Lava?" Olivia asks, nodding to the ground. Lailan's head turns at the strange word.

"Flood," Delan says, then explains *lava* to Lailan in Kurdish. The girl's eyes narrow, as if she has a bone to pick with fire that would dare flow from the earth. "You missed her shivering," he adds to Olivia. "The water's freezing. It was actually very realistic; I was impressed. There, Lailan, to safety! I see a boat."

"Where is boat, where?" Then Lailan stops, laughing. "Where-ah. Where-ah boat."

"*Were,*" Delan says, pronouncing it as she did, "means *come* in Kurdish. You're calling the boat to you; is that what you're doing, Lailan?" He turns to Olivia. "Soran only talks to her in English. She's better than I was when I came to the United States."

Lailan puts her hand to her mouth, as if holding an imaginary megaphone. "Where-ah boat. Where-ah boat." She's serious. Searching the street, squinting. Intent and focused.

Delan nudges the girl's shoulders. "The anchor's down. You'll have to jump for it. Go, Lailan, now!"

Lailan sees the spot where he points—the bottom step to her house—and makes a leap.

Delan gives her a thumbs-up, then turns back to Olivia. "You judge art on art, not biography. I see it, you know. The way you compare yourself to friends, to everyone, like they have some ticket to being an adult you don't. But when it comes to your talent"—he motions to her purse, to her camera—"it's your eye. What you're drawn to. What you see when you look at something. *Empathy*, that's it. Some people have it right off the bat. Others need to learn through hard lessons. If you didn't need to learn through hard lessons, to have an eye like you do, good for you. Don't question it. And a smile doesn't make you any less intelligent or creative. Just like a frown doesn't make you smart. I *choose* to be happy, and I'm lucky I have that choice, and I won't apologize for it."

And now she hears it. It's not just her he's defending; it's himself. Not for his past, which certainly has its share of torment, but for who he is now. Welcoming. Grandiose. Loving. The one who smiles at strangers and strikes up conversations with cabdrivers and people in checkout lines. "You feel like people pass you off because you're happy?" she asks. And then adds, "For the most part." Because she has of course seen when he is not.

"No one passes me off."

It was quick, but she saw it: insecurity. Slight but present in the way he leans seemingly nonchalantly against the house, the way he didn't meet her eyes as he spoke. Protection, she realizes. What at times must be a forced arrogance that prevents people from looking closer. She takes a couple of steps so she's inches from him, so close that she smells the detergent they use at home. "It wouldn't be proper to kiss you now, would it?" In the background, Lailan jumps over the threshold to her house, the door swinging shut behind her.

Delan's eyes find Olivia's lips. "Definitely not." With his finger, he pulls her collar so she's even closer. But he holds back, just barely. There's the sound of him breathing, then a door opening across the street. Thwacks of a rug being beaten. He glances toward the noise and stands up straight, and in response, she turns to see dust rising from the rug and Soran's car as it takes the corner.

The roads are dirt, and windshield wipers chase clear a path as they drive to another town for an early dinner, a town with a famous restaurant owned by Kurds. There's no parking nearby, so they find a spot blocks away, next to an old, tilted minaret. Men lean in the doorways of stores, chatting with neighboring owners, cigarettes wedged between stained fingers and smoke curling around eaves. Their eyes search for customers, and when they spot Olivia, they stand aside, smiling and gesturing into crowded rooms of clothing, rugs, and knickknacks.

"Where you are from?" one man asks. A gray suit jacket over a plaid shirt. He stands with his hands together before him and nods to her with his head, encouraging her answer.

A pause as she turns to address him. "California."

His hand goes to his heart. "America. We love the America. Please, you to have a wonderful visit in Kurdistan."

Delan salutes the man, and Olivia yells out a thank-you, waiting for the typical sales pitch, the imploring call to come inside, to check out a sale. But all the man does is raise his arm in a farewell, his face a broad smile. Once more, she nods a thank-you, and turns back just in time to sidestep a woman crouched on the sidewalk with a burlap bag piled to the rim with green fruit.

"Almonds," Delan says. "You eat the whole thing. The outside, everything. Delicious."

A man carrying a cage with chickens cranes his head to watch her as she passes. People, she realizes, are staring at her. "I look American."

He laughs. "You do. Sure. But that's not it. You're *tall*. The tallest woman they've ever seen."

But it's not just the women she's taller than. Passing through crowds, she realizes she's a head taller than most of the men. Faces tilt toward her. A woman kneeling beside a bin of walnuts peers up at her, her face weathered, black hair threaded with white.

"You failed to mention I'd be the tallest woman in the entire country."

"There is no hiding you," Soran says. "That is true. There, that is the restaurant, across the street."

But they're passing the opening to a bazaar. The thick smell of spices, a mix of voices. A long, narrow walkway of dirtied cement shoots through the chaos of goods. Each stall appears to have a different focus and a different merchant but is right on top of the other, the result a confusion of intents and rewards, a market that would render a shopping list useless. Overhead, tarps and canvases crisscross to protect against the sun or rain, everything lending itself to a beautiful chaos. A sensory overload, even from its edge. To be lost within the rows, to pry kebab off with her teeth and buy rugs or little brass dishes she'll have no real need for, it's all she wants.

"After," Delan says, then nods to an area with tall bags of lentils and beans: green, white, black, orange, and every hue in between. "We'll buy white beans for dinner tomorrow. And the next day, for the picnic."

Crossing the street, they pause to let a moped lurch past. A few older men smoke hookah on the sidewalk, and the air by the entrance of the restaurant smells of burning coal. Inside is already crowded. Against one wall is a chipped tiled pool with hazy water, and fish swim in repetitive, lethargic arcs. Toward the back, before the kitchen, is a rounded open fire surrounded by metal spikes on which fish are impaled and cooking.

"Well," she says as they take their seats at a table against the mirrored wall. "I actually don't like fish. But fresh is good."

"*Masgouf.* River carp," Delan says. "You'll like it. All netted today. Gone tomorrow." He leans back in his chair and smiles, while his brother holds his water glass with both hands.

"We took you to a restaurant of fish," Soran says, embarrassed, "and you don't like fish."

Delan turns to find the waiter. "She will like it. Trust me. It doesn't get better. I used to dream of this fish."

And there's something in his last sentence that makes her smile. Because it's true. He probably dreamed of this fish. And it's not that he thinks he knows better or doesn't care what she likes but that he wants desperately, more than anything, to open what he loves to others. To exist in a shared land, where one glance or *do you remember* is all it takes. And in his excitement to be in this place, he turns boastful and clumsy—a man who'd spill on a precious rug while hurrying to share his favorite meal or step on a toe while rushing someone to the dance floor.

"I'll be fine," she says. "As long as they have bread."

"I didn't think to ask," Soran says. Soran, the one who'd watch from the edge of the dance floor and who'd mop up the spill. Soran, who now glances to the back of the restaurant unhappily.

She touches his hand, and he turns to her, surprised. "It's okay. Really."

Delan waves to the waiter, who approaches. "They have bread; of course they have bread. Let's get drinks. The streets are swimming with food. If she doesn't like it, we'll buy kebab at the bazaar. Or *shifta*. You'll love *shifta*. The Kurdish hamburger."

Beside them, a couple drinks directly from soup bowls, bones of fish piled on saucers and charred tails left on rims of plates. At another table, a family uses their hands to eat, a platter of three fish lined with sliced tomatoes, cucumbers, and lemons before them. There are two little boys, one whose feet don't touch the ground and who's sitting on what looks like a telephone book. Bangs cut unevenly, a dimple on his right cheek. His face breaks into a smile when his mother spoons more tomatoes onto his plate, and as he eats, a seed catches on his chin. His father smiles and points to his own chin, miming the spot.

Delan doesn't so much order as indicate there are three of them, which starts the food coming. When the waiter sets the main dish in the center of the table, Olivia wonders if the Neanderthals caught these same fish. Did they use spices or herbs?

"We need to go," Soran says, having returned from the bathroom.

Delan looks up at his brother and then around the restaurant.

Soran doesn't even take a seat, just says quietly, "We need to go. I'm paying. I'll tell them I'm not well." Then he leans in to whisper in Delan's ear. There is a pause, and Delan's eyes flicker to the back of the restaurant. Then Soran is gone, joining the host by the front door and peeling dinars from his wallet.

"Is he okay?" Olivia asks.

"He might be right and we should go."

Now she looks around the room. Nothing appears wrong. The little boy beside them kicks his foot under the table, back and forth, back and forth.

Delan leans toward her and says quietly, "Too many political figures. Soran recognized them at that long table by the kitchen. And another one just arrived."

A table of men, all wearing dark-brown or gray suits. Most glance at menus, some drink water, and others are leaned in and talking quietly. Elsewhere in the restaurant, no one seems bothered. People eat, the fish swim, the fire blazes.

"But we didn't do anything."

Delan leans in so close, his lips brush her ear. Beside them, a man walking to another table stares hard as he passes. "It's not that we're doing anything wrong. It's that this restaurant just became a target."

A *target*. The word rings in her ears.

Then he sits back and points to the naan bread. "Take one to go if you want." Casual, as if he's just told her they need to leave now if they want to make a movie.

Soran motions to them from the door. As they stand, Olivia glances behind her and catches the eye of one of the men at the back table. He stares at her and then slowly looks down at Olivia's table: a spread of uneaten food. When the man looks back up at Olivia, it feels as though she's brushed against something cold. From the kitchen, something shatters. Hurried steps, laughter becomes louder. Suddenly she needs to be in a crowd, gone, and as she turns to leave, Delan glances to her to make sure she's following and must see the man as well.

"Come," he says quickly, pulling her arm.

The man's stare bears down on her.

In the bazaar, they wind through the aisles. The early-evening air is a cooling separation between where they were and where they are. She listens for gunfire, but there's only music that drifts from a radio and the chaotic din of voices. "Is he going to come look for us?"

"No. He's going to finish his dinner," Delan says. "Which we should've done."

"Better to starve than be dead," Soran says.

"No one is starving, not with all this food. And no one is dead."

Olivia glances back at the restaurant, to the men smoking hookah on the sidewalk, faces lost in swirls of smoke like identities obscured in a hazy memory.

Delan motions her forward. "Most likely we spent a lot of money on a dinner we didn't eat. That's the truth."

He's right that no one is dead. Nothing has happened. But that doesn't mean that the man stayed seated. Or hadn't sent someone to find them. A tap on the shoulder and any one of the men to his side could've slipped from the restaurant. Could be, at this moment, steps behind them, watching.

"Liv. Stop. Enjoy where you are. Nothing is wrong until it is."

Heating oil and dust and spices. The deep breath she takes catches on its way in, particles of choking worry. Be present, she tells herself. Don't dwell on the past and don't exist in a future worry. He's right: nothing is wrong until it is.

Mounds of almonds and walnuts and pistachios line a wall. Rows of shoes loom to the tarped ceiling, and bins of spices in every shade except blue crowd an aisle. She tries to forget everything except for what's before her—ropes of dried figs and the shocking gleam of bright brass kettles and trays. With a turn, there are stacks of rugs and a tower of fava beans and loops of shiny prayer beads.

"Should I get one?" she asks, touching the amber beads.

"Worry beads?" Delan says. "You worry fine on your own. You don't need help."

"*Tezbih,*" Soran says. "Prayer beads. There are ninety-nine beads. You use them for *zikr*. Each counts for a prayer."

"Sure. Or they are worry beads."

She turns to Delan. "Do I worry a lot?"

One brow raised, he looks at her, incredulous. "Is this smuggling? Is the man from the restaurant after us? Have I been tortured enough to be taken seriously?"

She bites her lip, smiling to piles of parsley and cilantro.

"You're ridiculous," he says and hooks his arm around her waist.

His hand on her hip. The smells of the bazaar. The music in the stalls. The day has a spark to it, good or bad she can't tell, only feels its intensity like a charge that could carry her through miles of boring nothing. From across the aisle, she catches Soran's eyes flickering to his brother's arm, and though she wonders if this is proper, ultimately she doesn't care.

Then they've made a loop and are near where they started. Pigeons drink from a puddle of water, and light skims the surface. An image she wants to capture, the birds and their thirst and the reflected chaos. So she starts to get out her camera, debating over angles and how much space she should allow in the foreground, when all of a sudden, she realizes the amount of attention this would draw. A tall American woman with red hair and a camera, crouched in a pathway, tripping people and taking pictures of birds. If anyone had been sent to find them, there she'd be. *There is no hiding you,* Soran said. If the man from the restaurant is looking for them, she's the giveaway. She looks up ahead to the opening of the market that's across from the restaurant. Right now, he could be there, waiting.

Delan pulls her around and points to a stand with the white shoes the Kurdish men wear, but in her turn, Olivia catches a dark-gray sleeve disappearing into a stall before them. Quickly, she faces the shoes. The world's gone hot. She lifts her hair off her neck, fanning her skin. She needs to relax. That could've been anyone. But once more, she turns to look, just as a boy with a cart of pomegranates cuts behind her. At the top of the pile, the fruits are split, red and gleaming.

"*Klash,*" Delan is saying. "The shoes. The top is woven wool cotton and the bottom recycled material and animal intestine. There is no right or left. The shoes are the same. The most comfortable shoe. And sturdy. First worn by Zoroaster." He adds that last part with a shrug, as if acknowledging it as a fact he cannot verify.

Soran calls to them, stopped at a tray of wrapped treats. "*Hallwa*. You know it as manna," he says. "From manna trees. Sap falls with the dew, hangs like icicles. People stretch cloths beneath the branches and shake the trees."

Manna from heaven. Connections between stories and terms come to life. There's something about it that's comforting, a feeling that all the world is a web and though she'd started in only a little corner, if she keeps going, things will make sense, patterns will unfold, and everything will prove to be part of the next. She touches a wrapped piece of candy, imagining how a starving and faithful people would believe that the food that dripped from branches had of course fallen from the sky and was a gift, a saving, when suddenly there is a blink of light and a gust of dusty wind and a sound that hits with two punches. The first sound is distant but in no way far enough, and the second travels and in a split second is around her.

The sound of metal bending, cement breaking, a world falling.

Already she's on the ground—Delan's arm around her—before she realizes he must have pushed her down. She stays bent, hunched, and through the ringing in her ears, she hears the muffled sound of her breathing mix with the sound of rain falling after thunder. But it's not rain. Of course it's not rain. It's glass, falling like rain, like ice, like every chime in the world had hovered in this spot and been released. Her fingers press white into the cement, and there is a jagged cut on her wrist, from what she's not sure.

Time no longer has a hold. It might be seconds that she stays like this or minutes. Sounds grow louder, voices and cries in another language, even the radio that had been playing in the stall begins again, and with this, she realizes the sounds have been there the whole time but her hearing has not. When she turns to Delan, he's looking over his shoulder. Another cloud of dust billows toward them but stops, like anger without the fuel to continue. People who were on the ground get up, scrambling, moving closer to the buildings. No one wants to be out in the open. A primal instinct.

And then Delan is lifting her at the waist and Soran is beside her, and they're moving through the shambles of the market, past the shoes on the ground, past spills of beans and spices, through the tangles of prayer beads. What wasn't knocked over from the blast must have been pushed over by people trying to get away, and when they get to the opening of the bazaar, she pauses, trying to focus, to find the men with the hookah pipes in front of the restaurant, but all she sees is dust. She waits for it to settle, and when it doesn't, she realizes it's because the restaurant, for the most part, is not there. Sirens bloom. And then she sees the rest.

Blood and dust. Shoes in the street. A man crawling. A woman gagging. People are slumped at strange angles—over chairs that have been tossed, over the sidewalk and into the street, against a wall but with legs up like children playing a game. Stomachs are exposed from shirts that have been pushed or blown away. For an irrational moment, she wants to go to a woman on the sidewalk whose abdomen is fleshy and pale and cover her, because she feels her embarrassment, to have her stomach bared like that. But with another breath, she realizes the woman feels nothing, of course.

A man passes by, covered in powder, staggering as if drunk, murmuring *Yallah* over and over. Olivia stops. This is one thing she can help with, to find this Yallah, but when she slows the word down in her mind, she hears the separation. *Y'allah*: Oh God. Now a different man passes by slowly, as if he has all the time in the world, with someone short flung over his shoulder, head and long hair swinging. *Someone short.* Her mind will not think *child.*

Then there is a synchronicity with a new sound—a wall coming down—and everyone flinches at once, shoulders tensing, hands on ears.

They're in this together now, a sick choreography. Beside her, a man stands against a light pole, rubbing his temple back and forth, smearing blood as if painting his face.

"Do we help?" Olivia asks. She might be shouting. She's not sure. But help is what you do. There is an accident and you help, though she knows, even as she thinks this, that this was not an accident and that new rules apply and that really she does not want to help, that in fact the last thing she wants to do is help because she wants to be gone and safe and somewhere the air doesn't make her eyes sting. She wants to not be out in the open.

"No," Delan says. "Help is coming. We go."

"Delan, we have to help." She's trying to convince not just him.

But he grabs her arm and looks into her eyes. For a moment, she thinks it's to check if she's all right, to look for pinprick pupils or signs of a concussion. But then he's talking. She watches his mouth moving before registering his words.

"We were seen leaving that restaurant with a full table of food right before. *We go.*"

With that, everyone looks different. Every man's face becomes one who could've been there, who would've left to find them and now needs to find them even more.

He pulls on her arm, with Soran on her other side. "This way, through that alley."

They walk and with every step shed the event. At first they pass people who reach to them, offering to help, handing towels or water. Arms gesture them inside; mouths move with foreign words. But farther along, the concern fades and becomes curiosity. People watch them, wondering. And then there is disinterest. A perimeter passed, normal life breached. People in bright windows. Men playing dominoes. Life, quite simply. An evening like tonight will be endured, and people will go to work tomorrow. They will tuck their children into bed and find smiles for them in the morning. Even as she breathes in the dust, she can barely fathom what's happened, much less imagine a lifetime of this or begin to comprehend what that lifetime would do to a person. To him. All the ways it's raised his voice in a moment of quiet. The ways it darkened him in the glare of a bright morning.

"What about the car?" she asks. They drove here, she now remembers.

"Tomorrow," Delan says, taking her hand as they cross a street. "We parked far enough away, but I don't want to go back now. We won't make curfew if we do."

The cab they hail picks them up without question. Exhausted, Olivia leans back into the seat. Her ears ring. And only then, in the buzzing silence of the cab, does she remember the camera that's been inside her purse.

CHAPTER 8

This past January, a couple of months after they'd started dating, Delan disappeared from bed in a time that seemed more night than morning. When Olivia wandered downstairs, he'd already eaten breakfast, showered, and was sitting at the kitchen table with a newspaper before him. His hair was damp and clumped with curls, and the light through the window was strangely intense, one of those bright Los Angeles winter mornings with no clouds but a cold, devious bite in the air. Deceiving, like a candy lure from a stranger. On the radio, the newscaster's voice rose with excitement over a freeze warning, and Olivia pictured silvery orange groves and farmers glaring at the sky.

A kiss on his cheek. Then eggs cracked on the edge of a bowl, whisked practically to a froth. As the flame beneath the pan spread, she asked why he'd gotten up so early.

At first he said nothing, just watched the window with the paper in his hand while the radio announced that the Hillside Strangler had been arrested in Washington and a blizzard was pounding Chicago. As she poured the eggs, she realized he might not have heard her question, so she switched the radio off till he looked at her—or, rather, not so much at *her* as to the absence of sound. There was a vacancy in his eyes, a distraction. "You got up early," she said again, tracing the spatula in the pan in a figure eight. "How come?"

"Dreams."

"Of what?"

"Home." Still he held the paper in his hand and went back to watching the day. "Your eggs are burning."

By this point, she was used to sparse words when it came to what upset him, but still she tried. "Do you want to tell me about them?" she asked, though it was clear he did not.

He shrugged—not to indicate he might talk about the dreams but to categorize them as not worth the effort of explanation. "I just didn't want to be asleep anymore."

She shut off the stove and accepted his response without pushing, then watched him as she made her lunch, waiting to see if he'd offer more. Recently she'd inquired about transferring to the photo department, just as a secretary, an idea that made her boss roll up one sleeve of his shirt as if preparing for a mildly restrained fight. *Let's keep our eyes on our own desk, shall we?* Disillusionment had begun to thicken her days, filling and spreading into each minute. Though making a lunch might mean she'd be late, she didn't care—or so she told herself while her eye was on the clock.

"The Kurds. Fighting," Delan finally said, motioning to the newspaper in his hands. "That's what's happening. Always."

She sliced an apple. Apples reminded her of her childhood, and with each cut, she smelled their crush in driveways, that lazy bite of fermentation in the air. "You're worried about your friend?"

"This," he said, tapping the article with his index finger, *one two, one two*, "is about Iran. The Kurds in Iran. An uprising coming. Aras, though, him I always worry about. But it's a given he'll die."

She looked up sharply, and he smiled sadly.

"Everyone will. He, sooner rather than later. He's a Peshmerga; it goes with the territory. His life might be short, but he will make a difference. *Kem bizhi kell bizhj*: Live short, live proud."

"Live big and bold and brave. That's what my dad says. Similar. About impact. Making the most of your blip in time."

He let go of the paper. With his hand, he went to push back the hair on his forehead but stopped midmotion, pausing as if stunned in the glare of morning. For a while, he said nothing. Then he took a long, deep breath. "And yet here I am." Hand lowered, he traced his finger on the black of the headline.

"Delan. You do things. The protest at the federal building. The letters to Carter. Hundreds of people know who the Kurds are just because of you."

"Let's grill tonight. Make some calls, see who can come over. This weather is too good."

She looked to the window. "It's freezing outside. Literally. They just said that."

"It's not. It's fine. And I'm the one at the grill."

She loved the parties and he knew this and it was true, he would be the one at the grill. And she needed something to look forward to, to get her through the day—as did he, it was clear. So she finished making her lunch, set it next to her camera on the counter, and decided to pick up ground beef that was cheap and could feed a crowd. When she looked back at him, he was lost in the paper once more, side lit by the kitchen window on that biting January day, and she saw there were tears on his face. It took her a moment to spot them. So often had she seen him angry when he talked about home that to see this was as confusing as their Los Angeles day of sun and blue skies and air that stung with cold.

Right at the end of the counter was her camera. *Always get the shot,* he'd once told her. *Art makes a difference. And if someone's story, their pain or sadness, if that can impact someone else, it's worth the invasion.* She watched him now, knowing that if he could see what she saw, he'd want this as well.

Choices in terms of where to stand were limited without breaking the moment. So she went back to the counter, knelt on the linoleum, and without him noticing, lined up her shot with the window to his right. She inched over to exclude a stain on the wall but then moved back, liking the way it looked in the frame, then made sure there was more space before him than behind. The curtain on the other wall was drawn closed but thin, and light fell in diffused chunks, broken by the windowpanes. She waited till he looked up from the paper that was still in his hands, and when he did, his face shone just enough to catch those silent, gleaming tears, and she pressed the button. He must have heard, but he never acknowledged it. Just sat back and let the paper fall onto the table.

That night they had the party, and she had to stand outside with a blanket on her shoulders and grill because he was asleep. She'd known he would be the second she came home and found him grinning loosely in his chair. So she stood in the biting air and was mad. Mad that he'd arrange for this whole thing and invite all these people over and then check out and leave her in the cold. Mad that everyone had shown up hungry. Mad that he had so much to cry about, and she couldn't help with any of it. And when at last she went to wake him up, the spatula still in hand and the blanket around her shoulders, she found him on the couch, his fingers skimming the rug. His breathing was steady even while the Eagles sang about a hotel in California and the people in the room caught the beginning and sang along loudly, relishing in location and fame and their luck to live in such a lovely place. His chest rose and fell. Without waking him, she reached down and lifted his hand so it was by his side, so no one would step on his fingers. Then she let him sleep, gone from wherever he'd wished to leave.

And now they are there.

She's washed her hair, but the smell still lingers, clinging like a campfire. A sickly scent. With every turn, she catches it. What she'd been wearing got dumped into an enamel tub in the backyard, and tomorrow they'll wash everything and watch the dust of buildings and tables and people and fish disappear into a drain, then hang it all to dry in the sun, to be held in a new day.

Alone, she's barefoot under the grape trellis. It's infuriating, that smell, that it won't be left behind. Another breath in and she realizes it's inside her. In her nose, her lungs. Reaching from her pores.

She hears him behind her. "The smell," she says, not turning.

"It'll be gone soon. We'll wash the sheets too." There is a pause, during which he waits for her to turn to him. "Hey," he says when she does not.

But now she's thinking of the times he stayed silent. The times they've edged around his past, circling it like something unwilling to be approached. And she understands that his silence was because there was too much that lacked proper words. There was no real way to tell her what he'd been through and nothing much she could do even if there was.

Now he says her name, and at last she turns. Her linen pants legs are long and wide and have dragged against the dirt, making it appear as if she's left no footprints. He watches her take this in, her strange absence of proof, and then reaches for her.

"You want to forget what causes you pain," he says, lifting her hand and studying her skin, tracing his index finger along the crease of her wrist. "Life. The faster you forget, the better you are."

"I don't think I'll ever forget."

He nods, as if he'd both known and feared the answer. "I had to go to the United States, you know. To act, sure, but it was everything. I felt myself there from the beginning. Film, I thought. Movies. It was all anyone talked about. But I went because I wanted to be there, not because I wanted to leave."

"You don't have to defend yourself. I understand. After tonight, I get it."

When he looks up, she sees she's said the wrong thing. "I'm not defending myself," he says. "I'm explaining. It was hard to leave, but it was worse to be gone. The guilt that I was giving myself what people called *a better life*. Why me? Why not them? Why not anyone here?"

By the wall, there is a long, loose grapevine, trailing without support. Aimless. He reaches for it, letting its end, the small leaves, rest in his palm. Then, patiently, he winds its tendrils around another for support. "At first I thought about it all the time. Where I left them. Beautiful in so many ways—I mean it; I'm proud of where I'm from. I'm proud of being a Kurd. I never left because I wanted to be gone and that, I know, is hard to understand after tonight." He touches a leaf, angling it in the blare of moon. "You asked me before why I didn't come home much."

"Delan, it's okay. You don't have to."

"No, you want me to talk; this is what I'm saying. It's because I wanted to forget. I wanted to forget *them*. I wanted to love them a little less." He turns to her. "What son says that? What son wants that?"

At last, he's let her in. And yet there is no joy, no feeling of *there, now we will work, our secrets are falling*. Instead, she feels pain. His pain—the pain of leaving his parents, the pain of wanting to forget, of having reasons to forget. And a pain from the realization that his letting her in was only the first step, and with it comes the question of whether she's strong enough for the rest. If she's even capable of handling the rest.

She doesn't know what to say, so she goes to him. Arms around him, she pulls back to look him in the eyes. "There is nothing, *nothing* you should be ashamed of."

And she means it. And if need be, she will stand here holding him till the next call to prayer, listening in case he chooses to say more.

Later, she sits with him in the darkened garden, trying to only survive this evening that's done so much. The moon throws an imprint of the pomegranate tree to the ground, and the wine they drink smells of hay and berries. Now and then, the electricity cuts out, and lights from houses disappear as the sky takes over with brightness. Sound changes as well, the natural world suddenly amplified. A minute, two, maybe more. Then everything seems to lurch as the power returns.

After a while, Gaziza comes out to the garden with a plate of stuffed grape leaves.

"*Yaprakh,*" Delan says, "but you know them as dolmas. That's right—no one got dinner."

He sounds surprised, as if the lack of meal had been an oversight. But now Olivia's thinking of the people in the restaurant, how someone might have died hungry and waiting. How of course that happened. Eye on the kitchen, fork in hand. A sip of water to try to fill a stomach, an anticipation of fulfillment that was trusted to come—and then life ended. Such a mortal quality, to hunger. Born from a body that is vulnerable and capable of ending in a flash. And to crave. To ache for something. To identify that thing you long for and seek it out, it's heartbreakingly human. *He just wanted yogurt,* she remembers Delan saying about his cousin. *I hate that. Dying, having been hungry for something.* It hadn't truly resonated with her until now.

When she looks up, Gaziza is still there, standing before her as if deciding what to do with her, this American who's ended up in her house. At last she opens her arms and nods as if to summon her. Without a word, Olivia stands and wraps her arms around the woman's thick back, and though she has to bend to put her head on the shorter woman's shoulder, it feels good. There is the night air and Gaziza's smell of pepper and tea, and Olivia tells herself not to break down. She will not cry. But it's the feeling of being in a mother's arms that finally does it.

At last, Gaziza lets go. Her dress is a faint *swish* in the dark as she returns to the house.

"No hug for you?" Olivia asks Delan, smiling as she wipes her tears with her thumb.

"It's different for me."

He's looking at her, and in his eyes are apologies.

"You didn't do this," she says, because only now does she realize he thinks he did, and she needs him to know that if there's something broken within her, he did not break it.

He tilts the wine bottle above his glass. A stream that's black in the night. "I never wanted this to happen to you."

"Delan, I wasn't hurt. I'm the last person to feel bad for."

"The first night is worse, for anything. Even tomorrow will be better." At their feet, the shadows of leaves change and shift with a breeze. "When you were mad at me," he continues, "when you thought I was calling you *naive* in Baghdad, and I said no, I meant *innocent*—"

"It doesn't matter." *Whatever* it *is*, she wants to say, *I'm no longer that.*

"What I was trying to say is there's a difference. Between naive and innocent. One is something I'm not interested in, and the other is something I should have done anything to protect."

"This was not your fault."

Light spills into the yard as the back door opens, Soran now approaching with a plate of baklava. Together they eat in silence. After a few minutes, Delan refills her wine, then leans against her on the bench, pressing his shoulder to hers till she sees his hand, palm facing up on his thigh, waiting. She places her own on top, and together they sit as the night deepens.

"Were they Kurds?" she asks eventually. "The political figures. The ones who were there."

Soran stands with one hand in his pocket and the other holding a glass of wine he's barely touched. As he answers, he glances over his shoulder as if to make sure no one's wandered into the garden. "Some of our best."

"How did you know what would happen?"

"I didn't. I guessed. There were too many. Someone would have seen them, would have made a call. The temptation to take them out." He shrugs. "Opportunity."

"I had my camera," Olivia says. "And I didn't take one photo."

Shame and doubt. She feels them at her back, her heroes—Dickey Chapelle with her Leica camera and cat-eye glasses running to the sounds, into dust and mud, and Catherine Leroy parachuting into combat though at any second the air around her could've hailed with bullets. Their eyes are on her back. Disappointed. Not that Olivia ever intended to be a combat photographer, but the fact is, her camera was the last thing on her mind. She did not get the shot.

Soran's words are slow. "You were trying to stay alive. Even the dead would want that for you."

Now Delan moves to the path before her, sitting on the ground and peering up at the moon. "No," she says, watching him. "They'd want justice."

"And that comes from a photograph?"

"Sometimes it starts with one."

"And sometimes it is just a photograph. And that photograph could get you killed."

She takes the last sip of wine from her glass, the sediment a grit on her tongue. "There was a family. Next to us."

"I saw them," Delan says. "They were almost done. I'm sure they left." Moonlight shines on his face as he continues to stare at the sky. Somewhere, a mourning dove calls in the night, searching. Again, he nods. "I know they left. They were long gone."

The boy with the tomato seed on his chin. Feet that didn't touch the ground. She tries to conjure his face, to picture him somewhere safe, but now can't remember what he looked like—which only solidifies the grief inside her. And the other boy. There was a second one, and yet she can't even remember the color of his shirt. Why hadn't she noticed him? Why hadn't she paid him any attention? The thought of a boy, a child whose life was about to end, not even being noticed—she draws in a breath, trying to hold everything back, but it doesn't work. The tears are silent, but she turns her head so no one sees. "They were right next to us." As if the proximity should not have allowed for such different outcomes.

"That family," Delan says, "they left. I promise. Olivia, look at me. *They left.*"

He holds her eye until at last, she nods. In her mind, she adds minutes together, the time it would take for them to finish, to pay the bill, to maybe stop in the bathroom before leaving. Kids always take longer, playing with the door, eyeing someone's dessert. Did they make it? It's futile, she knows, because even if they did, there was an entire restaurant of people who did not.

After a moment, Delan lies back on the ground, his arms folded beneath his head as he stares at the sky. She watches him, then goes to lie beside him. Without pause, he moves one arm down, placing it around her, then turns his head toward her, his mouth against her hair. His words are quiet, the heat of his breath a comfort. "I've never thought you weak," he whispers. "You don't have to prove yourself to me."

Above them, the clouds seem to buckle, curling in the night.

Inconsolable hours. The hours you're alone in bed and can't be talked away from thoughts. Can't be distracted enough to stop seeing a boy's shoe under the table, swaying back and forth, back and forth. Can't stop remembering the restaurant's glass window, filled with the reflection of people who were not long for this earth.

Olivia goes from outrage at anonymous death, the very concept that someone can be next to you and then gone and you'd never even known their name, to wishing that on her way out, she'd simply pulled one person with them. *One person.* One life could've continued, and with that so much more because that one person could then have children, and their children could have children, and eventually an entire family tree would emerge from the place in the ground where there was almost nothing. That little boy. His brother. A waiter. Anyone. What one person could've gone on to do. The lives they'd impact, the love they'd give. Caught on a spiral of regret, her thoughts shoot out possibilities that were never there, options that work only in hindsight.

And she never took a photo. All that happened will slip beneath the radar, will remain unknown, and she realizes that here, that is life. The reality of this world is that tragedy occurs undocumented and daily, and what happened this evening was a mere flash within a greater explosion and is one most people will never know took place. Whereas before, Olivia would've spun this toward inspiration, toward a need to fix things, now she feels only futility. Who is she to make things better? In a world in which tonight happens and not even a ripple is felt, who is she to cause an impact?

Cold, she pulls the blanket around her shoulders. A trick to fall asleep: think of words in nonsensical arrangements. A reenactment of what actually happens when you drift off, her father used to say, as if the mind could be fooled into thinking it's already on that chaotic ledge. Words plucked at random: *Linguine. Window. Fog. Tomatoes. Forests. Table. Shelf. Fall. Broken.* The words mistakenly lead into each other, and suddenly there's her mother's leg at the wrong angle on the black pavement and she jerks fully awake. Heart pounding.

All she'd seen was her mother's leg, her body not completely shielded by the policeman's coat. Those toes her mom had painted pink while Olivia watched Huckleberry Hound sing "Oh My Darling, Clementine." Those brown sandals she kept by the front door in a basket. Olivia stared only at that leg in the street until someone grabbed her hand and pulled her back into the store where they'd been, books lining shelves and lamps lit in corners. Her mother had just gone back to the car to get her checkbook to buy a book for Olivia. *Little House in the Big Woods*, the first of the Laura Ingalls Wilder books. That night, they'd planned on making marshmallow Rice Krispies treats from a Kellogg's ad in a magazine and reading the book. Her mother had forgotten her checkbook, so she'd crossed the street and was, essentially, no more. A family went to eat and was no more. Countless people took a breath and were no more.

The burning car and child, her former daydream of heroics. She thinks of it now and laughs and then cries because all those fantasies in which she'd reach within herself to find some unexplored magnificence were just that—fantasies. She is not brave. She helped no one. And those daydreams—she used to think they were about the powerless finding power, about a world in which the unjust could be stopped and she could do something to help, to maybe even save the mother about to cross the street. But now she sees they were about more than that, because they never occurred on an empty street, and the stories never went untold. They were about being seen, being at last acknowledged by those who would never think her capable of importance. They were more about recognition than about doing something good. And they were wrong.

The next day, it rains. A day given to them to gather themselves, to hide and huddle and swim in a mood that won't let Olivia go. Though Delan, she sees, seems remarkably improved, smiling and joking and helping his mother with a stew. An acceptance, she realizes, that's been learned over the years. A tolerance or a numbness, though perhaps the two are the same. While she feels this as a deep cut, he's barely felt the scrape and this, somehow, is a difference she never considered. The fine print she'd not known to look for.

Lailan shows up on the front steps with a tarp over her head. Water drips from the edges, darkening her light-pink shirt to fuchsia. In her hand is a plastic bag with crayons—nubs mostly, pieces Olivia would've tossed when she was a child—and a stack of yellowing lined paper that she holds to her chest. Her lashes are wet from the rain, as is one side of her cheek, and Olivia knows she must've struggled to hold the tarp and her supplies and in the process, half her face was bared to the downpour.

Within seconds, Miriam is behind her, chaotic with bags, an umbrella, and a towel, speaking rapid Kurdish. She said to wait five minutes, Soran translates, but Lailan was gone before she even finished. The girl beams, proud of her speed.

There is a quality to Miriam that confuses Olivia. Even, smooth skin but hair that's graying. Eyebrows that slope downward, making her appear apprehensive or perplexed by the world but at the same time open to surprise and oddly hopeful. Though she could be much older than Olivia, she might also be the same age, and when she speaks, she nods as if firm in her belief or far too used to doubt. And though it's clear she's in a hurry for work, she doesn't leave—instead she sits, draws the girl toward her, then tilts Lailan's chin back. Looking her in the eye, she deliberately, slowly, and gently wipes the water from the girl's forehead before tossing the towel over the girl's head, grabbing her, and drying her off. Both mother and daughter erupt with laughter. A routine, Olivia recognizes. Most likely done every night after baths, something dreaded turned on its edge.

When at last Miriam leaves, Soran blows on the pages of paper, separating them. Olivia sits with Lailan on the floor. "What should we draw?"

In the chair beside them, Soran doesn't look up from his book. "Yes, thank you. English. Your being here is a lesson."

From the doorframe, Delan watches them. "Why does the nurse carry a red crayon?"

"Why?" Olivia asks and in his pause hears the joke he'd told on the plane. That moment, the timing, much like now. Combined with the events of yesterday, his instinct to distract angles into an instinct to avoid. But how could it be wrong to lighten a mood?

He grins, already proud of his punch line, before saying, "In case she needs to draw blood."

Despite herself, Olivia smiles. Then she turns back to Lailan. "So what do we draw?"

"Dog," Lailan answers. But her hand hovers above the page. Frozen, as if she's unsure of how to begin.

"You just do it," Olivia tells her. "Dive right in." She touches Lailan's hand, and the girl abandons her drawing to run a finger over Olivia's orange nails.

"Dive right in," Lailan repeats and then picks a bright-red crayon and leans into the page. Wild squiggles appear below her small fist. Then an oval for a head. Dots for eyes. Olivia touches her head, realizing it's now a portrait of her and fearing the girl isn't far off. But suddenly Lailan stops, alarmed, and sits back.

"What?" Olivia asks.

Soran sets down his book. "Lailan. What's wrong? *Chi buwa?*"

The girl's eyes are wide as she looks between the two of them, and her tongue presses on her lower tooth. Slowly, as if afraid of what she'll find, she puts her finger on the incisor.

"It's loose," Olivia says, trying to mime the meaning of the word as she speaks. "Wiggly. Lailan, it's a baby tooth."

"I made wiggly?" Her voice is small.

"No. No, they're *supposed* to fall out."

Seeing her fear, Soran resorts to Kurdish as he explains, and Lailan goes from terrified she'd done something wrong to proud, standing as tall as she can, as if suspecting she might have also grown. When Delan walks into the room, she's before him in a flash, making him feel the tooth—"wiggly," she says, latched on to the word. He feels it with much exaggeration as Soran watches, entertained, until Lailan crawls into his lap and makes him test every tooth. Solemnly he touches each one, shaking his head *no* till he gets to the one that's loose and his eyes go wide. "Wiggly!" she announces.

What if one day Olivia and Delan have children? She's seeing how different they are, even in the way Delan seems okay, in his acceptance of what's happened. What would their difference do to their children, and to them at the end of the day? Would he pass off an early heartbreak as insignificant? Would he shrug off a fear of thunderstorms? Then the questions make her feel ridiculous. Of course he wouldn't. She knows him. But even the consideration is something—worry where before there was assurance.

After an hour of the girl being there, Olivia quietly asks Soran about Lailan's parents. In the distance, the booming has begun, that fight that has far-reaching arms, nothing truly contained.

"There is only Miriam," he says. He stands in the threshold of the room, tired, and glances in the direction of the mountains. "Miriam's husband died years ago. But they are not her parents. Her parents—" He stops, watching as the girl begins to trace her hand onto a page. "One day, I will tell you. But Lailan has me. She is here when Miriam works. She is the reason I took the job, for my friend. To be here when she needs me. I am good at math, but I do it for her."

The rain lessens as the afternoon drones on, drops heavy from the eaves of the house. Eventually Olivia takes her teacup to the kitchen and finds Hewar standing at the window, looking outside. On his face is a smile that deepens his wrinkles, a pull of pure amazement, and her first thought is to get her camera to capture his expression. But then he sees her and motions her to him. There, outside the window on a wire, is a bird with dark, almost iridescent, black-and-green feathers tipped in yellow, giving itself a bath in the mist, its call dipping and rising and clicking from one song to the next. When it ruffles its feathers, its chest puffs out, sheened in purple, and when it stretches its wings, the feathers spread like many fingers.

By the time she hurries back with her camera, the rain has stopped, and steam seeps from the cement. But the bird is still there, shivering itself dry. She shoots through the glass, moving slightly to play with the depth of the wires. The bird is beautiful, but not what she wants. She wants Hewar. His reaction. Him but more than him. The reverberation. Because his joy—face open with childlike bliss and those large, lovely ears—affects her, and thus could affect others, and with that, this click of a camera feels like the beginning, like the first undulation of a wave. Hope shudders itself loose. She stands farther back to get him in the shot. *Click.* He turns to her, eyebrows lifted, expectant, asking her to share in what he loves.

And then he is talking, and Olivia realizes Delan is behind her, watching the bird as well.

"It's what you call a starling," Delan says. "Usually you see them in flocks. He's telling you what they do, how they move in giant swarms, dancing in the sky. They move together, thousands of them."

"A murmuration," she says. "I've read about that."

"Reading about it is like reading about love. You need to see it. To feel it. We're talking thousands of birds, and not one bird leading. All synchronized but without a leader. Because each one connects, *really* connects, to its neighbors, to the ones around them. And with that, thousands move as one."

From the hall, Lailan emerges. "Tell her," Olivia says.

And so he does, with sweeping arm motions like someone casting a spell, and the girl's mouth hangs open as she stares at the bird on the wire as if it were a representative of this wizardry. Olivia, too, is captivated. Drawn in by his flourish, by a moment in which there is just joy, spun from a tale and a telling. It feels good to laugh, as much as it feels wrong. Lailan, mesmerized, suddenly grabs on to the counter before anyone can stop her, kicking her legs till she's at the window. The bird, startled, flies away.

Night, morning, afternoon. The rusted, inching turn of the world. Somehow it feels as though life is flaunting its continuation. Sun bright. Clouds triumphant. The world is gorgeous and unruffled and unnoticing. This is what she's trying to reconcile: blinks of destruction amid beauty. Everything combined with the unfazed tick of the clock.

The picnic is still happening. Up in the mountains, but not where the fighting is. When Delan tells her this, his distinction falls short of comforting.

"Just key places is where they fight," he adds, seeing her doubt. "High up. We don't go there."

So she finds mountain-appropriate clothes—tennis shoes, long pants, a lightweight shirt. And she feels guilty to do just this, to keep going and be the one to wake up when others do not. To wash her hair and decide what to wear and think of photographs and love and fears and a future. In the mirror, she spots her necklace. The tree of life. A reminder of an eternal connection between this realm and that, the tree's branches touching the heavens. *Every time you raise your arm,* her father told her when he gave her the necklace, *I see your mother reaching for your hand.*

"It's a choice," Delan says when he finds her in his room, watching the street. "You're thinking about what happened. But it's a choice not to. You put it out of your mind."

She turns to him. Thrown. His tone borders on demanding. Impatient. Body angled as if he's ready to leave the room, as if he were ready to go from the moment he entered. "How," she manages to ask, "is that even an option?"

"You, who wants to control everything, your thoughts too—you ask how?"

"Not this. This is different."

"If you were to surrender after something like this, you would never live your life."

Flippant almost. As if he's just told her to deal with the fact that it's hot outside. "Here," she says, trying to keep her voice level, "that might be true. Because this happens. Things like this happen. But I can't just *do* that."

"Anywhere, this happens," he says. "Where we live, you see a man fall on the sidewalk from a heart attack or someone who's overdosed in a hallway—do you let it destroy you?"

"I let it *affect* me. Yes. And those are different than a *bomb*."

"Death is death. The same outcome. You who saw your mother—"

"Stop," she says. Anger splayed. Every inch of her pulses with it. She tries to breathe in, to clear a space within her for logic and rationale, but all she sees is this man she thought she knew, accusing her of being too soft. A man who's suddenly callous in the light of tragedy. "My mother," she says. "That did destroy me."

"But *this* was not your mother. That's what I'm saying. These were people you didn't know. You don't fold after this."

"I'm not allowed to feel for people I don't know? How *dare* you come after me for this."

"Come after you? I'm trying to help!"

"By telling me to move on? To get over it? How can *you* just move on? How can you be so unfeeling that you just move on?"

"I never said move on. You move *with*. You move with, but you move. That's the point. You cannot stop. But to do that, you need to put it out of your mind so you can. So you become a politician and fix things or be an artist and put it in your art. If you crawl into a cave and let this defeat you, *everyone loses*."

For a moment, he just watches her, as if making sure his point landed. And this irritates her even more. As he opens the window to scan the street, she feels her words honing, pressing to a point.

"Is that what you do?" she asks quietly. "Put it in your art to help?"

Her words are like a jolt. His back tenses, body gone rigid.

"That's why you feel bad," she continues. "You think you don't do enough."

Now he turns to her. Shocked and irate. "Don't tell me I'm living my life wrong."

"There's no standard for what you have to do to feel okay. But *you* know. You know what you have to do, and maybe you're right and you don't do enough. The only thing I know is you've spouted a whole bunch of made-up rules that allow you to look the other way—all so you don't have to feel."

His eyes seem to actually fill with what he's about to say. And she feels it, an undertow of anger. The start of whatever he's about to say that will pull them in and strand them. From his words, there will be no getting back.

"You," he finally says, "don't come from a world where you get to judge how *I* handle this."

A slam that renders her speechless. But one she's been waiting for, that she practically asked for. Words strip in her mind: *There it is.* All this time, it's been there, off in the corner, waiting. Now in the open. Thickening, filling into the silence. Her youth. Her vastly different childhood. The weight of his past, compared to the relative ease of hers. It's all right there. And the problem is that he's right. In some way, she's always known this. But what does it mean? That, she realizes, is the question. The crux of what she's needed to learn.

"You're right," she says.

There's surprise on his face, as if he's just glimpsed a swerve in the road.

"What you've been through," she continues, *"nothing* I've known will ever compare. But does that mean I don't have a point? That I can never tell you I wish you'd do something differently, because I didn't grow up the way you did? How does that work for our relationship if I get dismissed for my past? If nothing I say is valid?"

The questions hang. They're everything, these questions. She's never conjured them this clearly before, never assigned them these words, but they've always been there. A simmer beneath recognized worries.

"Of course not," he finally says. Outside, a horn sounds. "If that were the case, no couple would work unless they grew up in the same house."

A pause, and he leans away from her, searching the street through the window. Maybe he's just saying what he knows he needs to. He's still angry, that she can tell. And so is she. Despite his response, the questions remain unanswered.

"But you can't presume to know," he finally says. "You cannot tell me *me*."

"Then likewise. That works both ways."

From the street, a car honks again. And then another. For a beat, they are silent, held back as if tied to their own points of view, until again a horn sounds, and he leans out the window, calling to a man in an off-white pickup truck. Behind it, a caravan of cars stretches the length of the road.

"Maybe we just do things differently," she says.

"Clearly."

There will be no resolution. Not now. She watches him yell to the man again in Kurdish, watches his profile, and feels, starkly, sadly, the borders of themselves in a way she never has. All the memories tied to what passes before them, the layers of fears and hopes and regrets, the events that have made him see the world as he does and pass off what's happened as not that bad—all of it kept separate by the simple lines of his skin. She cannot know him. Not truly. *You cannot tell me me.* And though she knows that's the case for everyone, for no one can exist within another's mind or skin, it's how far apart they are in their history, their beliefs, that ultimately matters. After all, it's the distance of separation that creates the impact.

An assortment of cars and trucks curves around the base of the mountain, each one with multiple men crammed in the front seats and women in the back. Though Delan was offered the front seat, he wisely chose to sit next to Olivia, and in this, their battle at least hasn't escalated. On her other side, an older woman in a traditional dress that's a brilliant, iridescent beetle green stares only at her folded hands in her lap.

The road is unpaved and rocky, at times more an idea of a road than an actual road, and after twenty minutes of views heavy with green and the shock of pink plum blossoms, they swoop upward on a road so narrow that the side mirrors brush shrubs and catch on branches. Now and then, there is a blind curve, a switchback, and the sheer cliffs and the absence of land pull with a vacuum's energy.

You put it out of your mind. She closes her eyes, chin against her chest.

That family, they left.

You *don't come from a world where you get to judge how* I *handle this.*

They've barely spoken since they left the house, and now she's thinking of all the ways he lives in denial, even at home, in mundane ways, such as with a phone bill shoved into a drawer—*don't look*—or a bottle of gin that eases him toward sleep. Only now does she see how deep this goes, how dark the source. She feels sick. His life, his world might not be one she can be part of. All the lines she fed herself about differing pasts and backgrounds not mattering were just that—lines. Hopeful lies from the mind of a romantic, from someone who thought differences would fall in the way of true love.

That loose flutter of sadness. Never have they done this. Arguments over inviting another couple over for dinner, sure, or if it was time to fold and call a plumber, of course. But nothing that spoke to the core of them. To the core of *if* they work.

Green branches whip along one side of the car. Nothing is over, she tells herself, though it feels that something has indeed ended. Maybe just the glow of a new relationship. At best, that's it. She tries to not think, to just take in the world around her. Flares of dark red in the grass. Poppies. Growing in clumps, cupping the sunlight. Then a wide stretch of aspens, an ancient orchard. Bees rise from short white wild-flowers in the grass. These rocks, she tells herself, long-gone shepherds once sat on these rocks. Again there is that pull, that connection, an anchoring to the earth, to the simple essence of their lives. And sadness. Because with the end of each distracting thought, she is right back to this: never has she felt this far apart from him.

Out of the car, people file to Delan. Embracing him, hands flurried with talk. *Hollywood,* they call him, and the name makes him blush. She looks away, unable to take his smile, his bashfulness, without feeling a desperate sorrow within her. A regret that they went where they did, despite how inevitable the direction might have been. Around her, the women are in traditional dresses, each an explosion of color and sparkling layers, sleeves long and flowing and tied loosely behind backs, and so quietly Olivia loads film into her camera and fires off a few shots, drawn to the shimmer—but ultimately she's just going through the motions. None of the shots has feeling.

Then there's a hand on her pants leg.

"Hi-lo," Lailan says, peering up at her with the sun hard in her eyes. She blinks twice and then seems used to it, defiant of its brightness. On the opposite hill, a shepherd watches with his flock. "Will you to please take my picture?"

Olivia smiles. "Of course. How about there, at the rock?"

Huge chunks of white marble, Delan had told Olivia on the plane, already so long ago. The ruffled edges of Lailan's long green pants have collected bits of sticks and leaves and gather more as they walk. When at the rock, Olivia sees the veins of gray in what is indeed marble, and the truth of his statement lands like an argument in his favor.

Telling the girl to stay where she is, Olivia steps off for a bit of distance and instructs Lailan to smile when she says *cheese*.

"Cheese?" Lailan repeats, and it's the funniest thing she's heard. *"Cheese?"* she says again. "Rice! Bread!" she yells out, cracking herself up as she lists off all the English words she knows for food—every word but *cheese*. Olivia's drawn in to the girl's rebellion, laughing as she fires off almost a dozen shots. But then there is the fight with Delan, shoving its way back into her mind. He's watching her from the path a ways up, and the simple fact that he's waiting for them breaks something within her. Joining him, she can't meet his eyes.

And then there are tulips. Folded, waffling leaves and red petals that rise to a point. Some of the flowers are missing sections as if nibbled on or windbeaten, and as she stops to frame another shot, trying to capture a plant that sneaks from a crack in white marble, she sees Lailan has stopped as well and is now posing and smiling in case she's the subject. A better photo, by far. Lifting her camera, Olivia gets the shot of the girl, just as she notices that all around her, people are stooping over a certain plant, then pulling it up and placing it in baskets. Like a thistle with spiked edges.

"Kinger," Delan says. "Good in spring. We eat the bottom of the stem, right above the roots. Fried with egg."

But then Lailan has found her way to the path and is demanding their attention. Hand out, she orders them not to walk. The cause for concern is a caterpillar, reddish brown and tan, its fur like mink, body gathering and extending. Olivia explains what it is to the girl, the impending transformation, as the people behind them peer over shoulders for a glimpse and then veer past, unimpressed.

"Where it goes?" Lailan asks, scanning the plants as if looking for a small house.

"Leave it," Delan says. "It'll go where it needs to."

Now Lailan's face opens in shock, right before it narrows in anger. "Leave in walk. How you leave? How?"

She wants an answer. It's not rhetorical. She's waiting, and Olivia can't help but get caught up. "She's right, Delan. How could you leave it here?" She adds a smile, but he glances at her as if he senses the inclusion of their earlier fight.

"I'm outnumbered, I see. Okay. If I were a caterpillar," he says and surveys the plants, "I'd want that one, there. With the fuzzy leaves."

"Borage," Olivia says. Purple-blue flowers bent at their necks. Little downcast stars.

Gently, Lailan scoops the caterpillar in her hand and then kneels with her palm held beside a leaf. A waiting game now. The caterpillar is in no hurry. With her other hand, Lailan pets it gently, whispering something Olivia can't hear.

"You have a big heart," Olivia tells her when she's done, then explains the saying. "It's good to have a big heart. To allow yourself to be open and to feel things."

Ahead of them, Delan doesn't turn around but angles his head toward the sky as if refuting her words with a careless glance.

Soon Lailan is pointing out everything she knows. A child's encyclopedia of life, a simple narration that takes them halfway up another hill. *Girl. Man. Mother. Camera. Flower. Sky. Tree. Head. Tooth. Foot. Shoe. Cloud. Rainbow.* Olivia peers at the sky, finds no rainbow, but still nods her approval. Then she sees the women in their bright colors on the hillside and realizes that the girl was right.

Suddenly Lailan points to Olivia, and Olivia's hand goes to her throat, to the necklace that must have come out from under her shirt.

"The tree of life. A symbol from where my family's from. A symbol is something small that has big meaning." She pauses and looks to Delan, who's stopped alongside them. Every word feels loaded. "Like the eyes people have on bracelets or necklaces. Those evil eyes. Those are a symbol for protection. And this is a symbol of the connection of heaven and earth. The stone is called green jasper," she adds, "which is also supposed to be protective."

Delan turns to the girl, speaking Kurdish to fill in the gaps of language. As he does, Lailan watches the pendant, then points to an oak tree on the hillside with long, gnarled branches.

"You got it," Olivia says. "That's it. An oak tree. The most sacred tree. The Druids—those were my people long, long ago—they believed family and spirits in heaven spoke to humans through the trees." She glances at Delan, knowing he'll have to translate at least a portion of that, but instead he studies her.

"That's why your dad gave it to you, isn't it? So you could hear your mother."

A nod. The copper's gone hot from the sun. "Something like that."

The sooner you figure out easy is good, her father told her, *the better off you'll be.* His words come back to her and remind her of something Rebecca had said after Olivia complained about Delan's temper, how a pleasant night could take a turn with any mention of politics: *We all love him. But I live in this house, too, and I see his baggage, and I don't know why you'd sign up for that.* If they were to make it past this hurdle, what would await them? Hard years of trying? Long sprawls of rough patches? Would they go through all that only to eventually succumb to the fact that ultimately they are too different and the issues too great?

"Soran's done a good job with her English," Delan says, nodding to Lailan. "He told her she can be an architect like him. She said she wants to be an artist. Her favorite color is pink but the other is *khal*. Dots. Like polka dots. Not a color, but that's what she told me yesterday."

Olivia keeps walking. Then, finally, "When I was her age, I wanted to work a cash register. Pressing buttons."

"For your birthday, I will get you a cash register."

He says this, and his words sit before them, a reference to a point suddenly she's not sure they'll be at together. She wonders if he feels that, too, if he sees this question within her.

"September fourteenth?" he asks.

She nods, trying to soften her demeanor. "Double Virgo. Not an easy job."

"You say that as if it should have meaning."

"It means I overthink and worry."

He laughs. "I never believed in astrology till now. And me, what am I?"

"Sagittarius. You're the life of the party, Hollywood."

He watches the trail, the backs of legs of the people before them. "They're not calling me that because they're impressed, you know. Yes, they are, a little—but that's not the name; that's not why. The West they love, but I loved it more, and they thought I was too good. That *I* thought I was too good, because of where I wanted to go. I'm *Hollywood*, the one who thinks he can make a living doing something that to them is like playing in the park. It's not real. It's not a job."

Ahead, Lailan climbs a small boulder only to jump off without pause. Dust rises around her feet. "Well, it is like playing in the park."

He shrugs. "If the park made you memorize thirty pages of lines, work every night with almost no pay, and then insulted you so you never wanted to leave your house. But sure. Compared to what most people here do, it's playing in the park. So the name, in a way I like it, because it's true and I'm lucky and I have worked for it and taken risks. But you see why it shames me."

Everyone stops alongside a creek. Old branches lodged between rocks, the current rolling white at the bend. There is a smell that Olivia at first thinks of as *cold* but then realizes is *fresh*. When has she last smelled something so fresh? Already Lailan is in the water, holding up her pants legs as much as she can without an older woman scolding her. Does she know how to swim? The creek could barely carry the girl, but still Olivia keeps an eye on her till she sits on a rock at the edge and churns pebbles with a stick.

Neighbors, cousins, aunts, and uncles. Friends he grew up with, who he went to school with. Everyone seems to have poured through the mountain to this one spot. Bright blankets and coolers and bags unloaded. Fires going, the nearest one topped with parallel cast-iron poles with legs that lift them from the ground. Upon one side is a tea-kettle and the other kebabs.

Delan talks to everyone, to old men in traditional dress and young women who shyly approach, glancing at Olivia when they think she's turned away. He embraces all and jokes with kids who clearly look up to him, and again Olivia feels that tug in her heart, because she *wants* to be with him. And truly, nothing is over. A bump, a new ingredient. It's possible that's all this is. With this consideration, there is a small surge of hope.

Then there is a man, a bit younger than Soran, whose eyes are dark like obsidian, like pebbles of black. Something about them makes Olivia nervous. Impenetrable, that's it. Eyes like a wall through which nothing can pass. Unknowable. "Wassim," Delan says when he introduces him to Olivia, and Wassim nods and studies his shoes and in his timidity, Olivia understands that this is how he is with women, that most likely he's not had much experience, and she wonders how much of that has to do with his eyes, with women unable to find themselves within them, unable to feel that they've made it past his surface.

"A cousin," Delan says. "Everyone's a cousin. I've known Wassim since he was a baby. Almost everyone here, since I was a baby or since they were babies."

The cousin who's to be married, Ferhad, arrives in a wave of greetings he accepts with his right arm, as his left is bandaged and held to his body with a sling, and the second he sees Delan, he goes straight to him, tears in his eyes as they embrace. His betrothed, a tiny woman with waist-length black hair, disappears into a flurry of well-wishes.

Ferhad is smiling but looks pained. He faces Olivia. "I sorry. I—" He shakes his head, looking to Delan for help before adding something in Kurdish.

"He says he didn't know you were here," Delan explains, "that he heard only about me just this morning. And a gift, he wishes he had a gift for you."

"I don't need a gift. Tell him I don't need a gift."

In scattered English, Ferhad thanks her for coming, then turns to Delan, shaking his head in disbelief. A man worn thin, Olivia decides. On a journey much longer than promised, at a picnic but masking an internal frenzy. "Weddings must be hard," she offers.

He shrugs but looks thankful for these words, like someone who would deny a compliment but repeat it silently later. Then she remembers there was a woman he'd refused. An arrangement turned down in order to pursue true love. Drama that went with that, drama that perhaps was the cause of his broken arm. The divisions within families from such a refusal, Olivia has no idea of the extent but assumes that as happy as any of this must make him, everything would be edged with a sort of betrayal. Then she thinks of Delan's family, of his parents. *They'll wish I was Kurdish,* she told him. *They will love you,* he replied, an avoidance of her point. Looking around now, she knows that if they had to pick for him, they'd pick a woman who spoke their language, who knew their customs, who would live near them and give them grandchildren they would actually get to see. They'd pick a Kurdish woman. Someone who'd know exactly what he's gone through, whose past was composed of the same worries and the same sounds in the night.

"I've heard stories about you," she says to Ferhad, trying to loosen these thoughts in her mind. "You and the flute in the tree, when Soran had his first kiss."

Now Ferhad throws his head back and smiles to the sky as Delan puts his arm on his shoulder and says something in Kurdish that makes

155

both men bend with laughter. But then something occurs to him, and he points to Soran, saying something in Kurdish.

Delan looks confused, and when he responds in Kurdish, Ferhad just nods.

"What was that?" she asks Delan when Ferhad has joined his betrothed.

"My cousin wanted to know if Soran has a new business, something that has him leaving town. Ferhad has an office by the checkpoint and sees him pass in the mornings a few times a week. But Soran works in town, mostly at home. It's the other owner of the car, I'm sure. The wedding is tolling on my poor cousin. Refusing the other woman cost his family."

Olivia watches Ferhad, his slow walk alongside his fiancée. "The saddest-looking happy man I've seen."

"It's hard to make someone understand tradition. What it meant to do what he did."

"No," she says. "You're right. I don't get it."

A sigh, as if he's reached the end of a fight and is disappointed to find her still entrenched within it. "If you don't want to understand, you won't."

Which, she knows, is true. But his world has made him tolerant of that which she disagrees with—marriage for something other than true love—and vice versa, their differences sifting loose. "This picnic is serious business," she says, trying to step away from their argument.

"If the sun is out," he says, "Kurds picnic."

Metal and brass samovars heat water for tea, and small, clear glasses are placed upon platters. While the youngest boys and girls play with one another, those a bit older have split off; boys play soccer while girls gather on blankets, helping with food or quietly whispering among themselves. Shy, searching glances. Questions through that murk of adolescence. Against a rock, a transistor radio leans, music hazy with lack of tuning, and in the middle of the field, men divide into sides for tug-of-war, which is so pure, so wonderful, and so contradictory to anything she's ever seen from adults that for a moment, Olivia forgets her worries and simply smiles into the sunlight. Soran, who must have just arrived with others, is on one side and lets go to wave in her direction.

After a moment, she leans back on her elbows. Grass bristles from under the blanket, and the sun is pleasantly warm. Illogically, she feels a distance from everything. From her job, from her worries, even from what happened at the restaurant and the distant bombings in the mountains. It's a comfort, this separation. Because she feels isolated. Protected in a field that is just a field. Small. The way grasping your own insignificance can lead to a sort of freedom. She breathes into it, trying to keep this essential existence without complication, without importance or past or future.

Like her, Delan is lying on the blanket, facing the sky. Past him, Lailan is in a tree, and a couple of men are below her, pointing out the branches she should take—not to get her down but to help her go higher. A few blankets over, Gaziza spreads out food while Hewar scans the mountainside with binoculars, searching for birds. All around them are white flowers, the smell of meat and spices thick. Nearby, the creek is fresher than anything she's known. And in this moment, with Delan beside her, she misses him.

"I'm sorry," she says. "For our fight."

"We're allowed to fight."

"About who we are?" she asks.

He turns his head toward her, and she sees he's about to answer, but his eyes go past her.

"Don't move," he says. "Pretend you're asleep."

It's then that she registers the silence. There's no singing. No talking. No taunts from the men playing tug-of-war. There's no music, even; someone must have shut off the radio.

"What is it?" she whispers.

"Soldiers. They're looking at our papers. It's fine, but better you're asleep."

She feels heat on the back of her head, the side that faces the soldiers, the exposed side. She hears Delan stand, then shuffle through his bag. Hears men speaking. Delan's voice is steady in whatever he's saying, but as the conversation continues, his mother and then his father join in. Soran as well—by now she knows the steady quiet of his voice.

She needs to know what's happening. Slowly she sits up, taking in the soldiers. Six of them with rifles.

"Olivia," Delan says, using her full name. "I showed them your papers. They have questions for me."

One soldier has turned away from Delan and is talking to Wassim, who gestures toward the path they took and then to Delan, saying something in a voice that is at once respectful and yet commanding—itself an accomplishment, to have mastered such a tone with a gun inches away. A sidelong look at Delan and the soldier is speaking and just like that, they have Delan's arms. Olivia jumps up, but he shakes his head at her. There are no handcuffs, but the soldier's grip shows little choice. Delan is calm. He is smiling, even. But he is an actor and he's telling her it's okay and she doesn't know what to believe. They want him for questions about a friend, he tells her and adds a shrug, as if the friend could be anyone. As if the friend is not his best friend, Aras, the one who's always known him as well as he knows himself.

Olivia feels a little hand within her own and looks down to see Lailan, the sun an angry bronze upon her hair. And then Soran is on Olivia's other side, his hand on her arm to keep her in place, to prevent her from moving. Because now the soldiers are leaving, and they are taking Delan with them.

Shock clears a space within you. There is a new emptiness. A place without feeling but with a spiked strip of anxiety. Panic without understanding. Nothing feels real but rather like a nightmare, something only vaguely familiar upon the telling.

Strangely, the picnic continues. Of course everything changes, prayer beads stringing through hands, women gathered on Olivia's blanket with comforting snippets of English and pats on her hand. But the fact is they can do nothing, and to follow in any way, even from a distance, would be an invitation for trouble. And so the music gets turned down and the games are put away. People eat and talk quietly. Olivia sits on her blanket, emotions a seesaw of panic and stunned incomprehension. Lailan, beside her, sits silently, wiggling her tooth and barely looking up. On their blanket, Hewar and Gaziza speak in low voices, solemn, their eyes on the trail that took their son. Another hour continues in the shadow of the event, and all Olivia can think of is getting back down the mountain.

They want to know about Aras, which she gathered. "Questioning, it is just questioning," Soran explains. "This happens all the time." He tells her of a man who is higher ranked than any of the soldiers who'd taken Delan. "A cousin. I will drop in to his office tomorrow. Delan will be back by then, I am sure," he adds, but he says it looking up, either in prayer or as a way to not meet her eyes. "And if not, he will help."

In the midst of this, in the midst of the long walk down the mountain and the dizzying car ride and a house gone silent, Olivia feels herself back in Geneva. On the night Delan told her he had a feeling they shouldn't go. The night she'd not listened. Had she listened, they would be in Switzerland still, arms dangling from the heights of a gondola, spring grass below and the air crisp and safe. But that didn't happen. Regret spirals wildly within her, paths that led to this fateful choice lit up.

"He will be fine," Soran tells her. "Do not worry." And indeed, he doesn't look worried. Her only consolation.

When you can't sleep, her father used to say, *it's because you're awake in somebody's dream.* When she wakes after midnight, she thinks of this and hopes it's true. Rolling onto her back, she sees the moon, solid and bold, and stares at it with defiance and anger, as if it's the watchful eye that's let too much pass. But then a beat later, she's plaintive and closes her eyes and says a prayer to anyone or anything that might intercept it. Her mother. God. Allah. The little boy at the restaurant who she can't stop thinking about.

Bring him back. Please.

The next day, she wakes with the panicked start of someone hit by memory. Sleep a respite that's ended. Recollection, a wall that's hit.

He's gone.

Their fight. Worries that loomed so large. Everything has fallen aside. All she wants is him.

If she could just call her father. If he could fly here, just so she could sit next to him, him and his comforting scent of woodsmoke and cigars and sweaters on rainy afternoons. He would know what to do. He would remind her it will be okay, and she would believe him. For a moment, she thinks of actually calling him, but to admit that any of the events of their trip had occurred would send him into a frenzy. No. She needs to be calm. To take the cues from those who know, who've been through this before.

Soran leaves as soon as morning curfew lifts, planning on talking to anyone he can, to try to get a message to Aras that Delan has been taken. She watches the window, waiting for his return, for news, and when he's finally there, he doesn't say much, only tells her that the person he went to find, Kak Zuhdi, was home and will do what he can. "Give me an hour," he tells her. "I have others to go to."

The day catches a sudden heat, as if it's spun too close to a fire. Only the second day Delan has been gone, but already the world is inflamed and angry. Does he feel this same swelter? Or is it simply that without him here, the ordinary has turned unsparing?

Delan's parents are kind to her, feeding her breakfast, patting her shoulder, making sure she's comfortable. She wants to tell them it's not right, that she should be the one doing this for them, because it's *their* child who's been taken and she knows that that trumps everything. But then she sees Gaziza's preparation of the food, the way she hands the plate to Olivia and watches, that this is what they need. Routine. Kindness. To do anything else would be to admit a great wrong, and now everyone needs to believe that he is okay. It was just yesterday he was taken, after all. Getting out of jail often takes longer than this in the States—though of course this is not jail or the United States, and it's these thoughts that sit like rocks within her.

Then Soran is leaving again. "Please watch Lailan," he says. "Miriam must work. And I must see if Kak Zuhdi is home, to tell him what happened. He will be key."

"But he was home. Earlier. You spoke to him."

A pause at the door. "Yes, you are right. Of course. I'm tired. There are others is what I meant. You can watch Lailan?"

A welcome distraction. Olivia throws herself into caring for the girl, playing with her and going on a walk, collecting bits and pieces for her art. Seedpods and sticks and pebbles. When they wander too far, Olivia turns them around, thinking Delan may be back, convincing herself with every step that he is. She pictures him in the living room, watching through the window. Even Lailan seems to catch sight of the vision, skipping and then stopping, turning with a grin and parroting phrases she's learned from Olivia. *Yes? You think so? I think so!* When they reach their block, they hold hands, silent. She feels him there. It's palpable. So palpable, she's waiting for the door to swing open. For him to step before them. The belief is so strong that when the door stays shut, when they step into a silent living room, it's as if he's been taken again. Beside her, Lailan holds her hand tighter.

Soran appears, heading upstairs. "I need to close my eyes. She could use a nap. If you can try, I would appreciate it, and then I can give you a break. Naps are her enemy, though, be warned."

Quietly Olivia leads Lailan up to her room, where she tells the girl stories in a whispered hush, hoping to ease her toward a nap. Lailan, however, has other plans and listens and kicks the blankets, fidgeting just enough to keep awake. "More," she says whenever Olivia stops talking, and Olivia searches her childhood for stories.

"Maybe *you* should tell *me* a story," Olivia finally says.

As if she'd just been waiting to be asked, Lailan jumps up, standing tall on the end of the bed. Eyes closed, she conjures her story with raised arms and then launches into an epic tale. There is what sounds like a frog who flies. A dress made of gold. A girl in a forest of faces. Though at times Olivia is lost from the roadblocks of language, one thing is certain: the girl is a born actor. Yet another thing to tell Delan when he's back.

"Wait," Olivia says. Something's occurred to her. "Faces?" She gets up to turn on the fan, remembering what they'd said on the hike about spirits in heaven speaking to humans through the trees. Maybe that wasn't appropriate to say in front of a child. She's not sure. She's never had to think this way before.

When Olivia lies back on the bed, Lailan is nodding, touching the wall. "Faces. Girl's mother father."

"The girl's mother and father. Her parents live in a tree?" She's hoping they're fairies, elves, or some Kurdish equivalent.

"Yes. Her parents in a tree. Her parents *dead*." The word drawn out and solemn.

A beat while Olivia absorbs this. What had Soran said about Lailan's parents? Just that it was a subject he'd revisit later, which was ominous in itself. "When I was little," Olivia says, "my mom died."

Lailan nods, as if she knew, then turns to face the wall, tracing a slender crack with her finger.

"But here's what was wonderful: my dad told me a secret he'd learned. That people we lose become stars. I don't know who he heard it from, I forget, but his sister, my aunt, she'd also passed away and there were two stars, right next to each other. That was them." Seen from a rocky shore on a clear night. Olivia's hands stained with blackberries. Toes dug into cold sand. It was the first time they'd walked to the water after her mother passed, and every wave was one she'd never hear.

"My dad said you can look at the sky and feel which star is watching you. And that's the person you knew. And he was right, because I felt it. She's up there, helping and protecting us. Keeping us safe. Even now, my mom knows I'm here with you. If we go outside tonight, I could probably find her for you."

Lailan shakes her head.

"No? You don't want to?"

Still facing the wall, Lailan shakes her head again. "Here, big clouds. Big. We see stars; stars are big big. But stars not see us."

"Because of the clouds?"

The girl shrugs. "Where I born, all people stars."

Olivia's unsure how to respond, if Lailan means that the stars must not be able to see because there's been no protection. Cautiously, she says, "Stars are very, very powerful. And I've heard that if the clouds are heavy, if they're having a hard time looking, sometimes they send someone to help. You might not even know who it is, because it's a secret. *The person* might not even know."

Now Lailan turns. Intrigued. She bites her lip, then remembers her loose tooth and touches it with her thumb. "Soran?" she finally asks.

Olivia smiles. "I can't tell you. How would I know?"

"You?" Said loudly and with a jump and a landing on the bed.

Olivia motions Lailan to lie beside her, and though the girl obliges, she can't seem to stay straight or still and so props one leg up on the wall. "Tell me another story," Olivia says, just as the power goes out and the fan slows to a stop.

And so with one leg on the wall and a small hand patting Olivia's arm, Lailan talks about a mountain and a treasure and lava, and when she says the word, she glances at Olivia, proud. Olivia nods, encouraging, but sees Delan in her mind. Outside the sky appears erased, wiped out by the heat.

Downstairs, Gaziza's kept vigil by the window, perched in the gold chair with prayer beads, her hair covered in a dark headscarf. She is willing her son to appear, and her love for her child is so concentrated, so intense that it seems at any moment it could break into something tangible, something so powerful, it could reorder the world. The woman's eyes shine and move with any shadow of clouds, any flicker of change upon the empty street.

Late in the afternoon, the heat has settled. Soran heads to the garden, plunging his hands into the soil at the potting table, while Olivia takes a seat on the bench beside him, listening for any changes within the house. A voice. A telephone ring. It's hot early this year, he explains, snapping the little leaves and tiny branches off a tomato seedling. When planted, he tells her of the stem, the spots of the injuries will become roots, the plant healthier. "These will go there," he says, nodding in the direction of the grapes. "That area, that's where I need to get ready." Beside it, the chukar birds are out in an enclosed pen, their *wah-ooo-ooo, wah-ooo-ooo* sounds constant as they stab at the ground with red beaks.

In the United States, there'd be a fist pounding a desk, demanding answers. A lawyer. A group outside the jail with signs. Calls to a news station. Here, they sit in a garden. Or a chair by the window. "There must be people we can call," she says.

"You do not make phone calls. Our phones are tapped—they have been for a while. We set meetings, go for tea. I have tea later today. Please, will you hand me that water?"

A pail filled with water sits by the faucet, inside a chipped porcelain teacup. Using the cup, he drenches the soil around the plant. Olivia fans her shirt, hot with stagnancy. She needs to pace. To run. To do anything to burn off her frustration. What she'd said to Delan comes back in bursts, how she'd made him feel. A fight at the worst time.

Just then, the chukars scatter within their pen as Lailan bursts outside, racing to greet them. "Bird," she announces and shoves grass between the holes in the fence, "bird time to eat," until Soran says something to her in Kurdish that makes her stop. Then he turns to Olivia. "There is work to do, if you want."

Gardening gloves. Her sneakers. The sting of sweat in her eyes and the burn of sun on her back. Eventually Lailan settles and sits on the path beside them, drawing on lined paper, as Olivia twists and pulls the weeds from their roots, relishing in an absence of thought, the physical motions that blank her mind and place energy into her body rather than her worries.

Hewar lugs compost in a wheelbarrow, and Olivia and Soran mix it into the cleared section. His sons, their love of gardening, it's clear it stems from him. Her own father, she remembers, discovered his love for gardens a few months after her mother's sleep—as they called it—began. Bags of soil had slumped at his feet like something defeated. For hours, it seemed, he'd studied an area in the backyard that was all grass gone to seed. *She will love this,* he'd finally said, his voice solid with belief. Seeds covered and hidden, plants that would bloom later in the year—a garden was not just for the present but for the anticipation of a future day. Such hope, inherent in its essence. And though her father's ability to keep a garden alive was lacking, it turned out to not matter after all. The moment never came.

"Stop," Soran says.

Olivia freezes, unsure. He motions her out of the way and pulls on a larger rock near where she'd been about to dig. A trapdoor. Two feet square, a wood plank that's been glued with gravel, each piece carefully arranged like a small sculpture of rocks. With the top off, she can see inside—a plastic-lined hole with nothing inside. "Kurdish books. Histories, poetry," he says. "Anything written in Kurdish could be called propaganda. They would be burned, and we would be labeled resistance. One book, that is all that's necessary. When there's a raid, everything is put in here. As long as we have warning."

A raid. The word is chaos and motion, and without thinking, she looks toward the side gate, almost surprised to see it shut, the boughs of trees undisturbed. "They happen often?"

"Not lately. But they can, if they have reason. And sometimes if they do not. Everything depends on who is in charge and what mood they are in."

He lowers the cover, setting it back into place. Would she remember where it is if something were to happen? On the wall above, plaster is missing in the shape of a hand, exposed bricks underneath, as if someone had stood there with their palm in place and chipped around it. Which, she realizes, is probably what happened. Nearby is a large bush of pink oleander, its poison sweetness thick and luring and a bit like apricots.

"Hi-lo," Lailan says, on a hunt for rocks she adds to a collection she's placed in the hammock of her shirt, her pale, slightly rounded stomach glaring in the sun, a jagged scar near her belly button. A flash in Olivia's mind: the people in the street, the wobbled flesh of stomachs exposed. She blinks hard, then focuses on Lailan, who's now lined her rocks into the shape of a star.

The girl stands back. "Art. Lailan art!"

Olivia smiles for the first time all day. "It is. That *is* art. You have to sign it now." A request that involves Olivia teaching Lailan how to write her name in English. An entire column of *Lailan*s is soon etched in bark on the concrete, most with the lines of the *A*'s on the wrong side. Then the girl goes to the bare rosebush and carefully inspects the thorns. Olivia is about to stop her, but Soran holds out a hand. "Let her," he says quietly as Lailan carefully bends a dried thorn off the cane. She studies the point, then sits on the ground and flattens a patch of dirt before using it to draw a delicate line for the *L*. Soran, watching, nods admiringly.

The rosebush. Olivia leans in. She'd thought it dead but now sees the starts of bright-green leaves, tight but ready to unfurl. "My neighbor across the street," she says, "he planted a rose but I figured it was dead. Just spiky canes."

"Roses are not weak. Look at their armor. Where it is hot, you must take off the leaves, to help the plant start over. No, someone cut that rose back, and when you return, you will see it bloom. This, I can promise you."

She smiles at his certainty, his faith in a plant he's never met. "Really? You can promise?"

"If I am wrong, you can tell me."

"And if you're right?"

"You will have a rose to look at. And me to think of."

A break under the pomegranate tree. Face to the sun, she listens to Soran talk quietly to the plants. Whispered encouragements. He cares for them like children—guiding them, feeding them. The garden, she realizes, has his heart, and she wonders if this is because he misses the woman back in London, if the soil and plants are the recipients of his unlanded love.

The back door slams. Two men step into the yard. Dark trousers and button-down shirts, one with a vest despite the heat. Quickly, she turns to Soran, but he's smiling a greeting, and the men are heading to Hewar, who approaches them with arms held out for an embrace.

"My father's friends," Soran says. "The man with the black vest, he grows geraniums. The best geraniums. He won a competition. Very known. Very famous here."

But the men don't come bearing news. Instead they talk about the garden, with politics and Delan mentioned in between, walking with their hands clasped behind their backs like thoughtful, wandering professors, stopping now and then to pull a weed or snap a dried bloom. To talk only of what worries you, Soran tells her, is too much. So they will garden.

A tray with glasses and white liquid is brought out. *Do*, a thin yogurt drink. She takes a sip and cringes because there's nothing sweet about it. It's sour, brawny. "A treat," Soran tells her, smiling when he sees her face. But expectations, once they are adjusted, allow for the true experience, and subsequent sips go down smoother. At the end, she realizes she might actually like it.

"It's good, is it not?" Soran asks. "Refreshing. For us, it is like beer to a German, only without alcohol. Now you are an honorary Kurd, if you like it."

Close to the back door, Lailan whispers to herself, lost in an imaginary instruction, until suddenly she stops, places her finger on her tooth, and moves it back and forth. Tempered with her mission but also purposefully out of the way. Though there's a wildness to Lailan, a streak of energy that flashes bright and fast, it's as if she knows she's on something like borrowed time at this house and with this family and so she's learned how to blend in at the right times, just as a child who wants to stay up past bedtime walks quietly. She's learned how to make it easy for people to care for her. How not to be a problem.

Olivia turns to Soran. "Does she have friends?"

"Some. More when she is in school."

"A girl's school?" To that, he nods, and she watches him, curious. "Why is it okay that I'm with Delan? Here, I mean. When men and women don't hang out. Is it because I'm from a different culture?"

"Partly. But mostly because you are engaged." He laughs and then quickly explains. "He told me later it isn't true. But to everyone else— you are engaged. It's more proper than coming home with a girlfriend.

They wouldn't have approved. No one would've approved. And he told my parents not to throw a party, that it was too much distraction. And they are listening, though my mother finds this difficult."

"They think we're engaged."

"Is it so unrealistic?" Though he's the one who asked the question, he blushes as if the inquiry was turned to him. "Sorry. It's not my place."

Engaged. A ruse, but realizing his parents believe it heightens everything. Alters meetings. The way people have looked at her. What they must have said that she'd not understood. It explains all the pieces of jewelry his parents gave her. The regret his cousin expressed that he'd not brought her a gift. Through the kitchen window is Gaziza, who thinks Olivia is her future daughter. The thought makes her want to cry, to be her daughter.

"So you thought we were engaged when you met me. But you didn't look happy. When you first saw me."

"Not because of that, I promise you. It was the risk. I didn't think it safe or a good time to come."

"I guess it wasn't safe. The verdict has been reached." A smile. "So that's what your fight with Delan was about?"

"He frustrates me."

She laughs. "Me too. But why you?"

"He is blessed. You know this. Everything has fallen into place for him. The American Friends of the Middle East helped him. The I-20, the student visa. And then he is discovered for a big movie."

A big movie but a little part, she wants to say but stays quiet.

"Paid enough money to buy a big house."

Now she says something, in part because she wants him to feel better, to not feel small in his brother's shadow. "A big house that's falling apart in a not-so-amazing area. I live there too."

"It is in *Hollywood.* He bought a big house in Hollywood."

Olivia smiles, letting him keep his glittering streets of stars versus hers of stepped-on cigarettes and crowded bus stops.

"And citizenship went through," Soran says. "He met someone who knew a senator. Those applications, usually they are lost. But not his. He gets work. A house with a yard, friends. Oranges. Even an empty lot behind the wall should he want to grow more. He said he wants to learn to ski and then meets the Norwegian trainer for the Olympics; did he tell you that? In London, when he visited me. Of course we did not ski—we were in London—but the man said, *Anytime, you call me.* That is how these things work for him."

"You're proud of him."

"Of course. It took bravery for him to leave. But his luck has made him lazy. He believes that what he wants will happen, that fate will make it happen—so often he does not act. How long before he told you how he felt? He waits for things to fall into his lap."

"Fate. I know. It's his crutch."

A quick glance at her. Guilt on his face from the sway of talk to something slightly negative.

"Yes. Fate. The lazy man's religion. But what happens if one star is not in alignment? And does not go into alignment? And chance never comes and time is wasted? What if you wake up only to die that day?"

"Maybe that faith is good," Olivia says. "Maybe it's good to not be so worried."

"Is that faith? Or an excuse? Perhaps that depends on the person. But Delan, he is a man so accustomed to life going the direction he wants that he becomes reckless. And his gambles, in his life, he has won. But you do not gamble with another person."

In its cage, the pigeon beats its wings. Soran says nothing more, just turns back to the house and raises his hand, shielding his eyes against the sun.

CHAPTER 9

In the morning, she wakes to the sound of the front door closing, the rest of the house silent. Within seconds, she's at the window, and Soran's car is pulling down the street. A whip of orange as it turns the corner. Back in bed, she wants to lose herself in a dream. Sunrise shoves through curtains in darkened red.

Darkened red. The first time Delan went into the darkroom with her, the first time he saw her photographs and maybe even truly saw her, was only a year ago. A time that now feels ancient, a relic of an easier world. Upstairs at their house. In the bathroom with a tub that allows for three trays and late-night black-and-white printing, which is easier than color. Often she wakes in the middle of the night and tapes a sign on the door. **DARKROOM. USE DOWNSTAIRS. SORRY!**

One night, he told her he wanted to see the magic. Though she'd obliged, she was suddenly nervous. Towel under the door. Black paper taped to the window. She flipped the switch and the world went black until the film was loaded. Then a click of the safelight, and everything shot red. Keenly, she was aware of where he was. Felt him. Saw him in the dusky reflection of the mirror and spoke just to fill the silence. Talk of fitting film sprocket holes. Ridding air bubbles in the tank. Test prints and exposure. Her words went on until the image appeared, and she forgot him because there was Rebecca, slowly coming into existence. Pulling on a high-heeled shoe while holding on to the kitchen counter, late for work. A teakettle on the stove letting off steam and morning light landing in heavy chunks through the window. The timer clicked, and the lines of Rebecca's short hair sharpened, and the expression on her face—hurry, irritation, acceptance—summed up everything. Because this was a woman who was told she could work the same job as a man as long as she didn't forget her job at home. A woman whose right to take birth control pills was too often seen as a ticket to noncommitment from those who no longer lived in fear of shotgun marriages and diapers. This was a woman whose mind was on a million things but who just needed to get her shoe on. A woman who'd come a long way and was tired.

"I don't know how you knew to take that," Delan said. "That look on her face. Even the kettle. It's tragic. And beautiful. Whatever you do, though, don't show it to her."

She'd not thought of that, that Rebecca wouldn't approve. "Should I not have taken it?"

He looked upset, disturbed that the photo's existence could be called into question. "*Of course you should have.* Always get the shot. Always. Art makes a difference. And if someone's story, their pain or sadness, if that can impact someone else, it's worth the invasion."

Soon he was riffling through her other photos but stopped when he found three taken right after Christmas. Each of a house in black and white, taken at night. The houses are bright, filled with light and activity—one with a family at the dining room table, another with a woman on the phone in a cheery kitchen, the last with children in the top window, jumping on a bed. In the foreground of all three images are the Christmas trees that just days prior had been lit up and loved within the houses but now are dried and discarded on the curbs, left in a haze of street light. Duty done. Life goes on.

"I was calling them *Kicked to the Curb*," she said.

"*Fickle Love*, I'd call them. This is a triptych. I want them on our wall when you walk in."

The next morning, the chemical smell still hung in the air, but when Mason complained, Delan held up his hand. "You have your own bathroom in your studio—use that one."

"The shower's shit—"

"No one yells at you about the brushes you leave in our sink," he said. "Even though you have your own sink. You are an artist and so is she. You of all people should support, not make it harder. In fact, frames. We need frames. For three photos. I want them in the entryway."

Mason looked at her differently after seeing the photos, as if having felt a hard shell beneath the silk of her shirt. All three images went on the wall, and the rest of the day, Olivia burned with the blaze of someone who for a moment had been truly seen.

When she wakes again, it's to the sound of Soran's car parking outside. "You slept," he announces when she walks downstairs to the kitchen.

"Did you find anything?"

He shakes his head. "I only went out quickly for bread."

With his answer, she checks her watch, and there is a falter in her step, because it's been hours that he's been gone. But then she sees the counter, a new bag of naan bread by the sink. Though there, in the far corner, is another bag. *My cousin wanted to know if Soran has a new business,* she remembers Delan saying at the picnic, *something that has him leaving town.* Now she watches Soran, the way he seems distracted. Distracted enough to not notice they already had bread, perhaps. Or maybe he just wanted to be alone.

Day three. The third day of them asking questions. The third day of Delan not answering. Or worse.

"Is this normal?" she finally asks Soran. "Him gone this long?"

"Nothing is normal. But I am not worried. Most likely they have forgotten about him because someone else came in whose answers they need more."

And then there's a knock on the door. A rush of hope. Olivia's standing in an instant. But it continues—the knock Lailan has established: *tap-tap, tap-tap-TAP.* When the door swings open, there is Lailan with a pot and pan to pretend to cook.

"Lailan cook *perde plau*," Lailan says. "Rice with goodness. Many goodness."

Later, after much invisible chopping, the girl leads her through the garden, through the streets, anywhere, pointing out items and saying their Kurdish names so Olivia can provide the English. *Rose, stone, fig, roof, branch.* Already Lailan's English has improved by leaps, whereas Olivia's Kurdish is meager at best.

"*Walla,*" Olivia said earlier to Soran. "I keep hearing *walla* and *ser chow.*"

"*Walla* means I swear, I promise. And *ser chow* means on my eye. Like with all my heart."

She smiled. "On my eye?"

"All my heart is better? Translations don't always translate. If you want to tell someone they're not very bright, we say something that translates to, *Donkey, don't die. It's spring and your saddle is coming from the city.*"

They both laughed, till circumstance caught up to them and the sound rang too loud.

On her walk with Lailan now, they pass a sheep that's tied to a rope by someone's side gate. Olivia stops to scratch behind its ears. Chewing, it looks at her, unimpressed, its coat dirtied and matted. "Sheep," Olivia says, and Lailan makes a motion as if eating.

"Food," she says plainly, because it is a fact.

Making the girl lemonade reminds Olivia of making lemonade with her father. Piles of spent fruit. The sticky counter. The sound of the spoon against the glass. Now she both misses Delan *and* her father, and watching Lailan drink from a cup that practically obscures her whole face only adds to the equation a sadness that this girl never had a father to miss. So Olivia holds Lailan extra tight, trying to forget it all by breathing in the crisp bite of lemons on her skin.

Dinner is silent. When finally the plates are cleared, Olivia lets Lailan show her how to feed the chukar birds the leftover tomatoes and fruit, their beaks stabbing into the white flesh of a melon that smells faintly like pineapple. The windows of Miriam's house stay dark, so Olivia gets the girl ready for bed at Delan's house, trying to scrub her face with a washcloth as Lailan ducks and weaves.

"Story," Lailan says when they're done. With her finger, she traces each copper bough of Olivia's pendant. "Story for trees."

And so Olivia tells her that in Ireland, oak trees were once called *daur*, the origin of the word *door*, and it was believed that if you fell asleep beside a certain one, you could wake in the magic realm of fairies. This was back in the day when Ireland was covered in oak trees, she adds, and then realizes that of course Lailan might have no idea where Ireland is, and so on the wall, she traces countries and continents and oceans.

When she adds that she and Delan live in a place called California, the girl becomes delighted with the mistake. *"Hollywood,"* Lailan corrects proudly. "Delan lives in *Hollywood*." Her laughter is a giggled, joyous spill. "You said wrong."

Olivia tells her she's right, that they live in Hollywood, and that back home, when Delan's onstage, he's all anyone watches. She talks and talks, pausing to listen for new voices downstairs, and then watches as the pendulum of the girl's energy takes a drastic swing, and suddenly her blinks become longer, heavier, until her eyes shut and she's out. With a finger, Olivia brushes her bangs aside on her forehead, watching her sleep that complete, encompassing sleep of a child. When finally Miriam's windows brighten, Olivia walks carefully down the stairs, Lailan's comforting weight on her hip and her small chin on her shoulder.

Three days. Now three nights.

And then it's two a.m., and she hears a noise. Someone down the hall. Water is running.

Delan has returned.

In a flash, she's out of bed. Delan's name gathers from her lungs, is on her tongue, her mouth open and about to call for him when she finds Soran running a bath. He laughs, fully dressed but embarrassed just the same. "I did not mean to wake you." He shuts off the faucet and averts his eyes as he explains. "I bathe at night."

"Why?" This will catch him, in what she's not sure, but she wants an answer to where he's been during those times of hazy explanations.

"Delan does not still bathe at night?" he asks. "He did for a while. I thought maybe still. But you would know."

"Why would he?"

Taking a seat on the edge of the tub, Soran seems to debate. Weighing pros and cons of whatever story sits within him. At last he leans back against old ivory tiles.

"People in our family, they've always been political. So even in peace, we had problems. Arrests. Imprisonments. But then the kingdom was toppled in '58 and the republic created. From then on, no Kurds had peace. And the government bombed during the day." He stops, as if this is all that needs to be said, but then sees that's not the case. "Imagine, not having clothes on when the sirens go off or when the ground starts to shake and you have to run. Imagine soap in your hair when you see the shadow of the plane."

She nods, a guilt at having even made him say the words.

"We learned to live at night. To work, to bathe. When the time came, you had to run. Take what you could carry to the mountains. That is where we would go. The mountains were safe."

Head for the hills, she remembers Delan saying. Such a common saying, so reduced from its meaning that never once did she truly understand what it implied. And never, she realizes, did he admit he himself had made the journey.

"Two, three, four families hiding in a space below a big rock. Or a cave—if lucky, a cave. We are blessed with these mountains; they have so many caves; they take care of us. I remember Delan, he had a suitcase. In it, he kept his treasures. A flute. Magnifying glass. A couple of books. I can't remember all. But really, truly, it was the suitcase he loved most. Blue like the sky. He cleaned it every day. Polished it, if you can believe. It was shiny, like a new car. But this, this suitcase he would drag up the mountain." There is a brief smile, and he continues. "One day, the bullets were too close, and we had to run faster. So he left the suitcase by a tree. There was no choice. When we went back down, it was gone. Someone took it. Friend, enemy. It did not matter. It was beautiful. Someone wanted it."

Soran continues, testing the water with his hand and shaking the drops from his fingers. "The next day, he went to school. Four of his friends were not there. They had not made it to the mountains."

Wordlessly, she tries to absorb this. A loss that would've upended everything. Delan, at school, alone at a desk. Eye on the door, waiting. How strongly did he believe they would come? How long did he listen for their voices before understanding? Beside her, Soran studies his hands, avoiding her eyes. And that, his evasion, makes her realize that his words tell only his brother's story, though his own, as a child, had treaded right alongside.

"His best friends, killed," he continues. "What do you do? He came home that day and the next, upset about the suitcase. Because he could not think of what he'd really lost."

A faint rust-colored stain rings the bottom of the sink. With her finger, she traces its outline. "He does that still. Said it's a choice, what to let your mind think of."

"A choice? The choice might be to see it as a choice. It would feel good, would it not?" A pause. "What do I know? He could be right."

"It's what we fought about. Before the picnic. Our differences in where we're from and how we see things. He told me I didn't have a right to judge him or tell him I thought he was wrong. That I could never understand him, because of where I'm from. Because of my life."

In a blink, the room plunges into darkness, the power out. All that's left is a weak trapezoid of light from an upper window. Piercing the silence, a drop from the tub's faucet hits the bathwater. One and then another. And then quiet. Neither of them moves. With the silence from the house and the darkness around them, there is a feeling of existing within a pause. As if the world has halted. An infinite arm holding everything back, granting a lull, a moment in which they are allowed to have this conversation.

"You could have said the same to him."

In the dark, she nods. "We're mismatched. I didn't really get it till then, what that meant. How big that could be. It's him not feeling understood and me feeling like I've not earned a place next to someone who's gone through what he's gone through. And what do you do about that? Does he want that? Do I?" A confession, to have spoken this out loud. To feel mostly unseen as she says these words. "I thought maybe I didn't. But now the idea of losing him—all that matters is him."

"His wanting to be with you, that's not a question. You were talking to someone who wanted to *not* change, asking him *to* change. When does that go over smoothly?"

A whir and the power's back. Olivia blinks in the light, and Soran continues.

"I assume your father is accepting of him. I know our family is accepting of you. True difference is when that does not happen. When there is much, much more in the way. When there is no option. Religion. Where you are from, religion does not cause impact like it does other places. Or being born too poor to marry someone above you.

Or too rich to marry someone below you. People have lost their lives for less. For even talking to someone they should not. *Loving* someone you should not, that is not an option for most. Those differences are what to be afraid of. The rest," he adds with a smile, "*that* is a choice. And earning? You earn your place beside someone by not walking away. Even when all you want to do is run."

The bath has gone cold when she leaves him. Though Soran's words were encouraging, she's left with a hollow ache. As much as she's wanted this, the *why* of who Delan is, it hurts to glimpse what he's been through—because she loves him. And he was right. This is no longer just *in love*; this is deeper. This is love that's true and certain and even at times unsettling. And not a new territory, she realizes, just one newly recognized. This is the place in which she sees the faults—his temper and denial and often irritating need to be liked—but will stay perched upon the broken land just the same. What had he said? You love someone because of who they are but also—and maybe more important—despite who they are.

Then she hears her father's long-ago words, caught on a horrible, prophetic slant. *You worry that if you really love someone, they will be taken.* Down the hall, the water starts again. *If you're worried you don't know him,* her father also said, *that's not a reason to leave; it's why you lean a little closer.* At the time, she asked him why she should bother listening closer when he never talked about what's important. Now, she realizes what her father meant. Not to lean in to *hear* but to be there. To allow for more. To allow for someone to be open and imperfect.

Day four. Each hour is an unchanged continuation of the one before, a never-ending knotted thread of worry. Soran tells her they need to buy her a traditional dress for the wedding, that Delan had a place in mind and he will take her there.

"I can't buy a dress."

"He will be back," Soran says. "He will. And you will need a dress. He wanted you to have a dress. Miriam is not working today, so there is no Lailan. No excuse."

She knows that if Delan's not back, she will not go to the wedding, but Soran does not need to hear this, just as she doesn't need to say the words. He needs to do as his brother wanted, and that Delan wanted her to have a dress is true; he described them on the plane as if talking about a woman. *Bright. Captivating. You want to be wrapped in the arms of these dresses—but they aren't soft,* he added. *Scratchy fabric but worth it to get close.*

After lunch, she will get the dress. While they eat, Soran tells her another bit of their past, and a collection grows. Though they are originally from this area, for a while they lived in another town. But in '63, the year before Delan left, they lost that home.

"It was taken," he tells her.

The Ba'athists wanted the oil-rich area as Arab so they could claim it, so Kurds were moved out and entire Arab families from southern Iraq moved in, doors flung open to homes with furniture and clothes and another child's toys.

"It was not their fault either," Soran says. "The families who were moved in. Everyone a pawn in a political agenda. But I thought it was. Once, we went back, and I watched a boy through the window in my room. And I hated him. I did not understand. He had lost a home as well."

Arabization. Wells destroyed. Farms burned. Cemeteries blotted out as if the land had held a troublesome crop. Teachers and other employees were transferred to far-off parts of the country and forced to sell their houses to Arabs. Ethnic cleansing. All to erase a people and a claim. Even the streets, he tells her, were renamed.

And then she knows. The house they'd first visited, the one close to the candy shop. The longing on Delan's face when he looked at the windows. The way he'd studied the door, the once-grand trees. The destroyed garden. That had been their home.

How much of what happened made him leave? How much pain will he never admit to, and what has that pain done? Forever there will be unopened years and tales kept silent, but does that matter? She thought it did. But in the face of what's happened, it's boiled down to this: she loves all of him. The sum of his parts, the conclusions of his stories. Who he is now. And the idea that she might not be able to be with him—*that* eclipses all the rest.

"Tell me something good," she says, because it's too much, the thought of their loss. And so she listens to him tell of his grandmother making bread, *naan i tandoor* in a pot installed in the ground outside, the way flames were fed with oak and how his grandmother thinned the dough with a stick before slapping it against the blazing-hot walls, the dough baking almost instantly. All day his grandmother would bake bread with three other women until there was a four-foot-high towering stack of still-warm bread that would last them the next few months. *You could smell it, that stack that was taller than we were.* One whiff and they raced each other for the honey. She listens to the story and asks questions about the bread and never tells him that when she said *Tell me something good*, she just wanted to hear *He'll be home soon.*

The fabric store is like a geode that's been split open. The outside bland on a faded day but the inside bursting with color. Taffeta in all hues drapes on hangers suspended from the ceiling. Embroidered with shiny sequins, threaded with tinsel, or embellished with faux pearls or gems, the fabric gleams. Still in her bag, Olivia's camera is like a child tugging on her arm. She didn't want to bring it, with Delan still gone, but Soran insisted. "How would he feel if he knew you didn't take photographs? Please do not make him feel that when he returns."

The dresses call for a stage. To dance beneath spotlights, to twirl and leave trails of glimmer. Long vests of taffeta. Floor-length sleeves that billow open and are to be tied loosely behind a back. Everything reminds Olivia of Renaissance dresses. Magic and spells and promises.

"Kurds like color," Soran explains with a shrug.

An older woman whose eyes are darkened almost wickedly with kohl looks at her kindly, almost sadly, and Olivia figures the woman has been apprised of the situation. She touches Olivia's hair and peers into her eyes. Then, inspired, leads her to a bolt of olive-green taffeta embroidered with gold swirls of sequins. It's beautiful, but the truth is Olivia doesn't care. She can't care. But choices are made. Even a gold headdress with a triangle-shaped net of gold coins. When Olivia tries it on, the tip of the triangle dips down to between her eyebrows.

"He will love this," Soran says. *He will love this.* "You are all right? I need to go to the bakery. She will measure you."

Four days, Olivia thinks.

The woman does her job, and as soon as she's able, Olivia forces herself to take her camera from her bag. *He will be back,* she tells herself. And she'll wish she'd taken the photos.

A raise of her eyebrows asks the question, *May I?* and the seamstress's nod confirms. From the ground, Olivia shoots up into stunning bolts of fabric. Then she shoots out, at such an angle where there's no flare from the outside, with focus that catches the brilliant blues and fiery oranges against the cement beige of the day.

When she's done, Soran has still not returned. Olivia riffles through an album the seamstress has on a table, each photograph of women displaying cuts and designs and fabrics throughout the years. It takes her a bit to notice that many of the photos are of the same woman, a woman who stares with heavily made-up eyes into the camera as if relishing in a sort of safety, a seduction without consequence. At the youngest, she is maybe in her twenties, flushed with youth and risk and shine. In the most current photo, the one at the start of the book, she must be in her forties, around the same age as the seamstress, with dark hair that's grayed at the temple like a current gathering its force. A repeat customer. Someone loyal throughout the years.

A bell chimes. The front door opens, and a young girl enters. Olivia catches the seamstress look up immediately only to look right back down, holding her hand to her head as if struck with disappointment, and it's then Olivia has a thought. Just a guess, but when she leans back in to compare the images, she thinks she sees it: love. Sparked in the much-photographed woman's eyes, pulling forward a shoulder, lifting a brow. Olivia glances back to the seamstress, who quietly folds fabric the color of honey, and wonders if she's right, then wonders how many others have noticed this love kept secret but right in the open.

The power of a photograph.

Right now, in Olivia's father's old oak cabinet drawer, there are loose photos of her mother, at least a hundred in black and white or faded color, some on deckle-edged paper whose scalloped sides Olivia used to run her fingers along. *Why is nothing in an album?* a friend once asked in high school, and Olivia—whose world hinged on order—just shrugged. The truth was that it was her father's doing and had been like this since the funeral, since he'd torn through albums to find pictures but never had the energy to return them. Instead he'd dumped the rest inside the drawer, and both he and Olivia had learned to love it because it was her mother's jumbled life, and there was something beautiful about the chaos, something that felt whole and complete and circular from the very fact that a handful of images would fly through time and reveal Olivia's mother at all ages, like a full life lived. Pregnant in a field of nodding sunflowers. A toddler before a Christmas tree. Catching salmon from a rocky shore. *Let's see who wants to join us,* her father used to say at their long-ago dinners, right before he'd close his eyes and reach his hand inside to feel for a photo that would then sit beside them at the table. Stories sprung from those photos. Everything a reminder made eternal.

Now Olivia wonders if all the seamstress has are these photos. If each time the bell rings, she looks up with hope, and if each night, she locks up and turns the key, looking forward to tomorrow with its slim and fragile chance.

Another ten minutes pass, and Soran has still not returned. From the door of the shop, Olivia watches the street. Men on bicycles and mopeds. Soldiers on the corner. When one turns toward her, she looks in the other direction to a couple of boys who chase each other around a car. An olive tree shimmers silver past a wall, and there are glares of brass and gold from the store that sells housewares. Then, beside it, the bakery. She crosses the street, heading toward a shining window display of baklava and sticky pastries. Inside, sweet rolls steam, fresh out of the oven, sprinkled with poppy and sesame seeds, and halvah is formed into giant blocks like fudge. Besides a woman in a bright-blue scarf who watches Olivia from behind the counter, there's no one else inside the bakery.

Back on the street, she's struck with the enormity of what could happen. What might have already happened. Because Soran could have been taken. Shoved into a car. Brought in for questioning as well. Who would she go to for help? She studies the street. Soldiers on the corner lean against a building. An old man sits on a plastic chair with tea and reads, and another man passing by drops his cigarette on the sidewalk, a trail of smoke snaking into the air. Her boyfriend has been taken, and now even his brother could be gone, and she doesn't know how to help either one of them. A dress. She was just fitted for a *dress* when Delan is missing. Delan, the man she loves, is gone. Four days. Four days he's been gone and they have no idea how to get him back. With this, everything goes loud inside her, and her breathing fights against itself, staggered inhalations that seem too shallow.

And then there is a voice behind her, saying hello in accented English.

Ferhad. His mouth opens when she turns, and he reaches for her as if she's about to fall. At the last second, she jams her hand against the wall to steady herself and lowers her head, feeling those pinpricks of panic, that swimming static that means she's about to faint. She focuses on his feet. Worn brown oxfords. One sock that is stark white while the other is an aged ivory.

"Delan?" he asks.

When she looks back up, he's searching the street.

"Where is he? I don't know. No one knows."

His eyes darken with worry, and she realizes he assumed Delan was back. And in this honest reaction, she understands that being missing for this long *is* reason to worry. That all the brave faces and positive words from others have been hopeful, but not truthful. And though Ferhad now tries to cover for her sake, nodding as if everything is fine, she knows it's not.

"Please," he says, trying to hand her a handkerchief.

Voices from inside the bakery. She turns to see Soran walking with another three men through a back door and into the main room. Immediately, he spots her through the window, registers the look on her face, and in a rush is beside her.

There is Kurdish. A frantic back-and-forth until Soran takes a couple of steps away, facing the sky. After a moment, he nods, as if affirming the situation, but there are tears in his eyes.

"I thought," he says, "when I saw you, there was news."

She shakes her head. "I'm sorry."

"Do not be sorry. Here," he says and hands her a white piece of candy. "Manna."

She takes the candy but lowers her hand. "At the bazaar," she explains. "We were in front of a tray of manna."

It takes him a second to find her meaning.

"Of course." He smiles softly and then turns to Ferhad, who looks confused, and tells him what happened in a mix of Kurdish and English until Ferhad says something in return. "He says we were lucky," Soran tells her.

"Lucky," she repeats, feeling the empty space beside her.

Ferhad must catch her meaning, because he again says something in Kurdish, to which Soran nods. "Ferhad feels your love for Delan. And he says you should see with your eyes and hear with your heart, because Delan is alive and will be back, and you know this. Have faith."

Later, in the shaded quiet of the garden, Soran tells her where he was.

"There is no meeting place for the resistance."

"You're in the resistance?"

He smiles. "Not me. No. I stay far from trouble. It shames me to say. Take care of my parents, Lailan. That is all I want to do. Simple. But I have friends."

"And they meet at bakeries?"

"Bakeries. Picnics. At a house for dinner. In a garden. Small groups. No one knows who is involved—you know only your four, five people in your group. Then one of those people, they are connected to another group. And so forth. The groups are connected, but you never know who. It is safer, if you are arrested."

The end of his sentence hangs. She does not need to ask *why*. "Ferhad thought Delan should've been back by now. I saw it on his face. This isn't normal."

He nods, accepting the direction of the conversation. "Well, yes. But nothing works the way it should. Remember too—Delan is here for Ferhad's wedding. This makes Ferhad feel responsible. Of course he is upset. Try not to worry. There is hope. The people I met with, they will help. And we wait, but the message is out."

Taking photos that afternoon is a stab at distraction. But it turns, her passion rebelling with its own anxiety.

Two boys play with a soccer ball. Their clothes are patched and dotted with stains, one brown shirt with Snoopy as the Flying Ace but with chunks of white worn away, Snoopy's existence precarious. Their ball is scuffed. Somewhat deflated. Most likely it was found, discarded by someone who had one better, and the empty lot they're in is scattered with broken slabs of concrete and thick, scraggly thistles. But the boys are in heaven. Olivia lifts her camera, wanting to capture their joy, the way they've adapted the physical obstacles into part of their game, but with one click, she realizes that in truth it's everything else that makes the photo interesting, that makes their joy stand out. It's their circumstance. Their stains and tears. Their broken field.

In her childhood, the grass was green. There were cleats and freshly laundered jerseys with silly team names and sliced oranges on the sideline. And to see the differences, to find these beautiful boys worthy of curiosity, of examination—it's the core of her chosen profession but it feels like human sightseeing. A tour of others. *Look at these poor boys, happy despite everything.* She lowers her camera. Within her, a sort of protective love for them, as well as a disgust with herself.

Now she turns, unable to watch. Everything within her a confliction. *The camera does not judge,* a professor said. *It captures. Judgment is what humans place upon the photo.* The logical side of the argument. She's halfway down the block when her own logic kicks in: to deny differences, to be afraid to look a little longer at something that is not us—what kind of insular world would that be? What kind of limited exposure would our lives be hemmed in by? And with this, she turns back. This is what she does. What she needs to be comfortable doing. And the boys, when they see her with the camera, they climb to the top of a slab of concrete and pose like Superman, small chests thrust out and hands wedged on their hips. She leaves only when she realizes she's started to cry.

Down the street from Delan's house, a fig tree is diffused with sun. A safe subject. Adjusting the focus on her camera, she tries to capture the lit-up undersides of the leaves, drawn to their texture, to the veins that seem to pulse with light. *Click.* Its base is thick and gnarled like an old man's knuckles. After what Soran has told her, she sees anything here of age as a miracle in survival, people and houses and mosques and even this tree that has no doubt seen its share of sadness.

Leaning down to shoot from below, she hears a voice and turns to see a short man with a Kurdish turban and khaki pants gesturing wildly to Soran at the front door. When she catches Soran's eye, he waves her over, but the man spots her and takes a few steps back. Quietly, Soran says something in Kurdish, and the man nods and gestures, indicating a foot above his own head as if talking about a tall man.

The message must have been received. But when she's with them, the man is already leaving, glancing at her camera, his white *klash* shoes dirtied from his travels.

"Where's he going? What just happened?"

Soran hushes her and brings her inside. "He knows where he is. He described him, had his name, told me of the scar by his eye."

"But he left."

"I need money. Bribes, transportation. Safe passage doesn't come cheap. There's a house where they've been holding people, and this man says he is there. This evening, right before curfew, I will meet this man with half the money, and tomorrow I meet him *and* Delan at the Bekhal Waterfall."

The relief is tremendous. But she stops herself—only when she sees him, *then* she will believe. But hope can be a cruel companion, and soon she's caught in the momentum of optimism, rehearsing what she'll say to him. *Lailan snores and got me with her elbow. The Kurds yell everything they say. And say everything they think. I love the raw sugar chunks with cardamom, and I know they're supposed to go in tea, but I ate one straight and I think someone scolded me and said I'd get fat. And we need to get your brother a longer hose. The one he has doesn't reach past the pomegranate tree and you need to use a pail for the rest.*

She pictures him seeing her in her dress, the look on his face. Thinks of their first hug, how he'll have to pry her arms from him. He is almost home; she can feel it.

I love you.

She will say it. Felt in some ways from the start but spoken at last.

Early evening seeps in. Soran is meeting with the man alone, so Olivia stays behind and watches images on their old black-and-white television set, the volume turned low. Lailan is there, curled into her, toes pressed against the couch's armrest. The wisps of hair by her face have curled from the day's heat, and the tops of her feet hold the tanned outline of her flip-flops, white vees like small, distant birds in flight. When Olivia adjusts herself on the couch, the girl burrows in tighter, resting her head on Olivia's thigh, her arm slung across Olivia's lap. Absentmindedly, she wiggles her tooth.

Soon Olivia forgets the TV and watches the window. The sun is dialing down, fading. It's after six o'clock. Minutes from curfew. Still, the street is empty, Soran not returned.

Gaziza as well finds the window, standing sentry at the sill. Though her prayer beads must be in another room, her hands still mime the motions, the gesture automatic and ingrained. What did Delan say would happen? Whatever the authorities want to happen. Jail at the least, and yet still the sun sinks. If this were Delan, in fact, she wouldn't worry. Delan and his rashness, his races against clocks and rules, but also his luck. Soran was right with that. But it's not Delan. It's Soran. Soran who is logic and preparation and quiet planning, and for him to be gone after curfew means something is wrong.

When the window goes black, the room suddenly skimmed upon its surface, Gaziza lets go of the wall. A nod toward the kitchen and she disappears, so Olivia takes over. One hand upon the wall, her face staring back at her, the street empty.

Then there is tap dancing on the TV, the reflection in the window a frenzy of movement. She turns to catch it and it's fast, a commercial maybe, but Lailan is up and inches from the screen, captivated, which is why a bit later, Miriam opens the door to find them both "tap-dancing" in bare feet and without music. Lailan's moves involve a lot of arm swinging and running in place, and Olivia is laughing until she sees Miriam in the threshold of the door, hand pressed against her mouth and eyes wide.

The woman's judgment comes down hard, mixing with Olivia's own shame for happiness in a moment like this. But then Miriam moves her hand, and Olivia sees that she's smiling. Is in fact watching with a sort of shocked pleasure, the kind that exists when something lost is found. It lasts but a moment, though, and then she's grabbing Lailan's hand and nodding thanks and from the front door, Olivia watches Lailan on the path, still caught in the throes of scattered dance moves, Miriam grinning beside her.

The clock ticks. The sky's gone black. From the kitchen, there are the quiet voices of Gaziza and Hewar, conferring, and with their whispered worry, Olivia thinks of the nearest soldiers, trying to remember if they'd be blocking the entrances to this street.

Then there is movement. Quick. Right outside the window. The door opens, and Soran slips inside. Within seconds, Gaziza is there, scolding him while holding his arm, as if needing a tactile verification of what's before her.

Olivia locks the door behind him.

"I took alleys," he says. "No one saw me. But there was no choice. The man, he wanted more. I had to find it. Medical care, he claimed." He sees the expression on her face as he sinks into a chair, worn. "It could mean nothing. But we are meeting him tomorrow, with Delan, he says. And Delan was asking about you. Telling people about a tall girl with dark-red hair."

With Soran's words, it's as if a cold current has swept through, because the man saw her. "Did he say my name?"

Soran shakes his head. "No. I asked. He said Delan described you and said you were waiting for him."

She sees it in his eyes, a shade of doubt that matches her own. "And you paid him?"

"How could I not? It's been days."

"Four days."

"Yes. I had to pay him, did I not?"

She's thinking of money. Of the expense of bribes and risk, how lucky that they can meet the demands but what of those who can't? "I'll pay you back. Everything. Of course we take the chance."

"No. You do not have to pay me back. That's not what I meant."

It's only after he's left the room that she realizes he just wanted an answer. A verification that he'd made the right choice, because at this moment, he doesn't know what was right or what was wrong. And with this, any assurance she had left is gone.

Morning burns orange on the horizon. Olivia's packed snacks and water in a bag that sits by her feet in the car. Day five. How can she eat if he does not? Are they giving him water? How many days can one go without water? Sometimes she finds herself thinking of his details—the disordered part in his hair, the vein at the top of his hand, a freckle behind his ear—as if the whole of him would be too great. But in fact, it's worse to see him that closely, because in those specifics is the frailty of being human. How much can he take? What is he having to endure?

"At the waterfalls," Soran says, eyes on the road, "where we are going, my mother and father were engaged."

"It wasn't arranged?"

"No. Encouraged maybe, but not arranged."

"And you, will you do an arranged marriage or marry for love?"

"There will be nothing arranged for me. Delan's fault is his reliance on fate. Mine is not being able to resist love. Love is the only thing that makes me not think. I cannot talk myself out of loving someone." He pauses, looks over his shoulder, and veers onto a road that dips on the right side, angling them toward Olivia's window. "If I am to be with someone forever, it will be because I cannot stay away. Right or wrong. There will be no choice."

"That doesn't sound like a fault. That kind of love."

"What if you should not love the person who your heart picks?"

"Right. Religion."

He glances at her. "I do not think when I love. And I do not trust myself when I am not thinking." A nod in the direction of the mountains. "There's another cave there. Bestoon Cave. Those are your undiscovered Neanderthal graves."

The morning dips to gray. As they drive to the waterfall, clouds in the sky seem to toy with becoming ominous, flirting against a white background. Soon mountain peaks flatten, becoming giant plateaus of layered rocks and jolting green grass. *The Grand Canyon of Kurdistan,* Delan had said. He should be here. His voice narrating the passing scenery. Instead there's just a whistling from a window seal that's not properly fit and now and then a clicking with a sharp turn. A car ride that feels longer than it should, both of them struck silent with hope.

When they arrive, the falls thunder even with the doors of the car closed. Water appears to emerge midmountain, bursting forth and raging past two trees that somehow grow from rocks in the midst of the chaos. "I feel like that tree," she says. Bent limbs, clinging roots, standing in a torrent. Defiant and stupid. Barely hanging on.

Beside her, Soran leans forward to peer through her window. "If that is you, then I'm the one beside you."

Outside the car, the sound booms, air wet with particles. Alongside the falls are vertical layers of rocks that jut straight up like stripes, and at the bottom the cascade widens, water like white streaks of fur on a giant splayed paw. She takes it in for a moment, searching for Delan, before they climb stairs that rise alongside the falls to a small platform with a view. Families on their way back down barely glance in their direction, but a few shake their heads and point to the sky in silent warning.

The face of Olivia's watch glistens. "We're early," she announces, but Soran, too, is scanning the thinning crowds. "What if it rains? Will he not come?"

"If that man wants money, he will be here."

There are chairs on the platform, and so they sit, from here able to see anyone arriving as well as the soldiers stationed on the road. The floor rushes with water. Each minute is a subtraction of possibility, a moment closer to something she can't even consider.

And then they see him. Just the back of his head, those loose, dark curls. She stands, waving, about to call for him, until the man turns and it's not Delan at all.

An unraveling inside her.

"Tell me about Lailan," she says. A distraction. Even thoughts of the girl are a comfort.

When Lailan was a baby, Soran tells her, her mother and father and even Lailan were taken from the mountain village where they lived, a place that harbored Peshmerga.

"The Peshmerga are in the mountains, and villagers love them," he says. "Everyone loves them. They are heroes. They protect us. But the government knows this, and they punish the villagers for helping them. There, like I said, you cannot have lights on at night or you are a target. Whole families have been taken as punishment for harboring Peshmerga. So Lailan's father was killed. Given a sulfuric acid bath, if I venture to guess. But Lailan's mother, she was kept with the other women and one day had a stroke—or that is what they thought. She slept and did not wake. Peaceful but with her baby left behind, only weeks old. Miriam was there. Miriam had just had a baby who was born into a room where the only cries came from the parents. So she didn't have her child, but she did have her milk. And there was a baby who was hungry."

Suddenly, as if pushed too far, the sky gives up, and rain starts to fall in a downpour. Quickly, Soran ushers Olivia toward an area covered with tin siding, and the furious pings against the makeshift roof battle the noise of the falls.

"Just like that," Olivia asks, "she took her? Nobody cared?"

"Who would care? The soldiers who wanted the baby to stop crying? A baby needed a mother, and a mother longed for a baby. Kurds do that. They help another's child. Shereena, you've not met her, she lives in Halabja with her husband, but her mother and my mother were very close. And her mother could not feed her, so my mother stepped in because I had just been born, and she had her milk. This storm will be fast. I can tell."

Olivia faces the trees that obscure their view. "But we can't see from here. If they came."

He confirms this with a nod. "Then I will stand there."

A spot where the roof doesn't reach. Within seconds, his shirt is soaked and his hair pushed around his face. Olivia stands as close to him as possible while staying under cover, watching as he scans the base of the falls while being pummeled with rain. Despite everything, it makes her smile. This man who loves his brother like she does. She wants to wrap her arms around him and thank him, but he'd hate it. He'd turn shy and bashful and lose his words, a thought that makes her love him even more.

"What I was saying," he continues, pushing his voice through the noise. "Shereena became what we call our *milk sister*. You cannot marry a milk sister or brother. Because you shared the same milk, you become related, even if not technical."

"Did she feel like your sister?"

"She *was* our sister. Is. As far as we are concerned. Off-limits. And beautiful too. Bad luck for us, but it's nice to have a sister." After a moment, he adds, "Family sometimes just happens."

Swiping his hair from his eyes, he leans forward. A flash of hope. Silently he watches something below, intent, and Olivia steps out into the rain, shielding her eyes with her hand.

"No, no," he yells, reaching his arm to stop her. "It's not him. Go back."

There is only the roar of the falls and the beating of the rain. Still, he watches, his neck shining with water as he swallows, drops hanging from his chin. If he were crying, she couldn't tell.

The sun, when it appears, emerges in a place that tells them the end of the day is approaching. *Five days* she'd not been able to imagine, but now there will be more. She takes it further: there's a little over a week and a half left of her trip, and with that brings the question of what she'll do if he's still not returned, an idea that makes her physically sick. How could she leave?

When finally Soran stands, there is only a faint, half-hearted glare on the water. She won't look at him, as if the lack of acknowledgment means it's not time to go.

"Olivia," he finally says.

Getting back in the car without Delan would be a defeat. Incomprehensible.

"If I thought there was a chance," he continues, "I would stay. Even with curfew."

And she knows this is true. And the fact that he is ready to go means that it's over. Delan will not come home today. So she stands, and the rushing water pushes her as she leaves.

Into the silence of the drive, Soran tells her they loved going to the cinema. His words feel loose, a string pulled from something in his mind, and the past tense bothers her—but of course he's talking about his childhood, which is in the past. Everything is fine. There was just a mix-up. Confusion. *The timing most likely was not right,* Soran told her. *It is all about timing.*

"Delan talked about the movies," she says. Films from the United States, Egypt, and India screened in his hometown. "There was a nut that people would chew—"

"*Qazwan.*"

"And people threw the shells on the ground."

He smiles. "He did tell you. Walking the aisles, everyone heard you. You did not want to move. Even to go to the bathroom, you would not. Or everyone would turn and see you."

"And the balcony seats were best. The most expensive."

"Perfect view. But under the balcony—did he tell you this?" She shakes her head, and he continues. "There were little rooms, and whole families would bring dinner. A curtain covered the rooms and opened when the movie began. So it was private. Sometimes you might meet a girl there." He smiles, embarrassed. "Girls and boys at a certain age do not go places together, as you noticed. So to meet a girl, it was in secret. And you had to leave before the movie ended, to not be caught."

I never saw the end of To Kill a Mockingbird, Delan told her. *But I saw the rest of it three times.* It hadn't made sense until now. "*To Kill a Mockingbird.* I had no idea what he meant. How it was even possible to *not* see the end of a movie three times."

Now he smiles. "Mostly we had to sit in the front. Forty *fils* for those seats because your neck hurt at the end."

"When he didn't see the end, was that the girl he rode in a tank for?"

"The tank?"

"He said he rode through a restricted area in a tank to be with someone he loved."

At first she thinks he's going to say it never happened, and she realizes there's a part of her that's been waiting for that. Denials. Reveal of embellishments. But he continues.

"No. My mother's sister, not the one you met in Baghdad, a different one, she's political. When she was arrested, my mother went to visit her. Delan did not want her to be alone. But he was teaching theater in Baghdad. The only way past the restricted area was, well, not proper."

To be with someone he loved. And she'd assumed it romantic—but it was his mother.

Then there is another question within her, and though she doesn't even want to form the words, she forces them out. "Have they given him that bath? The sulfuric acid?"

He doesn't look surprised. It's not a shocking question, not out of the realm of possibility. "No. They would not have done that. He is better for them alive."

"You promise?"

Now he turns to her, just for a second. "I would feel it if he were gone."

And she believes him. Because she would feel it as well. A magnetic tug or a slow, dangerous drag in her heart.

The next morning, Lailan and Olivia are in the garden, shredding fallen bark into thin strips for a project of whose details Olivia isn't certain. Soran talked to friends and learned that a man had come around asking about Delan, wanting to see a photo of him. He tells her this as she stands in the sun.

"It was the man who came to me," he says. "Delan's friends, they thought they were helping, showing him a photograph. But what they did was provide him with what Delan looks like. The man was a

197

swindler," he adds, and despite the situation, Olivia smiles, softened by the old-fashioned word that carries with it only a fraction of the evil it should.

Day six. A bludgeoning tally within her. There is no denying it. This is not normal. Choices may have to be made. Would she leave without him? She would have to. To go home and get the State Department involved. To gather his friends to action. To do something.

Soran snaps a baseball-size purple allium from its stalk. He touches Lailan on her shoulder to get her attention, presents the flower to her, and at once her eyes go to the plants behind him, to the one that's now missing its flower. Her face collapses, lips quivering. Olivia stands too quickly, and the world tilts. Head down, she takes a moment before going to the girl but still feels off, strangely slow, as if she's lifting her legs against an increasing gravity. Already Soran is kneeling and has his arms wrapped around Lailan, talking in a soft voice.

"What happened?" Olivia asks.

"I did not know what you were doing. And I took it from the plant."

Their project. The materials they've collected: bark that was already off the trees, leaves that had fallen, twigs that had blown free from branches. An unspoken rule, it appears, was that their collections involved only what had already been cast off, just the discarded bits of the world.

Lailan points to her chest and says slowly, "I hate heart."

Olivia starts to shake her head but stops when a pain sets in. "Why would you hate your heart?"

"This heart too big."

Everything feels faint, smudged out. That saying, that was Olivia, wasn't it? The day of the picnic. She'd told Lailan she had a big heart when she'd helped something. A caterpillar.

Olivia picks her up, and the girl hooks her legs around her waist. "Your heart is perfect. You're sad for the flower, for the plant?"

Lailan nods into her shoulder, and Olivia tries to think of what to say, her head heavy, while Soran talks and pats Lailan's hand, speaking in a soft, reassuring voice. After a while, the girl's breathing evens and she lifts her head from Olivia's shoulder, peering toward the empty stalk, the tall stem that reaches into nothing.

"Soran," Olivia says, suddenly thirsty, but conjuring a plan as well. "Could you get a few cups of water?"

The brown of soil. Gray from crushed granite. Purple of a hollyhock bloom that had broken, dried and dangling. In the cups, she adds the water and stirs, then brushes the color onto a piece of paper. Watercolors in their true sense. Lailan loves it and searches the yard for more material for new colors. Of course by the next day, this paper with its painted mountains and flowers will be faded or blank, with rises and dips where once the water sat. But it doesn't matter. Everything is for this moment.

A plate of snacks on the bench. Dried apricots and naan bread. Olivia has no appetite but moves with Lailan to a spot on the ground under the pomegranate tree, placing the artwork in the sun. "Yellow," Olivia says, pointing to the sun on the page. But it's not yellow; it's more orange. Or is it? Language, vision, everything seems a trick. The sun is blazing, her back hot.

When Lailan looks up, she looks above Olivia's shoulder and again collapses into tears.

"Lailan. The plant is okay. I promise."

But then Lailan raises her arms, her cue to be lifted, and so Olivia turns, figuring Soran is there, and shades her eyes with her hand as she looks up.

Delan. Standing, watching her even as he lifts the girl into his arms. He's in the clothes he wore at the picnic, though everything is darker, and there are tears in his shirt and rips at his knees. At last she stands with shaky legs, disbelief and relief and a rush of love bottle-jamming inside her, stamping down words. The sun flashes. He adjusts Lailan so she's on his hip and reaches for Olivia with his other arm, drawing her in. Then somehow he's setting the girl down and has both his arms wrapped around Olivia. They stand there. Her fingers pressed into the flesh of his back, her mouth at the base of his neck. And it's then she realizes that her throat hurts, as if her body has wanted to get sick this entire time but knew it needed him first. As they hold each other, her cheeks burn in the sun.

The fever fills her. Fast and heavy till she's lost and weighted inside herself, tucked in under covers she kicks off and pulls back on. A few times she gets up, trailing her hand along the wall as she walks. Delan and his family are in the kitchen, and the sight of food makes her sit in the corner with her knees up and her face in the crook of her arm. She watches them from over her elbow, not wanting to be alone and wanting to keep an eye on Delan, needing the proof that he's returned, because now and then, she doesn't trust herself. Then Delan and Soran help her back to her room, and Gaziza appears with cold washcloths for her forehead, abdomen, and feet.

It is assumed his release had to do with Aras. Someone Aras must have known, someone high up and with questionable government loyalty who'd made paperwork appear. That's all he says, and it's a hesitant speculation. "I'm back," he adds, and it's the final word and all that truly matters. But soon, he is not there, and Gaziza is the one with her, making her swallow aspirin, bringing tomato broth and trying to get her to eat yogurt or drink tea with honey. She cuts meatballs and brings them to Olivia's lips, and Olivia chews obediently, not wanting to eat but wanting to be good. She cannot remember the last time a mother fed her. She watches her, this woman. Sturdy and full. Black hair pulled back in a scarf. Just her presence makes Olivia know everything will be okay because a mother like this would not have it any other way.

Soran lingers in the threshold of the door. When she sees him, the fever erases Delan's return, and she asks when he's coming back, where he is. There is a panic in her question that narrows Soran's face in confusion, until he understands.

"He is here. In bed." He motions down the hall.

"Sick?" she asks when she's fit the pieces back together. Now she feels him there, his presence a murky light.

Soran tilts his head to the side, as if *sick* could be loosely interpreted, and says only, "Recovering. But he needs time. Like you. Your fever will break. You will both be downstairs soon."

Her eyes feel cold against the burning of her skin, and it feels good to have them shut, so even when not asleep, she sees only the bright orange of her closed lids. Soran sits beside her and tells her stories, weaving Kurdish history into her dreams. At one point, she wakes to him listing cultures that have disappeared. Akkadians, Phrygians, Hittites, Lydians, Babylonians. A parade of extinction. A lineup of loss. She feels them under this house, deep in the earth below. "Isolation helped the Kurds survive," he tells her, and in her mind, she sees mountains and clouds and below them, swarms of people with swords tearing down statues with ropes and dragging them off with elephants. "In Turkey," he tells her, "the Kurds were in Anatolia for twenty centuries before the Turks showed up. Twenty centuries. But the Turkish government calls them *Mountain Turks who have lost their way.*"

The *goranibezh*, she thinks. This is him. A Kurdish storyteller. Reciting history at her sickbed. She opens her eyes just enough to see his folded hands resting on his knee.

His voice goes deep as he says that Vice President Saddam Hussein, *that gangster from Tikrit*, will end up president and everything will be worse. Worse than before, when they bombed anything that moved in daylight and rounded up entire families like sheep into trucks. He clears his throat when he tells her that Kurds do not tell bad news to someone who is not with their family. "It is a kindness to lie until family can be there to help. My mother did not know her own brother was dead. For three months, she did not know."

Lailan in the hall. Olivia sees her through the threshold, lying on her back on the floor as if forbidden from getting closer, a pillow beneath her head and her doll in hand. She lifts the doll above her, twisting it as if it's flying. Olivia watches the doll's hair trail in a lazy arc, blonde and long like corn silk.

105.1. Soran is back and says this number as if it should mean something to her. "We cannot take you to the hospital," he says. "You would only get worse." The thermometer is then in a strange man's hand, someone who's appeared with a suit and a checked shirt that also has a pen wedged in its pocket, and she sees the meaning of those numbers like a shadow, here one second and gone the next.

"It's almost over," the man says.

"What?" she asks him. Or she thinks she asks him. "What's almost over?"

But then the man is gone, and Soran is in the chair. Through the open window, she hears the calls of the chukar birds outside, laughing in the face of her inquiry.

Nomads and goats whose milk becomes cheese and is sold all over the region. A citadel that is more than six thousand years old. Chewing the gum from trees. The special dish they make called *Saro Pè*, which Soran tells her means *head and legs*. Working construction on dams for foreign companies. "In one day, I made fifteen to twenty dinar. A teacher only made forty a month." She catches him looking down the hall, toward Delan's room, and realizes even through her fog of sick that Soran needs to be in here with her as much as she needs him. "Keep going, please," she says, because now she needs his voice to remind her she is here and not alone, and so he continues, telling her about women who circle around piles of yellow grapes, turning them to raisins.

Then it's Delan who is there, right next to her, the chair dragged against the bed, a window open to the sound of rain, heavy drops hitting leaves.

"There was a man," he says. "He had one arm. Born with one arm. Horrible already, his story, to be born with one arm. And they hung him by that arm. Till he told them what they wanted to hear, till he gave them information. But he must have not known what they wanted, because that arm came out."

A man who lost his tongue, the tongue shown to others. Ears cut from heads. She listens to him talk and is not sure what she's hearing. A confession or a delusion. Her eyes are closed. He must think she's asleep. Images dart in her mind, visions of taffeta and birds on wires and beautiful blonde hair and blood that runs pink in the rain. Maybe she is asleep. At times his voice does not sound like his, just quiet, hypnotic murmurings. Maybe none of it is real.

And you, Liv. I thought of you. All that you should have and none of it is this. Selfish. I was selfish to think it could be me. Liv, I don't have my toenails. They took my toenails. And the screams began to sound like silence.

The fever breaks with a pummel. Punishing and then gone. When she returns to herself, he is there, in a chair by the window. The curls of his hair knotted in the light. He tells her she was very sick for four days.

"Only four days?"

"You wanted more?"

"It seemed a lifetime. But I should be taking care of you," she adds, though now she is unsure of what was real. She doesn't know how to ask him and only looks to his feet. He's wearing socks, when usually he does not.

"No. No. You're the one who almost died," he says, standing. "A sheep. Lailan says you petted a sheep. The doctor said that might have been it—they're not clean. You and your love of animals. I should've warned you. And Lailan, speaking of her, she's glued flat pebbles to her shoes to try and tap dance. She's going to hurt herself, and she's loud. But me, I'm fine."

And though she lets him say it, she sees the way his hand holds the back of the chair, as if letting go is a risk he cannot take.

The wind in the trees sounds like the ocean, and blossoms tear from branches, petals on the path like confetti. Later that morning, they walk in the garden, and she finds herself saying "mmm" in reaction to anything, as if even small ideas have taste. There is a distance between them. Something has changed. Of course what he went through would change a person, there is no doubt, and she wants to lash the stupid girl within her for expecting anything different, for being impatient, for being hopeful that him returned was all that mattered and wanting nothing more than to wrap her arms around him and stand in the sun.

Normal, she tells herself. It's normal for him to be different—as much as anything can be normal with what just happened. But in her mind, there is also a stirring of his quiet murmuring at her bedside and a pull of something that had to do with her. Just the thought brings back the feeling of being sick. A weighted, sludgy feeling. And so she fills her mind with other things. The wedding the next day. Her dress that Soran picked up for her when she was sick. His father, who claims the pigeon is healed and ready to be let go.

"I got a dress," she says. A stupid thing to say. She's never been at a loss for words with him, and she's never cared for dresses, but there is a vacancy inside that part that used to know how to be with him. In the distance, a flock of birds makes a vee that folds and reorganizes in a turn.

"I heard," he says. "And I hear it's beautiful."

"Do you still want to go?"

He glances at her, confused. "Sure. It's why we're here."

Please be okay, she thinks.

I love you.

But she says nothing, holding the words inside as if clenched within a fist, because *I love you* should not be said to someone as a means to keep them going or as reward for how far they've come, and if she says them now, she worries that's how they'll be heard. As incentive. Or apology. So she stays silent and steps to him, about to link her arm in his, but he moves away from her. Just slightly, his arm straightens at his side. The move, though barely perceivable, hits her, and she must watch the path as she walks. *So this is what it is.*

"You had a lot of time with my brother," he says, moving a rock off the path with his foot.

"Not like that. Is that what you're saying?"

"I don't know what I'm saying."

"Well, don't."

They fall to silence. Walking the garden, separate and fragile. Straightening plants, patting back soil that's been dug up from animals, finding ways to occupy their hands and give their minds direction. The air is clean but surprisingly hot, rushed and rain-chased from a storm she'd not known had hit them. At the window, she catches Hewar watching them, then quickly lifting his binoculars to the trees.

"Your dad is spying on us." When she turns, she sees Delan was watching her as well, and she realizes that they are observing one another, searching for injury.

Again, he shrugs. "We're two ghosts walking in a garden. He's watching to make sure we don't disappear."

"You don't have to talk about it. If you don't want."

"I won't. I haven't. I never told you why I don't go into the basement at home, did I?"

"I thought spiders. Ghosts."

He looks at her, and a corner of his mouth raises. One of his first smiles. A half smile that slowly becomes full. "You thought spiders? You didn't."

"Or ghosts. I said ghosts too."

"No," he says. "No. Basements are where people are tortured."

She flinches at the word, which was unexpected yet expected all at once.

"At some point," he continues, smile gone, "everyone, I think, has been tortured. Even just a little." With his fingers, he indicates *a little*, a measurement like half an inch. Then he motions next door. "Ask Miriam what she went through. No, don't. It doesn't matter. I'm here."

She thinks of the man with one arm and wonders if she imagined it. Fever-wrought inventions. Delirium in its true sense. Testing, she says, "Not everyone made it."

"No," he says, but then his step falters, and she thinks he's about to say more, to at last let the words out, but he's looking to their house.

By the back door is a man in a Kurdish turban with a Brno Rifle. And above, in the open window of her room, another man with a rifle trained toward the garden. Olivia's reaching for Delan, for his arm, when she spots someone else walking toward them with black curls that dip past his turban in a widow's peak and a gold watch that catches the light in a moment of shock. His arms are open, and he is smiling.

And Delan, beside her, begins to cry.

She steps away. Goes to the side of the house where Gaziza has opened the door for her but is also watching her son. There is an embrace of the long-lost, of the rarely-seens. Olivia knows who this is—the man who need only glance at Delan's scars to remember the blood—and she knows that this is who he needs right now. His best friend. And at this moment, she is not that person.

CHAPTER 10

The day grew hot. Delan spent the rest of the afternoon with Aras, drinking tea, eating, laughing, even, giving him the gift he'd brought and then huddling close, whispering in a fading light. Olivia gave them space and only went back outside long enough to meet him. The lines on Aras's face looked deeper than they should be for someone Delan's age, etched with a heavier kind of time, but his eyes were rich and brown and took her in as someone he'd expected to meet, which was the smallest, thinnest thread of comfort.

That evening, Delan seems lightened. A pain shared, perhaps. Understood. He jokes with Soran, whose car is parked outside under what looks like a desert of dust and a mountain of bird droppings. He helps in the kitchen, slicing cucumbers and adding more seasoning to the meat when his mother's not looking, then holds the cage when his father lets the pigeon go, his face tilted toward the sky as the bird turns on a current. Still, there's a distance Olivia feels with him. A space of uncertainty. When he looks in her direction, he won't meet her eye.

After dinner, he quietly takes her aside.

"Was it him?" she asks, and he looks confused. "Was it Aras who got you out?"

"No. He said he didn't know, that the second he found out, he came. But he told me to put the books in the ground. Now. The books we have that are—"

"Something's going to happen." A raid. Soldiers pounding on the door.

"He said to be safe. For all I know, nothing will happen. But we listen to him, of course."

In the living room, Soran had showed her, there are certain shelves that would need to be emptied, all the books clustered together to allow for fast armfuls of the prohibited. And the portrait of Barzani. *Him especially,* he said. *A dead giveaway we're Kurds.* Olivia nods, anxious to get it done. "Let's go."

"No, no. Wait till everyone's asleep so no one panics. I don't have answers, so I don't want questions."

Through the window, she watches the walls of Lailan's bedroom. "But—we don't tell Miriam? Anyone else?"

"Tell them what? I don't know anything. If I tell them to put the books in the ground, there will be panic, and it will spread. Someone, he said, in my family is an informant. He doesn't know who, but it got to him."

"But you said no one in your family would do that."

The anger is swift and focused. "*Because they shouldn't.* But the *mokhabarat,* they want names, information. People tell them anything to make it stop. I was lucky when I got out. They threaten anything, anyone someone loves to get them to spy. To turn. What if I lived here? If I had a family and nowhere else to go? Would I throw someone innocent aside to save my parents? My children? You?"

There is, for a moment, a surge of hope completely out of line with their talk. Relief from the word *you,* from being included as someone he would still try to save. Maybe nothing is over. Maybe he was taken and in some ways just needs to come back.

But now he's waiting, and she's trying to decide what the right answer would be when she understands it doesn't exist. *You cannot make a perfect choice here.* What he'd said when they arrived. But then she thinks of him taken and knows her choice, as flawed as it might be.

"I would," she says. "I would lie, even if that makes me horrible. I would save you."

In his eyes, she sees the same resolution.

"So you know," he says, affirming. "The threat is real. Keep Lailan close. Tomorrow I'll find a way to tell Miriam."

The night is hot and the power off more than on, fans rendered useless. Because of this, they will all sleep on the roof. Delan tells her he'll put the books in the ground himself so no one catches them disappearing together.

Outside, the air is still, and an overlay of Kurdish rugs on the roof lends a rustic refinement. Oil lamps and mattresses with thin sheets. A breeze that catches with the sweet of oleander. Across the street, another family shakes out their bedding before they sit, disappearing from view.

Olivia's wearing her red sweatpants and T-shirt, lying on top of the covers. Truthfully, everything is beautiful, even with the heat, and so she tries to feel the night as a sort of festivity, a slumber party with a family gathered under the open sky—but every sound bangs like a fist on a door, and every dog barks a warning. Not feeling the threat, it doesn't take long for the lights to be turned down and Delan's family to fall asleep. Next to her, Gaziza turns onto her shoulder, a pillow beneath her head and her arm outstretched, palm open to a sky that looks like braille, like something that could be understood. On the floor by Olivia's bed, a glass of water holds the moon in a polished glare.

All day she wanted to touch Delan's hair. To run her fingers over his wrist or lean into him and tuck herself under his arm. Anything. And though there were moments of promise, the rest was marked with distance. Emotional and physical. Have they even touched? Once? She reminds herself that after what he went through, he's allowed. Let him be. All that matters is that he's home.

Now he sits across the roof. Leaned against the low wall, watching her, a glass of wine in his hand. With the shadows, she can't tell if he can see her face, if he sees that she's watching him in return, so she openly stares, willing him to come to her, to talk to her, to let her help. For a while, he doesn't look away, and neither does she. The rest of the roof falls from her vision so it's just him, until at last he tilts his head back and faces the moon. With that, she closes her eyes, trying to think of work, of the photographs she's taken, wondering if anything is good enough.

When the roof creaks, she wakes to see him at the door that leads to the stairs. Quietly she follows, finding him at the bookshelf. With a shake of his head, he motions to gather a certain stack, which she carries to the garden. Arms aching, bare feet warm on the still sun-soaked path. There, in the distance, is the mark on the wall, the place where a hand had been chiseled. Drawing closer, the air thickens with the powerful, apricot-like scent of oleander, that dangerous sweet. Everything around her is motionless. The garden still and patient, as if part of a peaceful time that's slipped from between the pages of chaos.

She's just opened the trapdoor when Delan appears with his stack of books. He pauses upon seeing her and then is by her side, his shoulder touching hers. She wants to freeze the moment. To simply sit beside him, the closest they've been. Olive oil and laurel oil soap, sandalwood and oleander. She breathes in, trying to plant the scent within her.

"You knew where it was," he says quietly.

"When you were away, I was out here a lot." She places the books inside. "It helped me not think, to do work. I couldn't think, or—" She stops and glances at him. "I know it's nothing compared to what you went through. But I wasn't okay. When you were gone. Because you were gone."

He watches her, and she thinks he's going to tell her something, anything, but instead he nods. "There's another stack, maybe two. Next to the radio."

There are no lights on in the house, and as she starts back on the path, she catches the garden's reflection in the windows. Faint, like an echo.

"Olivia," he says. "I lied."

When she turns, he's still kneeling on the ground, looking down at the books. But he must feel her there, a shift in the air with her return to him.

"About the code," he adds and stands, brushing his hands on his pants legs. Studying the indents of rocks left on his palms, he continues. "My mother. When I called her to say we might come, I think she said not to."

Her heart speeds up, even with the edge of meaning. "You think."

Now he looks up at her. "I know. She was saying not to come."

Their night in Baghdad. *Would you blame her? If she let us come when it wasn't safe?* That look, how concerned he was—it wasn't his mother he worried would be blamed. It was him. Everything's falling into line. His doubt in Geneva. Wanting to send her home when they were in Baghdad. The surprise on his parents' faces. His fight with Soran their first night here.

"That's why they didn't know we were coming," she says. "It wasn't because the phones were tapped and you couldn't say. It was because they said not to come."

He gazes past her, toward the roof. "The phones are tapped. That's true. But what I *believed* was that it was okay. That they didn't see the reason to spend money on a trip. Always she wants me to save, so that was why, I thought—nothing to do with safety. She was being a mother. Telling me over and over again not to spend the money."

Olivia's words are slow. "Could *that* have been her way of saying it wasn't safe? To not come?"

At first he doesn't answer, just continues to watch the roof. Then he nods. "I realized that later. I don't know. Maybe part of me knew then." The last part spoken almost to himself, an admission he hasn't fully accepted or understood. When he finally faces her, he's resigned. "But I see it now. It wasn't just you I lied to. I told myself it was fine. Because if it wasn't—how could I think that? How could I value myself more than them? Why should they be here and I be too good and stay away?"

She says nothing, and in the silence, he takes a step toward her. Beyond him, a palm tree's lower fronds hang broken in the night. "But it wasn't just you."

At this, he stops. "I know. You're my regret. That I took you here. When I was gone, all I could think of was what I'd done. Even now, I look at you and it's there. That day. The restaurant. What you went through that you will never get over. Because of me."

The picnic. The fight they'd had prior. She'd thought he was callous—but he was angry, with himself. Not just that she was still lost in what had happened but that there'd been an event in the first place. "That wasn't your fault. And I wanted to come. It was my idea. I convinced you to go—and wouldn't let you turn around."

"But *I* should've known. I know better. Even if it is safe, you can't predict. One day to the next—nothing is sure. But it felt like fate. You and me and the wedding, and I wanted it so much, I didn't think."

He swallows, hard, and looks up at the stars. At first she thinks it's guilt that averts his eyes, but then she sees the wetness on his cheek.

"Do you know," he asks but stops. His voice, meant for the stage, for convincing, for reaching last rows and even the unimaginative, has suddenly gone small. "It sounds horrible to say. Stupid. But you told me I didn't want to feel and no, don't apologize, because it's true. But it's because of this: I will love everything too much if I allow it. Everything." He swipes at his face and turns to her. "A tree, Liv. A *tree*. A stream of water. I look at it and it's perfect. How could it be more perfect? And people. How sad and scared they are. All of them. And I've seen how it ends. Even a tree."

She places her hand on his arm, the spot where the fabric of his sleeve meets his skin. "None of that is stupid."

"You were right, though. About not doing enough."

"Delan, I did *not* mean you didn't do enough. Only that you feel that way."

"And I do. I do feel that way. I didn't realize it, though. Not when you said it. So I hit back. What I said to you, though, that I didn't believe—not even then. You were right to tell me what you did. And I will do more. I decided. I will put it in my art. The poems, Liv. The epic poems, I thought of them while I was away. I'm going to find a way to put them onstage."

Now she touches the scar by his eye, bright with water. "I love that."

"I knew you would. I kept seeing it in my mind while I was gone—not the show but my telling you." A pause, and once again he studies her. "I just need you to know that never would I take you somewhere I knew was dangerous. Because what might happen, Liv. Even I don't know. A raid, it could be soldiers looking at papers, searching a living room, a basement, looking for someone. But it could be more."

More. They're at a precipice. The edge of something. Something that could simply be one step down or might be miles. She realizes she's sweating. In this night heat, with the constriction of meaning and possibility. Because now they're preparing for something that at best won't occur and at worst she can't fathom. And yet, almost irrationally, all she feels is relief. Simply for having pushed through what kept them apart.

"You should talk to Lailan," she says. "You two are alike. She wants to trade in her heart for being too big."

He smiles. "I knew it. The girl is an actor." After a moment, he wraps his arms around Olivia, his chin on her shoulder. "I don't know anything in life but that you deserve better. Like I said. You always have."

The dress shines. The woman was right—the olive color looks good with her hair, the two colors like poppies she'd seen in the mountains, green and red in a disappearing sun. Then she sees it. A difference in her face. She leans in. Older, maybe. Suddenly. The only makeup she brought is red lipstick, and with slightly unsteady hands, she twists the gold tube and dabs it on. A brightening. She looks more alive and then realizes that might have been it—she looked sapped. Drained from all that's happened. For a second, she sees herself as she used to be, the young woman with the tall boots and the short suede skirt. The one looking out the window, waiting for the party to start or waiting to go out, always waiting. Then she backs up and sees her dress and the long wings of her sleeves and knows she is no longer that person. She moves her arms, and the fabric sparks in the light. Under the copper of her pendant, the green jasper seems eager, emboldened by the green of her dress.

Downstairs, Soran and Hewar see her and both take to shyness, Soran saying something quietly that sounds like "incredible." Gaziza, leaving the kitchen, sees her and hurries to tie her sleeves, then studies her eyes as if mentally lining them with kohl.

"He's in the garden," Soran says, catching her peering into the kitchen.

Outside, Delan is moving potted plants on top of the trapdoor.

"It looks fine," she says, "don't worry."

"It's not fine," he says as he turns, then straightens. He blinks against the sun.

There's no smile, but his mouth opens. He looks surprised. Unnerved. "You're making me worry," she says. "Is it not right?"

"Olivia," he says, and her full name is again formed with his true accent, his true voice. "No one, ever, ever has looked so beautiful."

She gives a small, disbelieving laugh. "Then why that look?"

He takes her hand and studies her palm, the base of her thumb, before again closing his eyes. "Because I saw you exactly like this, in a dream when I was away."

His dreams. She wants to laugh but can't, because she remembers her restless nights and her father's long-ago words, *When you can't sleep, it's because you're awake in somebody's dream.*

"But I don't remember it," he says. "What does it mean that I just remember you?"

"That I'm all that matters?" A small smile.

He brings her hand to his lips, their eyes locked until she catches a glimpse of something next door and looks up to see Lailan in the window, mouth open. Delan, spotting her as well, blows the girl a kiss, and Lailan blows one back before ducking from the window.

"I told Miriam," he says.

"Good, thank you."

"For all I know, nothing will happen, and now she's worried. Don't thank me."

"Better to be worried and ready."

"Is it? Sometimes I think it's better to just never see it coming. Why end on a worry?"

The sounds: hollering, singing, music playing. Even the women are like bright chimes when they walk, gold adornments jingling. Throughout it all, the groom's family waits with horses for the bride, who eventually arrives in a bold red dress and a red veil edged in gold, walking behind a man who carries a giant mirror bright with her reflection. After a lifetime of weddings in white ordered silence, the day is a beautiful shock.

Sugar cones are rubbed together. Henna painted on the bride's hands. Swords get tucked into the men's waistbands while the women shine. Ferhad still has his arm in a sling and clumsily guides his horse, unable to take his eyes off his bride, so entranced that he lets the horse tromp through a bed of purple irises. An older woman with a sunken face and dots of tattoos below her chin shoos him off before bending to straighten the stalks.

Delan didn't exaggerate. There are four kinds of rice at the reception, which is a picnic in an open, grassy meadow edged with trees and a creek on one side and an orchard of pomegranate trees on the other. Behind it all, the mountains loom like solemn guests, rugged and protective, and when a man with a long wooden flute stands upon a ledge and begins to play, Olivia closes her eyes and the ancient world wraps around her, a conjuring by the spectral sound. "Ney flute," Delan whispers in her ear, right as the low notes soar high.

Rows of food in giant aluminum bowls. Layered rugs. Samovars that shine, polished and steaming. Songs indeed last for twenty minutes, with everyone dancing in a line that winds its way through the field, arms linked and feet moving in step. Drifts of clouds, even, seem stirred to movement. Nothing is unaffected by the celebration.

Delan dances with his family and friends, his shoulders lifting and dipping with each step, and yet still, with all the beauty and music, Olivia hears the words as if the warning's caught on a breeze: *Put the books in the ground.* Even the fact that he saw her like this in a dream has stuck with her, a whisper of fear. Still, she tries to shove past it by taking photos, by feeling the warmth and the ease of those around her. Nothing might happen, the alarm sounded just to be safe. Someone offers her tea, with a date placed alongside the cup, and as she tastes the two together, she tells herself that's all it was, just a little caution. Just in case.

Lailan, in a pink dress and silver-sequined vest, must glimpse the worry on Olivia's face because she pats her hand and says a phrase she's heard Olivia say many times: "It's okay." Over and over, she repeats this, like a mother soothing her child, convincing there's no hurt, until Olivia laughs and nods and agrees that yes, everything *is* okay, and then wipes powdered sugar off the girl's chin. Lailan lets her do this and licks her lips in case any was left behind. Mouth wide, she then presses on her tooth to show how loose it is.

"Soon," Olivia says. "A day, maybe less." Off to the side, there are men with *dafs*, handheld frame drums with metal ringlets that sound at once like thunder and rain, and *temburs*, lutes that seem to pluck ancient notes.

"You need to dance," Soran tells Olivia when he breaks from the circle and finds her sitting. Breathless, he reaches for her hand.

The next thing she knows, she's wedged between Soran and Delan, though mostly the men dance with the men and the women with the women. Still, as she's noticed, there are allowances for her, the foreigner, and though her shoulders move like the others, her feet are helplessly out of step. She laughs, flustered and amazed at how hard it is. *Kick, kick, knee lift, back, forward, turn to the side, kick, kick, knee lift.* The steps are too fast. Lailan, even—left in their charge so Miriam could take care of things at the house—has worked her way into the line, a fast-moving sparkle who dances in between two women. The woman to her right prods her with the steps till she gets it, then nods, back to singing and smiling in the sun.

"Watch me," Delan says to Olivia, and so she does, keeping an eye on his white *klash* shoes as she feels his hand in hers, the way he indicates what to do with a slight pull on her wrist.

Though she gets only a few steps right, she soon no longer cares because even her haphazard dancing takes her mind off any sad promises, and the gleam of the sequins on the dresses and the feel of the taffeta and sun combine with the fact that an entire field is dancing, the flute bright and the colors dazzling and the people happy, scarves at either end waved in the air like punctuations to their revelry. And there are only four days left of her trip, and the man she loves is holding her hand. They are laughing, their shoulders rising and falling and rising again.

It's only at the end of the day that they hear the news, and it is relayed with joy: a road dynamited by the Kurds to prevent the military from getting through. Sabotage. A minor strike against the major player. Some of the younger men celebrate quietly, while others wander off in small groups, talking among themselves. Delan takes Olivia's hand and leads her to an oak tree alongside the creek, the boughs gnarled and bent, the leaves longer, lighter in color than the oaks back home.

"Is that what Aras warned against?" she asks. Delan stands before her, her back against a thick, low branch. "The road?"

"Retaliation," he says. "If I had to guess. We're the closest town. Nothing might happen, but they could use it as an excuse."

"You think someone here did it?"

"There are two things. One, they want to find who did it. Two, they want to kill Kurds, for any reason. You see how both points work? How one is not needed for the other? All we can do is be ready. He gave us that, so even if they're waiting for us at home, we're ready."

Even if they're waiting for us at home.

"They wouldn't be, though, would they?"

He smiles. And traces her cheekbone with his hand. "No. All will be fine."

But she sees it in the way he's touching her face, the way he studies her, that he's looking with the eyes of someone who sees possibilities. She turns toward the water, watching it trick itself around rocks. "The last wedding I went to, everyone worried the groom's father would drink too much and hit on his ex-wife. And then we became bored because that didn't happen. It was a little different."

"But just as real."

She laughs. "Was it?"

"It happened, did it not? If you live in a room that is dark, you see a ray of light the same way someone else might see a spotlight. Everything is real. Everything is felt. That is perspective. But," he says, glancing back toward his family, "there is no denying luck. That you were born where you were. That you can choose. That you have the privilege of being bored. And do not have to leave your family. Or save your family."

"What if I can't make up for that?"

"Who says you have to? Sometimes living is all you have to do. Besides, you'd be surprised how you can save someone."

He gives her a light kiss, just a brush. Then, from his pocket, takes out a napkin folded around two cookies shaped like crescents and holds one to her lips.

Cardamom, a spice she's up till this trip associated only with holidays, dissolves on her tongue. "I taste Christmas."

"You love Christmas."

"What's not to love?"

"This Christmas, we'll get an eight-foot tree. A live one we can plant later." He watches her break more cookie with her teeth and then slowly, softly kisses the crumbs from her lips. After a moment, he says, "I almost didn't go into that café. The place with the pie."

She wants him to kiss her again, and it takes her a second to loop his words with meaning. "When we first met?"

He nods. "I saw you. Before you talked to the dog. And I knew it was you."

"But you were *supposed* to meet me. Why wouldn't you go in if you knew it was me?"

"No," he says, studying her as he speaks. "I knew it was *you*. You. The person I was supposed to be with. Forever."

Forever. A certainty he'd had from the start. "So you wanted to stay away?"

"I knew what it meant. I felt my whole life right then. Everything changed." He takes an orange from his other pocket and digs his thumb into the rind. A fragrant mist lifts into the sunlight.

"So all this time"—she smiles—"*you've* been the romantic."

Juice courses down his wrist as he tears the orange into rough sections. Gently, he places a slice in her mouth. A burst of California and home and their life together that is so hard to comprehend at this moment but that she's beginning to believe was fated from the start. And then it's as if something is coiled within her, and suddenly she is all urge and takes his arm and runs her tongue along his skin. Orange, salt, dirt. She eyes him as she pauses at the base of his thumb and sees him smiling, enthralled.

"Keep going," he says. "Please. But if they see us, it will be our wedding."

She smiles. "That's right. We're engaged, aren't we?"

"He told you. I knew he couldn't resist. I should've even said we were married because none of this is proper, but I want that to be real. When that happens," he adds.

In the field, she catches a flash of silver: the bride's sisters and friends are dancing with knives. "They're dancing with knives."

He turns. "They're about to cut the cake. That's to let him know they can handle knives. That he should be good to their sister. That they will protect her."

"A warning."

"Kurds aren't known for being subtle."

When he leans in for a kiss, she stops thinking. There's just the creek in the background, a sound that shimmers like a celebration, and him.

At Miriam's front step, a bird calls in the falling evening. The street is empty, everyone tucked in for curfew, and the moon is heavy, resting on the bough of a fig tree. The party will continue tomorrow, Olivia's told. A celebration that will last for days. *We can go,* Delan said, *or we could stay behind and do other things in an empty house.* A wink.

While Delan knocks on the door, Lailan is asleep against his brother's shoulder. Already their parents have gone to their own house, and lamps flick on, the bright quiver of television on a wall. Discreetly,

Olivia leans in to kiss Delan, and Soran shifts his weight and smiles to the door, pretending not to notice.

At last, Miriam is there. Soran turns to show her Lailan's face, that she's asleep, and as he does, the light from the street falls just so, and Miriam stops in her tracks. Her eyes take in her daughter, whose energy is at last spent, whose face is all ease and glow and who's fallen into that delicate, unguarded sleep of a child. There is an echo of roundness in Lailan's cheeks, a last vestige of infancy, and with one hand, Miriam reaches out to feel the soft curve, gazing with the awed amazement of a parent who is taken aback now and then by the wonder of their child. By the time Miriam reaches for the girl, Olivia's lifted her camera from around her neck and is ready. The woman holds her daughter against her chest, her thick hand against the back of the girl's head, and closes her eyes briefly, in prayer or thanks or maybe just simple happiness. Even as she takes the photo, Olivia knows the composition is off, but it doesn't matter. All she wants is the look on Miriam's face, her plain and ferocious love.

Back at the house, they watch a TV show that makes no sense to Olivia but is a comfort all the same and then find their ways to their rooms, the night cool enough to be back inside. Olivia undresses and puts on her white nightgown, the one Delan nicknamed her *Little House on the Prairie* nightgown, then stands at her window, facing the garden. The tops of leaves hold the sky's sheen and again she thinks of his confession, that he'd always known, and then thinks of his kisses of cardamom and orange and the vow of tomorrow with the empty house.

He's mere feet away. There's a charge at her back with the thought, and so she goes to her door, quietly turning the knob and peering into the hall. There he is. Standing in the threshold of his own room, still dressed, smiling. With a finger to his lips, he motions for her to come to him so they're farthest from his parents' room, and right as she takes a step, a plane thunders overhead.

She freezes. Delan, even, looks up.

But it's night. She remembers the security of the dark hours, the time Soran had said people were safe, but then remembers that the mountain villages are still bombed at night. But they're not a mountain village and they're not a target. Unless this is what Aras warned about. Without moving, she watches the ceiling until the sound fades. Another step, then another. Delan leans against the doorframe, watching her. Then he's closing his door behind her.

In his room, she spots herself in his dresser mirror, caught in a gold light from his lamp. For a moment, she sees what he must, rather than what she's always felt. Hair that's a dark blaze to her elbows. A white cotton nightgown that's actually quite sheer—the thin straps mere ribbons that fall loose on her shoulders. Hollows of her collarbone shadowed. He sees her looking at the mirror and moves behind her, eyes on their reflection as he rests his chin on her shoulder.

"You've always killed me with this thing," he says, running his hand on the neckline of her nightgown.

Then his hand slips under the fabric, and she closes her eyes, breathing into the moment. "I thought you were making fun of it."

"God, no. You have no idea what it's done to me."

With his hand on her thigh, he bunches the cotton of her nightgown, and she turns to him, lifting his shirt up and over his head and running her hand along his chest. Pressing into him, she feels his other hand in her hair, tilting her head back slightly as he bends toward her. She pulls at his belt loop until he undoes it himself, and as she slides her hand down, reaching, she catches sight of their reflection in the mirror. His arms, tanner in this light, hold her to him and are now lifting her, his mouth on her neck, and seeing this, feeling this, she sighs without meaning to and then closes her mouth, trying to be quiet, just as he takes another step and the floor groans beneath their weight. Her laughter rises in a flow and won't stop—the whole world, she feels, is ridiculous—and he has to put his hand on her mouth to silence her, holding in a laugh himself. And that's when they hear another sound.

Later, it returns to her as a keening, a word that has a ghostly feel, which is appropriate for such a sound in the black of night. A high-pitched sound that ends low. Over and over. As they listen, she tells herself it's an animal, though from the reaction of her body—hair on end, pulse quickened, a need to run—she knows it's not.

His window is covered with a heavy drape but faces the street. Later, she will realize that from the time they moved aside the fabric just enough to see, everything took mere seconds. But time starts its slow crawl in part because what she sees, the shapes in the street, do not make sense. Not to her, whose mind is unaccustomed to truly dark possibilities and thus provides alternate explanations.

A dog being dragged in front of Miriam's house. Legs to its stomach to protect itself. That it's a person, a woman, actually Miriam, hits Olivia a split second later when she sees men with rifles leave the house across the street, pulling a man who is standing but hunched and reluctant to follow. A shot is fired, and the man hunches into a complete crumple. With that, her mind realigns and all the shapes take forms: a soldier on top of a woman. A person dragged by their collar. Another soldier in the distance on top of yet another woman, while nearby a man is forced to watch with his arm bent at a hard angle. When the man leans forward to scream, Olivia hears it because sounds all at once attach to meaning.

A few seconds, this took.

Lailan. The girl's window is still dark. Olivia prays for it to stay that way, for no shapes to move against her wall. Within her an irrational conviction: as long as that room stays dark, as long as she stays asleep, the girl is safe. A mind's necessary white lie. A panacea for the heart.

Outside is chaos. Time inches and spreads. In a beat, she understands that the light could be enough for images, especially if she pushes the film later and develops it for a couple of extra minutes, and though her camera is downstairs in the kitchen, she can race back to this window to keep an eye on Lailan's room while taking photos. But to look away, to go downstairs, how could she? In a flash, she thinks of her own mother. Sees her at the bottom of a playground's slide, smiling as she waits.

Just then, a shape darts from Miriam's open front door. Lailan. Scurrying to a car. Now crouched by its tire.

Already Delan is in the hall, fist slamming on his parents' door as he pulls on his shirt, yelling to them as Olivia flies past him and down the stairs and only vaguely does she hear him shouting her name as she runs past Soran, who scans the bookshelves for anything they might've missed. Then she's got the front door open and sees the girl only feet in front of her, crouched in a yellow nightgown with pink flowers, huddled by the fender of a car and holding on to the metal as if she could pry it off and use it for defense, which of course she cannot. Before Lailan can say a word, Olivia has her hand on the girl's back and is clutching the cotton and pulling, dragging her toward the door. Low to the ground. She will remember that later, knowing to be low not just so they wouldn't see her but so there was less of her to shoot.

And then they are inside. And Delan is there just in time to catch the door she flung shut. Quietly, softly, he closes the door. Even over the noise from the street, she hears the click of the lock.

Everyone stands still. Quiet. A strange moment of peace. A family gathered. Mother, father, sons, and friends.

Then there is a scream like a falling rocket, something that plunges and is gone. A few short bursts of light through the drapes and a smell of burning. Gaziza and Hewar frantically race to the bookshelves only to see that everything is gone. Delan says something to them in Kurdish and Soran hisses, "Not in Kurdish! They are looking for Kurds. They—"

But Delan's not listening. He's turned to Olivia, who stands with Lailan frozen at her side. "You need to hide. *Now.*"

But time is a trick again. Sped up impossibly even as it draws out, and already there is banging against the door. Words spoken that need no translation. Without thought, Olivia sees the cabinet with the paintings, the woman with flowing dark hair who somehow senses everything, and quickly flings open the center door, the one that's just big enough. Inside is a stack of sheets, which she sets on a chair like freshly folded laundry. Quickly, she motions Lailan to crawl inside. "Shh." Terrified, the girl nods. And the door closes.

Just as the front door opens. And Delan sees that Olivia is still standing there.

Soldiers. Rifles and hatred and indignance. Their shoes dusty. Olivia sees this and understands that it has been a long night for them, that this house is one of many, many stops. And though she knows she shouldn't look up, she does, to one of the soldiers, who has sunken eyes and a thick mustache. There is a twitch in his face as he takes her in, as if his muscles cannot contain his thoughts. Beside him, a soldier who appears to be no more than fifteen watches the ground, his face marked with acne. When at last he looks up at her, he smiles quickly and sadly, as if knowing how the night will go and offering her this one fast apology that he hopes no one else will see.

Words are barked from the soldiers, and Hewar, the head of the household, answers. Brave, firm. But Olivia sees the back of his head as he speaks, his thinning hair, and then the tremble in his arm before he presses his thumb to his pants leg, steadying himself. His shoulders rise with a breath. When she looks back, she sees that all the soldiers are now watching her. There is an energy in the room, as if it's been tilted, as if with one slight adjustment, all of them would be on top of her, her in that white nightgown she loved just minutes ago, the one that upon returning to Los Angeles will be stuffed in the kitchen trash. Rebecca will dump coffee grounds on top of it before noticing but will know to not say a word.

Hewar and Gaziza both shift to block Olivia, and Delan goes to her and puts his arm around her. And in this, she feels the future and sees the unfolding, and now, when she has none of the anger or blame she might have later, she wishes to stop time and tell Delan that it's not his fault. That she is here only because she wanted to be, and it was her choice, and no matter what she says or does or what he might see, she does not blame him.

But of course there is no time for this, no world in which this can happen. The edges of her body burn under the soldiers' eyes, and she sees that one of them, the one who's clearly in charge, cannot look away from her. And just as quickly, she understands that she will be given to him first, and realizing that it will happen whether she goes easy or not spurs her to look up, to stare at him, defiant and angry. When she does, she sees that he is actually now looking at Delan—and Delan will not back down. Everything balances on edge, this one moment from which there can be only a fall.

Then the man closest to Hewar grabs Hewar's arms as the others move into the room, but that man who is in charge, the man who was staring at Olivia and now Delan, raises his hand. His right hand. A hand that is missing fingers past the knuckles, most of the digits nubbed halfway. Olivia sees this and then his face and only now places him, this man with his wounds and sorrow over his son who'd been killed that first day they got here, the man they'd found on the sidewalk in dangerous despair. His eyes go from Delan to her, and with that hand raised, the others have stopped, and there is silence. And he says something. One sentence that makes the man who's been watching her with that twitching face clamp his mouth shut so tightly, the knots of his jaw bulge.

And then, just like that, they are gone. And the door closes.

No one speaks. There is silence from within the house but not the neighborhood. Screams. Shots. They open the cabinet door to let Lailan out and then turn off the lights as they go to the back of the house to sit on the kitchen floor, huddled. Lailan crawls into Soran's lap, her arms around his neck, and stares at nothing. Olivia tucks herself against Delan and watches the knobs of the stove, bright with the outside light, as Hewar lights a brass oil lamp. Shadows move on faces.

In the corner of the room is her camera, in its bag on the floor. She moves to get it, and Delan looks at her sharply—but he needn't warn her. The thought of going anywhere past this room terrifies her, even the thought of her footsteps on the stairs. It seems there are a million ways she could draw the attention of a different set of soldiers. So instead she sits back with the camera in her lap and listens to the terror just past their walls. And then, after a moment, when everyone is lost in the sounds, she leans over to shoot slightly upward, resting her elbows on the floor, and snaps a photo: Lailan in Soran's lap and Hewar and Gaziza beside them, holding hands. All four are on the floor and looking up, toward the window, their eyes lit with fear.

Then a car door slams, and there is barking. A scream and a shot and an aching silence. She puts away her camera, her heart beating now not just from fear but from having captured this moment. If she dies tonight, if she's gone with the next raid, she hopes someone will find this film. That someone will see they had each other.

And then she remembers the soldier and his words that made everyone clear out. She looks up at Delan and asks him what was said.

The tips of his eyelashes are dotted with light, and for a moment, he doesn't answer, just watches the window. Finally he turns toward her. "He said, *There are no Kurds here.*"

"He saved us."

Delan nods. "He did. And then he went to the next house. And the next. And they, unfortunately, were not saved."

CHAPTER 11

During that tug-of-war between sleep and wakefulness, between the depths of her mind and the shallows of the outer world, she tells herself it was a dream. A strange dream of dusty shoes and noise and a girl in a cabinet. And then she opens her eyes to see Delan and his entire family, everyone asleep in the dining room, even Miriam whom they'd gone to, whom they'd taken home and cared for as best they could. *She took down the portrait of Barzani,* Delan had whispered to Olivia as his mother held her friend, rocking and crying. *But she forgot her Star of David.*

By early morning, the shocked horror has twisted to a sad, hard anger, and while the others sleep, Olivia scours the kitchen countertops, then quietly stacks dishes. The windows are still dark. The world outside unfathomable. The violence, the violation. What happened to Miriam, their friend, and to others on the street—Olivia keeps seeing it on a replay. Closes her eyes and hears the screams. Steadies herself against the sink and sees Miriam, the way she'd held on to Hewar's arm when they came through the door, unable to meet anyone's eyes.

When there's nothing left to clean, Olivia sits in the silence of the dining room, waiting, watching the others with her fist pressed against her mouth. When Delan wakes, he goes to her, taking a seat beside her with his back against the wall. Together they watch the two women on the cushions across from them, faces eased with sleep. After everything, all that can be done is comfort. They cannot stop this from happening again, and no law will make a difference because it was the government—the supposed source of protection for the people—that committed the atrocities. This understanding is like something seen from a great distance. It doesn't make sense to her. She doesn't want it to make sense.

Now and then, Delan glances to the window, as if weary of what awaits. Morning's begun its push into the room, and the sounds from the neighborhood are quiet but growing. With his little finger, he touches Olivia's hand, his voice soft as he watches his mother and neighbor.

"I wish they could keep sleeping. Even an hour more. I wish I could give them that." When he puts his hand on top of Olivia's, his fingers curl into her palm. "I'm not going to be able to say anything that makes this better."

The room shakes as her eyes fill. "I didn't think you would." A pause as she studies Miriam's hair, a dark spill on the pillow. When she speaks again, the words are an incensed whisper. "There's not even police to go to. No potential. Even that, just the potential—there's no *chance* for justice. Everything is too big. What can you do when everything is too *big*?"

He stares up at a crack in the center of the ceiling. "If it's too much to see how big a problem is, then don't. Get closer. Make it smaller." With his chin, he motions to the room. "Here. What you can do today. Look for that. For the people around you, because they will wake up, and they will remember."

And he's right. And now that the military is gone, grief can be expressed. A cry will not be answered with a bullet. Family members and friends arrive up and down the street, and through the windows there is a new sound: mourning. Olivia stands in Delan's room, at that same window where she'd stood the night before, before the world spun on its terrible new axis, and sees three women across the street in the spot where the man had crumpled. They are wailing and hitting their chests with their fists. They yell at the sky, and their voices rise and fall. Imploring or cursing, Olivia cannot tell. And then they are kneeling, their foreheads on the ground, and only then does Olivia hear the call to prayer and wonder what the women are actually saying.

He said, There are no Kurds here. The words come back to her. The reason they were spared. Saved. *Which is it?* she wonders. *Saved or spared?* One involves action, the other a passive assistance. A choice to look the other way. What the man did was spare them. What Delan did that day, she realizes, was save them. She'd started this trip thinking of her own hidden magic, daydreams of saving the day with feats of some unseen greatness that waited within her. And yet it was he who saved them.

They are alive, in truth, because of one small kindness.

An inventory has slowly, twistedly been collected throughout the day, funerals already begun, bodies under clean sheets with the *mullah* reading the Koran. Three killed on their block, one being a nine-year-old girl down the street. But other forms of devastation are widespread—as are theories. Revenge for the sabotaged road, it is known and accepted, fueled the attack. Justification from the government. The "resistance" was targeted, it is claimed—as if a little girl were *resistance*. But from there, the talk is jumbled. There is an informer among the Kurds who was spared, it is relayed from someone who knows someone, but then it is also said that the informer has not lived up to his bargain and was killed. Or will be killed. Or might never be killed. No matter who believes what, suspicion angles eyes and turns talk to a whisper.

And Lailan. Lailan has been quiet, has barely spoken, but when she does, Olivia leans in, peering at her mouth. "Lailan, open."

And the girl does and then realizes what Olivia is looking at. With her finger, she touches the spot where the tooth had been. Her shoulders hunch as she tries to not cry, and Olivia's heart breaks because it was her first tooth, and it's gone, most likely lost in a night that took too much.

The trip is drawing to an end. She's relieved to go, but to count the minutes while knowing that his family and Lailan will be left behind is like celebrating that she will be the only one lifted to safety. And yet. And yet she thinks of her father and life at home and her stupid job. The shower she can use during the day and the books on a shelf she never has to question. Even Mason with his snide remarks and Rebecca with her staunch, angry independence. All of it. And the urge to flee, to be home at all costs, to be safe is so strong, so dense, it swills like sediment inside her and makes her sick. To leave is to admit this is just a trip, while for them it is a life.

And her confliction, of course, pales in comparison to his. To leave his family before was one thing, but now, in the aftermath of this? She watches him, and when he speaks in Kurdish, she studies his face, worried he's making plans to stay, that she will board the plane alone. In her mind, this is the worst thing. A naive assumption.

Early evening, after funerals, everyone in the neighborhood pays visits to each other. Armed with food, they drop in to check on each other, to hold each other in a smothering dusk before quickly returning to their houses. Outside, leaves rustle in a growing wind, shimmering like something turned electric.

"I have a friend who has okra," Soran says. He's sitting on the steps to the back door, elbows on his knees. "The plants, I mean. They're babies. Very small, but I'd like to get them started. At the area in the back."

Olivia finds the spot. A small plot of untamed land against the wall. It won't take long to ready the area for planting, and even though tomorrow will be their second to last full day in Kurdistan, the garden and rote motions are all she craves.

"We'll do it," Delan says. "We'll have it ready. And stakes to hold the plants. Right?"

"Sure," Soran says, which makes Olivia smile because it's Delan's word, adopted now. "Maybe you can find sticks, tall sticks. I'll go to my friend, to make sure the plants are ready."

"And beans if he has them," Delan adds. "You could get them going up the wall."

Soran agrees, and as they continue to plan out the back garden, Olivia sees it, the need for normal. And she knows that Delan was right in some ways. You don't move on. You move *with*. Even if the other night is not found in her every conversation or thought, it lives with her. Tucked away. A hidden stash of meaning.

The next day, the sun is tangerine bright and the sky a stunning, deep blue but equipped with a wind, as if offering a slight undoing to its beauty. Soran is already gone, so Olivia and Delan join his parents for breakfast. Yogurt and naan bread, tea and fruit in the dining room. There are oval-shaped bruises on Hewar's arms where the soldier grabbed him, and he lowers his sleeves when he sees Olivia notice.

Clearing the back area won't take long, and Delan wants to go on a stick-finding mission in the hills sooner rather than later, so he tells her they'll work on the garden when they return. Again she has that feeling she'd had when they first arrived, that the garden is safe. The walls enclosing and protective. The last thing she wants to do is leave. But it's their second to last day, and there are photographs she could take of a landscape she might never see again, and so she agrees, straps on her yellow Nike sneakers with their orange symbols, and gets her camera. On the dresser in her room is the little tube of damask rose oil, which she dabs on her wrists and in the hollow of her chest. Already its deep, provocative scent reminds her of sugary treats and the warm gaze of others, the garden and old walls and secrets.

Soran's car is outside, so they find his keys and take a short drive to the base of the mountains, then walk along hills covered in oak trees and grass that's begun to dry. Truly, it's the most beautiful morning she's experienced since being here. Temperate. One of those days that draws you outside, charming you with waving flowers and full bursts of white clouds. Apparently they'd arrived in that fold of spring to summer, the perfect last chance, because even now, at the end of the trip, the land looks parched, though wildflowers remain, toughened and battle-weary.

Stopping in the shadow of a cloud, a little continent of shade, she sees Delan twenty or thirty feet away, bending to pick up a long stick before holding it up for inspection, and watches him for clues. Is he surveying this land with the greed of a last glance? Or with the ease of someone who will see it again? After a moment, she lifts her camera to her eye. Thankfully it's color film, because the sky has never been bluer than it is above him.

The grass whispers against her legs as she approaches him. Together they walk, gathering more sticks until the collection becomes unwieldy and they stop. Delan spreads out a long, thick strip of fabric; puts the pile on top; and ties the fabric around it, then hoists the pile on his back and holds both ends. In the distance, crooked boughs of oak trees angle toward the ground and sky, and all at once, the leaves shake with a gust of wind. At first, the sound that reaches her is the ocean but then becomes something else, something haunting, like hundreds of ancient whispers. A warning, she thinks. *You don't listen to warnings,* Delan said back in Baghdad, which could be true because she shrugs it off. Her camera with its MD-2 motor drive hangs heavy on her neck.

"I'm taking pictures," she says. "I want that view, there."

She points to a crest a ways up, one that promises a vista. Above it, clouds tumble from the top of the mountain like something released from the earth, and as she walks, she pauses for a photo. They look alive. As if they're speaking. Great rolling storytellers. *Click.* The MD-2 starts its automatic film rewind, and she realizes the film in her pocket is black and white. A disappointment, to remove the color from the day. Somewhere, an insect whirs alongside the rewinding, and she listens, trying to find it, at first entertained by the imitation but then thinking *snake*. Do they have snakes here? She thinks of the Garden of Eden, which surely must have been around here somewhere, and decides yes, yes they do. To be safe, she stands on a rock and thinks, *I'm on a rock in Iraq,* as she loads in the black and white.

Then she begins to walk.

At the crest, there is a view of the town and the streets that lead to his house, haphazard and jumbled. All the buildings are made of mud brick or stone or even beige cement, and they blend into the drying landscape as if built with the intention to hide. Trying to get higher, she climbs onto the first branch of a tree. Then back down. Kneeling to get the grass and a world that seems to drop away. Different angles, different views, like a study in perspective from her first late-night photography class. As she loads in another roll of black and white, there's a sound. A great flapping of wings. She turns, her eyes drawn to birds that scatter like buckshot from the ravine below. Lifting, they spread into the sky.

Her eyes follow them, and she's raising her camera to capture their flight when her vision catches what's underneath. Soldiers. And someone with a hood over his head.

She sinks to the ground. Heart slamming. The grass is tall and she's above them, but did they see her? She was standing in the open, thinking of clouds and sky and birds. She glances back the way she came. She could crawl back. Just to be over the ridge and out of sight, where she can run. But the camera is around her neck, as if the moment was created with this in mind—why else would she be here with film newly loaded? *Fate,* she thinks, now angry at her new way of seeing things, at the responsibility it brings.

Slowly she crawls to a large rock, crouches behind it, then raises her head and the camera just high enough to capture what's below. Through the viewfinder, she sees the soldiers beating the man. Savagely. There is no break between the hits. Yet still, he tries to stand, and with a great lurch she feels a love for him, whoever he is, for his determination and his pride that make him rise again. Another punch spins his hooded head, and she focuses there, on the hood, and starts taking photos, trying not to absorb what she's seeing, trying to think only of justice and payback and a reveal of this moment that could make a difference somehow. Her back burns as if blistering, exposed. *Click.* Anyone could be behind her. *Run,* she thinks. But if this man can keep rising, she can press a button.

Kicked onto the ground, the man rolls on his side and this time does not get up. Legs drawn to his stomach till someone behind him kicks him in the back, and his body lengthens in reaction. She cannot hear the sound and is grateful, so grateful, because another kick from a soldier in front of him meets his mouth, and she knows there would be a shattering of teeth, a choking on blood. Over and over, she clicks until two soldiers take him by the arms and prop him up, holding him in place while a gleam cuts through the air and meets his torso. His body hunches, as much as it can while being held up, and as the soldier retracts the gleam, she realizes it is a knife. And the soldier strikes the man again.

Still she clicks, though now she looks down at her feet. Dust and dirt coat her sneakers. Everything rises inside her, and she fights the urge to vomit on this hillside with what she realizes are this man's final moments below her. Her arms and legs start shaking, coursing with adrenaline, so she leans against the rock to steady the camera. Every shot from here on out will be blurred. Still, she takes them. She will not stop.

She doesn't know how many she's taken when suddenly the film begins to rewind. And all at once she remembers Delan, who doesn't know the soldiers are there. Right now, he could be looking for her, calling her name, about to stand in plain sight and scream for her. And so she straps her camera around her neck and starts to crawl. On her hands and knees, dried grass whipping in her face, rocks digging into her palms. Now and then, she has to lift her head to see where she needs to go, and when at last she finds the trail she took earlier, she stands and runs downhill so fast, her legs seem wobbly, faster than the rest of her.

And then she sees him. Tying more sticks to the stack. He spots her and straightens and waves, then registers the look on her face and is running toward her.

Olivia seems to just *be* in the gold chair in the living room. She doesn't feel herself there but is there. That's her arm on the armrest. Her fingers. Her chipped orange nail polish. Before her, Delan paces and Hewar stands at the window, watching the empty street. *Brown-colored pants. A white button-down shirt. A man.* With those words, she might've described half the population. Gaziza starts to give her tea but sees the tremble in Olivia's hands and so sets the saucer on the end table and carefully lifts the cup to Olivia's lips. Olivia takes a sip. The smell of tea and sugar now the smell of comfort as much as chaos.

Delan says something to his father in Kurdish and then translates to English. "I asked him who is Soran's friend with the okra. So we could call and tell him to be careful on the way home."

"Does he know who?"

"No. Soran has many friends. With many gardens."

The garden. "I'm going out there."

Delan looks at her questioningly but lets her go.

Outside, she spears the hardened soil with the shovel, stands on the edge to jam it in farther, and then steps back and lifts the blade to turn the earth. Over and over until she comes back to herself. She is here. She feels her body, at last and painfully. New blisters form on her hands. But she is alive, despite her stupidity. Her misguided bravery. Delan was angry from the start, that scared anger parents get when their child unthinkingly walks into a street, the *I almost lost you* anger. It wasn't aimed at her, of course, but at the situation. For the fact that a walk had turned into this. So she'd not told him of the photos, that she'd sat there for a full minute, maybe two, exposed to anyone on lookout who might have walked along the ridge.

The noon sun turns angry, temperate morning gone. Within minutes, she's sweating, and when Delan joins her, she wipes her brow with the backside of her hand to squint at him, to see what he wants. He doesn't say anything. Just gets the other shovel. Her eyes sting as she watches him begin to dig. And then she starts again. Turning the dry soil, mixing in the rich compost. Hewar even appears and kneels at one side, riffling through upturned earth and removing the weeds and grass. Now and then, he points to a bird in the trees, smiling as if seeing someone who finally returned.

The far back garden is ready. The soil turned and amended. Rows dug and ready. All they need are the plants.

Together they eat lunch outside, rice with almond slivers and raisins, chicken in a red tomato stew. In the distance there is a banging, someone building something. Olivia listens to the beat of the hammer and notes that Delan keeps glancing at the side gate when his parents look away. A strange flutter has begun in her chest, a sort of loose anxiety.

When they're done, Olivia helps Gaziza take the dishes into the house while Hewar and Delan stand before the cleared section and plan. Plates clink in the silence of the house. The refrigerator hums. In the distance, the chukar birds laugh into the afternoon.

Then there are voices. Gaziza is out the door, frantic, with Olivia close behind, just as Delan throws his shovel on the ground and Hewar lets go of his rake and there, at the side of the house, are Kurds carrying the same man who'd tried to stand in the ravine, a man whose brown pants are dirtied at the knees and whose white shirt is now almost entirely red. His head hangs and his arms are flailed, and Olivia can only look at the man's hands, but even that is too much because she knows those hands—the ones that were beside her when she was sick—and she only has to look at them to hear his voice softly telling her tales.

Everything slams to the surface. Fast, like a punch. Then a gauzy lightness takes over, and she can't move. Frozen in a moment of realization. It was Soran. Soran standing, trying to stand. Soran being stabbed. But even as she understands this, it slips away, despite the evidence before her. Not real, no. A humming builds in her ears, an enraged static.

Gently the men set Soran on the ground, his blood no longer flowing though still, the dry soil turns red. Gaziza is there in a second, holding his head in her hands as she yells something over and over, as if she could possibly wake him. Then Delan is on his knees, grabbing at his brother's hand, pulling on his arm, and Olivia kneels behind Delan and presses against him, her arms wrapped around his shoulders as she both clings to him and holds him up. Standing above them all is Hewar, watching with his hand covering his mouth, his face wet.

Then there is a sound. A wailed shock of understanding as Gaziza begins to pound her chest with her fist, stopping only to lift her arms to the sky, her voice soaring. And Olivia looks up and sees Lailan. In her second-floor bedroom window, watching. Frozen. Her mouth open and eyes wide, as in her hand, her doll hangs, forgotten.

Soldiers were seen driving fast, too fast, down a street at the base of the mountain. A man in his nineties was sitting in his window seat, keeping an eye on things, and said he knew right away that something was wrong. Standing, he went outside and asked his grandson and his grandson's friend to walk into the ravine to gather wild *toleke*, a bitter green that would be cooked with oil and onions later to help his ulcer. They in fact did not need to go that far for *toleke*, as it grew across the street, but the grandson did as asked. And alongside the road, they found the body. And then found someone with a car.

There is a swiftness to death in the Middle East. People appear immediately, and already Soran is in the mosque, washed and wrapped in white, about to be taken to the graveyard. Delan is needed everywhere. Dragged from this room to that, talking to people in Kurdish and pressing a cloth so hard onto his eyes, it's as if he's physically shoving back tears. Between the language barrier and the whirlwind of Muslim traditions that Hewar and Gaziza apparently practice only with death, Olivia is stunned. Uncomprehending. Though Islam mandates a funeral right away, she sees people appear, ready and crying and without pause, and feels that instead the briskness here is because death is well practiced. Tragedy, quite simply, lurks around too many corners.

At last, there's a moment. Delan finds her standing in the kitchen with the women and leads her to the stairs. "I need to go, but you have to stay," he says quickly, and it's as if his words have tumbled off an edge. "Please just listen. You stay with the women; I go with the men. There's an order; it's how it's done."

"Delan. Why him? What happened?"

Even in the darkened hall, his eyes go bright with tears. "*There is no why.* There is no reason. He's dead because someone didn't want him alive. It's that fucking simple."

"But—"

"I have to go with the men. *Please.*"

But she doesn't let him go. Instead she wraps both arms around him and presses her cheek against his shoulder. With his arms at his sides, he breathes in and out once, twice, three times before finally hugging her back. But it's quick. Done more for her benefit than his.

"I have to go," he whispers in her ear, and she sits back on the stair and watches him leave, helpless at the time he most needs help.

Translations do not happen. Trying to stay out of the way, she remains with the women at the house. Cooking has started and songs are sung, notes hitting chords of grief, each one bringing her closer to an edge. The women rock, swaying and crying, and soon she finds herself doing the same, the understanding of what's captured on the film in her camera hitting her in tumbles, rolling her stomach to the point where she must just think of the yard at home in Los Angeles, that essentially blank canvas, to not break down. She'll get tomatoes in pots along the driveway. The grapes Delan wants on the wall. To calm herself, she sways and digs holes in her mind and fills them with things that will grow, that will become lush and verdant and life-giving, all while the women's voices rise and fall and Olivia's camera sits with a wretched moment captured within.

When the men return, there is a last prayer outside the house. Then more people in the house: friends, neighbors, family, even his cousin and new wife, who canceled the remaining days of their wedding celebration after the raid. Olivia remembers when her own mother died, how her father sank to silence and hid in his room for days. Weeks. It might have been months. There were no voices in her house. But now people have brought food, and their reddened eyes commiserate, fists held to hearts or to the sky. Dark coffee is served without sugar.

"Nothing sweet," Delan explains, seeing her searching the table. "Sweet means happiness." A pause. "This isn't real."

Again, he's pulled away, and with the crowd, no one notices when she disappears to go upstairs. On her bed is her camera. Discarded upon her return from the mountain, inside a roll of film with Soran's last moments. The fact that it's there, on her bed, is so wrong, so horribly wrong, that she can't even touch it. Can't lift it or move it. To have sat taking photos while their son, his brother, struggled for another breath. And Soran. She's betrayed him as well. She *sat there.* Capturing last moments she had no right to capture. What's inside the camera—she feels it as a tiny, beating heart.

Like yanking off a Band-Aid, she removes the film. Quick. Never could she destroy it, but never does she want to see its images. Never does she want to accidentally develop and print and be faced with what's there. Riffling through her purse, she finds a ballpoint pen and then the canister and digs in over and over with the tip till there's blue on her finger and a deep, dented line like a strike. Even if the ink fades, never could she miss the indentation, the mark, the warning.

Olivia finds Lailan on Miriam's couch, hiding under a tangle of blankets, lashes clumped and moist, face streaked with tears. Curling behind her, Olivia wraps her arms around the girl's small shoulders. To say everything will be okay would be a lie. To tell her she is safe, another lie. That it gets better. That time heals all wounds. Every comfort, every reassurance, all of it, Olivia realizes, boils down to pretty words. Adages that are in no way anchored to this reality.

The hurt Lailan has been through—such an unfair allotment, more tragedy than most adults endure in a lifetime. But the girl knows none of this. Her life is all she's ever known, and to her this is just another dark hour. Now and then, her shoulders tremble as she cries, quietly and unobtrusively, already a professional at grief, and when finally the sun takes a darkened dip, Olivia gets up and reaches out her hand. Together they stand, and it's then Olivia sees Lailan's doll, discarded on the floor by a table, its blonde hair colored in with a red marker.

A car idles in front of Delan's house, the driver watching as if debating about paying his respects. About to open the front door, Olivia smiles a greeting—but the man looks forward and pulls away, as if the kindness was uncalled for. Lailan, however, doesn't notice. Just stares up at the window, unmoving, as if understanding that this is the edge of something else. A first step beyond. That was how it was when Olivia's mother died. *This is the first time I've been to the grocery store when my mom isn't on the planet. This is the first time at the movies with my mom dead. The first time buying clothes.* So many firsts to be had. Olivia shuts her eyes with the burden of being familiar with this one slightly similar journey. But then the front door swings open and there's Delan, eyes red, but with a grin for Lailan's sake. Immediately his hand goes to his heart, as if she's just the girl he's been waiting for, and Lailan beams up at him before he scoops her into his arms.

"My girls," he says.

The sound of Gaziza crying is constant, and Kurdish is all that's spoken. For once, Olivia is grateful to understand nothing. Holding Lailan's hand, she registers people on the couch, the last place Soran slept. His shoes left by the front door. A book he was reading splayed upon the end table. Remnants of his life are spread around them, and his absence is so abrupt, so jarring, it's as if he's been lifted by a hook and removed. At times she feels as though she'll turn her head and there he'll be, finishing what he was saying. She tries to remember his last words, but all she remembers is him talking about plants.

Plants. How many had he been about to get? Enough for the back row in the garden—enough that he should not have thought walking was best when his car was parked right here on the street. She stares at the front door, feeling he was either picked up by the military the moment he walked outside or that someone gave him a ride that went horribly wrong.

She pulls Delan to the hall to ask about the plants and the car.

"It could've been a tray. The okra, they were babies, he said. No bigger than a few inches. Easy to carry," he adds, though she sees that he's wondering. "He liked to walk."

She thinks back to that day in the bakery. And to the times he was gone, returning with some brink of confusion, things not adding up. "Could he have been in the resistance? He told me no, but—"

"No, no. He steers clear. I love him, but he avoids trouble." A pause as he hears the tense. "I was in a fight once, and he jumped in to help and then yelled at me for putting him in that position. Like a little old man," he says fondly. "He was in the wrong place. You look the wrong man in the eyes and that can be enough. And Aras, he would've said something. They would've talked more."

She needs to tell him about Soran's disappearances, but suddenly Gaziza is sobbing in the kitchen, her fingers burned on a pot of rice. Delan rushes to her side, wrapping her hand in a cloth and holding her to him.

There is food. The kitchen filled with well-meaning mourners making a feast. Ferhad unwraps the kebab he brought, a tray so large that Olivia knows it must be from his wedding. His wedding. Mere days ago. She danced with Soran and Delan. *You need to dance,* he said to her, breathless and smiling as he pulled her from her seat. His eyes, that sun-touched dark green, now closed beneath a shroud of white. Never to be seen again.

And then Delan's voice shoots through the room. She finds him in the corner with a man she recognizes, the man from the picnic with the almost-black eyes. Delan's anger is present and full, and in a second, Ferhad has stepped in, trying to calm both men. The moment Olivia is by Delan's side, Ferhad shakes his head apologetically. "Wassim talk what hear."

He's spoken in English. Either imploring her for assistance or not wanting others to understand. Ignoring him, she takes Delan's arm, and at first he turns to her, angry, his fury landing upon anyone he sees.

"Please," she says.

He studies her, needing the time, she understands, to pick an emotional path. At last he nods and follows Olivia to the garden.

"Tell me."

"In my own house. On the day of my brother's death. I should kill Wassim for that. I tell anyone what he said, he would not walk out alive."

"Tell me what he said."

"Rumors. Talk that Soran was the informer. That *that* was why we were spared during the raid."

"But you told them—"

"Of course I told them! *But this is what's being said.* That he'd turned and then did something the government didn't like and so they got rid of him. My own brother, and this is what they're saying."

"He would never do that." But even as she says this, she hears Delan telling her *they threaten anything, anyone someone loves to get them to spy. To turn.*

And he sees it on her face. This memory, this consideration. "How could you—"

"Delan, I didn't—"

"*I saw it.* You, thinking that my brother—"

"I *don't* think he would ever do that. I don't. He was good. He was sweet and wonderful, but there were mornings when he'd be gone and—it didn't sound right, where he said he'd been. His answers didn't add up. That's why I asked about the resistance. But I know there are other reasons—"

"*Of course there are.* A million," he says. But his words have a filed edge to them, worn from this new information. As he speaks, there is a distraction in his voice. "That's what Ferhad said. At the picnic. That he'd seen Soran leaving town in the mornings. But it means nothing. There was a reason, I know."

And then, perhaps in self-destruction or distraction, she brings up what she's been worrying over for days, something that was answered the moment of Soran's death but needs to be said aloud. "You're not coming home, are you?"

And he looks at her sadly, because of course he knows she's been worried about this and of course the answer is no.

"Not right away," he says. "But I will come back. I promise."

But how can you be sure? she wanted to ask. After what's happened, how could he know he wouldn't be next? But she said nothing, because he, too, must feel those dark possibilities and his own mortality, and yet still he was choosing to stay.

My family needs me. And I want the truth.

The accusation, though spoken by only that one man to Delan, must have made its way through town, because by the next morning, its spread is evident in downcast gazes. Gaziza won't leave the house, but Hewar looks boldly at people, daring them as he picks out lamb and desert truffles—a treat—for Olivia's last dinner. Everyone is silent, but everyone is thinking. Including Olivia, who sees sticky cubes of manna for sale and remembers that night at the restaurant, how Soran urged them to leave upon spotting the Kurdish politicians. *Someone would've seen them, would've made a call. The temptation to take them out,* he said. *Opportunity.* Had he been the one to make the call? The thought shames her with betrayal but once there seems to stretch out, at home. They could've threatened his parents, his brother. Perhaps that was even why Delan was taken—*you don't work with us, we'll hurt your family.* At the restaurant, he went to the bathroom and returned with orders for them to leave. Of course, he also could've just gone to the bathroom and seen the politicians—as they assumed. As is most likely.

Everything remembered now is cast under a different light. That need for reasons, that need invents links and connections and sees motive rather than coincidence. But memory lies. Like incident light in photography. The way a face seen at sunset will have an orange-red hue or a white piece of paper beneath a tree in which light falls through the leaves will look green. A lie, tinted by the situation. By the source. At the restaurant, Soran went to the bathroom and passed by the political figures and saw it was time to go. But in the light of her suspicion, she worries this may have no longer been the case.

The garden feels haunted. Leaves stir on the pomegranate tree and shadows move and everywhere she thinks she sees him. In quiet moments, she hears his voice, his soft cadence and even pace. And people come and go, leaving food behind. In the late afternoon, the second day's crowd has been gone for almost an hour when there is a knock on the door. They wait—usually a knock is followed by someone loudly announcing themselves, as if a knock alone would not be answered. When nothing follows, they stop what they're doing. Down the hall, in the living room, Hewar peers toward them before facing the door. Gaziza puts down her knife. Delan closes the refrigerator. From where Olivia stands, she catches sight of Hewar talking to someone in black. A black dress, as if in mourning, but exposed light-brown hair. A woman. When Gaziza heads down the hall, Olivia follows.

The woman glances over her shoulder before being brought inside. She's young. Eyebrows arched. Lips a muted pink, like the underside of a shell. As she speaks, there seems to be confusion, as if the group is settling on a mutual language or sifting through words to find the ones that work. Olivia understands none of it but watches, intrigued, till suddenly Gaziza sways back and forth, crying, and grabs the woman in a fierce hug. When Olivia turns to Delan for an explanation, she sees that tears are streaming down his face.

"This is her," he whispers. "Soran's girlfriend from London."

"She came from—"

"No. Liv, she's saying she lives here now. With her family. Twenty minutes from here. They're strict," he says, "and Chaldean. That's Catholic. They weren't allowed to see each other."

"But I thought it was okay."

"Not for her family. Their children would be considered Muslim, even though he doesn't practice. Her mother is sick. That's why she had to move back. And so he moved too. To be with her."

"But he wasn't with her," Olivia says. "He never even—"

"Liv. He *was*. They were. Every chance they got. When no one was around." He smiles through a saddened relief. "Mostly in the morning, right after curfew lifted. Just for a bit. At cafés. They sat at tables next to each other and whispered."

And then it hits her, and Olivia feels as if something in her has collapsed. Some pillar of worry that should never have existed in the first place.

The young woman's name is Nina. No one in her family knew about her and Soran, save a cousin who was sympathetic to true love because he himself had once loved a Shi'a girl from afar. The cousin heard what happened through a friend who arrived at his house without shoes. Just hours before, this man had been visiting someone when he was told to give his shoes to a soldier, a soldier who'd broken his own shoe hiking into the mountains. The sole, the soldier said, came right off. Still he *limped into the mountains to kill the Kurd*—and then limped back out and searched the street for someone his size. The friend made polite conversation with the soldier, not wanting to be identified as Chaldean, and when the soldier thanked him for his shoes, he gave him a tip: there were okra plants left behind, just a few blocks away. *Get them, because I cannot pay for these shoes.*

The cousin listened to this and asked the name of the town his friend had been in and felt dread inch as he remembered Nina telling him that Soran lived there and was going to plant okra, had found some small plants that he would add to the garden he spoke of constantly. Though of course okra is common and the town is big, an instinct in him trembled to life, and the world, with these bits and pieces, spun tighter. Without telling anyone, her cousin drove all the way there, to the mosque, and learned the name of the man killed: Soran. Still, he said nothing. And when he stopped at the store before going home, he listened to more gossip about this Soran and said nothing, just held the name inside him until he was with Nina again and his voice went low, fearful of her love and what it would make her do.

What it made her do was sink into isolated, un-consoled grief. Still, through her sobs, she questioned the information. There would be more than one Soran, wouldn't there? And who doesn't plant okra? So the cousin drove back to the town and to the street where Nina said Soran lived, and he drove slowly till he saw a house whose door opened to a room of people. Idling his car, he stayed till he saw a woman in black and caught the tail end of crying. Question answered.

More than anything, Nina wanted to pay her respects. To see for a first and last time his family and the garden that he loved, even just the window of his room so she could imagine the world he saw when he was not with her. But to do so would be to risk being found out by her family. And so she told her father she was sick, and the rest of last night, she faced the wall so no one could see her tears.

Until. Until this morning, her cousin told her what else he'd heard in Soran's town: talk that Soran left the city to meet in secret with the government, that he'd turned. With this, she knew she had to come forward. Not to her family but to his. So they would know their son was never a traitor—that he was, quite simply, a man in love.

What if you should not love the person who your heart picks?

His words beat in her mind. *Love is the only thing that makes me not think. I cannot talk myself out of loving someone.*

Nina takes in stories and sifts through pictures. There is a delicate, polite lift of her brow that changes right before a cry, and though Olivia knows that they're welcoming her like a new member to the family, she also knows it will be the only time they see her. They are kind and loving, their arm around her shoulders, their shaking fingers holding photos, but they are arming her with more heartbreak. This young woman will leave with the bittersweet taste of the family she never had and with more memories of the man she loved. She will go home to her own family and feel their judgments like a weight that now cannot be lifted. And Delan. Understandably, he begs for stories of his brother in London, and as he does, Olivia feels the tip of her own loss as well, because for her—though in a much, much smaller way—this is also a goodbye. Maybe Nina glimpses this. Maybe she senses the skipping beats of Olivia's heart, for at one point their eyes meet, and Nina holds her gaze, then reaches out to squeeze Olivia's hand. A look passes between them. An understanding of the love for these brothers that at the end of the day, maybe neither can have.

"Will his name be cleared?" she asks Delan that night. Her last night in Kurdistan. She watched the knob of her bedroom door turn when dark had settled and now is curled against him, her arm across his chest.

"We will say what we can. That there was a woman and that was why he left. But it's more important to keep her safe. If her family found out—it wouldn't be his wish to clear his name if it meant hurting her. Everything he did, he did to keep her safe."

A life lived in secret. Glances stolen through crowds.

"Imagine," she says, "the freedom and life they had in London with no one looking."

"At least they had that, then. That taste."

"They were allowed to fall in love and then told not to. Is that better or worse?"

"The age-old question. And I know the answer. It's better. Always better."

The past few days tug at her. Such a slender gap of time. Barely there in the calendar of her life, and yet that makes the days seem charged with the heat of compression. Her very cells feel changed. She lets her eyes close and feels him thread her hair in his fingers.

"Someone started the rumors," he says.

She opens her eyes. Readjusting. "But you know the truth."

"About him, we know the truth, but not why he was killed. He was accused as a traitor by some Kurds yet killed by the government. Why? Why would they target him? I need to find out. Then I can come home."

She props herself up on her elbow. "You said all it takes is looking the wrong person in the eye." With her finger, she traces the scar at the corner of his eye. A quill, she's always thought. An old-fashioned quill. As if with every gaze, a story was being told.

"Yes. That could be."

"You don't think it is."

"I don't know what to think."

When she lies back down, her head on his chest, she again feels him lift her hair to the light from the window. Just barely, she opens her eyes to find him studying the strands as if burning the shade to memory. Then he raises her hand. Examines the length of her fingers, the bones in her wrist. She watches him do this, and the act of such memorization undoes all his words. He's not coming back. At least not anytime soon. Because this, she knows, is the painful study of a last glimpse.

CHAPTER 12

A gray, sad send-off. Even her footsteps sound hollow, as if the acoustics have changed and her room's retreated into itself, sullen with her departure. Delan cleared it with the other—and now sole—owner of Soran's car, and after breakfast, he will drive her to Baghdad in time for her evening flight. She thinks of doing the trip alone, the flights and mix of languages, and realizes she's not afraid. There's too much sadness to allow for anything else.

Breakfast is drawn out and wrong. Eggs overcooked. Tea not as warm as usual. Everyone lost in their own worlds. The sound the plates make when Olivia stacks them is sharp in the silence, and for too long she stares into the drawer of spices, all those little bags of color, until there is a knock at the back door. *Tap-tap, tap-tap-TAP.* Lailan's code. Within a beat, the girl is clinging to her and has her feet on top of Olivia's feet and her arms around her waist. When Olivia takes a step, Lailan steps with her. With each move, she feels herself hold on to Lailan tighter, a burning in her throat from realizing this is one of the last times she'll feel the girl's arms.

They lumber down the hallway toward Delan, who stands at the front door with her suitcase. There is a pained look on his face as he watches them, as if someone has shown him a postcard of a place he can never go.

"Have you seen Lailan?" Olivia asks, trying to shake the mood with that age-old joke that somehow always works with children. "She was here a second ago. Maybe over here."

She steps toward the cabinet, and the girl laughs into Olivia's stomach, a vibration that settles sadness into her core. Then Lailan hurries to the curtain, hiding, and Olivia pretends to not notice when she then darts behind a gold chair. "Where am I now?" Lailan asks, her voice clearly coming from the chair.

Olivia goes to the curtain, and a tumble of laughter erupts with the mistake.

With each laugh, each gleeful reminder that Olivia's looking in the wrong place, Olivia thinks of the girl's future. Because Lailan is at the beginning of an entire lifetime, if she's lucky. So much sprawls before her: crushes and kisses and hopes and heartache. Skinned knees and friends who say mean things and long nights spent reeling in silence. And accomplishments. Burning pride and passion, that thrill when you surprise yourself. And all of it will be lived without Olivia, and though irrational, because of course this is how it will be, how it always was to be, the promise of such a void is a loss unlike anything she'd expected.

Finally, Olivia peeks behind the chair, and when Lailan looks up, there are tears in both their eyes.

"Come here," Olivia says, sitting in the chair. The girl crawls into her lap. "You and I," she says, but the words lodge in her throat. She looks up at the ceiling, at a faint stain like a leaf, and tries again. "You know you're one of my favorite people in the whole world. And do you know how many people I've met? A lot. *Thousands.* And out of everyone, you, you and your big heart, you're who I'm always going to think of. And wish I was with."

Lailan nods, as if she already knew this, and looks down at the rug.

In Olivia's pocket is her copper tree-of-life pendant, strung upon its dark leather cord. When she loops it over Lailan's head, it takes a bit for the girl to look up, to understand, and when she does, her eyes go wide.

"For me?"

Olivia nods. "This is a bit of me, and my family, for you. The stone will protect you. And the tree connects everything. Which means it connects me to you, always."

Goodbyes and wet cheeks and hugs that don't let go. Gaziza has packed them food, and Hewar hands her a square package wrapped in brown paper that she is told to open later. Outside the front door, Lailan buries her face in Miriam's shoulder and won't look at Olivia until Olivia is up against her, wrapping her arms around both the woman and the girl. Lailan, stuck in the middle, raises her face up for a gasp of air and twists her body so it's Olivia she clings to.

Olivia holds her. Sweet oil and seeds and flowers, a last breath of this little girl whose voice she's learned to listen for. The thin waves of her hair, the small bones of her shoulders. There is no choice, Olivia tells herself. No choice but to meet people and fall in love and live and lose. To work and worry and grow old, if given the chance. And hopefully, hopefully what adheres to it all is a bit of joy. Or maybe just an openness to joy. Because what she's seen is that sometimes it is a choice. A choice to let your eyes fall upon the sight through a clouded window that makes you smile or to find in plants a miracle despite the chaos and calamity that batters down the soil around them. She hears Soran's voice talking to the seedlings, encouraging, and realizes that Lailan learned this from him and his family—even in the way she never overlooks the abandoned bits of the world but rather sees in them an untamed potential and promise of transformation. The way she sees the magic. And it's this, his continued presence in the girl, that allows Olivia to finally let go. Because she knows he is there, his voice quietly breaking the silence.

The trip in reverse. Returning as if being reeled back, wound home. Mountains lowering, becoming hills, then plains. The loss of Soran is so monumental, it's unreal. Kept off to the side, unrooted and unfixed, a mind's effort to protect. But Lailan's loss is easier to process and therefore constantly triggered by a world that seems to flaunt a mutual interest in the girl, everything meant to be shared with her. A tree with branches low and wide and easy to climb. Clouds shaped like grapes. A flock of sheep that from a distance blends into barren land, seemingly invisible until all at once they run. Every view intensifies the girl's absence.

And anything she can think of to distract revolts, spurred by the ineffectiveness of language. *I will miss you.* How small those words sit in the shadow of their meaning. *I'm worried. Stay safe. Help Lailan. I will think of you.*

As such, they made idle conversation.

Do you think Mason will have destroyed the house?

I may plant things in the yard. Tomatoes, zucchini.

In Paris, get brandy at the duty-free.

And then there is a question he asks that explodes within her chest.

"What do you think about the photos you took?"

In her purse, the canister burns with betrayal. "I won't know till I look."

He glances at her. "You said you know the second you take it if it's good."

"I got some good ones. I just can't think about them. Not till the film is home safe."

But the checkpoints are a breeze. There is a daring within her that now sits at the surface, exposed with the erosion of so much else. Delan chides her with being an old pro, having perfected a respectful disinterest in the men with guns who demand their papers. To that she just shrugs, watching pale cars in the distance. Sometimes her eyes glide over the soldiers' banners of bullets, but she lets herself register nothing, stopping meaning in its tracks. Instead she takes in the wavered gloss of a distant river, realizing it could be a mirage but not caring because in either case it shines, and the simple fact that something could be made of nothing is itself a fascination.

Hours pass. He tells her to take a nap, but she can't waste their last time together. The air grows hotter. The landscape drained of its green.

They talk of places they want to visit in the future: Scotland, Hawaii, Spain. They talk of childhood: the first time a friend chose another, that cruel induction to life. And they talk about children. *I always wanted more than one.* A smile. A hint at their future. She wants to say, *I love you.* The words press against her, like something that could erupt without notice. He feels it too; she knows he does; she sees it in him, the way he looks at her. But those words, those beautiful, aching words, they shouldn't emerge now and forever be tied to what's just happened.

And then they are at the airport, in time for evening prayer.

At the ticket counter, she listens to him speak in Arabic, a difference she can hear though could not describe. She wants to know what he's said, if he gave a return, and he must see the question in her because he looks down at the counter, unable to meet her eyes. "A credit will be easiest. I'll set the date later."

They walk. The steady roll of her suitcase on the cement. Cigarette smoke that trails and spreads upon the ceiling.

"Everything," he says when she wraps herself around him, "always, is the beginning."

Of what? Of our future together? Of losing you? But she discards the questions. Later she can break down. Now she needs to not think. Now she just needs to get home.

His hand under her chin, he makes her look at him. "Liv. My Liv. I just want to be home with you."

Home. The thought—it's amazing and sad all at once.

"Us cooking," she says. "Picking things from the garden and cooking and sitting on the porch. You down the hall or in my room. Our room."

"Our room. It will be our room."

"And us at breakfast, you reading the paper and me making lunch and Rebecca in a hurry and Mason just being Mason."

He laughs. "Mason. Poor Mason."

"I might be able to handle him now."

"He was jealous, you know. Of us. There was always an *us*. It drove him crazy. He's annoying but smart. He saw it."

"And there will be. Us is not over. You just need to come home." And stay safe. Stay alive.

"I promise."

Then she rests her head on his shoulder and feels the slight lift of his breathing. Never did she see this moment. Never could she have imagined leaving him like this.

"I don't want to say goodbye to you," he says.

She lifts her head and watches the mountains in his eyes, his faraway land.

"Then it's not goodbye," she says. And with that she turns and forces herself to walk away—even as she feels his eyes upon her, even though with every step she feels as though she's falling.

CHAPTER 13

April 28, 1979

The gate at Los Angeles International. Plants with shiny leaves. Rows of orange chairs. People everywhere. Olivia waits for Rebecca to arrive, and the noise and the crowd feel foreign. This world is loud and bright. Color is everywhere. Jumping from walls, slipping from polyester, plush in velour. People swim in it, and it swims from them. And the touching, the hugging and hand-holding. Everywhere are embraces. People push around her and at times even against her, and Olivia finds herself fighting just to be still.

When Rebecca finally arrives, it's in a rush of apologies for being late, all while looking past Olivia for Delan. Olivia tries not to cry. "He's not coming," she has to yell. "Look at me. He's not coming."

And then she tells her the rest, or most of the rest, as fast as she can. And Rebecca continues to look to the gate and moves only when Olivia is halfway down the concourse, the people and all their colors simmering with tears she refuses to give in to.

A return to anywhere is strange, to see that a place has gone on without you, and Los Angeles is no different. Banks still have their tall, dark windows and the same strange sculptures outside. Billboards are unchanged; the ad for the upcoming movie *Alien* keeps promising terror while the Marlboro Man still rides his horse, lasso frozen midspin. It's as if no time has passed. As if nothing has happened. And it feels wrong, for their city to turn on them like this. To let her back in without a glance and not even notice that he's gone.

As they inch along the 110 freeway, she takes in the curves of the Bonaventure Hotel and remembers the boot-shaped glasses they got from the restaurant, how they drank strawberry daiquiris as the top floor rotated and the windows flared with sunset, and then how they took the plunge back down in the glass elevator only for Delan to say, *We need to go back up. We need a set of four.* Now those glasses are in their cupboard, and she understands that truly everything in their house will be like this. Tied to him. Because of him.

The tape dispenser he has no patience for. The kitchen table stained with rings. The stairs where he kissed her, where she was reclined and uncomfortable but loving every second until Rebecca had appeared, *Pick a room for crying out loud.* The whole house is a trap. And so a call is made, and Olivia's father tells her that there will be another plane ticket waiting, and Rebecca vows to call in to Olivia's work and say her flight got canceled, that she needs more time.

Numb, Olivia leaves her suitcase packed in a corner, ready to go as if the trip were just about to begin, as if the city had been right and nothing had happened. The only difference is the unopened gift from Delan's father, which gets placed against the wall.

Sweaters thrown into a duffel bag. Heavy jeans and close-toed shoes. Everything now for Washington, where the weather will match her mood. All the film will go with her, as well—all but that one roll, which she places in a box under her bed. And then the next day, she heads toward Rebecca's car. Pink azaleas line the path, blooms edged in white.

From the porch, Mason yells, "You're coming back, right? Wait, you leave a check?"

"Ignore him," Rebecca tells her.

"What?" Mason says. "We have the mortgage—"

But Rebecca cuts him off with a firm "shut the fuck up" and nudges Olivia's arm. "You take your time, love."

The plan is to create contact sheets and take it from there; a friend of her father's on the island is a photographer and already agreed to lend her his darkroom. Maybe it will help. But as the plane thunders into the sky, it occurs to her that if they crashed, last moments captured on film would be lost forever. Soran. To lose even one image of him would be a tragedy, but there is Miriam as well. That photo Olivia took of her holding a sleeping Lailan, the love on her face. That was the evening of the raid, only hours before, and though Miriam lived, it was in some ways a last moment as well. What if that was lost? Panic bolts through her, and the man beside her assumes she's afraid of flying and insists on buying her a drink when they reach cruising altitude. She downs it in a teeth-freezing head tilt.

"I used to be afraid too," he says, signaling the stewardess for two more.

"And then what?"

"Oh. I guess one day I just wasn't."

She turns back to the window. "I'm not afraid of flying. It's not me I care about."

He laughs, and she turns to him, confused.

"Sorry," he says. "I just realized. *That's* how I stopped being afraid of flying. My wife left me, and I didn't care if I lived or died. Made travel a cinch." He hands her the new drink and raises his in a toast. "All I have to say is sometimes you gotta boil it down and just do the bare minimum: live. That's it. All that's required."

Liv. She thanks the man and hears Delan's voice as the window grows blinding with restless, cloud-trapped sun. *Sometimes living is all you have to do.*

Maybe it's the clouds, maybe it's the exhaustion, but sleep is sudden and heavy and when she wakes, it's the end of the flight and the man beside her appears to be dreaming, his eyes moving behind closed lids. She watches him for a moment, this stranger who told her living was all she had to do, glad to be the one observing and not the one observed. Then she spots three freckles on his cheek, and the urge to connect them into a triangle is so overwhelming, she has to sit on her hands. Maybe she should find a pen and do it. A story to tell Delan at some point.

When her father meets her at the gate in Seattle, there is a hug that lasts so long, the people around them stare. Her arms are at her sides until he squeezes her tight. One squeeze, as if he knows she needs some cue to let go. And she does. Lifting her arms around him, she feels the shoulder of his sweater dampen beneath her cheek. People around give them a wide berth.

"This looks like a long goodbye," her father says when at last they pull apart.

In Baghdad, she'd walked away with *goodbye* held back. Refused the word as if its denial meant another day would be ensured. As if not saying it rendered their separation a mere pause. Already it's a regret she has, because the omission now feels reckless. Presumptuous. What if that was it? *Kurds say goodbye for too long. There's nothing worse.* And then she's thinking of Soran and knows of course that Delan was wrong. Because there is something worse—when goodbye never gets said at all.

The ferry with its wet floor and churning heart. The salted air. The petunias that line the boardwalk. Dark clouds fume on the horizon, leaving but never gone, and still puddles reflect branches and stop signs and windows of buildings. Everything is familiar, and that familiarity is double-edged. To have a place you can go, a place that is known and safe, where you can take deep breaths and finish dreaming and not fear something at your back, it's a sort of miracle. And to go through life never having seen that as a miracle, that in itself is miraculous. Everything a fun house series of good fortunes, a growing recognition that slows Olivia's steps and makes her pause a bit too long before remembering to answer when someone says hello.

At night, they have mussels with white wine and fennel, and her father talks about his new neighbor, a rich man who bought the property as a vacation spot and who's landscaping his backyard with zone-inappropriate plants he's had shipped in, his decision to include plumeria and the sacred flower of the Andes both baffling and irresponsible. The words barely make sense to Olivia, who catches only bits and pieces and tries to tape meaning together in her mind.

"Gorgeous but doomed," her father says of the plants—at least she thinks he's still talking of the plants. "The laws of nature, they don't care what you can afford."

She lets him talk about the island and everyone on it. It's all she wants. The idle talk. Now and then, he pauses, and though she knows he's waiting for her to fill him in, to start from the beginning and say what's happened, she can't—not yet—and so she stays silent, unspoken words on her tongue like grit.

The next day, he's home. Another day taken off work. The fact of him as he sits at his desk with his sweatered shoulders and combed hair, it fills her with love. And makes her think of Hewar and Delan and then the rest, and though she knows she *will* tell her father everything, she also knows that saying these words to him, out of everyone, will be the hardest because he is her heart, and she is his, and because of this, pain goes wider and deeper and is shared, and so to begin, to even find that toehold into what will undo them both, it's difficult. An hour more, she decides. Just one more hour without the events sitting between them, and then she'll start the story. *I wish they could keep sleeping,* Delan said the morning after the raid. *Even an hour more.* Little breaks of awareness, now she sees their tender beauty.

Then there's movement in the house. Fast and swooping. A hummingbird.

They try everything. Leaving the room to give it space and quiet, then a broom to shepherd it toward the door. The windows are open and the screens pushed out and both the front and back doors are splayed wide, red fabric draped atop as lures. No matter their efforts, the bird tries to find escape but fails, panicking mere feet, mere inches from the threshold to outside. So close yet frantic, and in its confusion, it returns to the one place it's decided is safe, perching on the hanging light fixture in the center of the living room. From below, Olivia can see the fluttering beat of its heart.

Her father, as he tends to do, takes to reference books.

"Hundreds of breaths per minute," he says, a book upon his knee. "And that's when everything is okay. Terrified, it would be more."

Outside is a crab apple tree, doused in ruby flowers. Olivia breaks off a small branch and, once inside, holds it toward the bird. Iridescent green and blue feathers flash as it moves away. Its black eyes watch her. "To help you," Olivia says, as if it could possibly understand. "Please."

"Each day," her father continues, "they eat half their body weight in sugar. When active, they need to constantly eat, or they'll starve. Sugar passes through them in an hour. Just one hour. Maybe that's it. Sugar water?"

But his words are like a gavel. Because it's been more than an hour. And with this information she understands that no longer is this a situation where eventually it will be figured out, and time will solve the problem. Now it's about keeping the bird alive. About every second being one too many for something so small that had so little to begin with. In the kitchen, Olivia fills a shallow bowl with sugar water and returns to hold it up—but the bird startles with a whirring buzz and water splashes and after another desperate attempt, it again perches, trembling, upon the fixture. Once more, Olivia lifts the broken branch, while her father turns a page.

Now Olivia's shaking. Arm raised and aching. Above her is a tiny creature who didn't know, who maybe saw the soft blue reflected in the mirror on the wall and couldn't have known it was going where it shouldn't, that another world had imposed upon the one it understood. A split second. And now there's nothing to do but stand with a broken branch and watch.

"I don't need facts," she says. "I need *help*."

Her face is wet. Her father looks at her, concerned, till suddenly he shuts the book. Without explanation, he heads out the front door.

When he returns, he's holding a plant with red flowers, still in its black plastic container. He hands it to her. "My neighbor and his ludicrous landscaping. The Sacred Flower of the Andes. When I saw you with that branch, it occurred to me. So I broke into his yard."

Clusters of tubular red flowers spill from slender branches. With both hands, Olivia lifts the plant to the light fixture, and within a flash, the bird is at a flower, the hum of wings steady as it drinks. All Olivia can do is watch, overcome. She's holding a plant, and a bird is drinking from its bloom, to live. The connection, it's magnificent and devastating. An unexpected breech into something wondrous. Never has she seen anything as beautiful as the quiver of its throat.

"Olivia," her father whispers. *"Walk."*

And so she does. Slowly and carefully, eye on the bird that's not once separated from the flower, its wings a blur. A few more steps and she's outside. Still, the bird drinks, but then must feel the air on its back, its feathers soaking in warmth, because it lifts into the air and hovers. A pause before leaving.

Back inside, she steadies herself against a chair.

"You know the nickname for this plant?" her father asks as he sets it outside. "Right there on the label. The Magic Flower. That things like this happen. This world, Olivia, I don't know what went on there, on your trip, but this world, as horrible as it can be, there are times like this you have to remember."

And though he's smiling again, it turns with a degree of sadness. Like when Delan watched her and Lailan lumber down the hall on her last day in Kurdistan, that look of having glimpsed a place he could never go. A look that makes sense when her father speaks again. "Man," he says, as he takes a seat. "She'd have loved this."

Her mother. And yet in Olivia's mind, she sees Lailan on Soran's hip, the two of them in the garden, with him pointing out the magic. The plant is just outside the door, red flowers drenched in what's left of the sun, a plant that never should've been here to begin with. Looking at it now, she feels her skin chill as if something's been traced against her back. "He would've loved it too."

Her father straightens in his chair. "You mean he *will*."

With a deep breath, she explains that she means someone else. And her father sits back in his chair and asks her to tell him. And she does.

CHAPTER 14

May 7, 1979

What if you wake up only to die that day?

Back in Los Angeles, these words come to her as the recollections have started to do. Insistent. Flashes mostly, but sometimes entire sequences descend upon her, and it feels as though she's somehow walking in her mind. No longer a part of this world but a part of that world. Smelling tea and spices. Feeling Delan's hand in hers. Hearing the cries. When she realizes where she is, it's as if she's woken, confused. A sleepwalker caught midstroll.

And Delan called. Just once, when Olivia was in Washington. Rebecca told him where she was, was even about to recite the phone number until Delan cut her off. "I just needed to know she made it okay. That she's with her dad—that's good. Good. Okay, listen, I'll call another day. It's expensive, so tell her everything's fine unless she hears from me."

There was guilt in Rebecca's voice as she relayed the message. That she'd been the one to talk to him. That she'd forgotten to ask how to reach him, just in case. *Everything's fine,* she repeated to Olivia, and Olivia held those words within her and then took them apart and searched for alternate meanings, ultimately whittling the statement down to the point where it could mean nothing or everything.

Today will be her first day back at work. The freeway she takes is packed, the windows of almost every car rolled down. Smoke drifting. A jumble of music from car radios. Los Angeles in May means ripening peaches and wilting lettuce, bougainvillea that's blinding fuchsia in the sun.

At least she still has a job; she called on Friday to be sure. "Your roommate Rebecca has kept us in the loop," the office manager said. "About the flight, and . . ." But her words trailed and ended. She was new, and Olivia couldn't remember her name, just the shade of her hair, which was file-cabinet beige. Shellacked to the same shine. "Don't you worry," she continued. "You haven't taken time off in *years* and with what you went through, well, you're just fine. We've got Helen Fisher on your desk, though I know Mr. Hensley is *desperate* to get you back. Big bark but soft heart, right? He's been telling everyone he needs his girl back."

The steps are wider, and there seem to be more people on them. The building's glass doors are taller, reflecting clouds and other places she'd rather be. When she steps into the bullpen, everyone turns, and she realizes that Rebecca must have said a lot, because people are searching her for scars. They're looking for a limp, a darkness in her eyes. She pulls down her sleeves—there are no scars, but she doesn't like them looking—and refuses to give them anything.

Phones ring. Someone tips a Styrofoam cup, and water rushes over a desk. People follow her with their eyes, and suddenly she remembers her daydream of walking in just like this, though covered in soot, a physical manifestation of disaster versus the internal mess she suffers. The thought of that fantasy, that disgusting, horrible fantasy where she was *excited* to tell of something dramatic, where in her mind she'd been brave and thought an audience would be reward for that bravery, shames her.

The second she sits, Helen Fisher rushes over. "You're back. You don't have to talk about it. I hope the wedding was at least nice?"

Olivia's eyes narrow and her voice falters and she forces herself to ask questions about dry cleaning and files and did he remember that his wife's birthday is coming up? The day continues as days tend to do, if you're lucky. At one point, she's typing when she sees a hand on a folder on her desk and looks up to find Ben.

"Lunch?" he asks. Behind him, people watch, and she understands he's asking her not because he wants to but because he thinks he can. Because he has an audience. Because he senses he's the one to get the scoop. Perhaps he even told them what happened, an achievement to have once bagged the damaged girl, and she recalls not that long ago when she thought this would've been the worst thing that could happen to her. For too long, she stares at his polyester shirt that's divided into diamonds, red and black. The colors of a darkroom. *A cloud goes over the moon, it's darkroom black,* Delan said, and for a moment she is back in his town and everything is still yet to occur.

"Lunch?" Ben says again, as if maybe she just needed another prompt.

"I'll be working. But thank you." She stretches a smile across her face, and he flinches, actually flinches, which makes her laugh. There are lines on his shirt from having been folded. Fresh from the store. A morning-after purchase.

"You're back," a voice says. Mr. Mosley's secretary.

"Let us know if you need anything," someone else adds.

A bit later, she finds herself in the break room, deep in her mind. A timer sounds. Lunch. She takes her bag from inside the refrigerator and on her way out sees that the notice for the contest is still taped on the door. The roll of film under her bed. She thinks of it, the only one she didn't develop while in Washington. The rest she developed and printed, an activity that oddly kept her mind off the very subjects she was studying, as if reducing what pained her to a rote activity, containing everything within the context of work—ultimately facing what happened in a safer way. There were, of course, a few times she lost her train of thought and simply felt. Hewar smiling at the bird, the lines in his face and his ears undid her. That glimpse of Delan's valley, as she thinks of it, when they'd pulled over by the hawthorn tree, a moment of pure *before*. Lailan in the garden, doing her art, the bend of her wrist and those fine, tiny bones as she positioned a stone, scolding it when it didn't stay in place. And the brothers at Shanidar Cave. Delan facing her but turned away. Olivia stared at the cuff of Soran's shirt, his hand in his pocket, then hung the photo to dry and felt her way to the corner of the darkroom where she sank and stared into the reddened black.

But that one roll. That will live under her bed until one day she moves, and then it will move with her. No one needs to see those images.

She's thinking this, feeling protective of its secret, wanting to contain it as if it were a seed that should never be planted, when she notices that Kyle Rudger—whose father is LAPD—and Trevor Miller—whose grandmother should be dead by now—are also in the room and watching her, observing her as if at any moment she could blow. Still, she can't look away from the damn flyer, and so she doesn't see when Peter Darrow, the photo editor, walks in.

He stops when he sees her, then notices the object of her study. "I heard you were there taking photos."

He's never spoken to her. Not once. Has he ever even seen her till now? Red, blonde, brunette, the women in the bullpen must be a long-haired calico blur. She looks him dead in the eye, and he must see that she's about to cry, which upsets her more. He tilts his head, and his mouth parts with something he's about to say, and his eyes are a kindness, a light amber like the color of just-poured tea, and with this thought, she has to bite the inside of her cheek to keep her here, in this moment, and not there, in that moment. When she speaks, she speaks the truth.

"I was. I took more photos than I ever had a right to."

Always get the shot, Delan said. If only he knew.

CHAPTER 15

June 1, 1979

Time's passage feels wrong. A betrayal with every trip to the grocery store, every TV show she watches, every tank of gas she puts in her car, standing by the pump as lights at the intersection change and people stop and start, stop and start. To go on. To do the little things, they're the worst. To indulge in the mundane, in the face of what's monumental. *You move* with. *You move with, but you move. That's the point. You cannot stop.* She reminds herself of this during the day, but at night it's different. A full devastation. The emptiness beside her a depression she can't help find herself in. A comfort, really, to swim inside this hurt.

Driving to work, she's got an envelope with Peter Darrow's name on one side and a number that corresponds to her on the back of the three photographs within. Photographs he will surely identify as hers, given the location and that he knows where she went. As she parks her car, she tells herself that what she's doing is okay, that she should still submit to the contest because the photos are good, and what happened does not take away from that fact, but by the time she's at her desk, she's found her apprehension again and leans the envelope against her dictionary, forgetting about it until a voice serves as the reminder.

"These them?"

Peter Darrow stands before her, on a pacing mission with his hockey stick. There is a coffee stain in the shape of Africa on his striped shirt, and it takes a moment for Olivia to look away, to realize he must have spotted his name on the envelope. Behind him, a few faces have turned, curious.

She shrugs, and the gesture makes her think of Delan. "What I can handle looking at."

"You haven't seen everything?"

"One roll, I haven't."

"You know, then—that's the one you should be looking at."

She shakes her head. "I can't. But it doesn't matter. The winning photo isn't there."

He picks up the envelope. "It's here?"

"I don't know," she says. "Maybe that doesn't matter either."

He looks out at the bullpen, over to Mr. Hensley's office. Behind his glass wall, Olivia's boss watches them, craning his head to see what Peter Darrow has in his hand.

"You know it matters," Peter says. "I know you do. And at some point, we need to talk. Because whether you can do it or not is one thing, but what you saw when you took the shot is a whole other beast."

When he leaves, he takes the envelope with him, and it feels as if she's given away something like a baby tooth or a lock of hair, something whose value only she could understand.

And then she is wearing her sneakers, dusty from the hike into the mountains, and the day beats beautiful around her. Birds sing as if in celebration—until another sound breaks through. A wail. High at first, piercing through like an arrow till it falls. The world goes quiet out of respect for this sound. Looking down at her orange shoes, she understands she cannot look up again, because she knows what she will find. Her back, exposed to danger, begins to burn until suddenly she realizes that she's no longer in the mountains but in fact at home, in Los Angeles, in bed, and beneath her, the roll of film has ignited and is on fire. Flames shoot from the canister through the mattress and into her spine, the intensity growing until finally she wakes, rolling over in bed and rubbing the small of her back, shocked to feel the skin intact. She doesn't need to look under the bed to know the film is fine, that everything was born from the dream, from her subconscious. It's not the first time she's had this dream. It's not the first time the film has called to her, trying to get her attention.

Her eyes go to the gift Hewar gave her, still wrapped in brown paper, propped against the wall by her desk. *Wait, then,* Rebecca said when Olivia admitted she was afraid to open it. *Wait till the trip doesn't make you fucking cry and* then *open it, because he intended it as a good thing, not something to make you sad.* But even looking at the brown paper, now dulled with a settling of dust, makes her want to cry, so she grabs the package, opens her closet, and sets it toward the back. Passing her dresser, she sees the gold and silver chains and beads that hang on a brass necklace tree. *Lailan.* What's she doing now? Maybe collecting bits and pieces for her art. Sitting on the path below the pomegranate tree, watching the leaves turn against a fading day. Or feeding the chukars leftover fruit. Back in bed, Olivia closes her eyes and remembers the smell of the melon the birds loved, the hint of pineapple from the white flesh. She sees the orange netted rind held in Lailan's fingers, the small beds of her nails. *Hi-lo.* Even the memory of the word is an undoing.

A sound starts up. Coyotes. A pack of them. Yipping. A haunting call that means they've got something. Someone's cat, most likely. *But they have to eat too,* Delan always said. *This is life.* This sound—there used to be a time when it was the most chilling thing she'd heard in the night. Now she listens to their celebratory chaos, the clamor that says something horrible has happened, and thinks *it is night,* because she knows that night is when danger slips in, unseen.

A few days later, all the photos that were submitted are displayed in a long glass case that lines the hall. The images catch her off guard. She'd forgotten this would happen. People cluster, whispering, pointing, and boasting. And though there are no names attached to the images, just numbers below each entry, it makes no difference because hints by subject or location provide obvious clues. Kyle Rudger and his LAPD photos. Hannity and his street scenes. Trevor Miller and his dying grandmother. And Olivia's. Scattered throughout the others, each of her photographs is of Kurds. Obvious. Seeing them there, it's as if a fierce and sudden wind has rushed around her. Everyone, she thinks, is looking at her. She will not meet their eyes, so she studies the other entries, some that were shot with wide-angled lenses and seem to ramble, jumbled with subject matter. Others that are landscapes with the horizon smack in the middle so any tension is erased and the composition's static. And many that are portraits with the subject's shadows pointing in different directions from too many sources of light. When she turns back to her photos, it's as if she's seeking the comfort of friends. And indeed she does feel comforted, just looking at their faces, but then gutted by them here, on a wall.

Delan, at their home in Los Angeles, the morning he sat reading the paper with tears on his face. His father, wearing the Kurdish turban, watching the bird outside, eyes bright with bliss as he found beauty in a world that should've proven anything but. And the family, sitting on the floor of the kitchen during the raid, faces turned to the window, the knobs of the stove bright. None of the photos blazes with risk or circumstance, but every image made her cry, and she figured perhaps even a tiny bit of her emotion would find its way to others.

Now she sees her mistake. People look at her on her way to her desk, and they're disappointed. Here she came back as if shell-shocked and provided only what amounts to portraits. They expected danger and death. Guns and explosions. A justification for her difference, for the change in her that's had her keep to herself, that's made her grit her teeth and stare back at people whose eyes she should avoid. Even that beige-haired office manager had whispered a warning as if she'd sensed Olivia nearing a cliff. *Careful now.*

She wants to go home. But there's too much to do. Before her is her steno pad with a to-do list that's fourteen items long, and as she tries to make sense of the words, she realizes it's someone else's because the handwriting is all sloppy loops, everything curling and tumbling and on a slope as if gathering speed on an incline. But then she focuses and recognizes the day's chores as her own. Flips back a handful of pages and sees that it is in fact hers, that she is the person with the untrained hand and the scattered mind.

For a moment, she sits with her confusion. Then gets up, needing coffee.

In the break room, Hannity and Miller are loading doughnuts onto plates.

Miller looks up, sugar on his lips. "Our Middle Eastern correspondent has arrived."

She nods a greeting, beelining to the coffee machine.

"Thank God. We need a new pot," Hannity says. "Tried making some but you'll see."

And she does. It's pale. Like water run through a teaspoon of grinds. As she dumps it in the sink, another editor walks into the room.

"Oh, good," he says. "Stronger this time, 'kay?"

This doesn't matter. She scoops the grounds into the filter, over and over till what will brew will be sludge. Then she pours in the water, flips the switch, and heads toward the door.

"Putting money on the game this weekend. You want in?" Miller asks Hannity.

"Nah, if there's one thing I hate more than wasting time, it's wasting money."

"Ever tell you I did two years premed? Talk about wasting time *and* money. Always good to know what you can handle. And what you can't. Some people just aren't cut out for things."

This doesn't matter, she repeats again in her mind. The machine begins to chug as she pushes through the door, frustrated that muddy coffee is her only retort.

People are still gathered in the hall, observing and scrutinizing the photos, and with this, all thoughts of coffee and insults are gone because the truth is she's violated Delan and his family by allowing them to be here for anyone to see. Hewar especially. To capture his joy like that and place it on a wall—how did she not see it as invasive? A betrayal? His wrinkles, the folds in his face from years of life hard lived. And those ears. What if people are making fun of him for his ears? The very thought makes her hunch at her desk, coffee from the morning rising in her throat. Him and his quiet kindness, his love for birds and animals—now he's on a wall and people are pointing. Everything inside her feels as though it's collapsing. Wrong. Everything she's done is wrong.

"Lunch?"

She looks up, angry, expecting it to be Ben coming in for the scoop, but it's Peter Darrow.

"Come on, come on," he says. "I told you we gotta talk."

Around them, the bullpen watches.

"Okay."

He nods, then knocks on her desk twice before heading toward the door.

The restaurant is ten tables long. Old newspapers shellacked on the wall. Tortilla chips served in red baskets with oil-darkened paper. Now and then, onions and meat sizzle, scattered on a grill, and in the corner of the room hangs a dusty sign advertising beer.

"This isn't because you won the contest," Peter says, sliding his menu toward the edge of the table. "You know that, right? Because I'm not saying who won. Not till the end. There are politics about who gets picked. You mighta guessed."

She's thrown. "But how? It's anonymous." Fair. Based on merit.

He unfolds his napkin to tuck it in his collar. "Even you know who took half the photos up there. Nothing's anonymous. And I know this bib business looks like I'm ten, but I've recently been told by Byron I need to up my caring percentage. As if my inability to eat a burrito without wearing it means I don't care. Might even have to shave, he said."

Her eyes go wide. "No."

"Worse than my wife, that man is. Even she just asks me to trim it."

"I guess he is the boss."

"Says anyone who hasn't met my wife."

She nods, staring at him, trying to figure out what he'd look like, where the lines of his jaw actually are. "What you said, though. I feel like you're telling me I didn't get it."

"I'm just saying *I* want it to be talent only, and that's not so easy. But that's my battle. You let me fight that. Now, we're talking. But first, figure out what you want to order because these guys are fast."

She studies the menu for only a second, then copies him and slides it to the edge of the table.

He nods. "A friend once told me that to be an artist, you have to have a little monster in you. I don't mean you gotta be cruel, though maybe some see it that way. What I mean is, you gotta be fierce. Taking photos of something means you're observing. You're not changing. Of course you need compassion—you save someone if you can—but in most cases, you can't. You're there to document. And though you know that, it can do a number on your head because there's a ruthlessness there. Witnessing and walking away. Lotta guilt."

"But I didn't even document when it mattered. Any bravery I thought I had, I didn't. My camera was the last thing I thought of. I thought of me."

"First and foremost, we gotta stay alive."

The waitress appears, pen in hand. Peter motions for Olivia to order first, and she asks for two chicken tacos. Then sees the sign in dulled red and green. "And a cerveza, please."

Peter's eyebrows lift, and for a second she thinks he's going to tell her that drinking on company time isn't wise. But instead he nods and turns to the waitress. "Same for me. Cerveza, as well." He waits till the woman is gone and then turns back to Olivia. "All right. Give me the skinny. Tell me what you saw when you weren't thinking of your camera."

So she tells him of the night at the restaurant. The dust, the blood, the shoes in the street and limbs that were torn away or angled wrong. The way her ears rang. The pull, as if magnetic, to cling close to walls and others, to not be the one caught out in the open. "We walked for a mile, I think, before I remembered my camera. In my purse. Loaded and ready."

Their food arrives, and she moves aside her plate and tells him more, only sipping her beer until he reaches across the table and pushes the plate back to her. "Eat. I can't return you tipsy."

So she does. And then tells him about the night the soldiers came, how at first it had not made sense but that once she ran for Lailan, it became real, no longer something that could be safely documented through a window, and that at that point, all thoughts of her camera were gone. Until she happened to see it in the kitchen.

He sits back. "That's the photo? You could tell something horrible was happening for those people to be on the floor. Haunting. That genie lamp. Like a wish gone wrong. The shadow play, thanks to your low angle and the lighting. Everyone looking toward the window. You could hear them listening. No caption necessary—you felt the fear."

Those people. She knows he didn't mean it that way, but the words stick with her. Then she remembers how they'd snuck outside to find Miriam. How they'd fallen asleep together, all of them in the dining room, on the cushions, afraid to be alone. How she wished it were a dream and woke the next day telling herself it was. A family she loved at one of their worst times. Now on a wall. *Those people.* "I shouldn't have submitted it."

"You're protective of them. I get that."

She nods and spears a piece of chicken with her fork.

"Tacos," he says. "A handheld food, by the way." He smiles and watches as she continues to eat with her fork, then takes a swig of his beer and yanks off his bib, done. "I went through this. With a kid. Only knew him for a day, one shitty day that you don't need to hear about and I talked about enough to kill some of the ache, but I couldn't look at those images for months. I'd seen firsthand that a camera could be more powerful than a rifle, but it didn't make it easier, coming back and just trying to *be* after everything. It's a catch. You gotta be invested in your subject. You gotta have empathy or it's obvious you don't. But you can't be so invested that you don't get the shot. So I learned it then. It's a mistake, getting close to your subjects. It's a mistake to care too much. And accepting that, it either destroys you or makes you better." Another swig and he seems to think of something. "That girl, though. You said you weren't brave. But you saved her. You know that, right?"

The tears are fast and infuriating. She holds her fists to her eyes, as if it would mask the fact that she's crying, and Peter awkwardly leans across the table and presses his napkin toward her.

"People are gonna think I just dumped you," he says, and she laughs and sees red taco sauce from his plate now on his shirt. She points and he looks down, shaking his head as the waitress drops off a damp cloth, which he uses to dab at the spot futilely. "Give yourself time. What you went through, it's a system shocker. Be kind to yourself. You didn't do anything wrong."

And then she takes a deep breath and tells him about the other roll of film, the one under her bed—the time she did do something wrong. She tells him that the film makes her dream back that day. And he listens and flags the waitress for two more beers.

"We can look at it together," he says when the waitress brings the check. "Use the lab at work. After hours. No one there to witness any of it."

"But I know what's there. Even when I wasn't looking, I know what happened. I just don't want to see it again."

"You lived it. But facing it after the fact, that's a different part of processing it. That's what your dream is telling you—to look at it. Trying to forget isn't making it go away."

"I don't know if I'm ready."

"Then you're not ready. When you are, you let me know. Next week, in a year. Whenever. I'm not going anywhere, even though I should. All you kids taking over." He grabs the check from the billfold and she reaches for her purse. "No. Paper's paying. This is a working meal." A pause. "You've got it, you know. I don't know if I told you that."

At first, she thinks he's talking about the check, which is in his hand, but then she understands what he's saying. Her smile is brief, but the words linger in her mind.

A half block from their building, Peter stops walking. The man behind him is forced to stop short and glares as he passes.

"It's not over," Peter says. "But I'm not gonna lie to you. The contest is looking like a formality. Politics. Like I said."

My uncle just shot eighteen with Byron. Hannity. The whole thing makes her sick. A farce. A way to get the staff invested. Toying with them for months, making them think they had a chance, upping morale with a false promise of opportunity. She can't look at him, still trying to understand. "So they're giving it to Hannity."

"I didn't say. And I didn't say I agreed with it, whatever *it* is."

"It's your department."

"But not my paper."

"Okay," she says, now facing him, "so why, then? Why are you helping me?"

He takes her arm and pulls her toward the side of the building, out of the way of others.

"Because I saw it in you. What I went through. When you came back, that look. You were a ghost of yourself."

We're two ghosts walking in a garden. He's watching to make sure we don't disappear.

"Most people, they take their vacation, they get Hawaii exotic or visit the in-laws, go see the Grand Canyon. Hotels and pool drinks. I heard someone was going to Iraq, I was interested. I heard it was you, and you were there taking photographs, I was more interested. Then you came back and I saw you were still there. And I know what that's like. You're an island. And no one needs to be an island."

A clenching in her chest. It's too much at once; she's grateful, devastated, and somehow, strangely, hopeful. But when she opens her mouth, the *thank you* she'd intended shifts, and different words emerge. "I left her there."

The sun is hot on her face. She closes her eyes, and her lids burn orange. All around her, people talk and horns sound and a bird scolds, while inside her is a realization that this, after everything she's said to him, is the hardest to admit. Because she will see Delan again. He is planning on coming back; their story will continue. But with Lailan, there was an ending.

"The girl," he says, taking her arm and nodding her forward, toward their building.

The broad steps narrow before her. The sidewalk specked with something that shines. She slows. It's the end of their talk but will be the beginning of everyone else's, just from watching them enter the office together. Colleagues back from lunch, in truth, but it will be told a million other ways. "I left her," she says again.

"Like I said. Witnessing and walking away. Lotta guilt there."

"But I didn't just witness."

He holds the door open for her. "No. You didn't. And I'm sorry about that." Already he's been spotted; one of his secretaries rushes to him with a manila envelope. He holds up a hand, demanding a moment. "Like I said, even if you didn't have talent, I was gonna talk to you. But when I saw that you did—it was just more reason to keep you going. So that's why. Just wanted to get you off your island."

CHAPTER 16

June 7, 1979

A moonlit heat. Olivia and Rebecca are on the porch in shorts and tank tops, their feet on the railing. Gin and tonics are on a melt and asphalt scorches into the night—one of those days that simply won't curl off in temperature, like a straight line of fever. Sweat snakes down Olivia's throat and "My Sharona" stutters from next door.

"He's coming back," Rebecca says. "That's why you didn't say it."

Then more music. The ominous blare of horns and throbbing bass of Van Halen's "Runnin' with the Devil," pounding from a gold-colored Firebird that's paused before their house. The driver leans forward to meet their eyes, his head practically upon the steering wheel, and smoke twists from the open window.

"I didn't say it because I was trying to force fate's hand. Like not saying goodbye would *make* him come back. Force him to come back to say it. Like something unfinished must be finished." Though of course she should've known this not to be true. She tries to think of Soran's last words, and still she cannot hear them.

"Dream on!" Rebecca yells, waving the driver away. "This is how they meet girls? Move! No one cares! Christ. You might be right. Maybe it's true. The unfinished can't be finished. And he *is* unfinished. He owes for the mortgage." She smiles. "Pretty sure Mason will make him come back, even if he has to go to Kurdistan to collect."

"Maybe we can leave Mason there in exchange." Olivia offers a smile to show she can still joke, that her life isn't strictly woven of sadness. Though she's not joking, she realizes.

"He's going through something too," Rebecca says. "With Delan gone. I think he always felt like the third wheel when you were together. Ever since you guys became lovey-dovey—he's just worried Delan doesn't need him."

Love. She no longer knows if holding back was right. Sometimes she would do anything to have told him she loves him. For him to know, for certain. And to hear his voice say those words. Other times, she knows it was held back wisely, as if they needed that one moment to still remain. Something else left unfinished that demanded another day. "I don't care what Mason's going through."

Mason has thrown two parties since she's been back, and he acts as though nothing is amiss while his friends watch the door, expecting Delan to appear. The last time Olivia went downstairs to lower the music, she got stuck talking to a man who went on about his Houston Oilers and then beat his chest as he made promises for their coming year. She heard the sound, the pounding, the thuds upon a heart, and remembered the women who beat their chests as they wailed and had to turn away, to lean into the wall and fight to stay present and where she was. But then she thought of Lailan. Watching from her room as Gaziza's voice soared into the air, seeing the man who'd loved her and cared for her lifeless on the ground below. *Soran. Lailan.* A tactile memory—Olivia could almost feel a little hand within her own.

But it's not about Mason, Olivia reminds herself. What she's going through is a result of loss. His loss, her loss, his loss. "He's not back and I still didn't say goodbye. It was stupid."

"You had your reasons."

"My reason was I couldn't handle saying it."

Rebecca takes this with a nod. "I'm sorry."

Since Olivia's return, Rebecca has stayed home with her, telling her boyfriend she needs space. This may or may not be the case, but Olivia doesn't care because the truth is she needs her, Rebecca with her fierce manner and sisterly protection.

"That book," Rebecca suddenly says. "With all his phone numbers. Can you find it? In his room? Call and say hi. Connect, even for a second."

His room. Shoes, tossed by the closet. A hairbrush left on his nightstand. Last moves, last choices. Both pillows still held an indent. She'd stared at the one on the left, his side, seeing his face against the white.

"I found it. Half is written in Kurdish. I would have no idea who I was calling even if I could read the numbers. *And* I don't speak the language. *And* the calls to his family are tapped. I say the wrong thing, I could make it worse."

Rebecca takes a long pull of her gin and tonic. "Good points. You've brought a new level to relationship issues. I'm not familiar with this one, and I've been around a few blocks."

Olivia takes a sip of her drink and holds the lime in her teeth, pain shooting from the cold. *A lime tree,* Delan used to say. *For our gin and tonics. Why don't we have a lime tree?*

"I'm getting a lime tree."

Rebecca nods. "He'll love that. All his gin and tonics."

The moon above seems alone in the night, center stage in a cloudless sky. The same moon he would've seen. Something about that makes everything worse, that they can be so connected and yet so apart, and so she looks away, back to their bare feet on the porch railing. Her toenail polish is chipped and dull. Meanwhile, Rebecca's is the perfect shining red of an apple meant to tempt. *You want this?* Rebecca asked the other day, when Olivia walked in on her painting her nails at the coffee table. *It wouldn't be the worst thing to go out, you know,* she added. *A drink maybe. Want to?* And so Olivia spent ten minutes staring into her closet as if reading a book that had slid into a different language. The suede patchwork miniskirt that used to be a constant familiar no longer made sense. Her wants and needs had changed, she realized. Going out was no longer about catching eyes and trying to outshine others at a bar but about being happy and maybe forgetting and coming back whole and in one piece. So she grabbed her jeans and a clean T-shirt and knew that the least she could do was paint her nails, but she couldn't. What she had on was the orange polish that she couldn't bear to wipe away, the last bit of the trip upon her. The last touch of *before*. Already a light bulb burned out in their kitchen, and changing it felt like a horrible admission. *He is not here, but life goes on.*

Again the dream. Again her back burns, the film below her on fire. When she wakes, she stares into the dark of her room and adds to a list she's started in her mind of all the reasons that Lailan will be okay, a list of what is good, because too often, Olivia thinks only of the bad. The land where Lailan lives is wild with beauty. Fruit tastes better there than it does here. There's a connection to the past, to the start of the world, and the very ground is soaked in history. People are friendly and neighbors wave to one another and call each other by name, and one person's tragedy belongs to all. Bright dresses and blue skies. Nights on a roof with a ceiling of stars. She is okay, Olivia tells herself, but still there is the fact that Lailan was born in a land wedged between people who want her gone, and with this, the girl's very existence falters with uncertainty.

In the morning, a heavy mist hangs in the front yard. Windshields obscured. Lawns silvered. Through it all, she spots a rose. One tall, bright-yellow rose in the neighbor's yard: the rosebush she thought was dead. The one Soran promised her was still alive. Leaves are full upon it and new branches have shot out—it must've grown two or three feet and yet she'd not even noticed.

You will have a rose to look at. And me to think of.

Tonight, she decides. Tonight she'll develop and print the film. Face whatever it is her subconscious needs her to face. But she thinks of how her hands shook when she took the photos. How sick she'd felt, unable to even look up. And that was when she believed the person a stranger. Now it will be worse, and there is only one chance with this film and many ways she could destroy it. Break down at the wrong moment and the images would be gone.

She slides the box from under her bed. Inside is the canister. With her fingertip, she feels its warning dent, then slips it in her pocket.

At work, the bullpen is a mass of ringing phones, slamming file cabinets, and rushing steps. Now and then, she catches Peter Darrow on the upper landing, talking with another editor and pacing with his hockey stick on his shoulders, a frightening, hulking presence with his arms spread out. When she finds an excuse to go upstairs, she passes his office but sees him on the phone and so keeps walking, relieved. Maybe it won't be today, she thinks. But on her way back, he's done—the time is now. Still, she keeps walking to the stairs and is halfway down when she sees her boss hovering by her desk. With that, she stops and quickly turns around.

Peter Darrow looks up when she knocks, spotting her through the glass. "Enter. Please."

Inside his office, she holds out the film canister. "I can't do it. But I want it done. And not messed up by Fotomat or someone else."

He takes the canister. "Got it. Won't mess it up."

She nods.

As she starts to leave, he holds up his hand. "Wait. I'll fight for you. I don't know if it makes it better or worse to know that."

"Better," she says. "Always better."

The sky is leaking blue, settling into a white blind of heat when she gets home, her car stifling even with the windows down. An early heat this year. A taste of a ruthless summer. The threat of what's to come matches the worry she feels about the film, about everything. Trying not to think, she peels her legs off the seat and gets out of the car. There, by the back steps, is a lime tree in a black container.

Rebecca sees her enter the living room and raises a glass of wine. "Did you see? That's for you. And him. Win or lose, 'you have it, you know.' What's wrong?"

"Anxious. Can't talk about it."

"Then don't," she says and nods to the spot on the couch opposite her. "I might move in with Gary."

"Wait, what?"

"I am, actually. Moving in with him. I didn't want to tell you and I know you need me, so I told him not for a bit. A couple of months. More if you need."

Olivia leans forward and touches Rebecca's hand. "You do what you want to do. I'm *happy* for you. You're happy, right?"

Rebecca smiles. "I am. I feel like it's lame—you know, maintain independence and all that. Like after all this proving myself, I shouldn't be content to move into his place and ask for half the closet. But I want to. Because I like his house. And he gets up early like me. Goes to sleep early. We're boring. But he cooks and I don't and, you know, I love him."

"You're going to be fine. And it's okay to love someone. And to want to be loved. It's not a weakness."

"Yeah, I get it. And I have a couple of bank accounts he doesn't know about." She smiles. "The mathematics of risk—I like them in my favor."

"Come on, a drink to this."

Friday night. Barry Manilow slides to the Bee Gees. Fans on high. Glasses poured full. The world pounds at the doorstep, chaos and bills and expectations and doubt all held back. Another splash of wine, another song. Sitting on the couch, rehashing childhood and loves and old dreams of a future that turns out to be now. It's not till the dregs of the second bottle that she remembers her anxiety and why—that she'd given Peter Darrow the film to print.

Just like that, the night skids to a stop. A threshold breached. Rebecca leans over in a wobbly flash, hand on her shoulder as she tells her not to worry—but Rebecca doesn't know. Olivia's told no one other than Peter about the film. Until now. As Olivia speaks, Rebecca sinks farther into the velvet clutch of the couch and rubs her forehead till a reddened streak appears. Then Mason swaggers into the room, with a girl on his arm and a wide smile on his face. "What it is, ladies?" And so she tells him. The girl he brought home says she should go, and he lets her.

The next day is cooler. Crows strut in the yard, stabbing at the ground, and Olivia's head's in a vise, Rebecca hiding in her room. When Mason enters the kitchen, he sees Olivia and laughs almost proudly, as if he should take credit.

"Can't say I didn't know this was coming," he says as he pours sugar into a cup. "And that's my shirt."

She looks down at a T-shirt stained with old paint. Somehow she'd also put on the red sweatpants from Geneva. "I found it in the dryer." She swallows heavily, watching him rinse lemons in the sink. "I needed something soft. Sorry."

"Take it. It's yours. God, you two last night. Laverne and Shirley on a tear."

She lowers her head back onto the table.

"Drink," he says after a bit, handing her a glass. "Water, sugar, salt, lemon. Down it."

So she does, so fast it rises back up. She tilts her head back and breathes in and out, forcing the rhythm. "I think I need to lie down."

"Obviously."

She's on the first stair in the living room when there's a knock on the door. "Mason," she says, barely a whisper.

"Got it."

She's just hit the second-floor landing when she hears Peter Darrow's voice. Everything rises in her—hangover, fear, guilt—and she doesn't move until Mason calls to her, as if perhaps she could've slipped through the moment undetected. Slowly she returns and there he is, in what must be his weekend wear: brown Adidas warm-up pants with white stripes on the sides and a matching zippered sweatshirt. His beard, miraculously, is even wilder, as if fed by the extra hours of sleep. She tilts her head, trying to understand, and in turn, Peter's eyes widen when he sees her.

Then, mercifully, he looks to the triptych of the discarded Christmas trees. "Yours?"

"An assignment. From way back when."

"I could tell. Not that it's an assignment but that it's yours."

"You can?" she asks, alarmed. "Isn't that bad?"

He smiles. "No. We are who we are, and we like what we like. And lucky for you, you know how to trap a gaze. You've got an eye and an awesome sense of composition. And a real ability to capture mood."

"I'm drawn to mood."

"I can tell. It's one of those intangibles you either get or you don't."

And then she sees it: the Pee-Chee folder in his hand.

He continues, holding it against his leg as if knowing she's spotted it but not ready. "I'll tell you the one that really got me. Of what you turned in."

"The one in the kitchen? When we were hiding?" *When we were hiding.* Said like *when we were at the lake* or something equally as nullifying.

"That's a damn fine photo. Haunting. Better than most of the crap I print. But I'm talking about the man reading the paper."

The man. "Delan."

He nods. He knew that but was encouraging distance. "Again, the intangible. Like the older man looking out the window. Pure emotion. Emotion is what's lacking in Miller's photos."

"I know. They're just of an old woman. You don't even know she's dying."

"Because there was no one else. No response, no reaction to the moment. They evoked nothing. But these Christmas trees—shit if you didn't nail the intangible. I feel worse for them than the dying lady." He motions toward the hall. "But the man—Delan—I'm assuming that was here."

She nods. "Guess I didn't even need to go to the Middle East."

"To take a good photo? No. You already had it. But for *you*? Only you know that."

Suddenly she can't take it and sits heavily, sloppily on the stairs. She leans her head against the wall, and the room tilts.

"That photo, though," he continues. "The blinds, the window, the angle. Your composition. Everything else can be a skill, but composition's where a photograph becomes art." He glances back at the triptych. "You know they see it too. The guys at work. They look at those photos and they see it even if they don't want to admit it. That's why they're hard on you."

"One reason, maybe." He's standing in a reach of light from the open door, and she averts her eyes from the brightness. "I don't know if I can," she says, nodding to the folder.

"I wouldn't want to either. That's why I'm here. Didn't want to give this to you at work. Some of it's blurry, but too much of it isn't. I used a color filter to bring out the subjects, which helped, but you might not thank me for it."

She looks at the yellow-and-orange folder, the drawings of a woman playing tennis, two boys playing football, and others off to the races. She used to color them in. Adding googly eyes and wild hair, back when the only goal was to escape a teacher's words.

He motions toward the kitchen, where Mason's most likely eating his cereal. "You've got someone here to be with you?"

A rush of car tires outside sounds like rain. Then there's a blast of light as he shifts, moving slightly to the side. She blinks. Behind him is a small point of yellow. The rose. Upstairs, a door opens and shuts and Rebecca calls to her, her name going long. *Oliviaaaaa.*

Olivia nods, and Peter hands her the folder.

Fear, apparently, chases away a hangover. At noon, she's at the nursery buying soil and compost and fertilizer. At the last minute, she throws in zucchini and tomatoes and anything else a man with a safari hat says likes hot weather.

Neither Mason nor Rebecca understands. They watch her in the yard with the shovel, sweating out last night's wine. It's only a very small section she's working on, but she will do it right. Dig out the weeds. Sift out the grass. Amend the soil. But the soil is packed and hard, and it takes hours to get the little bed ready, so when the first plant goes in, she stands back, exhausted in that earned way, the way that's edged with reward. There it is. One seedling with small leaves, just little flaps of green in a dark expanse. She kneels and plants the next one. And the next. Holding the new plants upright, tucking them in. *He will love this,* she tells herself. Those sad, hopeful words. Then she thinks of the vacant lot behind their house and decides that's next. A neighborhood garden. When he's back.

At last it's done, and she stands in their yard, observing. Baking in the Los Angeles sun and watching the windows of his room, feeling his absence like a draft. The folder is on her bed. After dinner, she decides, then she'll look inside. Now she cranks the knob on the faucet, and water pumps through the pipes and shoots from their sprinkler in a tinseling arc. The soil goes dark. Leaves drench and sag, but she knows they're being fortified. This is her favorite part. Like finally feeding someone a meal you spent all day making. She sits at the wooden table on the patio and watches the water, listening to its pulse.

The sun takes a turn. A moment of glow. Mason brings her a gin and tonic and sits at the table as well, opening his sketch pad. A mockingbird swoops from a wire to a tree, and gnats catch the light, becoming beautiful. Soon Rebecca brings out dinner. And life goes on.

Peter Darrow printed every photo in eight by ten. She can tell by the weight of the folder, the feel of the pages. Outside her door, she hears the floorboards groan and knows Rebecca and Mason are standing by. For a moment longer, she studies the drawing of the running men on the folder, the lines behind them that indicate a burst of speed. *Just look,* she tells herself. *Everything in here has been seen. Just look again.*

She flips it open. A piece of white paper is on the right, concealing the photos beneath, and with this she understands that they are the continuation and that he knew she'd need to ease her way in. He knew those images couldn't be the first seen.

So she looks to the left, and there it is. The first photo.

The valley, the houses. Damask rose oil mixed with the beauty of the day. Then the perspective changes—a new angle of the valley. And another one. One more and suddenly she hears the buckshot of birds, the frantic flapping wings. She'd turned, and then she'd seen. Now she flips to the next photo, and there it is. The man with the hood on his head, neck twisted from a punch. She's grateful for the hood. Perhaps the soldiers had been grateful as well—perhaps even they couldn't look him in the eye.

More photos. Him kneeling, trying to stand. Him on the ground, the soldier's leg extended to his stomach. The trees still beside them. Even now, she remembers the feeling of her back burning as if blistering, exposed. His body lengthened, a reaction to another kick. Still another, now to his mouth. Only when her hand comes away wet from her face does she realize she's crying, and for a moment she stares at her thumb, not wanting to look back because she knows what comes next. That gleam of the knife. But she has to do this. She flips to the next image, and there it is. A sheath of light from the blade. And the next photo, his body hunching. His body. She stares, adjusting the words. *Soran's* body. He was not the subject. He was Soran.

She lets herself feel this. Lets it wind through her, inching out, and then realizes she's shivering, cold, like those moments with a fever when blood goes to the heart in an effort at protection and the skin chills. She hears her own breathing, sharp inhalations that don't seem to bring enough oxygen.

But she forces herself to keep going. The next image blurs, just slightly. This is when her arms began to shake, her muscles trembling. The next one. From here on out, she realizes, she looked down. And just like then, she can't bear it now, to see this, but there he is. Soran folded over, dying. She looks away from him, to the side of the photo, to those unmoving trees. And that's when she sees it, something she'd not noticed before. Or not realized she'd noticed but must have, somewhere within her subconscious.

Quickly she flips through the rest of the photos, but all blur or worse. Then she flips back to the ones she already saw. And there it is again: a man who would ultimately be unable to escape his own burned image on film. In a few shots, he's beside a tree; in others he must be behind the tree. She grabs the sharpest photo and goes to her desk, shaking with the edge of understanding, then twists the shaft of her desk lamp to aim the beam at the image.

With her loupe, she leans down. Then sits back hard. After all this time, the answer was right here.

The man. Most likely *he* is why Soran had a hood on, so this man would not have to face the magnitude of his betrayal. Would not have to see it in Soran's eyes. At times, the man holds on to the tree, though in most other shots, he must have backed behind it. Not because he was hiding, Olivia realizes, but because he, too, could not stand the moment. Could not bear to witness what he'd done. But in one shot, there he is, turned in such a way that she can see his whole body. A man whose arm is in a sling. Their cousin.

CHAPTER 17

The phone bill.

Rebecca was the one who thought of it, who'd filed all their past statements in a cabinet in the kitchen, and so Olivia hunted for the one around when Delan called his parents, and there it was. A +964 number, connected through the operator.

Now she looks at the clock. Eight thirty p.m. here. Six thirty a.m. there. She picks up the phone.

Mason watches her with wide eyes. "What are you gonna say?"

But Olivia's not thinking. She's dialing the operator. Reading off the number. Oceans away, another operator answers and the call is put through. Ringing. And then a voice. Gaziza. The fact that it's this easy shames her. Why has she not thought of this before?

"*Choni,*" Olivia says. "*Eme Olivia ye.*" Nothing else comes to her, so she ends by saying, "Gaziza. *Delan?*"

"Olivia," Gaziza says and then follows with a flurry of Kurdish. Olivia's panic rises. Is he not there? At this hour, his absence would never be good.

Suddenly the line goes silent. Olivia shuts her eyes, trying to hear anything on the other end, but there's nothing. It occurs to her that the line could be disconnected, but she won't put down the receiver. Still, she holds it, placing a picture of him in her mind. He's sleepy. Going down the stairs. Going to the phone. *Please be there. Pick up the phone.*

"Is he there?" Mason asks.

"I don't know. Gaziza put the phone down, I think."

And then she hears a door close. A relief just that the line hasn't been disconnected. She takes a deep breath and then, for the first time in more than a month, hears Delan's voice.

"Is this you?" he asks.

Until this moment, she realizes, everything within her had been held with an unforgiving, unrelenting tension, one that finally, only now, subsides. A split-second change she feels in every inch of her body. And then she says his name, and simply saying it *to him* makes her eyes well. She stares at the bamboo kitchen light fixture, trying to settle herself.

"I had to call," she says, now wanting to get it all out, feeling the words jumble and scatter in her throat. "The photos. There's—"

"Did you win?"

"What?"

"The contest. At work."

"No. That's Friday, but that's not it." She stops. Because she hears a clicking on the line. *I heard clicking,* he told her. *That means the lines are tapped.* But did she imagine it? Could it be just a bad connection? "Did you hear that?" she asks. Which maybe she should not have.

In turn he's silent, as if listening, trying to hear what she's talking about. Or, she realizes, trying to figure out how to phrase his words. To warn her. "The knocking on the door?" he says at last. "Yes. Someone's here—I'll have to go soon. But my uncle, I'm sure you were going to ask, is the same. Not great. Nothing to worry about, though, I promise. But nothing to say."

Things are not okay. They're being listened to. He wants her to watch what she says. Beside her, Rebecca and Mason stare, questioning. Through the phone, she hears him yawn.

"Sorry," he says. "It's early. But I'm glad you called."

"You're all right?"

"In mourning. Let's not talk about that. But Lailan—wait till you hear this. *A weed.* She's grown like a weed. She kept saying she couldn't sleep, that her knees hurt, and sure enough, *an inch* this past month. Though I might have measured wrong. I don't know. But it was a lot, I'm telling you. And she talks about you all the time. Last week she colored her toenails orange, with a marker, to be like you. And she calls you Liv, like I do, but it sounds like *love* when she says it. And that necklace. She's not taken it off. But she gets sad because she didn't give you anything."

Olivia can't help it—now she's crying, arms on the table, face in the crook of her elbow. Beside her, Rebecca rubs her back in big circles. It's one thing to hear of this world in which she is a talked-about ghost, a world that, despite everything, she misses, but the futility is something else entirely. Because she can't be there. She can't help. She can't comfort Lailan or hold her. She can't even say why she's calling. Because if his cousin were working with the government, and the government is listening, to say anything to Delan would be dangerous.

"Are you crying?" he asks, and she hears it in his voice, that he, too, feels futility. A shared burden.

"No," she says, and he laughs, knowing the truth. "What about Miriam? How is she?"

And now he goes quiet, and in the quiet she hears what he doesn't want to say, and then hears that clicking, steady and spaced-out like a slow, dying heart. "Sick," he finally says, and then adds that it will be okay. That Lailan is with them. That she's a brave, feisty girl.

After a few more minutes, he tells her this will be expensive, and he should go. "But I can't come back now," he adds. "I still don't know why, you understand?"

"But that's why I'm calling." She's about to tell him she looked at the photographs when she realizes she never told him about them. He doesn't know they exist. How to tell him now that she captured his brother's final moments, and to tell him in code, no less? And then she hears Soran's words. *Kurds do not tell bad news to someone who is not with their family. It is a kindness to lie until family can be there to help.* Even if she could safely tell Delan, she shouldn't.

Suddenly, his voice goes low, as if he's attempting to dip below the surface of what can be detected. "We *can't*," he says. Then adds, "I'll be home soon," and it's fast, as if he's being chased, as if he'd spat the words behind him to make someone go away. She knows not to say more and listens as he takes a deep breath, becoming himself again. "I miss you," he says, his voice his own.

She can almost hear him lower his head, feel him push into the phone as if it could draw them closer. She presses the receiver harder against her ear, knowing there will be a round imprint later. "I miss you too."

Another moment of silence. She feels *I love you* unspoken but there, coming through between the clicking beats of the phone—until suddenly there's nothing.

"Sorry," the operator says. "The line dropped. Should I try again?"

What can Olivia say? Their whole conversation would be another attempt to not say what they mean, to hunt for meaning behind false words. So she tells the operator no and watches the reflection of the room in the window. Rebecca and Mason face her, waiting, the yard beyond faint, like a mirage. *The new garden,* she thinks, wishing she'd told him even that.

At last, she turns to her roommates. "There's nothing I can say. If I try to talk in code—what if he thinks I mean someone else? I can't use his cousin's name. I can't even describe him—I say his arm is in a sling and anyone listening might know." She motions to a bottle of wine on the counter. "Is that open?"

"No," Rebecca says, getting up. "But it can be."

"Ferhad. What they must have done to him. Broken his arm, who knows. Delan said it's so bad sometimes, what they do, that you give them a name. Any name. Just to make it stop."

Now Mason stands. "I have money. I got a credit card."

Both Olivia and Rebecca turn to him.

"I mean," he continues, "*I* can't go. I don't have an Iraqi visa."

"No," Rebecca says, understanding. "She can't go either."

Olivia turns to her. "But I could. To his aunt in Baghdad. Just there. I couldn't do more if I want my job when I get back." Even as she says this, she thinks of Lailan. *I wouldn't have time for her.* A pain and yet a relief. To have to say goodbye to her again—it's not something she can do.

"Call in sick," Mason says. "Or I'll call for you. When you're gone."

A swing of optimism. This will happen. With every thought, it's as if she's waking from a sleep, lifting from a stupor. "I know Soraya's address—we used it for my application. He can meet me there. I'll book and tell him the flight and call it a layover—in case the phone's tapped. What would the government care about a layover?"

"*No,*" Rebecca says. "You both need to stop. This is crazy. After everything. This is not an option."

"But this is what he needs. So he can come home. And Soran. For him."

Now Rebecca stands, walking to the sink as if needing distance. "Think about what you're saying. Does traipsing in there with photos of someone being killed by the government seem like a good idea?"

Silence. Rebecca sees she's landed her point and continues. "Even *he* wouldn't want justice at your expense."

You were trying to stay alive, Soran said that night at the restaurant. *Even the dead would want that for you.* She'd told him no, they'd want justice, and that justice sometimes starts with a photo. Yet still, he'd not agreed.

And sometimes it is just a photograph, he said. *And that photograph could get you killed.*

In her room, she tries to conjure Soran's voice, to hear what he'd want her to do. But instead there are just Rebecca's words about traipsing in with the photo of soldiers killing a man. Of course she can't do that, and the fact that she'd thought she could should be proof that she shouldn't take this trip. *Describe it, then,* Mason said. *You know it's him.* But what if it wasn't Ferhad? There's always the chance it's some other man with his arm in a sling. She'd looked through her other photos from the wedding and it looked like him, with the same arm that was injured. His features. But if there's revenge, if there's action based on this, if someone were to be hurt or worse, it can't be from interpretation.

Think about it, Mason said. *My credit card works the same tomorrow.*

"A sign," she now says to the ceiling, picturing Soran. "Can you help me with that?"

If anyone would want to keep her safe, it's him. But the room, of course, remains silent.

Then she realizes that, depending on where the soldiers are standing, she could cut the photograph and isolate the man with the sling. Delan certainly doesn't need to see the rest. And with this thought, the trip becomes possible once more, the idea of going, of returning. And again she feels that flutter of nerves, that beating of anxiety.

Just to see what the photo looks like cropped, how clear it is and if she could get him cleanly away from the soldiers, she decides to get her paper cutter. This doesn't mean she's going, she tells herself. This is only cropping a photo. In her closet, the box with the paper cutter is wedged under a shelf with shoes, and she's reaching down, fingertips skimming the corner, when she sees the present from Hewar. Square and padded. Still wrapped in brown paper and tied with twine.

She sets it on the bed. Unties the twine, then unwraps the paper. There are creases, the places where Hewar's hands had made the folds. Lightly, she touches one, wondering what was happening in the house when he'd pressed down, whose voices he was hearing. Then she keeps going. Inside is cheesecloth that covers something hard, and once everything is unwrapped, she sits back, shocked. On her bed is the center cabinet door. The door with the painting of the woman that's covered in glass. Part of a piece that's been in their family for generations. Olivia stares at the image: the woman's head with dark, flowing hair on the body of the white horse. Crown topped with red and turquoise ribbons that flow like the plumes of her wings as she sails over flowers in a sky of royal blue. The woman who somehow senses everything.

This whole time, the painting's been there. Mere feet away, hidden beneath its wrapping. People came and went below and music pulsed and beat into the night as Hollywood stretched around it, this ancient bit of a faraway family—and yet she'd not known. *It's beautiful. The paintings,* she said. *Careful,* Delan warned from the stove. *If you tell a Kurd you like something, even a small comment, it's custom for them to give it to you.*

Hewar had taken it off its hinges. On their cabinet now, what's in its place? An open wound or a makeshift door? Anything would be a constant reminder of her, something they'd face every day. Something Delan has faced every day. To have given this to her was a huge gesture, generosity like nothing she's known, and yet she'd cowered from her memories to the point that it went unnoticed. She takes it to her dresser, where she moves aside all her perfumes, all the reminders of other days. There she sets it. In the center. And from there, the woman appears to stand by, knowingly.

She dreams new dreams. There is no fire at her back, no film that sends its chords of need. When she wakes Sunday morning, she writes a letter to her father that begins with *I'm sorry* but then scratches it out and crumples the page. She's not sorry. She wants to do this. A flight tomorrow. A chance to help.

The night before, when she found the best image, she startled because she realized she'd been observing it technically. That somehow she'd turned everything off, like a stranger to a strange situation who could simply evaluate. That fierceness, that ruthlessness as an artist that Peter Darrow had talked about—perhaps it was true. And perhaps it's been within her. Because she'd gone back to photograph the boys playing soccer. She'd taken pictures that day in the mountains and did not stop. And the night of the raid, she'd thought of her camera when the world below her window seared with tragedy. But though it was fierceness, it sat alongside who she was. Because she adored those boys. And in the mountains, she both got the shot and looked away. And truth be told, never does she want to be the person who stares down tragedy, unblinking. Never does she want to be the one who remembers her camera but forgets her love.

And then it's early Monday, and her flight leaves in a matter of hours. Last night she called the number again and Gaziza answered, but Hewar quickly jumped on the line and managed to tell her Delan had just left to meet friends for tea. Knowing Hewar understands more English than he speaks, she listened for clicking and told him what she could, the details of her "layover" in Baghdad, her plan to go to Soraya's, and her hope that Delan could meet her there. *Please, can you let Soraya know that I will go to her? And tell Delan to meet me there?* And though Hewar agreed, it still hadn't felt real. Until now.

All she's taking is one carry-on suitcase, inside of which are clothes for Delan and gifts, including a collection of tea for Gaziza, a book on birds for Hewar, and for Lailan an Etch A Sketch and a set of watercolors and brushes and paper. Mason has determined—from an old medical dictionary he found on a shelf—that she has pneumonia and is on bed rest. *I'll call each morning and even tell them your symptoms. What are they gonna do, stop by and bust us?* Of course, there was only one person from the paper who'd have reason to stop by upon learning she was out sick—right after giving her the photos—but she knows that

Peter Darrow will most likely just give her space, and that if for some reason he dropped by, he would find her absent and yet return to the office with reports of her cough and tales of her fever.

A friend of Rebecca's is a travel agent and called with names of hotels nearby Soraya's, just in case, and though Olivia has folded the list in her purse, she knows she won't need it. If for some reason Soraya isn't home and Delan never shows, she will wait in the hall all night. She will sleep against her carry-on bag till the morning's call to prayer, and then she will slip the envelope with Delan's name under his aunt's door and catch her flight. *He was there,* she will write on a piece of paper. *This man. That day in the mountains.*

Concourses and gate changes and sleeping through sunlight. Before she knows it, they're lowering through a haze of smog to a land that is flat, becoming roads and fields and sand and shrubs, and when they touch the tarmac, there is a feeling that she is on his land and even that is one small miracle. No bomb threats. No diversions. Throughout everything, she makes eye contact and is not afraid to smile.

Key phrases in Arabic written in a steno notepad. The cabdriver nods at her request and her address and then chews *gat* the entire ride. Tearing the leaves with his teeth, he squints through a dusty windshield, then turns to her to offer a warm bottle of Coca-Cola.

"*Halha ltf mink,*" she tries. *That's very kind of you.*

His dark eyes find her in the rearview mirror. He nods before correcting her. "*Hadha ltf mink.* You are most welcome."

From his rearview mirror hangs a small photograph of two little boys that's been threaded onto a string, and as he takes a corner too fast, they swing to the side. The littlest one has no teeth and grins for the camera as if proud of that fact.

A thought has been working its way into the forefront of her mind: Lailan could be with Delan. Olivia pictures the door to Soraya's apartment opening and the girl standing by the walls of the painted garden. *Hi-lo.* Only a few hours they'd have before Lailan would tuck herself against her, head heavy, sleep overtaking. Only hours, but that's okay. For a moment, Olivia allows herself the memory of the girl's arms, but there is a physical ache to it and so she stops, as best she can.

Al-Kadhimiya Mosque is gold even in the veil of late evening. Her nerves are building. What if he's not there? She's prepared, of course, as she needs to be logical, but her heart would break because she *wants* to see him. To feel his shoulders and his chest against her cheek. Just the thought makes it worse, the craving for him, and so she turns to watch vendors on the sidewalk and date palms that stand tall and swaybacked, bent from time and circumstance. Night is falling.

When they turn onto Soraya's street, she looks up. Balconies are stacked one on top of the other, emerging from buildings in all shades of wrought-iron railings. Dark gray, she remembers, and scans until she sees one. Six floors up, with vines of a plant and a man who stands and faces the other direction.

She knows his shoulders. Knows the way he leans. Knows him even in the way one arm hangs slightly over the railing. Before them, cars are inching and honking, everyone stopped for what appears to be a donkey that won't budge. And Delan is right there. After all this time. Right there, scanning the streets, looking for her.

At last they pull closer, and as if looking away would snap the connection and wind him back into the apartment, she keeps her eyes steady on him. A white shirt against the night. He faces a breeze. They park one building over, and she has her head out the window as she looks up, not caring that she's smiling like a fool—and as if he feels her there, he turns and sees her. And takes a step back, as if unbelieving. But then he leans forward and shields his eyes from the lights of the city, trying to see her, to be sure. And she's still watching him when she opens the car door and steps into the noise and dust of the street. Still watching him when he must understand it's really her, her in her American sneakers and jeans and too-tight T-shirt and big knit purse. For a second she looks down, to the driver, and remembers Lailan and that it was only him on the balcony. Quickly she looks back up, but he's gone.

It's best, she tells herself. But already there is an ache within her for the lost hours with the girl. She peels off dollar bills, the only currency she has, handing over an amount that's way more than the ride was worth, but she doesn't care because she's missing Lailan and thinking of those two little boys in the photo. The cabdriver's face narrows and then becomes sad, as if bracing for a joke, for her to pull the money back from him, and when she doesn't, he looks up at her, and in a flash, he's smiling with half his mouth green from *gat.* Then, ashamed, remembering, he covers his mouth and looks down. *"Shukran,"* he says over and over. *Thank you.*

"You just paid him his whole year's salary."

She doesn't care about decorum, about rules, about anything. She's in Delan's arms and he's half lifting her, her toes brushing the ground. Around them, people must be staring, but she's got her eyes closed as she breathes him in, his sandalwood and olive oil and that mix of *here,* dust and kerosene and spices. And then he's kissing her, and it's as if she's stepped into an underwater sway, that moment in an ocean when your feet leave the ground right as a wave you'd not seen catches and holds you. When she finally opens her eyes, she sees the driver still there, watching and smiling with his hand over his mouth as if her generosity has at last made sense, as if he now understands the value of his role in delivering her to this place.

Dinner is waiting. Lamb and dolmas and cucumbers. Naan bread in a stack in the center of the table. Soraya appears, welcoming with a hug and cheek pinching and a long gaze as if trying to understand the situation through Olivia's eyes. Then she retreats back to her room, happy to give them privacy.

On the table, there are only two plates. "Either your aunt's made herself scarce or you didn't really think I was coming and this is her dinner."

"No, no. She ate. That's for you. If you did not come, it would still be there, waiting. As would I."

Outside, the city lights blaze in the dark, the mosque lit up. "Can we eat there?"

"On the balcony?"

She smiles and grabs her plate and slides open the door. For a moment, she stands at the railing, remembering when she was here before, how she'd thought it was the last time, and how that supposed certainty had turned out to be wrong—and the very fact of that is an unleashing of hope because suddenly the promise that the world will surprise is a good thing.

She sits cross-legged, with her plate in her lap, and Delan stands at the door with wineglasses in hand and the bottle under his arm as he watches her. Then he sets them down, and when he's back with his plate, he takes the spot before her. "It's not real. You here."

"And I leave again tomorrow."

He nods, as if he'd understood that from the message but hoped it not to be true, then leans back against the side railing and studies her. His hair is longer, wilder, though he's kept his beard trimmed. Skin slightly darker. The shirt he has on is new—short sleeves, white polyester, and a flared collar. She reaches out to touch it.

He looks down at her hand and places his on top. "I dream of you."

"And I dream of you."

"So. Why?"

"After dinner. Please."

His face changes, sharpens with alarm. "Something happened? To who, to you?"

She lets him know that everyone is fine. That she's fixing up the garden and Rebecca got him a lime tree and that Mason misses him so much, he could barely talk about it. And work. She fills him in on the contest, how it looks like a formality, but that Peter Darrow thinks she has talent and she thinks he will help her, no matter what, and that at some point she has a feeling she'll end up in his department. Then she admits to Delan that she'd taken a photo of him, in their kitchen, and that it's one of the images she submitted.

"Of me?" he asks, confused.

The newspaper. The day in the kitchen when he'd cried into the cold light. She explains and says she can get it back if he'd like, that she'd not thought about it until it was too late. That she'd not thought of any of the photos that way until it was too late.

"Liv, I'm happy. And my parents would be happy. Use it. Use everything. Show it to people and be proud. Hang them on walls and put them in the paper and *affect* people, any way and as much as you can."

One worry dislodged.

He tells her of his family, his father who found a falcon with an injured wing and his mother who still wears black and will for the next year. Then he looks as if he's trying to convince himself of something. "There are reasons I can't come home."

"Yet. You mean *yet.*"

"I need to talk to you about this. Soran is one. I still don't know why. And the other is paperwork and bureaucracy—"

"Soran is why I'm here."

A dart of darkness in his eyes.

Quietly, as if volume might soften the content of her words, she tells him about the photos. He looks sick, even with the memory, but then alarmed as she tells him that she kept taking pictures, as if with each word a bullet was fired and once again she was crouched by a rock, exposed.

When she's done, he's angry. "What they could have done to you."

"I know. But there's more. I need my purse." She finds it in the living room, the envelope inside. When she returns, he's watching the city.

"I don't want to see."

She stands in the threshold of the door. "I cut everything out. Everything except for one person."

With that, he turns to her. And in this, her standing while he looks up at her, afraid, she sees him not only as he once must have been, young and scared and at someone's mercy, but as he still is. Brave and open. He reaches for the photo, and though she has her loupe in her hand should he need it, he takes one glance at the image and covers his eyes with his hand. His shoulders begin to shake. Beside him, she kneels and wraps her arms around him, feeling a vibration within him as meaning takes hold.

The night passes quickly with them on the couch, trying to stay awake. She'll sleep on the planes and he'll spend another day in Baghdad before heading back. And the photo of Ferhad, he decided, will go to Aras. Aras who visited after she'd left and vowed to make things right. Aras who would know what to do.

Delan sits facing forward, while she's turned toward him, her legs across his lap. He's still processing the information, the betrayal. "This has been in motion for a while," he says. "Even before we got here, there were rumors someone in my family had turned."

"You think Ferhad started the rumors? Or were they *about* him?"

"No. If someone even suspected Ferhad was working with the government, he would've been stopped. The second we know about a traitor, it's done. This was gossip. Vague gossip, just mentioning my family, planting it for later." A pause. "At the picnic, Ferhad told me he saw Soran leaving town a few times a week, right after curfew lifted. You remember that. That right there—with no new job, no reason for Soran to leave as far as anyone knew—that worked. For both sides. So he could tell the Kurds Soran was a traitor meeting with the government and tell the government he was meeting with the resistance."

Then she remembers. The restaurant. Soran had told Ferhad he was there the night the Kurdish political figures had been killed. Outside the bakery, he had innocently offered information that could further sell himself as the traitor. As she tells Delan this, he turns to her, quietly taking it in.

"He said we were lucky," Olivia continues. "Lucky Soran got us out of there in time. And Soran had just met with men who were in the resistance. At the bakery, they were all in a back room."

"He was playing both sides. That was icing on the cake."

Ferhad feels your love for Delan, Soran had said. *And he says you should see with your eyes and hear with your heart, because Delan is alive and will be back, and you know this.* And Delan *was* back. The very next day. Now Olivia wonders, did Ferhad have something to do with his release? Or even with him being taken in the first place? "Delan, he was surprised to see me at the picnic. But he knew you'd be there."

She watches him absorb this. Silently, he traces a little circle on her knee with the tip of his finger. "The military," he says, "they patrol the mountains. I'm sure that was it."

But the idea is planted. Her mind is racing. If Ferhad had turned, could he have seen opportunity when he heard Delan was in town and offered up a cousin he barely spoke to, someone connected with a high-ranking Peshmerga, to try to appease the government? To put off turning in Soran? Then, maybe after the sabotage, they'd demanded more. Maybe at that point there was no other choice but to go through with it. Again she thinks back to when Delan had been taken, to Ferhad on the street outside the bakery, and the look of surprise on his face when he realized Delan had not returned. As if something had happened that shouldn't have. As if someone had not kept up their end of the bargain. "Maybe he thought they'd just take you for a day. Even a night."

"Stop," he says and flattens his hand on her knee. "I came back. That's what matters."

And she accepts this, because she has to. Because he doesn't want to know why he was taken. Because he can't add another wrong to the list.

"My cousin," Delan continues, "he was shocked, did I tell you? When I told him about Nina, Soran's girlfriend."

"Everyone was shocked."

"Not like this. He was going to be sick. Even then I wondered, why would he care so much that there was a woman he'd never met with a broken heart? But now I know. Because he caused it. He who believes in love, it's the last thing he wanted."

She watches his hand as again he starts tracing a circle on her knee. The lines of his tendons. The veins beneath his skin that rise and fall.

"My cousin," he says at last, looking up to the ceiling. "My god. What they must have done to him."

Legs threaded on the couch. So close that whispers are felt. Recaps of life until sleep steals in and one or the other wakes. A shake of the shoulder. "Hey." Then more stories, more kisses.

"So you're calling in sick," he says. "You'll be back to work when?"

"Friday."

"That's the contest. Am I right? June fifteenth."

She shrugs. The contest. She's told herself it's over. "You know it's Mason who's calling me in sick."

"No. He's in your good graces?"

"He paid for this trip."

"Mason has money?"

"A credit card."

"That's not good. I'll pay him back."

"You don't have money."

"I do. I told you, didn't I? By the oregano. That piece of granite. Lift it and there's some money."

"You have a trapdoor in the garden."

"It's a *hiding* place. Everyone looks under a mattress. I thought I told you this."

"No." She smiles. "It's okay, though. Rebecca's been covering you."

He nods, distracted. His mind no doubt wound back to his hometown, back to his cousin who'd at one time been like a brother. All at once it hits her that maybe she was wrong. Wrong to come here and make him relive it. Wrong to add to everything the injustice that it was his own family who caused the loss. Because despite everything, he loves his cousin—and any retribution will be more hurt upon his family, upon people he loves.

On the wall by the lamp is a faded painted hyacinth. She moves toward it, to the far end of the couch, and watches him. "Was I wrong? To come here with this?"

One of his hands kneads the other as he shakes his head. "No. You were right. I had to know. He loved Soran. I know he did, and I know he still does. And one day I will forgive him for this, because he must've saved someone he loved even more. And that's what I'm going to tell myself. That it was for love. And if that's not the case, *that* I don't want to know." He pats the place next to him. "But you. You did the right thing. So come back. Let me tell you about the garden."

And so she does, and he tells her of the okra they planted where Soran intended. The new pomegranate tree. *A baby with four blooms.* But when he starts to tell her about Miriam, how she's mentally not well, and then Lailan, Olivia shakes her head and untangles herself from him.

"Not her. I can't."

"You don't want to hear about Lailan?"

"You," she says, "I know I will see again. Leaving you is awful, but it's not *it*. With Lailan—I *wanted* you to bring her here. Just so I had a few hours with her. But I was relieved when you didn't." Because, she realizes, like him with his family and all the visits he never made, she'd wanted to forget. To love a little less.

He nods, then studies the rug below them as if reordering his stories, tucking all he meant to tell her about Lailan away. He looks worried.

Suddenly she looks down the hall. "She's not here, is she?"

He laughs. "No. No." But then he's serious again. "You really didn't want to see her?"

"I couldn't say *goodbye* to her again. I didn't want to reopen that. You get it. You said it yourself, about why you didn't want to go back."

"I want to be with you. You know that."

"And we will be."

"What I said before, I thought you'd be happy about it."

"You're talking in circles. *What* did you say before?"

"About the paperwork, the bureaucracy." He reaches for his glass of wine on the end table, brings it to his lips, but doesn't take a sip, just sets it back on the table and stares at the rug as he speaks. "I'm in the process of adopting her."

A pounding begins in Olivia's chest, one that fills her ears. "Adopting her."

There are reasons I can't come home.

"I know I don't have much. A house that needs work. Odd jobs."

He's not coming back. His new life is here. His parents, his friends, a daughter. She tries to remain calm, to keep herself grounded. *This is okay,* she tells herself. *This doesn't matter.* But the words are frayed. Worn. They don't apply, and she knows it. Still, he's talking, but she's lost inside herself. Realizing that though Olivia loves Delan, Lailan both loves *and* needs him. And if there is anyone, *anyone* in the world Olivia would give him up for, it's her.

"Miriam is not well," he's saying. "She wants this for her." And it's then that he finally looks up, away from the rug. "You're crying."

"*Of course I am.* I don't want us to be over."

"It only has to be over if *you* want it to be. *I* don't want that. She'll be mine, my responsibility, forever. No matter what. I'm not taking that lightly. And never would I want this to affect your work. I'm home during the day, so it shouldn't get in the way, and if you want nothing to do with her, then I understand. But maybe you can just see when we get there what you think."

When *we* get there. "You and—?"

"Me and Lailan. I'm sorry I didn't ask you first, but it has to be done. Whether I lose you or not, *which I do not want*. I want you. More than I've wanted anything. But Lailan has no one. My parents are old, but I can help. My brother, he would want this. *I* want this. I cannot leave her, this girl who is loved but has no one."

Understanding hits in waves. A possibility she'd never considered. A life with Lailan that can actually happen. "You wouldn't leave her here."

Now he's frustrated. "*This is the point.* I'm a US citizen and she'll be my daughter, and I'll need a lawyer, I know. I had a good one before; I'll find him again. As soon as I can, I'll take her to the States and we go from there. A month is what I'm told. It's who you know, and I know someone. I'm lucky."

Olivia swipes at her tears, which have only increased. Though he's pale and nervous, he must now see that though she's crying, she's also smiling.

Family sometimes just happens, Soran had told her.

"Delan," she says. "Bring her home."

CHAPTER 18

June 15, 1979

Friday. Gray and stormy. The words *June gloom* tossed about like everything is better with a label. News about the contest will send someone into a celebratory weekend, while the rest will need the time to armor themselves for the following week. She doesn't care. She made it back. A trip with no issues—a short one, granted, but proof that she could do it. That if need be, she could go again.

And both he and Lailan will be here. A month, he thought. Their night continued with talk of logistics, everything tinged with nervous excitement. Where would she go to school and would it be kindergarten? Which room would she have? *Mine,* Olivia said. *Or Rebecca's. Did I tell you? She's moving in with Gary.* To that, Delan just smiled. *You see how that worked?* And Olivia had no retort, because she did see. Still, there was an impetuousness that only edged their conversation, known but never settled, because in truth it wasn't crazy. It was risk, but it was good. It would be hard, but it was right. It was saving one person, and it was a choice she had no hesitation in making.

And like before, at the airport she would not say goodbye.

"It worked last time," she told him.

"I will say something else, though," he said as he pulled her to him, his lips to her ear. "Olivia. Liv. I love you."

And that, she decided, she could say back.

A breeze. It feels like there's a little gust that carries her into each room—and muffles the annoying gossip about the contest that is everywhere. In the copy room, a secretary with bright nails tells another woman from upstairs that Miller's got it. Then she turns to Olivia, as if just having remembered she, too, was in the race. "Sorry. I didn't mean—"

"It's fine."

"But did you hear? *That was his grandma's last breath.* He said her skin changed, became smooth. Monday he's bringing in a photo that'll prove she was all wrinkly before."

The photos of the dying grandmother were just of a woman in a hospital bed. Nothing more. The story existed outside the frame, not within. Peter Darrow had been right—there wasn't a reaction, not one other person to show the moment for what it was. Not only that, but the composition was off. But with this thought, Olivia scolds herself. His grandmother was dying. He wasn't thinking, and it was right that he wasn't thinking. She remembers the photos she took in the mountains, how her hands shook. How she'd looked down and snapped without seeing. Sometimes, she knows, taking bad photographs is all you can do.

In the hall, she walks with stacks of contracts and has just rounded the corner when there's Peter Darrow walking with a copyeditor.

"You," Peter says when he spots her. "You feeling better?"

She's confused till his eyes widen. Beside him, the copyeditor glances at his watch.

"Yes," she says, placing herself back in a world where everyone believed her sick. Very sick. "Thank you. Probably could've come in yesterday, but it was good to have another day to rest."

"Pneumonia comes on fast like that. I think." Then Peter puts his hand on the copyeditor's shoulder. "I'm gonna catch up with you."

The man looks to Olivia and back at Peter. Then he tilts his head as if he's just heard someone calling his name before continuing down the hall.

"For the record, I don't blame you," Peter says. "For needing time to digest it all."

"I didn't need time. I went there."

Peter's eyes narrow in confusion, and she sees he has no idea.

"I recognized a man in the photo. His cousin. He set it all up. So I went there. To Baghdad. Met Delan and gave him the photo—a cropped version—and came home the next day."

At first he continues to study her, unsure. But then it's as if a cord has been pulled and he's smiling, laughing, his head tilted back as he grins to the ceiling tiles. "Holy shit. *You went there.*"

"He was glad I did."

Peter looks back down, still smiling. "Well, I bet he was. And you?"

"Tired."

He shakes his head and pats her on the shoulder. "Get some coffee. And listen, I fought for you. Okay? It might feel like it's over, but it's not. Remember that. And then let's talk, because when you're ready to let them go," he says, nodding toward the display in the hall, "those photos should be seen."

Though she knew she wouldn't win, the contest's finality still settles within her, a letdown that makes her realize she'd actually held out hope. But then she hears what else he said: a future for the photos. A chance to make a difference. She nods and manages to say "thank you" before watching him disappear.

In the break room, the coffee is dark and stale. She makes a new pot, watching it drip and listening to the ferocious sound of its churning. When it's done, she stirs in sugar, thinking of Gaziza and her sugar cubes, her long skirts and broad back. Olivia's only regret is that she didn't see any of them. *Before, you came at a bad time,* Delan said to her. *We've had no problems where we are since. Other places, sure. But for us, it's been peaceful.* Of course peaceful, she knew, was relative, but it still gave her hope—for his sake. And for the future, that one day they would return.

"Is Peter Darrow still married?"

She turns at the question and sees Miller and Hannity, seemingly talking to each other—but obviously intending she hear.

"Happily," Hannity says. "Heard they're going on fifteen years."

Olivia knows she should just walk out of the room. Leave. Let them have their assumptions and accusations and be the bigger person.

"Good to hear," Miller says. "Marriage is hard. Danger lurks. People wanting things, knowing how to get them."

There is a silence as they let the words find her. She won't look at them. Her breeze is gone, and anger scratches in her chest. But instead of saying anything, she walks toward the door, where she sees the damn flyer still taped in place. Their stares press her to the point where when she stops, it's as if they've bumped against her. *The contest is looking like a formality,* Peter said. A formality. Hannity and his uncle, the one who knows Byron, their editor in chief.

At her desk, she sits and glares toward the break room till they emerge. They're smiling, and that's what does it.

"Hannity," she says as they near. "I've been meaning to ask you. How's your uncle?"

"He's good," he says, pausing, momentarily thrown.

Beside him, however, Miller has clued in to her meaning. And she would let this be the end of it, would go back to her work and slog away, dreaming of another day, another trip, another return, but for his response.

"What I don't get," he says, and his eyes gleam as if he's just spotted aces in his hand, "is why you didn't take photos of what you saw. If you really wanted to win. Isn't that what photographers do? Wouldn't *that* have been a better way?"

Hannity glances at him, as if he's made a sound he doesn't understand.

But Olivia understands. "Of what I *saw*? You mean what I *lived*."

In the distance, she sees that office manager she doesn't like stand. A shocked plea on her face, her hands lifting as though she's about to conduct an orchestra.

"Fine, then," Miller says, "worded it wrong." He shrugs at Hannity as if to say, *Yikes, you know how this goes.*

And Olivia does. Because she's been through it. And she knows how it will end, and so she doesn't care and keeps going, loudly. "Yes, *lived* it—not saw it. There's a difference, and if you don't know that, I'd say you've been pretty damn lucky."

"Oh, now." His face flushes with reddened shame, but his body goes rigid with pride. He glances to the upstairs landing, where a few editors stand, watching. "Let's not get crazy here. What I'm saying—"

But he doesn't get a chance to say anything, because she's talking.

"See, I wasn't safe in a car with people who had guns to protect me. I wasn't on a street with people playing chess or hitting a soccer ball. And, Miller, I'm really sorry about your grandmother, I am, but I wasn't in a room where the only hurt could come from someone dying *when it was their time.*"

With this, the room goes silent. Or as silent as can be. The phones ring. The machines in the copy room make their clicking hums. But the people are still. And when she looks up, she sees him—Peter Darrow, standing by his office with his hockey stick on his shoulders, his hands hanging on to the ends. Though it's subtle, he's smiling.

She turns back to Miller, now thinking of his grandmother and the *peace* on her face.

"You're not the only one who got a picture of someone dying. I got one too. Only he was being killed. Stabbed. Over and over. By soldiers. And even though they could've seen me, I got the shot. I got a whole roll of shots, and you know what? There is *nothing* about this contest that was worth handing over *the end of someone I loved's life* to be hung on a fucking wall. So maybe you're right, and you are a better photographer, since you had no problem doing just that."

CHAPTER 19

Nobody said she was fired, but through the chaotic hush of the bull-pen, she understood it to be true. "Everyone, back to work," one of the voices from upstairs yelled, and she casually sat and gathered her things. Faces turned toward her. People leaned in to each other. Theories whispered. The girls she was friendly with gave worried smiles. What she had done was not to be done. A transgression. A story they'd tell later. Though most everything, Olivia knew, would be explained as her losing it. Which was fine. Maybe she had lost it—some tie to who she'd been, a hook around her waist.

She pushes her way through a muggy heat to her car. Drives home with her knit purse beside her, stuffed with what few personal belongings she'd had at her desk: a couple of framed photos, her Parker's pens, the green Trapper Keeper with her favorite photos. Though she knows she didn't win the contest, she now understands she blew it. Right at the verge. With a connection, someone to help and possibly mentor her. Right then, she slipped. She'd found her voice at the one moment that demanded silence. But when she imagines not having said something, she knows it wasn't an option. Not anymore. No more muddy coffee as a retort. No more itching, silent screams.

At a stoplight, she looks up at the gray sky and sees it—a massive flock of birds moving together as one. Expanding and contracting as they shift midflight, circling and diving and turning and twisting like fire. A dance. A dance in which not one bird is out of step.

Behind her, a car honks. Without thinking, she pulls over to the busy shoulder, parks in the red, and gets out. The air has sprung to a light drizzle, haphazard and pulling. She leans against the hood and feels the mist on her face as she looks up. A murmuration. This is what Hewar talked about with starlings, what Delan translated. *We're talking thousands of birds, and not one bird leading. All synchronized but without a leader. Because each one connects,* really *connects, to its neighbors, to the ones around them. And with that, thousands move as one.*

A movement so great, created so small. It's incredible. She feels it within her, a vibration of hope, and turns, wanting to share this moment with someone, but red brake lights line the road and people stare straight ahead, just trying to get through. Her eyes continue to search the street because it makes her sad, to be in this alone. But then she sees one other person on the corner. A teenager with his hand on a telephone booth and a backpack forgotten at his feet. He holds on to the booth as if for balance as he looks up. Maybe he feels her watching him, because after a moment, he turns toward her and nods. *I see it too.*

And she smiles and looks back at the sky.

Later, she will call Peter Darrow and ask if he'd be interested in publishing one of her photos, the one during the raid. She will tell him she wants the world to know what happened, even just on that one night, in that one small part of the world. And he will, and the photo will help her land the job he sets her up for at a competing paper. And after years as a photographer there, she will be driving on a cloudy day from an assignment, wanting to get home to her family, but will be fascinated by a sky that's gone oddly dark and light at once. A confluence. Something underestimated that's found its power. And she will remember this day with the birds in the sky, that sometimes you must stop and look up because magic exists whether you see it or not, and it's so much better to get the glimpse. And so she will. She will be peering up when a cloudy hook lowers. Immediately, she will have her camera and snap photos but then will stop and simply watch with her Nikon at her side. A rare F2 tornado that touches down in Los Angeles. *How did you get that shot?* her editor will ask, and she won't tell him that there were better shots she could've gotten but didn't because she was too busy feeling the wind and the electricity in the air and that strange haunting alchemy from the sky.

And she will also think of this day in only a few months, when she's in her room upstairs getting ready for work and through the window sees a string of birds in the sky. Just a handful. But in midair they meet another string and join together, taking a new shape, and she knows that at some point, someone else might witness what she did back on the day she'd finally grown tired of looking down. But for her, through her window, there is only a small vee that slips delicately through the air—and then a cab that pulls before the house and the top of Delan's head as he gets out, his hair twists of wild and his arm extended behind him.

Lailan. Stepping out, taking in the yard. The orange trees and the pink azaleas. Her mouth opens in shocked pleasure when she spots her favorite color, and then she's looking up and seeing Olivia in the window. And so she waves. And Olivia's heart rushes. Full of love and promise for a future in a place where hopefully this girl will never be judged for anything other than her kindness.

Delan, as well, will see Olivia in the window. And he will stand with Lailan on the front path and squint against the sun. A moment of stillness before the rest begins. Before years unfold and one day Lailan announces she wants to go by *Lily*, and Olivia will remind her again of the woman who'd named her, who'd raised her as her own, alone but never alone, and she will bring out that photograph from the trip all those years ago, that moment that captured a mother's love for her daughter, a love that was plain and ferocious and true. And Lailan will go silent, and the next day Olivia will hear her correct her friend when she calls her Lily. *You did good,* Delan will tell Olivia. And she will shrug it off and credit the image. *The power of a picture.* And Delan will draw her to him and whisper in her ear. *The power of someone who loves.*

But now. Now the gray clouds seem to split in places, like a puzzle come loose upon a table of light. And now she watches the birds in the sky, their form twisting and expanding, ducking and turning. Thousands seen as one, moving against the scattered brightness.

ACKNOWLEDGMENTS

This novel is inspired both by my father's stories of life in Kurdistan of Iraq, as well as my family's 1979 trip to the region. During that visit, there were many events I drew upon, including a bomb threat on our flight there, soldiers who held us at gunpoint at a picnic, my father being taken in for questioning, and a restaurant that exploded only moments after we left (upon spotting too many political figures). But it wasn't just these experiences that were crucial—it was the memories of many Kurds, Kurds who often had to struggle to tell their tales. For that bravery, and that generosity of spirit, I am indebted.

Though inspired by true events, this is a work of fiction. As mentioned in the book, Kurdistan is spread over four countries, so isolation has been both geographic as well as political. Because of this, traditions, landscapes, dialects, and spellings all vary, and though I made every effort to stay true, some aspects were melded to create the world of my characters. That said, please know that the kindness and hospitality of the Kurdish people is accurate in all parts of Kurdistan. They are truly some of the most giving, loving people I've ever met. On my most recent trip to Kurdistan, I was embraced as an American (I am), fed like I was starving (I was not), and honored to witness the pride the Kurds have in their culture and history.

Growing up in Kurdistan of Iraq, my father and his family endured atrocities I could never fully capture with words. There were five children born to my grandparents: my father (Sardar), my two uncles (Sarchal and Baktiar Zuhdi), and my two aunts (Ronak and Anjum Zuhdi). Each one coped and thrived differently. Ronak, tragically, never made it out of her twenties, and to this day my father cannot say her name without crying. My other aunt, Anjum, became a Peshmerga who was jailed and banished to the south of Iraq, and she went on to become a high-ranking KDP member in charge of underground activity. Due to her invaluable work for the Kurdish cause, her face is immortalized with other key figures in the city of Sulaymaniyah. And my uncle Sarchal—a doctor. On that trip my family took to Kurdistan in 1979, my brother became extremely ill with a high fever, and my uncle (who at the time was living in London) dropped everything and returned to Iraq to care for him, despite the fact that he knew doctors were in demand and he'd not be allowed to leave again. A true lifesaver, may he rest in peace. My other uncle, Bak, is an engineer who worked under enemy fire on the front lines with the Peshmerga to keep roads and bridges open and was also exiled by Saddam Hussein to the south of Iraq. Since moving to the United States, he has worked to provide relief aid to help his community both here and back home. An amazing gardener, a fantastically knowledgeable tour guide, he is most importantly a central and loving part of my life. Without both he and his wonderful wife, Barham, as well as my aunt Anjum, my recent trip to Kurdistan would never have happened. (Bak, Barham, Anjum—words can't express how much I cherish your generosity and time and love.)

And my father, Zuhdi Sardar, who is not Delan but was the seed that grew both the character and this book. Out of all the children in his family, he went the creative route. An incredible visual artist, he is someone who does "put it in his art" and who is loved by everyone he meets. In fact, his kindness actually saved his family during a raid, much like in the novel. And despite what he's been through, he will smile at strangers and feed anyone who's hungry, and even those who are not (seriously, Kurds love to feed people). I must also mention his love of gardening, which clearly has had an impact on me. My father, my heart. Thank you for leading by example and for being who you are.

To all the Zuhdis—my family—none of this book, or me, would be possible without you.

Dr. Rashid Karadaghi, honorary uncle and brilliant scholar, a man who wrote the most comprehensive Kurdish-English dictionary—I am lucky to have known you my whole life, and your assistance in helping with translations (and so much more) was invaluable. Dear reader, please know that any mistakes I've made are my own.

My heartfelt thanks to photographers Randall Michelson and Diana Lannes. You both are immensely talented, and, Randall, the time you took from your day to answer my annoying photography questions was so valued. Again, any mistakes are my own.

Lucy Carson, agent extraordinaire—I can honestly say this book would never have happened if it were not for you. You pushed me to write the novel you knew I had in me. For the time you spent caring for this story, for your faith, and for so much more, I am eternally grateful. And my editor, Alicia Clancy, along with everyone at Lake Union, this book has benefited from your eye and intuition and enthusiasm, and I am so, so very appreciative. To say I'm lucky to work with such wonderful people is an understatement.

Stephanie Stephens, who might have read this book as many times as I have—after everything, I can't believe you still like this story (or me!). Thank you for so much. And Becarren Schultz, my supportive and loving cousin and reader, I feel like I won the relative lottery with you in my life. I also want to endlessly thank the talented author Meg Howrey—this book benefited from your wisdom and caring, as did I. Sieglinde and Ralph, you two made Kurdistan even more memorable and meaningful. I'm so glad I got to share the journey with you.

Though I mentioned my father already, my mother also deserves enormous praise and thanks. Mom, thank you thank you thank you, not just for your insight and memories of being an American woman in 1979 Kurdistan but for your support and love. You've fought for me and believed in me, and I love you. As well, a shout-out to my brother, Kam. Who'd have thought that your petting a sheep (as was the theory) and getting so sick all those years ago would end up in a novel? Stay safe, brother.

To Joe, my husband. None of my writing would be possible without you. Thank you for you, my eternal partner. And to my son, Maximiliaen. In your brown eyes, I see the family that we come from, and in your heart I see their strength and love. You are kind, smart, and a constant wonder to me. Your spirit makes me proud. Never stop seeing the beauty in the world.

DISCUSSION QUESTIONS

1. What, if anything, surprised you about the Kurdish culture?

2. At the beginning, Olivia wonders, "Is it possible to truly know someone if you cannot comprehend that which made them who they are? Can one truly love another without that understanding?" What do you think? Do you believe being from such different worlds is surmountable?

3. Though she wants to go to Kurdistan, in some ways she's driven to go in order to not live a life dictated by fear. Is there something you've done that you were afraid to do and had to push yourself to do? Or something you wish you'd done but didn't?

4. Olivia likes to "find the start of things" for the big elements of her life. Do you do the same? What are some surprising "roots" you've found?

5. What do you think of Delan's realization that he'd stayed away from his family in order to "love them a little less"? Does it make you think less of him, or is it something you understand?

6. Delan believes that *in love* transitions to *love* and that you both love someone for who they are but also despite who they are. Do you agree?

7. Olivia grapples with the moral side of taking photographs, feeling at one point that it's "human sightseeing." What did you think of her debate, and would you have the same qualms?

8. It's Olivia's belief that Delan saved them with one small act of kindness. Do you have a moment in your life that you believe similar? A time when an act of compassion had big ramifications?

9. Olivia thinks that "place can build or break a heart just like a person." Do you have a place you feel this way about?

10. Do you agree with Olivia that "pain inspires," and if so, do you think people subconsciously or consciously afford more credibility to people who've "been through so much"? In the same vein, do you think that people get "passed off" just because they're happy?

11. The fight that they have before the picnic is centered on whether "moving on" (in this case, after the bombing) is the best way to try to handle traumatic situations or if it's callous. Did you find yourself agreeing with either character more than the other?

12. What do you think the title *Take What You Can Carry* ultimately refers to?